ALSO BY PENELOPE DOUGLAS...

KILL
SWITCH

KILL
SWITCH

PENELOPE DOUGLAS

3

Proofreading & Interior Formatting by Elaine York,
Allusion Publishing
www.allusionpublishing.com

AUTHOR'S NOTE

I don't normally add a preface, but as this is the third installment in the Devil's Night series, I'd like to forewarn readers. While this is a series in the sense that each book tackles a new plot with a new hero and heroine, it has become a saga, of sorts, as well. There is a bigger story at play with the central characters all prevalent in each other's books and other mysteries playing out. It's recommended to read the series, starting with *Corrupt* and *Hideaway*. Getting to know all the players and connecting all the fun dots will assure that you have the best chance at understanding the full picture.

If you've already read *Corrupt* and *Hideaway,* then onward and enjoy!

If you haven't, both are currently available through Kindle Unlimited.

Happy Reading!

PLAYLIST

Stream the *Kill Switch* playlist here
(https://open.spotify.com/playlist/736UejcpLSuwKLzaxuMCoV)

"37 Stitches" by Drowning Pool
"And the World Was Gone" by Snow Ghosts
"Bad Company" by FFDP
"Beggin for Thread" by Banks
"Black Magic Woman" by VCTRYS
"Bloodletting (The Vampire Song)" by Concrete Blonde
"Cannibal Song" by Ministry
"Cry Little Sister" by Marilyn Manson
"Dark Paradise" by Lana Del Rey
"Deathwish" by Red Sun Rising
"Don't Say a Word" by Ellie Goulding
"Fear the Fever" by Digital Daggers
"Girls Just Wanna Have Fun" by Chromatics
"Go to Hell" by KMFDM
"Go to War" by Nothing More
"Hater" by Korn
"Holy Water" by LAUREL
"Human" by Rag'n'Bone Man
"Is Your Love Strong Enough" by How to Destroy Angels
"Me Against the Devil" by The Relentless
"Mouth" by Bush
"My Prerogative" by Bobby Brown
"Nothing Else Matters" by Apocalyptica
"Plastic Heart" by Nostalghia
"Season of the Witch" by Donovan
"Serenity" by Godsmack
"Seven Nation Army (Glitch Mob Remix)" by The White Stripes
"Sleep Walk" by Santo & Johnny
"S.O.S. (Anything But Love)" by Apocalyptica (feat. Cristina Scabbia)
"Something I Can Never Have" by Nine Inch Nails
"Then He Kissed Me" by The Crystals
"Voices" by Motionless in White

"THERE IS A REASON WHY
ALL THINGS ARE AS THEY ARE."
-BRAM STOKER'S DRACULA

CHAPTER 1

Winter

M y ballet slipper brushes the hardwood floor as I slowly step down the long hallway. The glow of the candles on their pedestals line the dark walls, and I fidget with my fingers as I glance left to right at every closed door I pass.

I don't like this house. I've never liked it here.

But at least the parties are only twice a year—after summer recitals in June and following the premiere of the annual Nutcracker performance in December. Madame Delova loves ballet, and as my school's benefactress she considers it a 'gift to the masses to descend from her tower once in a while to entertain the villagers and allow us into her home.'

Or so I overheard my mom say once.

The house is so big that I don't think I'll ever see all of it, and it's filled with things that everyone is always gushing over and whispering about, but it makes me nervous. I feel like I'll break something every time I turn around.

And it's too dark. Even worse today with the house only lit by candlelight. I suppose it's Madame's way of making everything look like a dream the way she kind *of looks herself: surreal, too perfect, and porcelain. Not exactly real.*

I press my lips together, pausing before I call out, "Mom?"

Where is she?

I step softly, not sure where I am or how I get back to the party, but I know I saw my mom come upstairs. I think there's a third floor, too, but I'm not sure where the next stairwell is to get to it. Why would she come up here? Everyone is downstairs.

I clench my jaw harder with every step away from the party I take. The lights, voices, and music fade, and the silent darkness of the hallway slowly swallows me up.

I should go back. She'll get mad that I followed her anyway.

"Mom?" I call again, itching at the tights on my legs as the costume I'd been wearing since this morning chafes my skin. "Mom?"

"What the fuck is the matter with you?" someone yells. I jump.

"Everyone is uncomfortable around you," the man continues. "All you do is stand there! We talked about this."

I spot a sliver of light peeking through a cracked doorway and creep closer. I doubt my mom is in there. People don't yell at her.

But maybe she is in there?

"What is going on in that head of yours?" the man bellows. "Can't you speak? At all? Ever?"

There's no response, though. Who is he mad at?

Leaning into the door frame, I peer into the crack, trying to see who's in the room.

At first, all I can make out is gold. The golden glow of the golden lamp shining onto the golden desk set. But then I shift to the left, my pulse hammering in my chest, as I see Madame's husband, Mr. Torrance, cross into my view from behind his desk. He stands, breathing hard with his jaw set, as he looks down at whoever is on the other side.

"Jesus Christ," he spits out with disdain. *"My son. My heir... Can anything come out of that fucking mouth of yours? All you've gotta say is 'Hello' and 'Thank you for coming'. You can't even answer a simple question when someone asks you. What the hell is wrong with you?"*

My son. My heir.

I inch down and then up, trying to see around the edge of the door, but I can't see the other person. Madame and Mr. Torrance have a son. I rarely see him, though. He's my sister's age but goes to Catholic school.

"Speak!" his father bursts out again.

I suck in a breath, and on reflex, take a step. But I accidentally go forward instead of backward and hit the door. The hinges creak, the door creeps open another inch, and I rear back.

Oh, no.

I scurry back, away from the door, and whirl around, ready to bolt. But before I can escape, the door opens, light spills across the dark hardwood floors, and a tall shadow looms over me.

I clench my thighs, the silvery ache burning like I'm about to pee my pants. Slowly, I turn my head and see Mr. Torrance standing there in a dark suit. The scowl on his face softens, and he lets out a sigh.

"Hi," he says, his lips curl in a slight smile as he gazes down at me.

On instinct, I retreat a step. "I...I got lost." I swallow, looking up at his dark eyes. "Do you know where my mom is? I can't find her."

But just then, the room's other occupant swings the door open even more, letting the knob hit the wall, and charges around his father and out of the room. Black hair hanging in his eyes, head down, and necktie draped untied around his neck, he rushes past me without a look and barrels down the stairs.

His footsteps disappear, and I turn back to Mr. Torrance.

3

Running around the hedge and onto the grass, I suddenly stop and inhale the rush of wind that hits me as it blows through the trees. Chills spread up my arms, and I glance back at the house and the windows on the second floor where I'd been. My mom might come looking for me.

But the party is boring, and my friends are this way.

Beyond the house and party, the land opens up into a vast lawn, lined and dotted with flower beds to my right and left as well as trees and rolling hills in the distance. It spans far and wide and looks like something out of a fairy tale.

I look over, seeing my sister in a tight group with our classmates. What are they doing? She glances over at me, smirks, and then says something quickly to them before they all rush into the garden maze, disappearing behind the tall hedges.

"Wait!" I shout. "Ari, wait for me!"

I take off down the small slope and toward the maze, stopping only briefly at the entrance and flashing my gaze to both of the hedges on either side. The path is only visible for several more feet before I'm forced to make a turn, and I didn't see where they went. What if I get lost?

I shake my head. No. This wouldn't be dangerous. If it were, they would've blocked it off. Right? A bunch of kids just went in. It's fine.

I push off my foot, breaking into a run as the wind sweeps through the cypresses, the promise in the gray sky and looming clouds making the hair on my arms rise. I turn right and wind around the trees, following the path and losing my way as the entrance to the maze gets farther away from me the deeper I go.

The smell of earth fills my lungs as I breathe in, and even though the ground is covered with grass, dirt scuffs my slippers, and I shift uncomfortably. They're going to be ruined now. I know it.

But Madame insisted we keep our full costumes on, even after the performance.

Laughter and howling echoes in the distance, and I shoot my head up, starting to walk faster to follow the sound. They're still in here.

After a minute, though, the sounds die out, and I stop, straining to hear where my sister and friends might be.

"Ari?" I call.

But I'm all alone.

I step timidly down the path, coming to an open plot of green with a big fountain in the middle. The space is about twice the size of my bedroom, surrounded by tall cypresses with three other pathways leading off from the big, open area. Is this the center of the maze?

The fountain is massive with a gray stone bowl at the bottom and a smaller one on top. Water shoots from the spouts, filling the upper bowl and pouring down like thick waterfalls into the lower one. It creates the prettiest sound. Like roaring rapids. So peaceful.

But not looking where I'm going, I crash into someone and stumble backward. A woman's arms rise with her palms up and away from me as if I'm dirty and she doesn't want to touch me.

I see Madame's surprised eyes soften with her smile, her body graceful and fluid like this is a theater, and she's always on stage.

"Hello, sweetheart." Her voice is drenched in sweetness. "Are you having fun?"

I step back and drop my eyes, nodding.

"Have you seen my son?" she asks. "He loves parties, and I don't want him to miss this."

He loves parties? I dig in my eyebrows, confused. His father doesn't seem to agree.

I'm about to tell her 'no', but then something to my right catches my attention, and I look over, thinning my eyes at the dark form.

The dark form inside the fountain.

It sits behind the water in the bottom bowl, almost entirely hidden.

Damon. Their son who was just getting yelled at upstairs.

I pause for a moment, the lie coming out before I can stop it. "No." I shake my head. "No, I haven't seen him, Madame. I'm sorry."

I don't know why I don't tell her he's right there, but after the way his dad just shouted at him, I guess he looks like he wants to be left alone.

I avoid Madame's eyes like she'll be able to tell I'm lying, and instead, stare straight ahead. Her black dress flows to mid-calf, glittering with little jewels and pearls as the top hugs her slender body and the bottom sways as she moves. Her long, black hair drapes down her back, as straight and shimmering as a cool stream of water.

I never hear my mom say anything nice about her, but while people are afraid of her, they are definitely nice to her face. She doesn't look much older than my babysitter, but she has a kid older than me.

Without saying anything, she glides around me and walks toward the entrance, while I stay still for a moment, wondering if I should follow and just leave, too.

But I don't.

I know he probably doesn't want to see anyone, but I kind of feel bad that he's alone.

Slowly, I inch toward the fountain.

Peering through the streams of the water pouring down, I try to make him out as he quietly hides. Arms clad in a black suit coat, resting on his knees, and dark hair hanging over his eyes and sticking to his porcelain cheekbones.

Why is he in the fountain?

"Damon?" I say in a timid voice. "Are you okay?"

He says nothing, and through the falling water, I can tell he doesn't move. It's like he doesn't hear me.

Clearing my throat, I harden my voice. "Why are you sitting in there?" And then I add, "Can I come in, too?"

I didn't mean to say it, but I got excited. It looks fun, and something inside me just wants him to feel better.

He shifts his head, his gaze flashing to the side, but then he turns back.

I squint into the thin slices of air between the spills to see his head bowed and wet hair hanging in his face. I spot a flash of red, noticing blood on his hand. Is he bleeding?

Maybe he wants a Band-Aid. I always want my mom and a Band-Aid when I'm hurt.

"I see you at Cathedral sometimes. You never take the bread, do you?" I ask him. "When the whole row goes to receive communion, you stay sitting there. All by yourself."

He doesn't move behind the water. Just like in church. He just sits there when everyone else goes up the aisle, even though he's of age. I remember him being part of my sister's first communion class.

I fidget. "I have my first communion soon," I tell him. "I'm supposed to have it, I mean. You have to go to confession first, and I don't like that part."

Maybe that's why he stays seated during that part of Mass. You're not supposed to take the bread or wine unless you've confessed, and if he hates that part as much as I do, maybe he just sits out altogether.

I search for his eyes through the water. The spray from the falls hits my skin and costume, and the hair on my arms stands up. I want to go in there, too. I want to see.

He doesn't feel friendly, though. I'm not sure what he'll do if I climb in.

"Do you want me to go?" I lean my head to the side, trying to catch his eyes. "I'll go if you want. I just don't like it out here very much. My stupid sister ruins everything."

She took off with my friends, running away from me, and my mom is...busy. Seeing what it's like inside a fountain for the first time seems like fun.

But he doesn't look like he wants me here. Or anyone, for that matter.

CHAPTER 2

Winter

PRESENT

I froze, fisting my hand and feeling him sitting across from me in the limo after the service. Damon Torrance. The boy in the fountain.

The kid in the disheveled suit with hair in his eyes and a bloody hand who would barely speak or look at me.

But now he was a man, and he had definitely learned to talk. Tall and sure, there was a threat in his dark words in the church, but I could still smell that fountain on him. He smelled like cold things do. Like sharp water.

"Your father guaranteed us a lofty settlement as long as I stay married to you for a year," my sister said as she and Damon sat side by side, across from my mother and me in the car. "I intend to see it through. No matter what you pull."

She was speaking to him, but his voice was calm and resolute when he finally addressed her. "We won't be divorcing, Arion. Not ever."

His voice sounded turned away, like he was gazing out the window or anywhere but at her.

No divorce? My heart pumped harder. Of course he would divorce her. Someday, right? I couldn't even believe it had gone *this* far. This was all just revenge on my family, after all. Why would he want to carry it out for a lifetime?

It was his plan to ruin us. Finding proof of my father's embezzlement and tax fraud and causing his flight from the country, the feds seizing nearly everything we owned, our bank accounts drained, and now...the perpetrator of all the havoc swooping in to take advantage of three destitute women who needed support. Someone to save their home and put them back into the luxurious lifestyle and community standing they were accustomed to.

But no, I understood. As much as I wanted to pretend I didn't know the end game, I did. Deep down, I did.

His plan wasn't to ruin us. It was to torture.

For however long it entertained him to do so.

"You *want* to stay married to me?" my sister asked.

"I don't want to be married to anyone else," Damon clarified, his voice monotone and uninterested. "You're as good as anyone, I suppose. You're beautiful and young. You're Thunder Bay. You're educated and presentable. You're healthy, so children shouldn't be a problem..."

"You want kids?"

My sister's question sounded almost hopeful, and I closed my eyes behind my sunglasses, cringing. "Oh, God," I breathed out, unable to hold in the curse filled with nausea and disgust.

Silence stretched the space of the car, and I was sure everyone had heard what I'd said, and while I couldn't see him, I knew his eyes were on me.

How could she still want him? And they were going to bring kids into this madness? What he did when we were children wasn't enough to convince her how bad he was, and neither was what he did to me in high school. She knew he couldn't stand her, but still, she wanted him anyway. She always wanted him.

Arion didn't care that she had to marry him because of the predicament he created in the first place. We lost everything, because of him, but no fear... Here he was, giving all of it back by marrying the eldest daughter and tucking us back in under the umbrella of his protection and his family's bank account. He made himself the cure, which wouldn't have been necessary if he hadn't also created the disease.

I hated him. My sister's new husband was the only man I thought I might kill someday.

"If you have extramarital affairs," Arion warned, "be discreet. And don't expect me to be faithful then, either."

"Ari..." My mother hinted my sister to be quiet.

But she kept going. "Do you understand?" she pressed her husband.

I stayed turned toward the window to hide my face—or at least half of it—or maybe I wanted to appear as if I weren't following the conversation, but the car was too small a space to escape his presence. I couldn't not hear every word.

Wasn't this something they should've discussed before getting married? Or wasn't this a deal-breaker for my sister?

"Let's get some things straight," he said calmly, "because I think you've forgotten exactly what your situation is, Arion." He paused and then continued. "You get my name. You get an allowance. You get to preserve your social standing in this community, including your lunches and your shopping and your fucking charities." His hard voice dug her grave deeper with every word. "Your mother and sister don't wind up on the streets, and that is where my obligation to you ends. Don't speak unless spoken to, and don't ask me questions. It aggravates me."

My chest rose and fell in shallow breaths as my stomach tightly knotted.

He continued, "I will fuck women who aren't you, but you can't fuck men who aren't me, because no one else can father my kids. Duh," he added snidely. "I will come and go as I please, and I expect you to be dressed and ready on the rare occasion we need to play the couple in public. You may not be the happiest wife, Arion, but I'm told this is why God invented Saks and Xanax."

No one said anything, and I tightened my fist around my skirt, suffocating with their lack of guts to fight back.

None of this had anything to do with her, and she knew it.

My mother guided me into the house. I felt my sister's gown brush past me as soon as we entered the marble foyer, and I let go, holding out my hand to find the stairs ahead. Once inside, I knew my way.

The stairs creaked above me. Probably Ari seeking out her room.

Some wedding day. No guests. No reception. No wedding night. At least not yet.

"Mom?" Ari called out as I swung around the bannister and headed to my room down the hall. "He and I will need a bigger room and more privacy, as well as the master bathroom."

I clenched my jaw, lightly skimming the wooden bannister with my hand as I charged to my room. Opening the door, I ducked inside and slammed it shut, locking it behind me.

My nerves fired underneath my skin, and I felt to my right, immediately grabbing the dining room chair I'd stolen. I nudged it underneath my door handle for additional protection.

He might've left for now, but he could be back at any time.

Any day. Any hour of the night. Any minute.

Mikhail brushed his wet nose on my leg, and I crouched down, petting him and holding his head to mine, savoring the feel of the only thing that made me feel good anymore. Other than dancing.

I adopted the golden retriever last year, and while I adored the company, it would be hard to leave with him if I was going to run now.

I stood up, rubbing my eyes.

God, I couldn't believe Ari. They were taking my mother's bedroom.

Anger boiled my blood, but I guess it was a good thing. We shouldn't hide under any illusions. We lived, ate, and slept under someone else's good graces. Now, we were simply guests in our own home.

How could my father leave us to this?

If caught, he would've gone to prison, which I was sure was Damon's desire. An eye for an eye. A little payback. A dose of his own medicine.

But my father had just enough time to run, and no one knew where he was now. If he had used some of the money to hide us away, get us out of the country with him, or put us under the protection of friends, I might've been able to forgive him. Or at least trust that he had a care in the world.

But he just left. And he left us high and dry at the mercy of anyone who came along. What was Damon going to do to us?

He would certainly have his fun. My sister was gorgeous. My mother still had her figure and face, judging from the comments I'd overheard around others. My sister would do anything he asked, and so would my mother. If she refused, he'd just threaten me, and she'd do anything.

She might've even been an option for this alliance, if not for the fact that she was still married to my father. And I wasn't an ideal choice, either, because I'd fight him and never stop fighting him. Ari was the easy choice.

But dodging that bullet didn't mean I was safe. What the hell else was I going to do? I had to leave. It was time. I knew this.

I should've just stayed gone. After high school, I'd completed two years of college in Rhode Island but quit to come home and focus on dancing, training, and trying to convince any choreographers or company directors to give me a chance. It had been a horrible year, though, and getting worse.

Kneeling down, I slid my hands under my bed skirt, feeling around for the nylon strap, and yanked a packed duffel bag out from underneath. The cool, oblong bag had been hidden in my closet since I sent Damon to jail five years ago, always ready for flight, because I knew I would lose in the inevitable fight. There were two changes of clothes, an extra pair of sneakers, a burner phone plus charger, a hat, sunglasses, a first aid kit, a Swiss Army knife, and all the cash I'd been secretly scrounging since then: nine thousand eighty-two dollars so far.

Of course, I had friends and family I could go to, but disappearing was the only fail-safe. I needed to be gone. Out of the country.

But I needed help getting there. Someone I trusted above everyone else who wasn't afraid of Damon or his family or the elite in this town. Someone who could outwit my new sister's husband and get me out of here.

Someone I hated putting in Damon's path, but I wasn't sure I had a choice.

• • •

"Hey," Ethan called out from the running car. "Are you okay?"

I nodded, feeling the car brush my thighs and knowing he'd opened the door for me. "I'm fine."

It was just after midnight, and a shiver snaked up my arms as I exhaled the chilly air outside my front gate and held on to Mikhail. Of course, my mother might see headlights, so I'd told my friend to pick me up down the road, honking three times in a pattern of two quicks and one slow to alert me he'd arrived.

Awareness made the hair on my body stand up. Damon hadn't come back tonight, but as long as nothing had changed, then he was still the same. He liked to be up at night, so he could still be on his way, and I needed to hurry if I was going to put miles between me and this town before anyone found out I was gone.

I should've left when the feds came after my dad more than a month ago. I knew more was going on. Or I should've left two days ago when my mother and sister were summoned to a meeting with Damon's father, and Arion came out engaged. But I was leaving now. I wasn't spending a single night with him in this house.

My duffel was pulled out of my hands, and I knew Ethan had taken it to toss in the backseat.

"Hurry up. It's cold," he said.

I climbed in, forcing the dog into the backseat and pulled the door closed, fastening my seatbelt.

A strand of hair, loose from my ponytail, brushed across my lips before getting sucked into the corner of my mouth with all of my panting. I nudged it out of the way.

"Are you sure about this?" Ethan asked.

"I can't stay in that house," I told him. "I'll leave them to whatever sick game they want to play."

"He won't let you go." I could hear him shift into gear again and the engine rev. "He won't let any of you go. Your mother, your sister, you... In his mind, you all belong to him now. You, especially."

The car took off, I pressed back into my seat, and with every inch we sped away from my family's home, the non-existent breath on my neck got hotter. I hadn't slept well in a while, but from this moment on, I'd always be looking over my shoulder.

You, especially. Ethan was one of my best friends, and he knew the whole story and how bad this was for me.

"He only married Arion because she was easy. She said yes," Ethan warned. "It's you he wants."

I remained silent, clenching my teeth so hard they ached.

Damon didn't want me. He wanted to torment me. He wanted me to hear him in the next room with my sister every night. He wanted to see me sitting quietly at the breakfast table, nervous with my knees shaking, wondering if he was watching me and what he was going to do next. He wanted to kill any peace of mind I'd achieved these last years with him tucked away in jail.

coming from outside. Gravel crackled under the tires, and I knew Ethan was veering off to the side of the road. He pressed the brake, my body lurched forward a little, and I planted my hands on the dash to steady myself as he shifted the car into *Park*.

Shit. I'd only been in a car that was pulled over once before in my entire life, and now, tonight of all nights…

A car door slammed shut, and a quiet motor hummed, telling me Ethan was rolling down his window. His shallow breathing filled the car. He was nervous, too.

"Good evening," a male voice said. "How are you tonight?"

I recognized the voice. Small town, limited cops, but I didn't mix with him enough to remember the name.

"Hey, yeah, we're good," Ethan told him, shifting in his leather seat. "Is anything wrong? I don't think I was speeding, was I?"

There was silence, and I imagined the officer bending down to peer through Ethan's window. I remained still.

"Kind of late to be out, isn't it?" he finally said, ignoring the question.

The hair on my arms stood up. What did he care?

Ethan let out a nervous laugh. "Come on, man. You sound like my mom."

"Winter?" The cop spoke up. "Everything okay?"

Heat brushed the side of my face. He had his flashlight on me.

I nodded quickly. "Yeah, we're fine."

But my hands started shaking. We shouldn't have stopped. If we'd just been able to get down into the village, around people…

"Can you pop the trunk for us?" the cop asked, his tone clipped. "You have a bulb out. I'll check it."

Us. There were two of them.

"I do?" Ethan shifted in his seat again. "That's weird."

The trunk popped open, and Ethan exhaled as I waited quietly, still feeling the heat of the flashlight.

"If you see any bodies back there, they're not mine!" Ethan called back to the second cop at his trunk, joking.

The car shifted under me a little as the second officer fumbled around at the rear, and I clasped my hands together.

"Congratulations to your sister, Winter," the officer still at the window said. "Looks like your family's luck is improving. You must be grateful."

I pursed my lips.

"So where are you two going?" he asked.

"To my apartment in the city," Ethan replied.

There was a pause, the heat left my cheek, and then he continued, "Planning on staying a while, Winter?" the officer questioned. "Is that your bag in the backseat?"

I swallowed, my heart suddenly hammering.

And then I hear the officer's low, taunting voice. "Tsk-tsk-tsk... Damon won't like that."

I turned my face away, out my window. *Shit.* I knew it.

"Excuse me?" Ethan interjected.

But he was interrupted by the officer shouting from the back. "Found something?"

"What?" Ethan blurted out.

I turned my head back toward their direction.

They found something? In his trunk?

"Step out of the car, please, Mr. Belmont."

No.

"What is this? What's going on?" Ethan argued.

But the next thing I knew, his door was opening, and I could feel him getting out of the car. I didn't know if the officer helped him or he did it of his own free will, but I opened my mouth to speak. "Ethan..." But I didn't know what to say. They had him now.

Shuffling and mumbling, I could feel the car shift under me as they dug in the trunk again.

But then...

"What?" Ethan shouted. "That's not mine!"

I twisted around in my seat, hearing Mikhail whine a little as I tried to hear what they were saying.

"Cocaine," one of the officers said. "That's a felony."

I shot my eyebrows up. Cocaine? As in... cocaine? I unfastened my seatbelt and opened my door. *No.*

Stepping out of the car, I got out, leaving the door open, and kept my hand on the vehicle, using it as guide as I walked toward the rear. I wasn't supposed to leave the car. They were going to yell at me, but...

"You guys have to be joking?" Ethan growled. "You planted that!"

I heard a scuffle and a grunt, and I sucked in a breath.

"Whoa, whoa," one of the officers said. "Are you under the influence right now?"

What was happening?

More grunting, gravel kicked up under their feet, and I knew they had their hands on him.

"Stop!" I yelled, my hands sliding down the hood of the car to the open trunk as I reached them. "He would never do drugs. What are you doing?"

I heard heavy breathing I assumed was Ethan's as the chilly evening air stung my nose.

"We've got at least fifteen baggies here," a cop said.

"That's intent to distribute," added the other.

Intent to distribute. Two possible felony charges? My head was reeling.

"You son of a—" Ethan growled but was cut off and shut up.

"Wait!" I burst out. "Please stop. This is my fault."

This was all a setup. There was no way he had drugs in his trunk. These cops stopped us for a reason, and it wasn't a busted taillight.

I stepped closer, careful of my footing. "*I* called *him*," I said, taking the blame. "What do you want me to do? Just please... Please don't do anything to him."

There was silence for a few moments, and then I heard some clicks. Someone was on their phone.

"Sir?" one of the cops said. "I have her here."

Damon. This was him. He was who the cop was calling.

A cool hand touched mine, and I jerked, pausing when I realized the officer had put the phone in my hand. My fear and confusion slipped away, replaced with anger. I breathed hard, seething as I clenched my teeth.

I raised the phone to my ear.

"I'm very disappointed you actually thought this would work," a hard voice said. "Although I am surprised you even got out of the house."

It wasn't Damon.

"Gabriel?" I barely mumbled, shocked.

Damon's dad had arranged all of this? I was pretty sure he hadn't been at the wedding. I knew he had to fully support what Damon was doing, but it escaped me that he'd have his back, too. He was watching me.

"Try not to worry," he went on. "They'll let him go in the morning."

"They'll let him go now!" I growled.

I wasn't having my friend suffer at all because of me. It was stupid. I should've known better. Even if I had made it out, I would've put Ethan in Damon's path just by involving him.

"Or we can keep him locked up until the trial," Mr. Torrance continued. "Your choice."

I ground my teeth together, too angry to think. Ethan wasn't tough. I loved him, but a night in jail wouldn't be good. Much less weeks, months, or years. Tears sprang to my eyes, but I forced them away.

"What do you want?"

"I want you to get your fucking little ass back home and in bed," he bit out.

I shook my head, knowing he had me—for now.

But not forever.

"You think I'll be easy?" I challenged.

"Of course not." His tone softened, sounding amused. "That's why he wants you, Winter. Just try not to be predictable next time."

CHAPTER 3

Damon

SEVEN YEARS AGO

I snake my arm around her, pulling her close and hanging on as I bury my nose in the back of her hair. The coarse little jewels glued to her costume cut into my arm. She's so small and fragile, like a toothpick in my coil.

The fountain spills around us as her teeth sink into my hand, but instead of yanking my arm away, the pain of her sharp, little bite fills my veins with warmth and my eyelids flutter. Tingles spread under my skin, and the breath I didn't realize I'd been holding finally leaves my lungs.

It doesn't feel bad. It doesn't hurt the way it should.

I look at her small face, not resisting her as the pressure deepens, and I'm sure the skin has torn.

Yes.

I won't pull away.

Not ever.

I squeezed her tighter in my arm, the curve of her body molding to mine as I refused to let go. Even as consciousness started to seep in, the fountain faded away, and the scent of her changed from flowers to my soap. The costume she was dressed in was now soft, like cotton, and her naked legs, free of their white tights, laid next to mine.

It was different. Something was different.

I blinked my eyes open, the weight of sleep heavy on my head as the dream floated away and the room came into view. As well as the body next to me.

Unfortunately, it wasn't the girl from the dream.

I stared at the back of my sister's head, her hair laying across my pillow and nearly as dark as mine. I could feel her breathing in my hold as she slept, and my fist clenched where it lay across her stomach.

I'd reached for her in my sleep.

I never used to do that. We'd been sharing a bed for four years now. Just knowing she was there was enough.

Uncurling my fingers, I accidentally brushed against the skin of her tummy where her shirt rode up, and I stopped, my eyes narrowing as unease burned under my skin.

I lifted the sheet and looked underneath, taking in the pronounced curve of her waist, deeper than I remembered it, and her round ass pressing into my groin.

There were dips in her thighs where the toned muscles were now more pronounced, and her skin looked so smooth.

Fuck. I closed my eyes, the relief of the dream long gone by now.

She was starting to look like other girls. Girls who were old enough for guys to do things to. She felt like the girls I went out with.

"Damon," she suddenly said, awake. "It's Banks."

I guessed I stirred her when I touched her. She probably thought I was thinking she was someone else.

Opening my eyes, I clenched my jaw and yanked away from her. "Yeah, I know who it is."

I threw off the covers and got up out of bed, grabbing my cell phone off its charger. "I thought I told you to wrap yourself up," I mumble, unlocking my screen and scrolling through my notifications.

She didn't say anything, but I heard her scoot up to a sitting position. "When I sleep, too?" she whined. "It's like a corset, Damon. I can't breathe."

You'll get used to it.

After thumbing through a couple messages from Will and some comments on posts, I tossed the phone down onto my desk and started some music on the computer. Walking to the closet, I grabbed some slacks and a white shirt and then stopped, staring at a pair of jeans hanging next to my black hoodie. Devil's Night was next week, and a familiar rush skated through my veins.

I grabbed the jeans, too, and headed for the bathroom to my left. I had a craving.

"Maybe..." I heard Banks say from the bed. "Maybe I shouldn't sleep here anymore, you know?"

I stopped, narrowing my eyes as I turned to look at her.

Her gaze instantly dropped. She knew I didn't want to talk about this.

Banks was my father's daughter, but she was mine and had been from the day she came to live here. Her mom was some lowlife slut, one of the many my father had kept on the payroll, and if her mother hadn't banged down our door for money four years ago, I probably never would have known Banks existed. My father certainly never acknowledged her and still barely did.

That was fine, though. She wasn't his. No one could take her from me.

After the first time we met, I spent days scrounging and stealing all the money I could find around the house and any valuables my mother wouldn't know were missing. It was thousands of dollars, and Banks' drug addict mom put on a show of struggling with the decision for a full twelve seconds before taking the cash and jewelry and giving Banks to me. I brought her home and no one fought me on it. My mother, when she still lived here, didn't let anything penetrate her happy, little dream world, and my father allowed anything that kept *me* happy.

Banks stayed in my room, she took care of me, and I provided for and protected her. She had her own mattress up in the little hideaway in the tower adjoining my room, but she'd barely ever slept there.

"Just in this bed, I mean," she clarified. "In... your bed. Maybe I should start sleeping in my cubbie again. We're not twelve and thirteen anymore. You're bigger. You need more room."

I cocked an eyebrow, angry and knowing I had no good reason to be. There was a reason I kept her a secret. A reason I didn't let any other girl in my room and forced her to wear my old clothes, bind her body, and would never tell my friends my sister was the only woman who would ever sleep in my bed.

I knew I was fucked up.

I just didn't care. As long as I was happy, I didn't explain myself to anyone.

When she turned away, I knew she'd given up the argument, and I continued into the bathroom. Turning on the shower, I stripped out of my pajama pants and climbed in, washing and shampooing. I rinsed under the hot spray, bending my head forward and letting the water run down the back of my neck.

I closed my eyes, my fingers pressing into the wall. *It's only a matter of time, though.* My senior year just started last month, but it was my last year at home. Next summer, I'd be leaving for college, and Banks wouldn't be going with me. I *should* let her set up her own room. Get us both used to the space. We had plenty of empty bedrooms for her to choose from, after all.

And I had no doubt she'd adjust easily and even love having her own room.

No, the problem was me. She was mine. She was the only person who knew everything, but we were growing up, and I knew she was going to leave me eventually.

I dug my fingers into the wall, feeling a face—anyone's face—fill my hand as I tried to crush it in my fist. The familiar burn crawled up the back of my neck, into my head, and I could feel heat rush through my dick, every inch of my skin begging not to feel anything I was feeling right now.

I needed to get out of here.

Finishing rinsing, I turned off the water and stepped out of the shower, grabbing a towel off the shelf to my left. I dried off, pulled on my jeans and T-shirt, and walked back into the bedroom, drying my hair on the way.

"I did the math problems and updated your research log," Banks told me, sifting through papers on a desk I never used and slipping folders into my bag. "You need to recopy the math in your handwriting, though, and don't forget to do the reading in Physics for your test today. At least absorb enough to pass."

I tossed the towel down and picked up my black hoodie, sliding my arms through. "I always pass. Ever notice that?" I shot her a look before pulling the hoodie over my head. "I could piss all over that test and still pass."

I heard her laugh under her breath. "Yeah, it's almost like they don't want to do anything that will keep you at that school longer."

Nope. I would never fail a test, much less a class. The administration was practically counting the days until I was gone. They would never hold me back.

I did whatever classwork I was inclined to in order to keep people off my case, but Banks did the homework, projects, and papers. It wasn't that I was lazy—I worked my ass off for the basketball team—I just didn't care. And it was too damn hard to force myself to do anything I wasn't invested in. I was selfish and completely fine with that.

Taking the bag from her with my uniform inside, I slung it over my head and stuffed my wallet, phone, and keys into the pocket. I walked out of the room and closed the door, not even half-way down the short, hidden staircase before I heard the click of the lock on the other side of my door behind me. She knew the drill.

It normally didn't occur to me to care that my house wasn't exactly a safe place for pretty, young girls, but I didn't want anyone messing with Banks. That door stayed locked until she was dressed and had her guard good and up.

Swinging around the bannister, I headed through the foyer, down a few more steps, and into the dining room, straight for the table.

"Good morning," someone chirped.

I blinked, aggravated. Some girl stood just out of the corner of my eye dressed in the standard white button-down the servants wear, but she must be new. I grabbed a slice of bread from the tray and began piling it with some eggs and bacon, then stuffing some water bottles from the rows on the table into my bag for the day.

Our cook, Marina, placed a silver bowl of fruit on the table.

"When is my father back?" I asked, tearing off the crust on the bread.

"Tomorrow evening, sir."

"Would you like something in particular for dinner tonight, Mr. Torrance?" the girl piped up again.

Jesus Christ.

I folded the bread in half, keeping everything tucked inside as the girl waited for an answer. I took a bite, shot Marina a look, and walked out, hearing her scold the new girl as I left.

• • •

Life felt like hell, because we expected it to feel like heaven. The quote I read years ago went something like that, but I never understood it. When you're in the thick all your life, living in ways you eventually figure out no one else is, you learn to sleep well in heat and eat fire. Until one day it's all you need.

It was heaven I didn't trust. High hopes and false expectations...

No, I *needed* the trouble.

I pinched the cigarette butt between my three fingers, feeling my phone vibrate for the second time in my back pocket as I brought my hand up to my mouth and took another drag. The faint sizzle of the paper burned to the end, the hot smoke being pulled into my lungs, and I blew it out again as I leaned against the column next to the bulletin board.

The school was still mostly empty, at least forty-five minutes to the bell.

And the third floor was my favorite place. The bustle of the cafeteria and gymnasium were far below, and there were very few classrooms up here, so it was quiet enough that you could hear every footstep. Every door. Every pen drop... You knew when you weren't alone.

And she wasn't alone. I wondered if she'd noticed that yet.

I turned my head and peered around the edge of the column, seeing the blur of her through the glass, across the open air, which allowed for the courtyard below, and through another set of windows. She'd gotten a little too big for her britches, but that was common with new teachers, especially the young ones. They thought college prepared them for this, and even if it did, it didn't prepare them for Thunder Bay. Things worked a little differently here, and she wasn't the boss, because I couldn't be handled. It was time to educate her that teachers fell in line, not the other way around.

She moved in the room, making her copies at the machine, and I licked my lips, my mouth going dry. *Come on. Go somewhere quiet, or I'm taking you right there.*

Images of her loose, little bun coming down. Those legs in heels as she was bent over a table...

My phone vibrated again, and I blinked hard, swallowing through my parched throat. *Goddamn him.*

Gritting my teeth, I dug out my phone, swiped the screen, and held it to my ear. "Fuck off."

"Well, top of the fucking morning to you, Grouch," Will said. "What's your problem?"

I swallowed again, raising my eyes to the prize once more. "Nothing my dick can't solve if you leave me alone for ten minutes," I told him, staring at her. "What do you want?"

"To make you smile."

I frowned. *To make me...* Jesus, fuck. I rolled my eyes. But just like that, I almost gave in. He had a gift for smoothing out my edges and really fucking quick, too.

"Haha. I can hear you smiling." I could hear his amusement. The laughter always present in his voice.

"You can hear me smiling, huh?"

He was the only one—the only one—who didn't walk on eggshells around me, and I damn near killed him for it a few times, but now I barely did anything without him. "I told you," he pointed out. "We're connected. It's spiritual and shit."

I let out a little grin he couldn't see. "I fucking hate you." Idiot.

Will, Michael, and Kai were my friends, and I'd walk through fire for any one of them. Will was the only one, though, who I was sure would walk through fire for me.

"So, what is she wearing?" he asked.

I kept my eyes on her, following her as she left the copy room and started down the hallway. "An engagement ring."

"Kinky."

I laughed to myself and took a step and then another, matching her pace as she walked down one hallway and me another. "Be even kinkier if she were wearing the wedding dress, too."

"I'll take a piece of that."

"You're welcome to it. I'm good about sharing."

And sometimes sharing was necessary. When it came to women, I didn't always keep my promises. Will finished them off if I lost interest.

She was approaching the corner and would turn left. It was almost time.

"Gotta go," I told him. "Meet you in the parking lot at seven-thirty."

"Yeah. I left my gym bag in your car, so I need to get it before practice. See you—"

I didn't let him finish. I pulled the phone away from my ear and hung up, never taking my eyes off her. She rounded the corner and reappeared through the windows perpendicular to me, making her way closer and closer. Pulling to a stop, I slid my phone back into my pocket, leaned my shoulder into the wall, and slipped my hands into the center pocket of my hoodie, waiting for her.

She took another left, briefly disappeared from sight, and reappeared again, stopping as soon as she spotted me.

"Mr. Torrance," she said.

I nodded once. "Miss Jennings. You wanted to see me?"

She took a step back, looking around her. I wasn't sure if it was instinctive or if she was confused, but it amused me. She wore a short-sleeved, black V-neck dress that hugged every curve, far from the little cardigans and floral, knee-length skirts she wore at the beginning of the school year. A first-year teacher who started out looking very much wife-of-the-town-pastor seemed to like the lustful eyes of her teenage male students on her and couldn't help but dress for it now. She still wore her glasses and her hair in tight, little buns, though.

She swallowed, a blush crossing her cheeks. "Um, during school hours, yes. I'm, uh…" She dropped her eyes, shifting in her black heels, and I held in my smirk. While she dressed sexier now, she was still shy.

And I loved that. Confidence annoyed me. I didn't like being hunted.

"Well, you're here, I suppose," she said, giving me a curt smile. "Come in."

I followed her into the classroom, feeling the blood suddenly pump a little warmer through my body.

This was what it took for me.

There were any number of girls downstairs right now. Girls my own age. The cheerleaders, the gymnastics team, the work-study students in the cafeteria... I could get laid in five minutes if I wanted to, but sex for me had little to do with my body.

It was right here. With my eyes on her back. With the door I closed and locked behind me. With the fear and the attraction and the danger I felt rolling off her at being alone with me. With the idea that she'd have to look at me every day for the rest of the year until I graduated, knowing what she'd let me do to her today and the panic that she let it happen but also the desire of wanting it to happen again.

Sex for me was in the head. Almost entirely.

She set her little pile of papers on her desk and turned around, her eyes darting to the door she just realized I'd closed. A heavy pause followed, and I saw her body go rigid, but she pressed on.

She threaded her fingers in front of her body and put on her stern face. A pretty cute attempt for a twenty-three-year-old who thought the seventeen-year-old guy in front of her who was broader—and half-a-foot taller—actually saw her as an authority figure.

I took the two steps to reach the first desk in the front row and planted my ass on the edge.

"Look, I'm not skilled at beating around the bush," she said, "so let's just cut to the chase."

I stared at her.

"There is a significant difference between the work you complete at home and the work you complete in class," she continued. "And I notice the difference in the handwriting, as well. I'm not going to ask you to defend yourself, because we both know what's really going on, and I'm not going to waste either of our time."

I cocked an eyebrow.

She paused, licking her lips and clearing her throat. "All I'm going to say is 'stop'." She tipped her chin down at me. "Do the work, or you won't pass."

Uh-huh. I kept my eyes on hers, but I could still see the hard, little points of her nipples jutting through her dress. Maybe it was cold. Maybe it wasn't. I just wanted to see them.

My breathing quickened and my cock started to swell with the image of her undressed, and I ground my teeth together to keep my urges in check for as long as possible.

When I didn't reply, she prompted me. "Do you understand?"

I cast my gaze upward again, imagining her glossy red lipstick smeared all over my pillow from being 'face down, ass up' in my bed all night. "Yes, ma'am," I replied.

She stood there, looking confused like she didn't expect it to go that smoothly, but then nodded and offered me a goodwill half-smile. "Okay, then. Have a good day," she said, dismissing me.

I almost snorted. We weren't done.

My turn.

"May I ask you a question?" I said, pulling up a picture of her on my phone. "Is this you?"

I stood up and strolled over to her, not stopping until I was close enough to look down at her. Her eyes shot from the phone in my hand up to me and back down again in our suddenly intimate space, trying to take a step back but only meeting her desk.

I held it up, speaking softly. "You don't look a lot different."

She swallowed again. It was one of many pictures I found on her social media, apparently from after her junior year of high school when she was away at summer camp. She posed with friends on her bunk, smiling and innocent, hair down, tan legs in cute jean shorts, no makeup and braces...

She pursed her lips. "I know how to use mascara now."

Turning her back to me, she lifted the chalk and began writing on the board.

"You're blushing," I commented. "Are you embarrassed?"

"That's enough."

Young Miss Jennings was a dork, but she had potential. I let my eyes wander down the curve of her waist to her ass and sexy legs. *Obviously.*

"You see, I'm not lazy or dumb," I said, coming up behind her, just out of reach. "I'm just not interested in doing anything I don't enjoy. But things I love doing?" I lowered my voice, playing with her. "I could go all night, Miss Jennings."

She twisted her head to the side again, her hand paused mid-sentence on the chalkboard. Her mouth opened and closed twice before words came out. "I have work to do."

I shot out my hand, planting it on the board in front of her and leaning in so close, her hair tickled my lips. "Guys like me didn't go for you in high school, did they?" I taunted in a low voice. "No one ate you out in the backseat of a car. No one took off your panties and dry-humped you on your parents' couch while they were in the next room." I slowly ran my finger over the zipper at the back of her dress as her body went rigid and her breathing turned shallow. "No one sucked your tits and made your pussy wet on someone else's bunk beds in a room upstairs at some party in a house you didn't know."

She whipped around, her teeth slightly bared. "I'm going to report you."

"Please don't." I smirked. "If I were there, though, I would've broken your cherry." I dropped my voice to a whisper, leaning in. "I like the quiet ones."

She shook her head, the brown of her eyes warm and dark. "I was warned about you boys. This won't get you an A. Someday you'll learn the world will make you work for something you want."

42

"Oh, I don't mind working." I planted my other hand on the board at the side of her head and looked down at her.

My little Lit teacher was only six years older than me, and while every guy in school loved to look at her, I was the one who would have her, because nothing else would do. I was bored. So bored all the time with the brainless twits downstairs who never said 'no' and couldn't satisfy the sordid need inside me to be deviant in everything I did. I didn't want to fuck. I wanted to get dirty, and I wanted to get her dirty. I didn't want to be the only one who…

I couldn't finish the thought. My friends—as much as they liked to play at being bad, they were still always clean. Their desires were normal, getting off was physical, and fun was just around the corner.

But for me, everything was harder. I couldn't detach from my brain, and I wasn't happy unless it was a mindfuck. I didn't want Miss Jennings to enjoy it. I wanted her to hate that she enjoyed it.

I inched in, holding her eyes and moving in for her mouth.

But she planted her hands on my chest, halting me. "Stop it."

I let the weight of my body slowly press into hers, the heat of her breath falling on my mouth as I shook my head.

She breathed faster, her eyes dropping to my lips, and I could see that look on her face that I'd seen a hundred times before. Everyone lets themselves indulge in a moment of consideration.

"I don't need an A, and I'm not afraid of what you can do to me," I said, flicking her top lip with my tongue and hearing her whimper. "I just want you to slide up your dress, lie down on the desk, and spread your legs like a good teacher who just wants her student to eat his breakfast."

She growled, raised her hand, and fucking slapped me.

But I barely moved, the sting of her hand filtering down into my neck within seconds.

Grabbing both of her wrists, I held them against the chalkboard at her side, trying to hold in my grin. "You just hit a minor. It hurt, Miss Jennings."

Her chest rose and fell hard as she seethed and tried to squirm out of my hold.

"I know you want this." I let my eyes fall down her body. "Your skirts are getting tighter. Your tops lower cut. You're not my first rodeo. I know how to keep this a secret."

"No matter what a woman wears, she's not asking for it."

"So that's not you then?" I gestured my head toward the windows. "Peering down from the window when the team's exercising on the field? Watching me?"

We were nearly eight weeks into my senior year, and coach had us on the outside courts after school as much as possible while the weather held. I started noticing her gazing down a few weeks ago and then quickly ducking away when I would notice her. Just went to show, we want what we want and we were built to burn.

"You stare especially long when I have my shirt off." I dropped my eyes to her lips. "Which I take off more now, because I know you like it."

She lost her breath, opening her mouth as she stared at mine.

"If I had been in your high school," I told her, leaning in to her ear, "I'd come up to you in front of your friends and whisper in your ear 'I want to touch you.'" I whispered the last and then came back around, holding her eyes. "And then I'd take your hand and lead you down to the basement and into the dark wrestling room where no one ever is, and I'd start to take off your clothes."

"Mr. Torrance," she choked out, and then pleaded, "Damon, please."

Fear etched across her face, but not the fear of not being able to stop me. It was the fear of wanting something but not wanting to get caught.

"And then I'd push you down on the mat," I said, "lift up your skirt," I let go of one of her wrists, and wrapped one hand around her neck, "and fuck your tight, little body while I sucked on your tits."

She panted, and before she could say anything, I sank my mouth into hers, her groan getting lost down my throat. I kissed her hard, tasting the strawberries she had for breakfast and feeling her arms wrapped around my neck.

I pulled them off and lifted her off the ground, turning us around and planting her ass on her desk, immediately pushing up her dress.

Reaching under, I slipped my fingers under her panties and pulled them down her smooth, tan legs, over her heels, and dropped them to the floor. I squeezed my eyes shut, feeling my heart pound a little harder.

I'm gonna fuck her. I'm gonna have her begging to come and take pleasure later today as she tries to lecture the class knowing her fucking panties are in my pocket. I'm gonna come back for seconds tomorrow and maybe bring Will and watch her ride him in her own desk chair.

Yeah. My heart skipped a beat, and I stopped breathing for a moment. My dick hardened, and I licked a trail up her leg to the inside of her thigh as I stood up.

"Why me?" she asked, leaning back on her hands and biting her bottom lip.

I pushed her down, forcing her back onto the desk. "Because it's sordid," I growled.

Hiking up her skirt the rest of the way, I checked the door again, remembering I'd closed and locked it, and then dove down, covering her goddamn cunt with my mouth, the little gasp and cry that followed making my eyes close in satisfaction. *Just spread your fucking legs and let me have my way. That's what you're here for.*

Wrapping my hand around her thigh, I held on as I sucked, kissed, pulled, bit, and penetrated her, tasting her clit and making her squirm and moan with every inch

I teased. She wasn't the first teacher I'd seen like this, but she was the first one I'd touched, and I looked up at her as I sucked on her, seeing how much she liked it. This was almost too easy. It was less of a turn on when it was easy.

"Pull down the top of your dress," I ordered her, flicking her clit with my tongue.

She let out little moans again and again as she pulled down one side and then the other, baring her naked breasts. *Better.* She looked vulnerable. Half-naked, legs spread for one of her students, glasses...

"You're so good at that," she panted.

I bit her lightly, making her gasp. *Don't talk.*

She started moving into my mouth and took my head in her hands. I shoved them away and pressed a hand on her stomach, keeping her ass on the desk. I licked and sucked again and again, liking her in my mouth, because I was in control and she was at my mercy. Everything was happening to *her* right now and whatever I wanted to give her.

"God, yeah," she moaned. "That's so good."

I snapped out of my head for a moment, hearing another voice instead.

That's a good boy. You're getting so good at that, baby.

I stopped working Miss Jennings, needing to swallow, because my mouth was suddenly dry.

Forcing myself on, I pushed the voice out of my head and slid two fingers inside her as I played with her clit with my tongue.

"God, you're doing so well," Miss Jennings said, refusing to shut the fuck up. "Don't stop. Keep going, baby."

Baby? What the fuck?

I clenched my teeth and stood straight, breathing hard and damn near ripping at my belt buckle to unfasten it. She might have some duct tape in her desk. She needed to be shut up. Heat flooded my neck and chest as I fought to get back in my head where I was distracted.

But she rose up off the desk, trying to kiss me and take over unfastening the belt. "I want to suck you," she breathed out. "I want to taste you."

It gets hard when I do that. That means you like it.

The memory of those words knotted over and over again in my gut, and I pulled her hands away. "No."

I didn't like that.

"Do as your told," she said, trying to play.

But I lost it. I grabbed her neck and held her still as I got in her face. "I don't like that."

Yeah, you like it, don't you, baby? You're such a good boy.

I shoved her away and backed up, refastening my belt. My pulse pounded in my ears, and my skin crawled as the walls closed in. I couldn't catch my breath. I couldn't breathe.

Fuck.

"What?" I heard Miss Jennings say as she held up her arms, covering herself. "I want it, Damon. You knew I wanted you. This was so hot. Come on." She reached for me and stood up, trying to wrap her arms around my body. "Finish me," she whispered, her sticky, snake-arms like fire on my skin.

I pushed her off and ran a hand through my hair. "Stupid bitch."

And I walked away from her, unlocking the door and throwing it open as I charged into the still mostly empty hallway. Nausea rolled through my stomach.

Why couldn't she shut up? Why couldn't she just shut her fucking mouth? Most people did what they were told.

I bolted down the stairs and then the next flight as well, turning the corner and pushing through the door into the men's room.

I shouldn't have touched her. I walked to the sink and spit, still tasting her and spit again. I turned on the water, filled my hands, and splashed my face to try to cool down. I did it again and again, wiping my face on my sleeve.

I stared at myself in the mirror as I ran my hand through my hair, dragging my nails over my scalp and down my neck. Down my neck, digging in, deeper and deeper.

Come sleep with me, my sweet. And the memory of climbing in her big bed with the thick comforter as she held me to her naked body.

I let my eyes close and my forehead fall into the mirror as I breathed. "I should have fucked her," I mumbled to myself. "I should've taped her mouth, turned her over, and fucked her."

Everything turned black behind my eyelids, and I was sinking into a black hole. I felt the needles prick at the back of my throat.

I dug out my phone and hit all the buttons without even looking. It started to ring, and I held it up to my ear.

"Damon?" Banks answered.

I paused, breathing hard. "Banks..."

"Do you need me?"

I blinked my eyes open, checking the door to make sure no one was coming in. "There's no time."

We had to do this over the phone.

But she started to argue. "Damon—"

"Fuck, what good are you?" I squeezed the phone so hard I heard it crack.

She fell silent, and I pictured her in my room where she was cleaning or reading or taking care of my snakes, and I wished she was here, because this would be so much quicker.

Do it. Just do it.

I heard her clear her throat and let out a sigh. "You know..." She gave me her best annoyed tone. "I got shit to do. Is this all you're calling me for? Jesus, you're such a fucking baby."

My fingers twitched with the urge to fist. *Good.* Keep going. I slid into a stall and locked the door. "Go ahead," I egged her on. "Say that again?"

"Or what?" she shot back. "What will you do? You're so goddamn weak, you have to call me because someone hurt your feelings? Someone stepped on your toe, baby, is that it? Michael, Kai, and Will must be doing Jesus a favor to even consider breathing the same air as you."

My jaw locked.

"The only reason I stick around here is for the money, but I don't even care about that anymore," she continued, "because I want to fucking vomit every time I have to look at your stupid face. Jesus, I really am sick of this shit."

My chest shook, and I balled my fist over and over again. *She's lying. She's doing what she's supposed to do. I need her to hurt me, because pain covers up pain, and if I feel one, I won't feel the other. I need her to push back down what tries to crop back up.*

"What?" She smarted off. "What are you going to say? Nothing, that's what. You can't even manage an hour away from me before you're having a Malibu-fucking-Barbie panic attack. No wonder Daddy likes me best. I'm the son he always wanted."

And I feel a slice inside my stomach. That one cut.

Because I thought she might be right. My father wouldn't even acknowledge her as his kid, but he trusted her. He entrusted her.

Her. A bastard gutter rat who would be turning tricks just like her junkie mother if I hadn't literally bought her ass when she was twelve. She lived in a mansion, because of me. She had three meals a day, because of me. She was safe, because of me.

"What did you say?" I gritted out.

I could hear her breathing shake. She was losing the nerve. "Damon, please..."

"Say it again!"

She gasped, choking down her tears and forcing the words out. "We laugh about you every day while you're gone." Her voice grew harder. "He can't trust you to grow up. He can't give you any responsibility. Everyone laughs about you. Especially the guy doing me in your bed right now."

I shook my head, gripping the top of the stall door. No one was supposed to touch her.

"God, you weren't even out of the house before the first one was inside me," she said, digging deep. "I've been getting pounded all morning. Why don't you get to class and leave us the fuck alone?"

I clenched my teeth, seeing her in my bed with a line of my father's men taking their turns. Smiling at her. Enjoying her. Using her. Treating her like trash.

And I kicked the door. I kicked it again and again, growling until it gave way and swung open, hitting the wall behind it.

Fuck, yes. And just like that...everything relaxed. My limbs felt exhausted, and I saw my sister, in my room at home right now, fully dressed with her collar up to her neck, crying, and her books spilled onto the floor, because she was innocent, pure, and the sweetest girl I would ever know.

Everything she said, I made her say, because we could only feel one pain at a time, and maybe if I could pile on enough dirt, I'd get so buried I wouldn't be able to think.

And sometimes, I could overpower whatever was in my head by making my own victims.

Like Miss Jennings. Like Banks. Maybe I didn't like being alone, and I wouldn't be if everyone else was as dirty as me.

At home, there were other things I'd ask her to do to stop the pain, but when she wasn't in front of me we had to improvise.

The memories that had sprung up in Jennings' room were so far away now, I couldn't even remember what had set me off. I walked to the sink, turned on the faucet, and pooled some water in my hand before taking a drink, feeling the cool water soothe the heat in my head.

The last twenty minutes never happened.

"Damon?" I heard Banks call. "Damon!"

I stood up straight and held the phone back up to my ear.

"Better?" she asked.

"Yeah." I checked my face and hair in the mirror, seeing the rage start to fade, and my skin turn pale again. "Yeah..."

"Please stop making me do that..."

I pulled the phone away from my ear and hung up, ignoring her. What she wanted was ultimately unimportant. We would do what we had to do.

Straightening my clothes, I felt the phone vibrate in my hand again and looked to see who it was.

Damon K. Torrance
Please see Mr. Kincaid in the dean's office
before the first bell this morning.
cc: Gabriel Torrance
Thank you.

Goddammit.

I checked the time on my phone, seeing that I had eight minutes till bell. I wanted to smoke.

Sticking the phone in my back pocket, I let out a long breath and tilted my neck to each side, hearing it crack. Every time I got summoned, my father got the same text, keeping him abreast of whatever was going on as if he cared. He knew if it was important enough, they would call him directly. Which they had done plenty in my tenure at this school.

I used to want his attention. Now I just hated it when they reminded him that I existed. I wasn't excited to leave town for college next summer, but I couldn't wait to get out of that house, either.

So what bullshit did I do now that Kincaid needed to hassle me?

I left the bathroom, brushing the shoulder of another student as I crossed the hallway and entered the school office. Swinging the door open, I walked up to the long, dark wood counter and shot a glare to Mrs. Devasquez, the secretary.

"Have a seat," she said, her short gray hair unmoving as she nodded to the chairs behind me. "The dean will call you when he's ready."

I simply turned around and propped my elbows up on the counter, waiting.

Drumming my fingers as my hand dangled over the edge of the counter, I noticed no one else was in the office, but I perked my ears at several voices coming from Kincaid's office to my left. I looked over, seeing bodies rise up, as if from sitting positions, behind the frosted glass.

"Why aren't you in uniform?" I heard Devasquez challenge behind me.

"Is it 7:45 yet?"

I didn't turn around to look at her, and she didn't open her mouth again.

I hated this room. Most of the classrooms in this old school had been updated over time, the fancy gray stone exterior preserved, and everything in a condition which was expected from parents who paid a substantial tuition every year, but this room reminded me of home. Dark wood, shiny with a noxious odor from years of layers of furniture polish, high ceilings with rafters that collected dust, and cobblestone floors that never quite made me feel like my feet were firmly on the ground.

Kincaid's door opened and voices flooded out.

I turned to see Margot Ashby lead the way out of the office, saying as they all left, "Thank you, Charles. I know you and the teachers have gone above and beyond to help Winter re-assimilate."

Winter... My eyes narrowed.

And then she appeared. Holding her mother's arm and trailing slowly behind.

I stopped breathing for a moment. *Jesus Christ.* What the hell was she doing here?

The little girl in the fountain. She'd grown up. She couldn't be more than fourteen or fifteen now, but the baby fat was gone, her white tutu gone, and her eyes on me... gone. She would never look at me again.

Her older sister, who was my age, squeezed out first, while Kincaid and their father, the mayor, trailed behind.

"We'll keep her up here until Miss Fane arrives," I heard Kincaid say as they all drifted into the main office. "She has all the instructions to help Winter through her first few weeks, and since they're in the same grade, it was easy placing them in the same classes."

Same classes.

Miss Fane. Erika Fane? She and Winter were going to be in the same classes? Then that meant Winter was a freshman.

And she'd come home to go to high school.

I fought not to smile, practically fucking delighted with the potential of this new distraction.

She came up alongside her mother and dropped her hand when everyone stopped, not needing to hang on any longer than necessary, and I couldn't take my eyes off her. Her blue eyes still looked so innocent and carefree but probably only because she didn't know I was less than five feet away from her. I wondered how well she remembered me.

But there was a defiant lift to her chin that intrigued me.

How easily one pain replaced another. How I could barely remember the hurt in my head just a few minutes ago and Miss Jennings seemed like a distant memory. I inhaled a deep, quiet breath, filling my lungs with the welcome fresh air.

"Does she have to wear the blazer?" Mrs. Ashby asked. "We tried to get her to wear it, but—"

"Oh no, it's fine," Kincaid answered. "As long as she's in Thunder Bay colors, we're good."

Winter wore the standard blue and green plaid skirt, but while most everyone wore blouses or Oxfords under their blazers, I could see a white Polo hanging out from under the hem of her navy blue hoodie.

Rebel.

"What's the dress code say about wearing shoes from dumpsters?" Arion, her sister, chimed in as she knelt down to tie Winter's Doc Martens that were scuffed beyond repair on both toes with laces dragging. "You'd think someone who needs a hand to walk everywhere so she doesn't trip would know how to double-knot."

"Bite me." Winter yanked her foot away and felt for the counter next to me. I wasn't sure how she knew it was there, but she found it and then knelt down to tie her boot, her long, layered blonde hair hanging around her.

Everyone in the room suddenly fell silent, and I looked up to see her parents staring at me, suddenly realizing I was in the room. Three inches from their daughter.

Winter rose, her hand brushing my jeans.

"Oh, excuse me," she said, finally noticing someone was here.

Her mother inhaled, darting toward us. "Um, actually, Charles, we'll wait with Winter in the library." She came up and grabbed Winter, pulling her away from me. "If you could send Erika there when she arrives..."

"Of course."

Margot, Arion, and Winter filtered into the corridor, and my head started swimming with all the possibilities now laying in front of me. I wasn't sure if she thought about me or what she thought about me, but I knew she wouldn't forget me. She would never be able to forget.

The door closed behind them, and I saw Griffin Ashby, our city mayor, start to follow, but then he stopped as he reached me.

I stared at his profile, his dark gray suit and blue tie perfectly pressed as he focused ahead, refusing to spare me any eye contact.

"Someday you'll be in a cage," he said. "And hopefully sooner rather than later, so you can't do any more damage. Mr. Kincaid will fill you in on the do's and don'ts while my youngest is in attendance at this school." And then he finally turned his head to look at me with disdain "Mark my words, if you fail to behave, I will end you, and it'll be for good."

Turning away, he left the office, and my lips twitched with a smile. Six years ago, his little girl and I changed each other, and while I couldn't change her back, I could certainly give her some new memories of me.

Now that... I could do.

It was settled, then.

I heard Mr. Kincaid clear his throat as he held his office door open for me. "Mr. Torrance, if you please?"

CHAPTER 4

Damon

PRESENT

"Ten moves and you have me," Mr. Garin told me. "Do you see it?"

I stared at the board between us, calculating the moves I needed to make for checkmate while trying to anticipate his counter moves.

Yeah, I see it. But what fun would that be?

I reached for my pawn at E2.

"Don't," he scolded.

And he shot me the same look I'd seen since I was a kid.

But I couldn't resist. Unable to hold in my small smile, I ignored him and moved it to E4.

He let out a sigh and shook his head, exasperated with the lack of control and strategy he failed at drilling into me all those long afternoons after school, years ago, when he worked for my father.

Or he *thought* he failed at drilling it into me, anyway. People assumed I behaved strictly on impulse, when actually, it required quite a bit of strategy being this fucked up.

House music pounded downstairs, the club already packed with college girls, young professionals, and anyone else in the twenty-something set able to spring for the three-hundred-dollar bottle of vodka or champagne just to be able to sit at a damn table.

I'd spent plenty of time down there in the crowd and noise in high school with my friends. Now I just kept a private room upstairs on reserve to catch up with Kostya Garin, one of my father's old bodyguards who now organized security for this club. Fifty-nine years old, gray goatee, and the same black suits he always wore when he worked for my father, he still had more muscles than me, and he was one of the few people I had, at least, some regard for.

I would do business with him.

I would trust anything he had to say.

I would attend his funeral.

There weren't many people I'd sit through a whole service for.

But we weren't friends, and we never discussed anything personal. He taught me things, but he never complicated it with trying to be my father. He was one of the perks I came here for.

The other...

"I want to leave," a girl spoke up from the other side of the room as if on cue.

As Mr. Garin contemplated his next move, I turned my head toward her.

She wore a tight pink dress of sequins, glittering in the dim glow coming from the sconces on the wall, and her ass was planted on some little prick's lap whose name I didn't know. Her boyfriend across from them, on the edge of the black leather couch, watching his buddy putting his hands on his woman. I observed them, trying to put myself in each of their skin.

Did she like another man touching her? Was her boyfriend jealous? Turned on? Angry? Was his best friend living out a long-held fantasy for her? Was he enjoying this? Was he hard?

I blinked, waiting for it to come. His jealousy. Her degradation. His desire. Their fear and excitement at being watched.

But it didn't come. Not yet. It was getting harder and harder to empathize over the years.

Fuck.

Maybe if it was my new little wife being fondled?

Or...

The guy touched her hips lightly and hesitantly as his mouth grazed a path across her shoulder, probably trying to hold back so they didn't know how much he was enjoying himself.

"Can we leave now?" she asked me, the man underneath her not giving the slightest hint he wanted to leave quite yet.

But I ignored her, turning back to the board and seeing that Mr. Garin had matched my move with his pawn to E5.

I smiled to myself.

"Look closely," he continued. "You can still get me. Ten moves."

Ten? I grabbed my knight and moved it to F3, hearing Mr. Garin let out a sigh as he plucked his knight and sat him back down in C6 as if on auto-pilot.

"Damon..." he scolded, growing angry with me.

I could hear it in his voice, and my pulse raced a little as he continued the game, going through the motions as if we'd gone 'round and 'round about this for years, and he was done with my bullshit mistakes and impulsiveness. He just wanted to get the game and his inevitable win over with so he could get back to work now that my head wasn't in the game.

My bishop to C4, his pawn to D6, my other knight to C3, and as he reached for his bishop, I stopped breathing as I watched him move it to G4, pinning my knight to my queen.

You idiot. That actually fucking worked, and he didn't see what he'd done yet. I moved my knight to E5, snatching his pawn and leaving my queen completely vulnerable to his bishop. He saw the opening, shook his head, and captured her, removing her from the board and moving his bishop into my queen's spot.

My heart jumped into my throat. He thought he had me.

But it was my move now, and as soon as I moved my bishop to G7, I had his king in fucking check.

He paused, realizing what had just happened and re-examining the board. His eyes flashed to mine.

As expected, he tried moving his king to E7, but the look of defeat was already in his eyes.

I slid my knight into D5. "Checkmate," I said.

He stared at the board, scowling like he wasn't sure how that just happened. "Seven moves..." he mumbled.

Yeah.

Not ten.

His eyes darted up to mine. "You hung your queen. I didn't teach you to do that."

Just then there was a knock on the door and my driver moved to open it. Erika Fane entered, and I stood up, fixing my jacket as the driver closed the door behind her.

"The queen is the most powerful piece on the board," I told Mr. Garin, keeping my eyes locked on Rika's. "Why not use her?"

Rika, the fiancée of one of my high school friends, stepped farther into the room, looking ready for anything except a night at the club. A smile tugged at my lips. Her tan baseball hat sat low, casting a shadow over her eyes, while her long, blonde hair spilled down her back. She wore jeans with the hood of a gray sweatshirt sticking out the back of a tan jacket, her hands tucked into the pockets. She stopped when I started to approach, no doubt trying to keep a safe distance.

I veered for the couch, sitting down on the opposite end as the boyfriend, who still watched—or tried not to watch—what his girlfriend and best friend were doing.

"Have a good night, Damon," I heard Mr. Garin say.

I nodded, and when I looked up again, he was gone. Rika stayed back, watching me as I dug out my wallet from my breast pocket and pulled out a stack of bills.

"I want to stop," the young girl said, pulling away from the guy's mouth.

"You can stop whenever you want," I said. "Door's not locked."

And I started slowly laying down one-hundred-dollar bill after another on the frosted glass table between us. Next to the cash I'd already paid them for what they were doing.

"Or you can stay there," I continued, laying down another hundred and then another, "and keep doing nothing while your little boyfriend lets his best friend put a hand inside your dress." I put down the last hundred. "And you can earn next month's rent money while you're at it."

"What the hell is the matter with you?" Rika demanded.

I glanced up at her, seeing her shoot a glare from them to me.

"You can look," I told her. "I won't tell Michael. I'm good at keeping our secrets."

She looked away, and I cast my stare back down at the girl—who'd arrived earlier, trying to sneak into the club with her boyfriend and his friend, none of them twenty-one. She was hot, they looked fun to play with, so here we were.

The young woman's brown eyes dropped to the money on the table and lingered for a moment. And just like with Mr. Garin, heat coursed slowly down my arms, through my stomach, past my groin, and into my thighs as I waited to see if she would do what I wanted her to do.

Her young tits rose and fell as she got more nervous, no doubt wanting to do it but afraid of what seeds this would sow between her, her boyfriend, and his friend once they left this room. *Did she just want the money?* I swallowed, watching the indecision on her face. *Or did she like the kink? The danger.*

She threw a look to her boyfriend, whose face was etched with discomfort, but he sure as hell wasn't standing up and taking her out of here either.

Come on, man. *Make a decision.* Get your woman or sit back and enjoy the show.

What a pussy.

But slowly, she made that decision for him. She relaxed into his friend, he fisted the back of her auburn hair, and buried his mouth in her neck as he slid a hand into her dress and took hold of her breast. Her eyes fell closed, her breath shook, but she remained rigid.

For the moment.

And after another moment, I was him, with her in my lap and taking what someone else didn't want me to have. The boyfriend on the couch saw his friend's desire and knew the truth now. Something his buddy had been hiding. They were changed, and pleasure fluttered into my chest.

Yes.

I closed my eyes for a second, finally fucking feeling something. Just a twinge, but it was better than nothing.

I heard Rika's sigh. "You wonder why everyone hates you."

I opened my eyes, shaking my head. "I don't wonder."

I stood up and tucked my billfold back into my breast pocket.

"I like chess." I approached her, noticing her hands were still tucked into her pockets. "Knowing and seeing what I want in front of me. Knowing that it won't come easily. Knowing that it takes patience and a series of carefully constructed maneuvers all plotted into a specific sequence." I paused, looking down at her. "Knowing that the longer I have to wait and possibly alter my course makes getting what I want so much more enjoyable."

I loved making her uncomfortable. Mindfucks were sometimes more fun than actual fucking.

And for a moment, it was like I was looking down at *her.*

At Winter.

They had the same hair, although Winter's was a shade lighter, and the same colored eyes, except Rika's were darker. Winter had this ring of darker blue around the outside of her pupils that made them...piercing. I was glad she couldn't use them, because if she could look at me with those eyes...

Yeah, Winter and Rika were both so similar, and not just in their looks. They were both defiant. Both liked a little danger. And both fought back.

"And knowing that the path to success changes based on the game pieces I choose to use," I continued. "And people are my favorite pieces, Rika."

She narrowed her eyes but didn't say anything. She was probably trying to look bored, impatient, or unimpressed, but I knew better.

"Look at her." I nodded once to the girl in the chair. "That beautiful body, hesitant at first, but now she's responding. She wants to touch him." I glanced at Rika and back to the couple making out. "You see how she's fisting her dress in her hands. She's turned on, but her boyfriend is watching, and she's scared of what he thinks. She doesn't want to show how much she likes his friend's hands and mouth on her, so she's feeling her man out. Waiting for some sign from him that it's okay to enjoy it."

"Then why did she say she wanted to leave?" Rika retorted.

"Because it's what girls are supposed to say, isn't it?" I fired back. "It's risky to bring out your king or queen too early."

The couple continued playing, nibbling, kissing, and touching as we talked.

"That's what they teach you, isn't it?" I went on. "That's what I taught Banks?"

Women weren't supposed to want it as much as a man, right? And they certainly weren't supposed to like it casual. That was what I taught my sister to keep her safe.

I pressed forward. "So why did she stay?" I questioned Rika.

Her jaw flexed, and she looked away as if she wasn't playing, but then I saw her gaze slowly flash back to the college kids and then to the money on the table.

"Because it was your move, and you pushed back," she replied.

"Yes, very good."

The girl might be doing it for the money. Or maybe she needed a good enough excuse to agree.

"Now him." I eyed the best friend under her as he kneaded her tit under her dress. "He'd do this for free. I told him to kiss her, but he's eating her alive right now. He's wanted her for a long time." I saw his eyes open, probably having heard what I'd said. "Probably fantasized about her and looked at her when his friend wasn't watching. I'll bet he really wants both hands on her tits now."

And then I looked down at him, asking, "Don't you?"

He nodded, his mouth on the girl's. He dropped his other hand from her hair and placed it on her hip, getting ready for when he got permission.

"And her boyfriend," I told Rika. "It's driving him insane. He wants to be angry, but—"

"He wants the money," she finished.

"Or it turns him on maybe, and he doesn't want to admit it."

She gave me a condescending look. "Yeah, sure."

How naïve she still is. "Not every man has to be paid to watch his woman get fucked by another guy."

"Why would he enjoy that?"

"I think you know," I shot back, eyeing her with amusement. I knew all about her little romp in the steam room at Hunter-Bailey with Michael and Kai.

And as much as I thought I'd be turned on by the reality of what Rika had enjoyed in that room, it actually pissed me off. I wasn't quite sure why, either. Maybe because I didn't get my turn, and I felt left out of the fun?

Or maybe, even though I knew her enough to know she didn't let anything happen to her that she didn't want, a small part of me still felt like she'd been... I don't know...

Used.

I didn't know why I gave a shit, though. Michael and Kai had shared a woman before. I just didn't want to think about it with Erika.

But it did mean one thing good. My old friends still liked to play and they'd be prime game pieces.

"You see, Rika," I told her. "There are people in the world who are destined to be played. Victims who wouldn't be able to change their fate even if they went back and lived life over a thousand different ways." I made a show of letting my eyes fall down her form. "And then there are players. Like you and me." I gestured to the threesome. "Which piece would you move next?"

She didn't look away from the challenge this time, only hesitated before finally surveying the group. Her gaze finally rested on the boyfriend. "His instinct is to be the better man."

Very good.

"He feels competitive, yes," I replied, impressed. "It pisses him off and gets him hard. He wants to fuck her and show her who the real man is. To keep him in the game, we need to use him. Make him feel important."

She was quick. She had the same thought I did.

"Boyfriend?" I called to the guy on the couch but still stared at Rika. "Tell your friend what you want him to do your girlfriend."

Rika held my eyes, both of us locked in a challenge to see if we were right. To see if he'd stay on the board or fold and run.

The dude was quiet, nothing but the sounds of kissing from the couple on the chair and the music thrumming downstairs, and then...a clear voice, quiet but sure spoke up.

"Pull down the strap of her dress, Jason," the boyfriend told his friend.

Rika and I were locked, watching each other, but I heard the shuffle of clothes, heated breaths, and a moan.

"Yeah," the girl in the chair panted, now having the full blessing of her boyfriend to enjoy this.

Out of the corner of my eye, I could see skin, the top of her dress having been pulled down, and their movements quickened, more excited and ready.

I couldn't read Rika's expression but I definitely knew part of her enjoyed this. She might hate herself, but that rush of power felt good, didn't it? There was nothing like playing people.

And she was good at it. No one had ever indulged me before. Except Winter. Not one of my friends had the patience or the interest.

I liked Rika. Michael had barely tapped into everything she was capable of.

But this wasn't why she was here. She wanted to talk.

"All right, you three," I spoke up, inhaling a full breath. "Take your money and get out. I've got business."

"Huh?" The guy sounded out of breath.

"Are you serious?" The girl suddenly pulled her arms up to cover her half-naked body.

"Out," I growled. "Now."

They stood up, heaving sighs of aggravation, because they were all finally into it, wet and hard and ready to go.

"Go finish it in your car," I mumbled, heading over to the cabinet and taking out a pack of cigarettes.

They left, taking their money, and I waved off the driver to leave us alone, too. Once the door was closed, I turned my head to Rika as I unwrapped a new pack.

"I want to play chess with you someday," I teased.

"Haven't you been?"

I turned back to the cabinet, smiling to myself. Having her as an opponent would be a real challenge, but I think I preferred her on my side.

I packed the cigarettes, hitting them against the back of my hand, and feeling it again.

The pressure. The need to release.

Winter.

I had her close now. Finally.

But I was being pulled with the need to end it quickly and the desire to drag it out long and slow.

She was home. Right now. Probably trying to devise some way to escape, and let her try, for all I care. I'd enjoy hunting her ass down. That stupid, dumb shit I married might make some good-looking kids, but she wouldn't be half as enjoyable as owning that little girl will be.

Yeah, Ari's little sister was nothing like her. Winter would put up a fight. She'll give me hell, and not only was I getting my revenge on her for what she did to me years ago, but I was going to have it all now. The head of the table, domain over my own house, and my favorite fucking toy.

The city lights glittered out the windows as I walked to one of the tables. Meridian City, the metropolis less than an hour from my hometown and where Winter slept, shimmered and shined below, but I had no ambition to be a part of it tonight. Sometimes I liked the clubs—the music, the noise, the sex—but that was the thing about me. I only loved one thing at a time.

A smile curled my lips, and I unwrapped the pack and stuck a cigarette in my mouth, lighting the end.

"You better have something good for me," I said to Rika, inhaling a puff and getting down to business. "Our little rendezvous come with strings attached, girl."

"Healthy relationships require a little reciprocation," she replied. "What I brought you last time was the motherload, Damon. Now it's your turn."

I let out a little laugh, pinching the cigarette between my thumb and finger as I took another drag. "I gave you info."

"You gave me no proof," she retorted.

I sucked on the cigarette again, filling my lungs with the sweet sting and tipping my head back to blow it back out in a stream above my head. *Such a fucking little monster, that one.*

"Come here," I told her, not turning around to look at her.

Winter wasn't the only woman in my head. This one and I still had a score to settle, too.

I didn't hear anything for a moment, but then I saw her emerge from the shadows out of the corner of my eye.

But she stopped short.

"Closer," I taunted.

Another couple of steps, and I could see blonde hair falling down her form to my left.

But I still didn't look at her.

"Closer." I grinned.

Slowly, she approached, stopping just short of arm's reach.

Picking another cigarette out of the pack, I finally turned my head, met her eyes, and held the cigarette out to her.

She looked like she was undercover or some shit, dressed like she was, but that was okay. I liked that our meetings were secret. This was a part of her Michael didn't have.

I raised my eyebrows, waving the cigarette back and forth for her to take it. I knew she liked them.

But a little smile crossed her eyes, and she pulled her hand out of her pocket, holding up her palm with an entire un-opened pack of Davidoffs that she'd already stolen from my stash tucked in her hand.

"Jesus Christ," I mumbled.

She plucked the cigarette out of my hand, taking it anyway and skimming it under her nose to smell. "Thanks."

I shook my head. She must've snuck into my apartment at Delcour to look for me there first and raided my stash.

Sticking the cigarette in my mouth, I closed the cabinet and walked away.

"Those are my rooms," I warned her. "Stay out when I'm not there."

I didn't want her going through my shit.

"They're not your rooms," she argued. "Michael doesn't know you're still staying there, and I can change that at any time." She slid the cigarette into her breast pocket. "Thanks to me, you can still hide out right under our noses."

"And thanks to me, Michael doesn't know that you're *letting* me hide out right under your noses." I pinned her with a look. "Your ass would be grass just as much as mine, so stow it."

She cocked an eyebrow but didn't press further. She knew she had more reason to be afraid of me than I did of her.

Still, though...as much as I kind of enjoyed our little exchanges, it pissed me off she wasn't wary of me anymore. After everything I'd tried to do to her and could still do to her.

I looked up, seeing her staring at me.

"What?" I took another drag, walking over to the windows.

"I thought you'd blackmail him with the info I got," she explained. "Or ruin some of his partnerships."

She was talking about Winter's father.

"I must say, you exceeded my imagination."

"Impressed?" I glanced over my shoulder at her as I flicked off the ashes on my cigarette.

"Scared," she clarified.

I chuckled. "I can live with that."

"And guilty." She sat down on the arm of one of the couches, and I could see her watching me out of the corner of my eye. "I can't believe you did that today. You went for the jugular, and man, you know how to commit, don't you? What the hell have I gotten her into?"

"Aw, don't worry. She was going to answer to me with or without your help sooner or later anyway." I blew out smoke and turned around, heading for the ashtray on the table.

"Don't hurt her," Rika said.

But I just breathed out another laugh as I ground the butt of the cigarette into the dish. "Coming from the woman who offered up all the info I needed to take her father, her home, and her fortune."

Winter's father shared the same accountant as Rika's family. The same disgruntled and anxious accountant who hinted that Winter's father, Griffin Ashby, might have swindled Rika's late father on some real estate deals years ago. I'm not quite sure how she got the proof, but she didn't show up at my door until she had it, knowing it might be exactly what I needed to take down the Ashbys.

And in exchange, I'd help her get something she needed, as well. Something I wasn't entirely sure I wanted to give her just yet. I liked her coming around, and I didn't want it to stop.

"You know what I mean," she continued. "Don't *hurt* her."

You mean other than taking everything Winter owned and putting her in a perpetual state of dependence on me?

Or hurt her as in...

Yeah, that was what you meant, wasn't it? Don't *hurt* her.

"Do you know how much Will bled in prison?" I asked her. "Do you know how hard Kai had to fight to hold down any food because his gut raged with nerves and fear from constantly having to look over his shoulder?"

Her stern look remained steady on me.

"Do you know that no matter what Michael paid or who he bribed, there were people paying more to see the rich, entitled sons of the Thunder Bay elite suffer in prison?" I kept going. "Do you have any idea how sick they both got from lack of food and sleep to balance the fucking excess of fear and pain?"

Her gaze dropped for a moment, uncomfortable, but she stayed quiet.

"Yeah, well, neither do I," I told her. "Because I wasn't there."

Her eyes shot up, looking confused. I walked, circling the perimeter of the room as I continued. "Three levels below cell block six, in the basement, down a dank corridor, below five feet of concrete, is where I was." I fisted my hands, the anger returning almost immediately. "For three years. You didn't know that, did you?"

Her eyes, so blue even in this dark room, pierced mine.

"Banks thought she was doing me a favor," I said. "And Gabriel agreed with her. He had too many enemies and those enemies had soldiers on the inside. I was more at risk than Kai and Will, so I was put in solitary confinement." I drew in a deep breath, the blood under my skin growing hot. "Twenty-three hours a day, seven days a week, all day, every day, for one-hundred-sixty weeks. That's one-thousand-one-hundred-twenty days. Twenty-six-thousand-eight-hundred-eighty hours, Rika."

My fingers tingled with the urge to dig into my skin, but I held back.

"I was allowed outside one hour a day, but even then I was alone." I walked around the room, glancing at her as I spoke. "I ate alone, I walked alone, I did everything alone. My father didn't want me killed, so I was cut off from everyone."

I started circling the couch she sat on, and without thinking, I skated my hand over the portable bar, tugging on the corner and making the bottles clink together. Heat trailed up my neck.

"The first day, you're wondering what's going on," I explained. "No one's saying anything. No one will answer your questions. You can't see anything but your little plot of cement. And after the first week, you start talking to yourself a little just because there's nothing to do, and you're getting really fucking bored."

"You mean lonely?" she jabbed.

"Pissed off," I gritted out, correcting her. "No one is coming to visit. Where's Banks? She would be there. Why are they keeping me from her?" And then I nod at her. "But you know you can take it. You can take anything they dole out. Will's fine. Kai's fine. They'll be fine."

I kept circling the room, the muscles in my neck suddenly tight as I dragged my hand over the surface of tables and walls, going a little faster now and my fingers digging in as I held her stare.

"But a month in, you start to find that your head is heavy," I said, growing breathless at the memory. "Really fucking heavy, Rika, like you can't lift it. So you start doing things to snap yourself out of it, like banging it into the wall over and over again."

I brushed past a vase and sent it crashing to the wooden floor, but I didn't stop. I was in my cell again, circling the eight-by-eight-foot square and going mad.

"And your skin feels tight, and the walls are pressing against your lungs, so you can't breathe, and your brain starts slipping sideways, because the world looks so different now than it used to." I sucked in a breath and squeezed my eyes shut for a moment. "And you just want to run—run hard. And breathe. You're crawling inside yourself. You don't just want out of the room. You want out of your skin."

I winced, and I couldn't inhale. Something was on my chest. Sitting there.

"And when you finally get a visit—four guards your dad pays to beat the shit out of you on the first of every month so you don't get soft in solitary—you start to look forward to those visits." I bared my teeth, still looking at her as I walked. "Because pain in the body quiets the pain in the head. It feels good, like a kill switch for your brain. And then you remember that fucking little cunt sitting in that courtroom, even though she didn't have to be there, to take pleasure in hearing you accused and sentenced, while people lied about you and said you forced her into it." My throat grew thick, and I almost couldn't speak. "Forced her to get naked and to open her legs, going into vile detail like I made her do things I couldn't already get from her sister down the hall or any other girl I wanted." I was yelling now. "Acting like that time with her wasn't the only fucking time I didn't hate fucking."

I gasped for breath, my mania replaced with fury, and I saw Winter in my head and then only red. I stopped and stared at Rika, but my anger was still hot.

"And maybe she couldn't have stopped me being convicted, but she could've told them the truth. She could've stood up and said something. She could've opened her fucking mouth and talked," I growled, my throat tight and burning. "But she stayed quiet, and you went into solitary for three years, and your friends fended for themselves while your mind slowly slipped off its axis and you'd rip out your own hair because animals do insane things when they're caged for too long."

I panted, trying to lower my voice. "Three years," I said, seething. "Three. Years. Rika."

I paused, evening out my voice and calming my breathing back to normal.

"So, yeah," I said, mocking her. "You bet your ass I'm gonna hurt her."

She sat there, her gaze faltering and her eyes glistening, but her shoulders still squared. She wasn't a stupid woman, and I knew that. She had to suspect the can of worms she was opening by giving me those documents, but ultimately, she decided what I could give her was worth the damage I would cause. There was a bit of "not-so-honorable" inside her, too.

She did what she did to get what she wanted, and I couldn't lie. I felt a pang of pride at my new, unlikely little friend here.

But again...she wasn't a stupid woman. She knew the can of worms she was opening between Winter and me, and it was entirely possible she was planning for it. And while I was enjoying our newfound camaraderie, Erika Fane wouldn't stand silently by and let me do my work. She'll try to protect Winter.

And let her. The more she put herself in my path, the more it would bring everyone else into play.

Michael, Kai, Banks...

Will.

Balling my fists, I walked over to the bar, poured two fingers of vodka, and downed it in one gulp, immediately pouring another.

Will.

And Winter.

Will and Winter.

I downed the second shot, liquid heat coursing through my chest as I closed my eyes and heard Rika clear her throat.

"So, do you have anything for me yet?" she asked like she hadn't just heard all that. "Or are you just ready to admit you're completely incompetent?"

I squeezed the rocks glass, the subtle burn of alcohol still stinging my throat as I whipped it across the room in her direction.

Fuckin' girl.

It shattered against the wall above her head, and she turned her face to the side, barely flinching as she let out a quiet laugh.

She was hardly afraid of me anymore.

"Call or text Banks," she instructed, ignoring my tantrum. "She's worried about you."

"She's not." I lit another cigarette and refilled my glass. "Banks knows me best. She knows I take care of myself first."

"And Will?"

I walked for the couch, tossing her a look.

"He has an alcohol problem," she told me.

But I just smiled to myself. "For men, it's not a problem."

Every man I knew or grew up with drank. You held your liquor and you got shit done. Women were the lightweights, which is why I never let Banks drink.

"And he has a drug problem," Rika continued.

I leaned back on the couch, tucking an arm behind my head and staring at her.

And she was telling me this because...?

I brought the cigarette to my lips with my other hand and took a drag. I met Will at the beginning of high school, and he'd played around with drugs for as long as I'd known him. Weed, X, pills, coke... It all ran rampant in our school. The only reason we didn't have the heroin epidemic the inner city did was because we had the money and access to good shit from the town M.D.

And Mom's medicine cabinet.

It was almost the only thing Michael and I ever agreed on.

We didn't do drugs. We were the drugs.

"I'm sure you all will take care of it," I told her.

"You whined earlier because you weren't there for him in jail, but you can be there now."

"Go home," I said.

For someone so smart, she was good at stupid. I was the last person Will wanted or needed help from.

She paused a moment, as if waiting for me to say something or still holding out hope maybe, but then finally turned around and headed her ass for the door.

But something caught her eye, and she stopped, lifting up a small black box off the sofa table and inspecting the contents.

My heart thudded a beat, recognizing what she was holding. I clenched my teeth so hard my jaw ached, and then I was up, dropping my cigarette into the ashtray and charging toward her.

Ripping the box out of her hands, I slammed it close, hearing the contents jingle inside as I tossed it on the sofa again, and then grabbed her collar, backing her up into the wall.

Her blue eyes glared up at me, all tough and ready, but her little panting gave away the small amount of fear she still held of me.

"Keep me in this perspective." I stared down, towering over her. "At any time I could snap you in half and shut you up for good. You need me. I don't need you. We're not friends."

Stay out of my place. Stay out of my shit. No more chit-chat.

"Glad you know that," she replied, her voice surprisingly steady.

I released her and turned, going back to the sofa, tucking the contents of the box back in, and fastening the latch. I'd cleared some stuff out of my father's house and brought it in for the driver to take to my apartment at Delcour tonight.

"I look like her." I heard Rika say. "Don't I? That's why you've always hated me."

I hesitated.

Like her. Like Winter.

Blonde hair, blue eyes, same age, same wild purity... Like the innocence of a tornado or a raging hurricane.

"I hate all of you," I mumbled. I don't even blink saying the words.

I hate all of you. Hate all of who? Their little group I was once a part of? Women? People, in general? Who knew, and she didn't ask.

But part of me wanted her to understand.

Jesus Christ.

We needed to get back to business.

She reached for the door, but I called her back.

"Erika?"

I saw her stop out of the corner of my eye as I walked for the cabinet and pulled out one of the two handguns I had stored there. I ejected the magazine from the Glock and checked the chamber to make sure a bullet wasn't loaded and then held the gun and clip out for her to take.

Her eyebrows shot up.

"It's untraceable," I said.

I wasn't allowed to own firearms, being a felon and all, but oh well.

Her eyes shifted side to side, and she looked confused.

Impatient, I closed the distance between us and pushed the shit into her hands.

"Learn to use it."

"Why do I need this?" she asked, still holding the handgun like she was debating on whether or not to drop it and run.

"Because my father is smarter than we are. He'll be onto us eventually. You might need it."

"So if your dad comes after me, you're giving me a gun to kill him?" she asked, sounding sarcastic. "So he doesn't kill me instead?"

I let out a sigh. "Fuck, you're dumb," I said. "Like he'd come after you himself. That's for the guys he'll send. If anyone kills him, it'll be me. Now get out." I jerked my chin toward the door, pulling another cigarette out of the pack. "I'll call you when I have your shit."

I lit the end and tossed the lighter onto the table in front of me. "Unless you want to stay," I said, softening my voice and letting my eyes fall down her body. "Your fiancé is out of town, and it's my wedding night. We could...play chess."

And by chess, I meant...

But she just shook her head. "That's how I know you're not half as dangerous as you pretend to be," she said. "You only ever threaten."

I tapped the cigarette into the ashtray, my mood turning solemn as the smoke streamed into the air. "Sometimes," I nearly whisper. "And sometimes I mean exactly what I say." I looked up at her. "So trust me when I say you'll never escape me. None of you will."

I watched her, trying so hard to look defiant, but the barest hints of awareness, fear, and doubt still seeped through. She knew I wasn't going anywhere.

Without a word, she turned and left, leaving the door wide open and letting the music pour in as she disappeared.

Fuck you. This won't go how you think it will go.

You won't change me. I'll change you.

My phone rang, and since Rika just left, there were only two other people who had my number. My father and my security.

"Fuck," I breathed out as I picked up the phone.

"Yes?" I answered.

"Well done today," my father said. "I thought for sure I was going to have to strangle you at some point."

I took a drag and set the cigarette in an ashtray as I blew out the smoke. "I'm sure it would've been difficult."

"Yes, I don't really want to kill you," he added. "You're my only son, after all."

"No, I mean I'm not eleven anymore." I grabbed a clean T-shirt and hoodie out of my duffel bag and kicked the door closed again. "I'll be more difficult to strangle now."

Prick.

He was silent for a moment, and I could just imagine the look on his face. My father was a master at not losing his cool. He rarely did.

But it would be in his eyes. That hint of aggravation. The distaste for my childishness.

If I weren't his blood and sole heir, I have no doubt he would've killed me long ago.

"The town is buzzing with the news," he continued, changing the subject. "I want to capitalize on the momentum. The Crists are having an engagement party for Michael and Erika in a week. You'll go with Ari, and bring the other two, as well. They're your family now, too, and their reputation needs repair."

"And they'll achieve that by showing up with me?" I thought out loud. The irony of my presence helping anyone's reputation was not lost on me.

"I have to go." I cut him off. I'd do what he asked, so no argument from me on this one. I wanted to go to the party because everyone would be there.

"Just a heads up..." he told me. "Luka and Dower stopped Winter and some guy on the road tonight. She had a bag packed."

I stopped, waiting for the rest. "And?"

"And she's back home where she belongs."

I relaxed, knowing she wouldn't have gotten far, but I still needed the confirmation. I knew she would try, though. I hoped she'd try again.

Some guy...

Ethan Belmont. I fisted my hand on instinct. I hope she'd done him. Done him a lot and was still doing him, so I could get an eye full. It would give me one more reason to hate her and to hurt her. It was all the fun I was going to have in this marriage to her sister.

But my father chimed in, as if reading my thoughts. "Let's make something perfectly clear," he said. "I want Arion pregnant before the year is out. You know the rules. Do your chores before you play."

I cocked an eyebrow. I'd never done chores in my life.

"And we need to talk about you taking on some responsibilities with Communica. It's time you start earning what you're going to inherit. I need you to come—"

I pulled the phone away from my ear and hung up, tossing it down on the couch. Communica was one of his companies, and nope. He'll be angry I hung up. He'll call back later or tomorrow or have his guys drag me back to him for a face to face to finish the conversation, but I didn't care about any of it.

I'd always had tunnel vision when it came to things I wanted, and it was always one thing at a time. I couldn't concentrate otherwise.

The choices I made probably wouldn't ensure me a long life, but it was like I'd always known that, and I'd accepted it. I would die young. I had never thought about working, and the idea of walking into one of Gabriel Torrance's offices every day made me want to puke.

Maybe I was lazy.

Selfish.

Self-absorbed.

Or maybe my head just wasn't built for a long life of no consequence. It was "hard and fast" on everything, and I didn't have the discipline for anything other than a one-track mind.

I changed my clothes, pulling on jeans, a T-shirt, and black hoodie, and then walked over and picked up the black wooden box Rika had held and noticed there was something stuck under the lid, preventing it from closing all the way.

I opened it, nudging the razor blade back inside and hesitating as I surveyed the rest of the items. An assortment of desserts that had been constant and reliable during a time when I was a kid, and they were the only things I could trust.

A paperclip, sewing needle, push pin, pocket knife, scissors, tiger tooth, small animal antler, and a bird skull for the sharp nostril edges. Most of them were sterilized, having not been used in a long time, but my gaze dropped to the lighter, and I absently rubbed my thumb over my index finger, feeling the raised skin from the old burn.

I looked at the push pin. *I could sleep tonight. If I really wanted to.*

I tapped my fingers silently on the box, indulging in the thought of the temptation, but then I heard a knock on the door, and I blinked, inhaling a deep breath.

"Sir," Matthew Crane, the lead security detail my father had given me, said behind me. "The extra equipment you asked for is at the site."

I nodded absently, closing the box and fastening the clasp. "You can go home," I told him. "I won't need you for a few days."

Tucking the box back in the duffel bag, I walked to the sofa and finished getting dressed, lacing up my boots and grabbing my bag, stuffing my suit inside.

"You're going tonight?" he asked, probably noticing my attire. "You won't have much light, and it's supposed to rain, sir."

I shot him a look as I finished gathering my shit.

He didn't press further, simply dismissing himself. "Congratulations," he said. "On your nuptials, I mean. We'll wait for your call."

I followed him out the door, he and the other man both flanking me as we descended the stairs and left the club.

They may as well get their rest while they can. When the shit hit the fan, they'd be getting some sleepless nights.

Just like me tonight.

It was time to head back to Thunder Bay.

I've done so much more than what I went to prison for—and far worse. Winter has no clue how bad this can get.

CHAPTER 5

Winter

SEVEN YEARS AGO

"So you could probably just be homeschooled, huh?" Erika—or, Rika—asked as we treaded down the school hallway slowly.

She led me as I held onto her arm, just above her elbow.

"The textbooks are on audio," she went on. "And then the teacher sends you the lecture notes, and the computer reads them for you, so..."

"Yeah, my parents would prefer it," I admitted. "Actually, they would've preferred if I'd stayed in Montreal. But I need to learn how to be around people."

I'd been attending and living at Penoir, a school for the blind in Canada for over five years now, and while I enjoyed it there, comfortable around others who had to live life like I did, I wanted to come home. I wanted to learn to live here again and cope with being who I was now in an average environment. I missed the smell of the sea around our house and the ballroom at home where I always danced.

It was for my own good, too. I wanted to do more ballet and start regular classes again, maybe shoot for something professionally with the support of my family around me.

"Must have been lonely," Rika offers.

Someone brushed my shoulder as they rushed by, and I took a moment to steady myself. This was the part of school I wasn't going to like. The crowded halls, the shouts, laughter, and chatter, and all the eyes. I lifted my chin, hoping I looked relaxed.

"Uh, well…" I joked. "I didn't really say I *wanted* to be around people. I just need to learn to be."

She let out a little laugh and veered right. "Turning," she whispered, alerting me.

"Actually, I had lots of friends," I continued, following her. "It wasn't lonely. It was comfortable. Too comfortable, I guess. I annoy my sister, so since she graduates at the end of the year, I thought it would be my last chance to be around for that."

She chuckled again. "How fun. I'm an only child."

I wonder if my parents might've kept me around if I had been the only one instead of tucking me away at some distant school for others to deal with.

My face started to warm as we walked, and I wasn't sure if it was my nerves or what.

"Are people staring at me?" I asked her.

"They're staring at *us*."

"Why?"

I heard her inhale. "I think… they're confused. We kind of look alike."

"Do we?" I replied. "Are you hot?"

If she was hot, then I was hot.

But she just laughed.

"When I think about how I must look," I told her, "I still see the kid I last looked at in the mirror when I was eight."

"So you can think in…pictures?"

I blinked. Pictures?

She must've seen a look on my face, because she rushed to apologize. "I'm sorry. I'm so sorry. That was a dumb question, right?"

I shook my head. "No, I... I'm just used to being around people who understand, I guess. I'll have to get used to questions." And then I added, "And making people feel comfortable enough to ask. It's fine." I let out a small laugh and licked my lips. "And yes, to answer your question. My brain still works, just not my eyes. When I try to picture things I've never seen before, though, like you or the inside of this school, it gets more complicated. Sometimes I map it out in my head, and I can create an impression. Other times it's just like a color or a feeling or a sound that helps me identify it."

Then I went through some of the pictures in my head, reflecting on how I drew things in my mind.

"Sometimes," I continued, "it's a memory. Like when I think about trees or I'm in the forest around my house, I always picture the last trees I saw. No matter where I am. Every tree looks like the trees in that garden maze with the fountain. Tall hedges, dark green..." I trailed off, the memories of that day flooding me again. "A fountain..."

"Garden maze?" she questioned. "Not the one at Damon Torrance's house..."

My face fell, and I almost stumbled. *Damon.*

She said his name so casually, like she assumed I knew exactly who he was, heard his name every day, and he was just any other boy, living and breathing right here in Thunder Bay. All of it so normal to her.

Of course, I knew he still lived here, but having her so casually confirm it all of a sudden reminded me that I'd let my guard down.

The truth was, I hadn't heard his name in six years. It was never spoken in my house, not since the day I found him sitting in the fountain and ended up covered in blood. Everyone said it was an accident, but he'd scared me that day. He made me fall.

But I knew he'd be here. I just hadn't let myself think about it, I guess. I was a freshman, and he was a senior, on his way to college in a matter of months. My father wanted me to wait until he was gone—start here my sophomore year—but I wanted to start now. My classmates would be transferring from their middle schools, just like I was transferring, so we'd be on an even keel. In that respect anyway. I wanted all four years with my graduating class.

I'd just avoid him and his circle, but he probably didn't care to trouble himself with me anyway. I couldn't imagine how he'd forget, because I never would, but it was possible. Given the time that had passed, maybe I was just a faint memory to him.

"Well...," Rika began after I didn't say anything else. "It might be nice to live in my good memories forever."

I nodded, letting the misconception go. I wish I could remember any other trees but those trees.

We stopped at her locker, and I heard the hollow clunk as she dumped her bag of books into it before taking my bag, as well. Not that I had much in there. Some headphones, a digital recorder the school made me buy to record lectures even though I have an app on my phone for that, my wallet, and of course, my cell.

All of my text books and reading material were downloaded on Audible and on my phone, and I'd left my MacBook in my own locker before Biology, since I'd been told I wouldn't need it for that class. The text-to-speech feature, where I could type out homework and hear it read back to me to make sure I'd typed correctly, had always been useful, but working in groups *and* having my earbuds in during class was going to be an obstacle I hadn't thought of. The learning curve coming here would be steep.

"We'll pick your stuff up after lunch," Rika told me.

My locker was at the other end of the hall, and the cafeteria was right here. Something about the way she just took my bag into her space, and reaffirmed that we'd be together this afternoon, too, kind of comforted me. Like I had a place.

Lunch. I let out a breath. It was the part I was dreading the most. Even though the entire morning so far was a running contest for "most awkward."

The whispers in Algebra.

The awkward silence in French.

The laughter in the science lab when the class president introduced herself and offered to be of any help she could in a *really loud voice* like I was deaf instead of blind.

The nervous verbal exchange with the P.E. teacher who'd forgotten to accommodate for me in her basketball lesson plan, so she ended up putting me on the treadmill for thirty minutes all by myself.

It was to be expected, I guess. I was the only visually impaired student, and I was the mayor's daughter. People were curious, while others were just unaware or flustered as to how to interact with me. I supposed the learning curve applied to us all.

"Whoo-hoo!" Loud shouts descended down the hall, and I turned toward the noise, hearing a door swing open and closed a few times as it banged the wall.

Students jostled on both sides of me, squeezing between me and Rika and forcing us farther apart as they tried to get to wherever they were going.

Finally, she took my hand, leading me away. She hadn't taken my hand all morning, and my mother had made her aware that I didn't really like that. I preferred to hold on to them, not the other way around.

Plus, it made me feel like a kid.

"Ow, ow, ow!" someone howled, and I jerked my head toward the noise, wondering what was going on. It was a lot noisier at this school.

My thumb brushed the cuff of Rika's shirt as she held my hand in her slender one, and I continued my slow steps through the crowd.

Hadn't she been wearing a short-sleeved shirt, like a Polo shirt? With a sweater vest, I thought? I felt them both as I'd been holding her arm all morning.

I narrowed my eyes.

And just then, I heard my name.

"Winter!" Rika's voice called.

And it wasn't coming from the person holding my hand, either.

I halted.

"Winter!" she shouted again. "Put your hand up, so I can see you!"

I yanked my hand out of the grasp of whoever had me and was just about to raise it, so Rika could find me, but the person grabbed me, I heard a door creak open, and I was shoved, stumbling into a completely different room with a tiled floor under my boots, humid air, and a strange smell, like a mixture of sweat, sporting equipment, and perfume.

Or...a body spray.

I shot my hands out in front of me, breathing hard and noticing the noise around me had changed, too. The distant shouts and chatter from down the hallway were gone, no doors opening and closing, and...no female voices.

"I think you're in the wrong place, honey," some guy said, chuckling.

"Whoo-hoo," another boy cooed as he walked by me, and I heard some whistles go off around the room.

Oh, shit.

My stomach sank.

Who the hell had grabbed me out there? Had Rika seen where I'd gone? *Oh, my God.* I whipped around, feeling for the door and finding it just a few feet away. But when I pushed on it, it wouldn't budge. Laughter spilled in from the other side, and tears sprang to my eyes as I pounded on the door. It gave way just an inch, I thought, more giggles filtered in from the outside, and then their weight was against it again, keeping me in.

Goddammit. My heart pounded in my chest. I wasn't in the locker room. I closed my eyes, praying. *Please tell me I'm not in the locker room.*

"Need a shower?" a male voice said behind me.

"I think she needs a cold shower, man!" another guy called from farther away.

Laughter echoed around the room, the noise level stinging my ears as more people turned their attention on me. I turned around, holding my hands up just in front of me a little, but blinking away the tears and straightening my shoulders.

The less I reacted, the less they'd react. There had to be a coach in here or a teacher or something.

Stupid me. I knew the teasing or pranking or even bullying was a possibility of someone in my shoes, but I arrogantly thought my status protected me. Or my father's status, anyway.

But whoever pushed me in here thought of something I didn't. If I couldn't see them do it, there was no one to punish.

"Damn," someone said, and I turned my head toward his voice.

"Is that...?" Another voice trailed off. Younger, like he was my age, maybe.

"Yeah, it's the mayor's daughter," a raspy voice added. "The blind one."

"Oh, shit. I heard she was coming."

"She's cute."

Heat covered my face, but I kept my jaw locked to keep the panic from rising. I spun around again and tried the door.

I pushed my body into it, it gave way, but it was pushed closed again by the same weight. More cackling from the other side.

I shook my head. I was going to kill them. Whoever they were, I was going to kill them. I wanted to scream—to demand they open the damn door and let me out—but it would just entertain the boys behind me even more.

"It's okay, babe. You can stay," one of the same voices told me. "Not like you can see our shit anyway, right?"

"Shower's all yours, babe." A towel hit my body, and I caught it on reflex. "Unless you don't want it all to yourself."

Heat rose to my cheeks, and I swallowed a couple times to wet my throat. "Hello?" I called, hoping to alert a teacher that a girl was in the room so I could get some help. "Hello?"

"Hello!" a voice called, mimicking me.

And another. "Hello!"

"Hello!"

"Hello!"

Male voices around the room laughed and joked, and I gritted my teeth together, aggravated. I didn't know why I was surprised. The guys in this town...

"What the hell's going on?" someone asked.

"Winter Ashby wandered in, man."

I backed up to the door, my hands at the ready as it sounded like more guys came in from the showers or the gym, I wasn't sure.

But before I hit the hard doors, I hit something else. I stopped, feeling a body behind me.

"Hey," he said. "I'm Simon."

I jerked, but there was suddenly a body to my left and in my ear. "I'm Brace."

And then another one in front of me. "I'm Miles," he said, and I sucked in a breath and held out my hands.

I tried to slip in any direction I could, but they were everywhere.

"Guys, come on, leave her alone. Get her out of here!" someone barked from farther away.

"Oh, come on, Will..."

I stepped to my left, but there was someone's bare skin there. I shot to my right, and I ran into someone in a towel. I growled and darted out my hands, pushing at the body of the boy who said he was Miles in front of me.

"You guys are assholes," I said. "Let me out of here!"

Suddenly, a hand swung into me from the front as Miles grunted, and the boy behind me shoved into me as

90

he was pulled away, knocking me forward a little. I lost my breath and held out my arms to brace myself, but they were suddenly gone. All three of them.

Someone took my hand, and I jerked on reflex, about to pull it away, but then he asked, "Are you okay?"

His tone was light and gentle and immediately put me at ease. Or at least more ease than I was. I stopped, letting his fingers hold mine by the tips.

It was a small gesture, but it didn't scare me. Just more reassuring.

"I'm Will," he said. "I'll find someone to get you out of here, okay?"

I inhaled the fragrance of body wash and fresh laundry on him and nodded, his presence helping me calm down a little.

But then our hands were knocked apart.

I went rigid, stunned for a moment. *What the—*

"What?" Will asked someone.

"Get off her and go get dressed," the new voice said. "I got it."

I got it? Who was this?

"I wasn't *on* her," I heard Will say, but his voice faded away anyway.

Wait...

I backed up, pressing the door again and finding it still not giving way.

"Are you hurt?" the dark voice asked me.

I shook my head. His tone wasn't taunting like the others, but there was something about it that gave me pause.

"Are you going to class?" he pressed, his voice growing closer. I couldn't back up anymore, just kept putting all of my weight into the door.

I opened my mouth. "I have—I have lunch."

He leaned in close, his body brushing mine, and I sucked in a breath and put my hands up.

"Let me get the door for you," he said in a low voice.

"I…" I planted my hands on his chest to keep him away from me, feeling a crisp shirt, stiff collar, and skin. I let my fingertips linger a moment too long in the strip of bare chest where his shirt wasn't buttoned.

Shit. I moved to pull my hands down, but just then, my thumb brushed an object—a little ball or…bead—peeking through the opening of his shirt.

Déjà vu washed over me.

Grazing it with my finger, I felt another and then another, tracing the beads on the chain—warm from his skin—down his torso where the two strains joined into one as it draped down his stomach.

Wood. I could feel the grooves under the gloss coating.

My stomach dipped. *No, no, no…*

I couldn't help it. I followed the line of the beads, feeling his stomach tighten under my fingertips, and his breathing quicken.

Reaching the crucifix I hoped wasn't there, I pinched it between my fingers, my nerves firing hot under my skin as I instantly recognized the carefully crafted definition of the fingers attached to the cross.

Oh, my God. I let the rosary go like it burned my fingers.

But he grabbed my hand, pressing it back on the beads and his skin.

"Oh, why stop when you were doing so well?" he taunted.

"Damon," I murmured, trying to pull my hand away.

"Mmm," he affirmed. "Missed you, kid."

I tore my hand free, clenching my jaw.

Jesus. In my head, I still saw him how I last saw him. A kid, not much bigger than me, with a lanky body and a shaky voice.

But everything had changed. His hand in mine was bigger than I remember, his voice was deeper, he was taller, and he had a voice now. He wasn't eleven anymore.

Why did I feel like I was just now realizing that?

And any hope that he'd forgotten about me was now gone, too. He knew exactly who I was.

But before he could say anything else, the door behind me gave way, I fell back, and he caught me, pulling me forward again and into his body. I didn't have time to push him away before someone grabbed my hand, pulling me off him. I stumbled.

"Winter," my sister snapped. "What are you doing?"

But she didn't wait for my response. She hauled me out of the locker room and into the hallway, and the door slammed shut behind us as a trickle of sweat glided down my back. My head was swimming, and I could still feel him near me.

I jogged to keep up with my sister as my heart pounded painfully.

But my body buzzed with warmth, too. I frowned, rubbing my fingertips over my thumbs and still feeling the beads between them.

• • •

Ari was probably the one who stuffed me in the damn locker room in the first place. Or she had her friends do it. How else did she know where I was?

She was probably just pissed when I didn't make it back out right away and she had to go in there and fetch me. Were she and Damon friendly?

They were in the same grade, but I had no idea if they hung in the same circles. My parents would've advised her to stay away from him, but it wasn't like she would listen unless she wanted to. I had absolutely no idea what he was like anymore or about my sister's life at this school. The former I couldn't admit I wanted to inquire about over the years, and the other, I really didn't care. My sister and I had been struggling through our growing pains for about ten years now, and I wasn't sure why. There just seemed to be a layer to her I couldn't crack, and we didn't have much in common, either. Especially not anymore. She'd gotten used to life as an only child while I was away and obviously liked it.

"God, he's looking at her," Claudia, one of Rika's friends, said across from me as we sat in the lunchroom.

I perked my ears, an earbud still stuck in one as I half-listened to music and half-listened to the conversation. I didn't want to be rude, and I should've been concerned with making friends on my first day, but after the locker room debacle, I needed to recharge for a few minutes.

"Who?" Rika asked.

But no one answered her—at least not verbally. It was times like this when I realized how aware people were of my disability. Answering with nods or body gestures I couldn't see.

My disability.

I hated that word.

But it was what it was, and people, without meaning any harm, used it to their advantage. They could communicate with their eyes, their hands, their gestures...all in a possible attempt to keep me out of the loop.

Who was looking at who? Someone was looking at me?

"His attention has been on her for longer than seven seconds," Noah, another of Rika's friends commented, "and longer than seven seconds is not good."

Who and who?

But Claudia cursed in a whisper. "Oh, shit."

Rika shifted on my left, and the next thing I knew someone sat down on my right, their knees blocking me in, like they were straddling the bench and facing me.

"What are you listening to?" a deep voice asked.

I had a moment to process whose voice it was before the earbud was plucked out of my ear.

Damon. They'd been talking about him. He'd been staring at me in the lunchroom. The scent of tobacco and cloves wafted off him, and I searched for ways to get rid of him.

He was bold. A lot bolder than I remembered, and I wasn't used to it.

He was quiet for a minute, and I guessed he was probably checking out my playlist. The oldies I listened to when I needed something fun, light-hearted, and peppy to get me out of a mood. The same mood he put me in this morning.

The earbud dropped back in my lap, and his voice was low but sure. "It won't be like that with us."

Like that?

Like what?

And then I realized what song had been playing. "Then He Kissed Me" by The Crystals.

He and I weren't going to be like that couple in the song?

I tightened my jaw. Yeah, no shit. *There was no 'us'.*

"Leave her alone, Damon."

"Suck me, Fane," he shot back.

I stopped breathing for a moment, registering the sudden sharpness to his tone. God, he was different.

I swallowed the lump in my throat. "I don't want to talk to you. And you're not supposed to talk to me."

He didn't say anything for a moment, and he didn't move. Was he staring at me?

I faced forward, ignoring him.

After a few seconds, he cleared his throat. "I was Winter's first kiss, ladies," he told everyone, despite that we had another guy at our table. "I was eleven. She was eight."

I felt him nudge closer, and his voice dropped a hair. "I wonder how many guys have kissed you since. But then, I guess I don't really care, because I was first, and that's all that matters."

I balled my skirt in my fists. I wanted him to go away. "Don't think for a second that you were any good at it, either," I replied.

"And don't think I'm going to go easy on you just because you'd trip over a speck of dust if someone wasn't holding your hand to walk ten steps."

I heard a snort from somewhere farther away, my lips tightened. "I'm not scared of you."

"It's early."

I shook my head. "What do you want?"

"To pick up where we left off."

Where we left off? He nearly killed me when we were kids. There was no moving forward.

"Honestly, I don't know," he mused. "I have a short attention span, and you interest me at the moment. I have questions. Like, can you see anything?"

I narrowed my eyes.

"Anything at all?" he pressed. "Shapes, light, dark, blurs...? And is it true that when you lose one sense, the others heighten? Your sense of smell, hearing, ..." he paused, his voice dropping to almost a whisper. "Your sense of touch?"

The little hairs on the back of my neck rose up, and my blood heated under my skin. Everyone was watching us. I knew they were.

Just ignore him.

"And since you don't have the use of your eyes," he kept going, "do you have the reflex anymore to squeeze them shut? Like when you're in pain or...when you're excited?"

Another little laugh somewhere down the table. I turned away a little, worried they could all see how hard my heart was beating.

His words were filled with innuendo. I almost forgot he was older for a moment, our age difference at eight and eleven seeming much bigger now that we were in high school. I was too young, and he was being inappropriate. I kind of got the impression—judging from how he spoke to Rika—he was like that with everyone, though.

"Do you remember what I look like?" he asked. "I'm bigger now."

I turned toward him, knowing my eyes wouldn't meet his. "I remember everything. And I don't hurt as easily anymore."

"Oh, I'm counting on it."

The edge back in his voice spread chills up my arms, and every inch of my skin felt electrified. I could feel his eyes on my face, watching me, and there was a mixture of dread and anger inside me, but also anticipation.

Excitement.

While he hurt me years ago, and there was no doubt he was now ten times the asshole I knew back then, a small part of me liked that he didn't tread softly around me. He didn't coddle me. He didn't ignore me.

He didn't act nervous, scared of me, or treat me like I was fragile. Maybe he thought I was an easier target, or maybe he didn't scare as easily as some. Whatever it was, part of me kind of liked it.

And part of me wondered how he would respond if he found out I didn't scare so easily, either. It was obvious from the others that *no one* liked to deal with him. He was used to having things his way.

"What are you doing?" someone spoke up, making me blink.

I turned my head away, coming back to the moment and registering that Ari had come up behind me. Before I could figure out who she was talking to, though, Damon slowly rose from where he straddled the bench next to me.

"Just saying hi to your little sister," he said, and I could hear the smirk in his voice.

I felt him leave, and Rika shifted next to me, blowing out a long breath like she'd been holding it.

"He's not supposed to come near you," Arion said, and I guessed she was talking to me.

"Tell him that," I muttered, feeling for my sandwich where I'd left it on the table. "I didn't make him come over here."

"Don't tell the administration or Mom or Dad. The basketball team needs him, and I'm not having him get in trouble because you can't deal."

I picked up a half but didn't take a bite.

"He was here first," Arion pointed out. "You get him expelled, and everyone will hate us."

Yeah, no doubt. I knew about the order Damon got to stay away from me this morning before school started, but I hadn't entertained the possibility he'd actually disobey it. Was he stupid?

Or maybe he just thought he was that untouchable. He came right over here and sat down, knowing that at least half the eyes in the cafeteria would be on him and witnesses to what he was doing. And he did it anyway. Maybe he was overly confident, purposely reckless, or...uncontrollable.

Uncontrollable. That was the boy I remembered.

But my sister was right. He'd been here longer, and no matter what he did, they'd blame me if he got in trouble. For now, I'd handle him myself if he didn't quit. And I'd do it quietly.

It still pissed me off that my own sister's first instinct was to protect the basketball player, though.

I lifted my chin a little. "Thanks for your concern," I told her. "It's touching."

"Oh, gimme a bre—"

"You can go now."

"What are you—"

"Jesus, you're still here?" I blurted out, cutting her off. "Well, make yourself useful then and open this."

I reached for the bottle of O.J. on the edge of the table where I'd left it, found it, and handed it to her over my shoulder.

Juice splashed out from where the cap wasn't tightened properly, and I heard her gasp.

"Ugh, Winter!" she yelled.

I winced. "Oh, it was already open? Sorry. I'm so blind."

Laughter broke out around the table, and she let out a growl, her mumbled curses fading away as she stomped off. Or I pictured her stomping off. Not sure if she actually did.

"Oh, shit, girl," Noah said, knocking me lightly in the arm. "You are my hero."

I gave a half-smile, a little pleased with myself. Also a little aggravated that Arion and I were at war at all, but like Damon, I kind of appreciated the normalcy of it. Arion didn't put on airs to protect my feelings. She just treated me like I was stupid, as if learning how to live all over again six years ago didn't make me tough and quickly adaptable to change and new challenges with a hard heart ready to fight for all the things they told me I couldn't have and couldn't do.

Maybe that's why Damon treated me like I wasn't made of glass. Maybe he knew.

I thought back to the boy in the fountain, bloody with a silent tear streaming down his face, because something—or many things—happened to him that he didn't want to talk about, and now he was nearly a man who would never cry again and only made other people bleed.

I hated him, and I would never forgive him, but maybe we had that one thing in common. We had to change to survive.

CHAPTER 6

Winter

PRESENT

"Arms up!" Tara called out.

I reached up, leaping across the floor, the muscles in my back and shoulders stretching tight as I tilted my head back and my face toward the sky.

"There's the energy!" she shouted. "Let me see it again! Good!"

I exhaled as I hit the ground again, my right foot landing on the border of sandpaper lining the perimeter of the "stage" to signal when I was within two feet of the edge. Beyond that, there was another six-inch-wide border to alert me I had no more room and to stop.

Sweat trickled down my back, and I swung around, veering right again as I stepped, glided, and then arched my back before coming up on one toe and stretching high for a moment's pose and coming down again to continue the dance.

The music filled the room, my unconventional number of Nostalghia's "Plastic Heart" choreographed by me and soon-to-be performed at nowhere for no one.

No one would hire me. I tried to stay positive, especially since I needed out of here more than ever, but it was getting harder and harder to not feel stupid for leaving college.

Tara was one of my instructors growing up, and I continued to rehearse at home, but I also came to the studio from time to time, since my father had paid for five hours a week for room rental until the end of the year. I didn't want to use anything he left for me, but I sucked it up as an excuse to get out of the house. Damon hadn't been back since the wedding days ago, but it was only a matter of time.

And I loved it here. I only thought about dancing here and nothing else.

This was where my earliest memories of dancing were, and I guessed I was luckier than some. There was a time I could see, and I'd had four years of ballet training before I lost my sight. I knew how pliés and arabesques felt and looked. I knew movements and steps, and I knew a little technique. I'd continued with a private trainer when I went to Montreal, even though I knew my prospects weren't good for a career later on. I'd always known the reality.

I'd have a hard time in a chorus with other dancers and especially with a partner. It wasn't impossible, but everything took longer to learn and not many would accept that challenge.

And I certainly wasn't the first ballet dancer with a visual impairment, but I was the first in a five-hundred-mile radius. I held out hope. Someone had to start the phenomenon in other parts of the world. Why couldn't we have it here, too? The only major problem was finding a company and a coach to take on the work.

I slowed with the music as the song ended and finished, bringing my arms down, wrists crossed in front of me, and fingers displayed gracefully. At least I hoped they looked graceful.

"Here," Tara said. "Stay like that."

Walking over, she ran her chilly fingers over the bend in my wrist.

"Straighten them," she instructed. "Like this."

And she took my hands and placed them on hers, which were in my ending pose. I ran my hands lightly over hers, feeling the bends in the joints of her fingers, the tendons on the backs of her hands, and the smooth line down her wrist to her arm, so I could emulate it.

"Thanks," I told her, breathing hard.

I put my hands on my waist, my light, billowy top falling off one shoulder and baring some skin to the welcome cool air of the old, drafty building.

"Again?" she asked.

"What time is it?"

She paused a moment. "Almost five."

I nodded. I had a half hour, so may as well soak it up before the money ran out.

I heard her steps as she walked over to restart the music, and I counted my own steps from the sandpaper glued to the floor to the center, finding my starting mark.

"You don't have to stay," I told her. "I have the driver. I'll be fine."

The Torrances insisted on our own personal drivers, and while we sporadically hired them for certain occasions growing up, we never kept any on the payroll. My sister loved the new perk. The new perk that came with her new name.

But I knew the ulterior motives behind the gesture. A driver reported our comings and goings to the one who paid them, so Gabriel and Damon were aware of our every move.

The driver was my leash.

"You know," she started as the music began, "they offered to pay...for you to continue classes."

I stopped. "What do you mean? Who?"

"Gabriel Torrance's assistant called and said to have your classes billed to him," she told me. "In case you'd like to get on the schedule again."

She had guided me and offered feedback sporadically since my father left and I could no longer afford her. Bits here and there when she was on her way in or after a class had ended. Or like tonight when she was on her way out.

But this news of Gabriel's offer was like a slap in the face. Another reminder that I was destitute and couldn't have the things I'd been accustomed to.

Because of them.

Because of him. This was Damon's idea.

No one else cared if I continued my dancing except him. He liked it. I was probably the only person who knew that he loved it, in fact. He'd watched me. I'd danced for him a lot before.

Fuck him.

I got back into position, lifting my chin, and craning my neck. "Can you restart the music?" I asked her, ending our conversation.

After a moment, the music cut off and restarted, and I began again, letting the volume of the song drown out everything else. The world swayed around me, and even though I couldn't see it, I sensed everything.

The space. The scent of pine needles from last year's Christmas tree. The cold bricks around me that I knew were there. The barre with chalk crusting the wood and the way the ceiling felt torn away and there were miles of sky above my head. I could reach and feel endless.

I was flying.

The singer's voice burrowed into my stomach, and I broke away from my classical moves and let my hand fall down my body as I slowed, feeling every inch of my skin come alive. My feet ached in the pointe shoes, but my body was alive.

I closed my eyes, the strands of my hair spilling around me and tickling my face. My stomach flipped as I spun, and a smile twitched at the corners of my lips. God, I loved this. I was free here.

I wanted to see if you'd dance for me.

I slowed in my steps, hearing his voice in my head.

But then I picked up the pace again and slid into a closed position doing several échappés in a row as I moved my arms.

You'll hate me.

I'll love you.

We have to stop. Make me stop.

I can't. I won't.

And pressure hit down low, between my legs and making my stomach dip. I opened my mouth, filling it with the same, silent cry as that morning he was arrested as I twirled and twirled, tears stinging my eyes and hoping to spin the world so fast I'd lose sight of him in my head.

But then I lost my footing, hitting a piece of furniture as my leg slammed into wood and a sharp pain shot up my shin.

"Shit!" I exclaimed.

"Winter!" Tara called out.

I snapped my eyes open and growled, stumbling as my hand came down on the piano to steady myself.

The bench. The damn piano bench. Did I miss the markers on the floor?

"Whoa, I gotcha," a male voice suddenly shouted. "I'm coming."

Ethan? When did he get here?

The music cut off, and I hunched over, squeezing my leg as the shooting pain throbbed harder and harder. I winced, blowing out a long breath as footsteps scurried across the wooden floor.

"You're bleeding," he said, steadying me under my arm, while Tara took my hand. "Come here."

"It's okay," I blurted out, shaking my head and pissed at myself. "I haven't done that in ages. What the hell?'"

Distracted. That's what I'd been.

"Sit her down," Tara told Ethan. "I'll go find the first aid kit."

I limped, but pulled myself up straight. "It's in the bathroom. I'll be fine."

"But you're bleeding."

"And I know how to operate a Band-Aid." I laughed through the pain. "Go home. Ethan will help me. See you in a couple days."

I heard a little sigh as she debated on whether or not to make sure I was okay, but she knew this wasn't new for me. I'd gone through my fair share of Band-Aids.

"Thanks for your help tonight," I told her, slipping out of Ethan's hand to grab hold of his arm instead. "Later."

After a moment, I heard the shuffle of her feet and belongings as she picked up her jacket and bag. "Well, have a good night, then. I'll text you later, okay?"

I nodded, guiding Ethan toward the direction of her voice to follow her out the door and toward the bathroom. He tried to put an arm around me, but I waved him off.

We pushed through the doors—Tara veering left to the exit and us heading right, toward the stairs.

"How long have you been here?" I asked him as we descended to the lower level.

"Just arrived," he said. "I had a study group that went late, but I knew this might be the only chance to see you."

Yeah. With the trouble on the road the other night, who knew if he'd be admitted to the house. And if he were, how would it play out once Damon came home.

Home. I held onto the railing as we took the stairs two flights down, still holding onto Ethan with my other hand. Damon—or his family—owned my home now, and while he'd been clearly sleeping elsewhere all the nights since the wedding, he could still come and go whenever he liked. Without knocking. Without permission. Without an invitation.

He controlled every key in the house. The realization curdled my stomach.

"Are you okay?" Ethan asked. "I mean...not just the leg."

"Yes, I'm fine."

I knew what he was worried about, and I was grateful for his concern, but he couldn't help. And I wasn't sure I would tell him if there was something to worry about.

"Don't worry," I assured.

I may not be able to handle Damon, but Ethan definitely couldn't.

He led me to the women's bathroom, knocking and calling out before we entered to make sure it was empty, and I walked in, releasing him and reaching for the wall to the left I knew was there. Coming around the corner, I found the sink counter and hopped up on it, immediately reaching for the paper towel holder.

Ethan reached for it, too, trying to help.

"I got it," I told him. "Can you grab the first aid kit? It should be inside the box on the wall."

While he walked over and lifted the lid, I wetted a couple paper towels and dabbed at the skin where it hurt. They said I was bleeding, but I had no idea how much.

I groaned as the cool water stung my cut. It was always the smallest things that hurt the most. Forming a little circle of claws, I dug my nails lightly into the skin surrounding the pain to deflect it a little. A trick my dad taught me when I was about six. The sharp ache eased a little, and I stayed like that for a moment, enjoying the slight reprieve.

"Hey, there's nothing here," Ethan called out. "Let me run upstairs and see if the girl at the desk has it."

I nodded, not sure if he saw. The bathroom door creaked open and closed as he left, and I pulled the paper towels off, folded them, and re-applied them to my leg, leaning back on the mirror and closing my eyes.

What the hell was I going to do? I was twenty-one, no job prospects, and I was scared. I would never be free while he was alive, and there was still so much he could take from me. He was already heavily at work on my peace of mind.

He'd been out of prison for over a year before he made contact, and two years before he set his plan into motion. I'd gotten complacent in my sense of security, thinking he might've moved on. I was wrong.

My eyelids grew heavy, and my head started to float as the pain in my leg subsided. I yawned, letting the sleepiness take over. At least when I was tired, I couldn't worry.

Just as I was about to nod off, propped up against the mirror, I heard the whine of the unoiled hinges on the bathroom door. *That was quick.*

"Did you get it?" I asked, keeping my eyes closed and breaking into another yawn.

He didn't answer me, though, and I opened my eyes, blinking. Someone had just opened the door, right?

"Ethan?" I called, sitting up straight.

The theater was about to close, and other than the front desk attendant, I didn't think anyone else was in the building anymore.

And then...he was there.

He rested his hand on top of mine where it laid on my thighs, his chilled fingers making me suck in a breath and laugh. "Hey, you scared me," I said. "Did you get the Band-Aids?"

Fingertips came up to my face, brushing a strand of hair out of my eye, and I recoiled at the icicles on my skin. What was he doing? I took his hand off my face and held it in mine, reassuring him.

"I'm okay."

His body came in closer, though, forcing my knees apart and his clothes chafing the inside of my thighs. He took his hands off me, and I stilled, feeling the warmth of his breath right in front of me, on my face, as he leaned in.

What the hell was he doing?

"Ethan..." I protested but wasn't sure what to say. He'd gotten close a few times, and while I knew he wouldn't say no to more, it just never happened between us. He wouldn't try again?

"Shhh..." he said.

And I stopped breathing. The heat of his mouth was centimeters from mine, and suddenly, my heart started hammering. He'd never felt like this. He was never forward, and I was instantly uncomfortable, old memories coming back.

Please don't try to kiss me, I begged.

Water pumped through the pipes above my head, and I could hear the dull hum of the furnace somewhere in the distance, but otherwise, it was quiet down here, and we were all alone.

"I need the Band-Aid," I told him, forcing a little smile. "Come on..."

"So pretty," he whispered over my mouth. I could taste the smoke on his breath.

Smoke...

"Okay, I got them!" Ethan suddenly shouted from around the corner, stunning me out of the quiet as the bathroom door swung open again.

I gasped, rearing back. *Shit!*

I darted out my hands, looking for the man who was just here, but finding only empty space.

Tears stung the backs of my eyes, my pulse throbbed in my neck, and I couldn't catch my breath as I sucked in lungfuls of air.

Motherfucker. Goddamn him. Where was he? I searched with my hands. Where did he go?

"Hey, hey, hey, what's the matter?" Ethan asked, coming to my side.

But I just grabbed onto his sweatshirt, fisting it as I breathed hard.

If Ethan didn't see him, he was already gone through the exit on the other side of the bathroom.

I shook my head, trying to calm down.

I'd relaxed. Like an idiot, for five minutes, I'd relaxed, and he never did. He would always be at the ready.

"Just get me out of here," I told Ethan. "Right now."

"What about the Band-Aid?"

"Now!" I cried out.

And he didn't need to hear anymore. Pulling me off the counter, he took my hand, and we left the theater as quickly as possible.

• • •

I let Ethan take me home, followed closely by my driver, I was sure. Even though I had transportation at my disposal, I couldn't stomach anything to do with Damon. I got in Ethan's car, told my driver to "go to hell" when he protested, and we left.

Once Ethan dropped me off and left, albeit with some hesitation, I walked into the house, Mikhail trotting up to greet me and hearing my mother's voice coming from the dining room.

I leaned down to pet him and give him a kiss. "Feed you in a minute, boy."

Walking into the dining room, I felt their footsteps and heard pages flipping from the dining table.

I hadn't spoken to my family much in the past few days. Angry, I stayed in my room, chewing my nails and trying to figure a way out.

"We could do wallpaper in the kitchen," my sister said. "Like just one wall. It's back in style now."

Decorating? They were fucking decorating? *Jesus.*

"I tried to leave a few nights ago," I finally told them, brushing my hand against the doorframe and stopping there. "Back to Montreal."

Silence suddenly filled the room, and I could guess both of them were trying to process if they should be angry or not. My mother wanted me safe, even though she wouldn't do anything to ensure it herself, and I was pretty certain my sister would love having me out of the way. They would both know, however, that it would displease Damon, and there might be consequences if I ran and he couldn't find me fast enough.

"The police," I went on, "on Gabriel Torrance's payroll, no doubt, caught up to me and turned me around."

"Ethan was helping you?" my mother asked in a tone that said she already knew the answer.

I nodded. "And if I want him to stay safe, then he'd better not help me again. That was the gist of the warning anyway."

I heard a slow but deep intake of breath and a quiet exhale, and I knew my mother was trying to stay calm, but I was done pretending to be. Damon was clever, diabolical, and patient. All of the things I wasn't. At least not right now. I was too fucking angry.

It finally dawned on me that no one was actually on my side.

"I hate you," I said to my mother, letting it go with my chin trembling. "I would rather live in the gutter than have him in our lives!"

I gestured to where I'd heard my sister chatting. "I know why she'd do this, but you're supposed to protect me," I told my mom. "He raped me!"

"He didn't rape you," my sister snapped back, pushing out of her chair. "We all saw the video. The whole world saw the video! You wanted him. You were in love with him."

I shook my head. "Not *him*."

I had never been in love with him. Not with *Damon*.

That damn video.

Tears spilled, and I couldn't stop them. I folded my lips between my teeth to keep from sobbing. A video of us was leaked, he was sent to jail for statutory rape, because he was nineteen, and I was still a minor, but nearly everyone in this town took his side. He was a little richer, a lot more popular, and two of his friends went with him for their own misdeeds leaked on other videos, as well.

But he got the most time.

He was the only one convicted of a sex crime, and in everyone's eyes this was a grave injustice, because their basketball star, golden boy only had sex with a willing girl who just happened to be a couple years shy of the legal age of consent. Big deal.

Hey, in some other states sixteen is old enough, isn't it?
This is a technicality.

Did he even do anything wrong? How many of us were having sex at that age?

Don't ruin his life. It's not like he hurt her.

Hey, she seemed to love it well enough.

The backlash was sickening, and while other girls claimed he'd taken advantage of them, too, by the end of it, they'd all folded, and it ended up just becoming an example of how warped our justice system was when there were "actual" predators out there. I'd ruined a young man's life. To-may-toes, to-mah-toes.

All they saw in that video was me willingly kissing him.

Touching him.

Holding him.

In their eyes, I'd wanted it, and he was 'the man'. But they didn't know what was really going on in that video. They didn't know what he'd done to me to get what he wanted from me.

Footsteps approached, and I smelled my mother's Chanel No. 5.

"Winter," she said calmly. "Do you really think he needed to marry into this family to get anything he wanted? He could've easily threatened Ethan anyway to keep you in Thunder Bay and under his thumb. Or threatened us, your grandparents, or any other friends. No matter what, this was going to play out how they wanted, because they have the money and we have nothing anymore. Nothing."

KILL SWITCH

'Because of my father', I finished for her.

Yes, I knew. She wasn't entirely wrong.

And in that moment, I hated my father, too. His crimes didn't put us in this mess, because Damon would've eventually found another door if that one had been closed. I only hated him for leaving. Gabriel and Damon Torrance could do anything they wanted with us now. And given their reputations, I tried not to think about how bad this could get or I'd be sick.

"At least now," my mother continued. "We have something to work for. A light at the end of the tunnel."

The divorce settlement? Was she actually that stupid? Damon would get Ari pregnant, and there would be no way out after that!

"And what were you planning for us to do in the meantime?" I challenged. "As we wait for this year to pass?"

What would I do as she tried to wait this out, day after day, week after week?

"We survive," she finally answered.

Survive.

Submit, you mean?

After a few moments, I left the room and made my way upstairs, shutting myself in my bedroom for the rest of the night with Mikhail. I fed him but forwent dinner myself, not hungry anyway, and I only left briefly to shower.

I couldn't make my mother's decisions for her, but she also couldn't make my choices for me, and there was no way I'd do whatever it took to survive. I had my limits, and I wasn't going back to that place with him.

If it even came to that.

But hopefully I'd find a way out of here before it did.

• • •

I blinked my eyes open in my bedroom hours later, my lids still way too heavy, but the air was chillier than usual.

113

Was it six yet? My alarm hadn't gone off.

I reached over and hit the button on my bedside table, the male voice in the machine saying loud and clear, "Two-thirteen a.m."

"Two-thirteen?" I breathed out, painfully awake now.

I closed my eyes again, hoping to fall back asleep, but my brain was already working and assessing. The night was silent outside. No rain or wind, but we would probably get snow in the next month. I allowed myself a moment to feel wistful for it, but the weight of all our troubles descended again, and I wanted time to slow down, not speed up.

I loved wintertime, though. And not because of my name. It was just a festive period, and happy things made me happy. I always decorated my room, because I could still feel the lights and the garland, hear the music from the snow globes, and smell the scent of pine. But I wasn't sure I wanted to decorate this year. My pride was planted firmly, and I refused to make the best of this. Hopefully I wouldn't be around for it anyway.

Turning on my side, I adjusted the pillow under my head and stretched my legs out under the sheets, feeling the space, smooth and cold.

Not warm.

Wait. Where's...

"Mikhail?" I called out, popping my eyes open and my head up.

The dog slept at my feet, but he wasn't on the bed. I listened for the jingle of his collar as it did when he rose to answer me, but there was nothing.

"Here, boy." And I clicked my tongue a few times, calling him.

He couldn't have gotten out. I locked the door.

Then I noticed the scent of something buttery and sweet, and I sat up, throwing the covers off. My heart picked up pace. *She didn't,* I groaned to myself.

I made my way over to my desk, my fingers grazing a ceramic pot with what smelled like tea and a small dish with a flaky croissant. My mother had broken in to leave me food.

Christ.

I walked over, finding my door open, thanks to her. Really, it was probably useless to lock it. If Damon lost the master key to all the rooms, he could, you know, just kick it down, but still... I couldn't *not* lock it, so...

I stuck my head into the hallway. "Mikhail?" I whispered. Nothing.

I pinched my brows together. It wasn't like him not to respond, and there was no way to get outside without someone to open the door for him.

"Mikhail?" I whisper-yelled a little louder.

I stepped out of the room and slipped quietly into the hallway, the floorboards creaking just a little under my weight.

I rested my left hand on the bannister as I followed it around, the only sound being the tinkling of the crystals on the chandelier above as the draft seeped through the old house. Carpets laid softly under my feet, and the grandfather clock ahead of me and at the top of the stairs ticked steadily, the small noise amplifying how eerily quiet the house was in the middle of the night.

I would've heard him bark or growl or felt his sudden movement in bed at least if something made him nervous, right? He was always alert. No one was here now except my mother, sister, and me.

Trailing down the stairs, I held onto the railing with both hands as I took each step, and then I let go, walking carefully to the front door. I checked all the locks, making sure they were twisted into position.

And then I heard a little whine to my right.

"Mikhail?" I turned my head toward the sitting room.

Walking over, I took small steps and reached the rug, feeling him rush up to me, his wet nose hitting my knee.

"Hey, where did you go?" I teased, reaching down to pet him. "What…"

The scent of a cigarette hit me, and I trailed off, my face falling.

My stomach sank, and I stood up straight, my chest rising and falling, steady but quick.

He'd had my dog.

"Don't touch him again," I bit out.

"He came to me."

Damon's voice came from somewhere deep in the room, and I guessed he was probably in the high-back cushioned chair in the corner by the window. I pictured him sitting in the dark, the only light the small embers from the tip of his cigarette.

I reached down to take hold of Mikhail's collar.

"You gave your dog a Russian name," Damon mused.

"I gave him a dancer's name."

Mikhail Baryshnikov. I couldn't help the fact that most of the revered ballet dancers were Russian. It had nothing to do with it being a fucking nod to Damon's heritage.

Just about to turn around and take my dog, I sensed him rise from his chair as the last of the cigarette smoke dissipated into the air. Keeping my dog close to me, I stepped back to the table against the wall and swiped the pen I knew sat there with a pad of paper for messages. I kept it in my hand, hidden behind my thigh.

There was a time when he scared me, and I liked it. I didn't like it anymore.

"I don't want to be here," I told him. "I'll find a way out. You know that."

I faltered for a moment, realizing this was the first time Damon and I had had any semblance of a conversation—albeit reluctant—since he went to prison five years ago. Any other interactions we've had have either been brief attacks or bitter threats in passing.

"You have nothing to say?" I prodded.

"No, I just don't feel a need to respond." His voice grew closer, and he took a drink of something, the ice in his glass clinking before he set it down on a table. "You can say and make whatever declarations you like, Winter, but ultimately you'll do what you're told. You, your mother, and your sister," he pointed out. "You don't run this house anymore."

"I'm an adult. I can go where I like and leave when I wish."

"Then why are you still here?"

My lip twitched in a snarl, but I hid it quickly. His meaning was clear. Yeah, I could've tried to leave the other night. If I were willing to see my friend get arrested for something he didn't do. He and his father had advanced on me, and I'd retreated, so the truth was, I *couldn't* go and do as I pleased, could I? Not without consequences.

"I do love your anger," he said. "I'm glad it's still there."

Yes, it is. My anger seemed to be all I had anymore, and I missed laughing and smiling and the freedom of who I used to be. Before he happened, and the threat of his inevitable return didn't always linger. Would I have things of my own again? Could I even fall in love anymore? After him?

"Ethan Belmont is the mediocre third son of a CEO of a failing coffee shop chain and a second-grade school teacher," Damon said. "He spends his entire day locked in his parents' house playing video games—"

"Designing them, you mean—"

"And sucking on an inhaler, because of pollen, or clutching an EpiPen, because peanut butter touched his bagel," he went on. "He wouldn't be able to haul his own body weight out of a burning car, let alone save his wife and kid."

And you would? Please.

Damon Torrance didn't save anyone but himself. Not that Ethan and I were seeing each other, but I'd choose him any day over Damon.

"Mikhail," I said. "Mikhail, come here."

"Now the question is..." Damon continued, and I heard him approach again. "Do I keep him or give him to my father. I haven't kept a dog as a pet in years. Not sure I have the knack for it."

My nerves fired. "Give me my dog."

"You want him back?" he asked, getting closer. "Then beg me."

"Fuck you!"

He grabbed the back of my neck, fisting my hair. "A dog is a dog and a bitch is a bitch," he bit out. "Neither of you is very much use to the world, so I don't care either way."

I planted my hands on his chest, trying to pull away.

Mikhail.

No.

"Beg me," Damon taunted. "Beg. Just whisper it. Just say please."

He couldn't take my dog from me. What was he going to do to him?

My face started to crack as I thought about Mikhail, and I wouldn't know where he was or if he was okay. If he was hungry... Would Damon take him away?

Damon kneaded my scalp, still gripping my hair. "Whisper it," he said, his breathing turning ragged. "Whisper it like I did your name the morning they found me in your bed and arrested me, Winter. That's all I want to hear. A little whisper."

His hand shook where he held me, and my stomach knotted so hard, I was in pain. *Please stop. Don't do this.*

"Killing him would probably be more merciful than giving him to my father," Damon added. "He's not good with dogs—"

"Please," I burst out, a tear falling. "Please just give me the dog back."

"On your knees," he ordered.

I closed my eyes.

Goddamn him. He knew exactly what to do. Every time. I wanted to rip him apart.

I hate him.

But slowly, I lowered.

I fell to my knees, my teeth clenched but still shaking as his hand stayed in my hair.

"Please," I whispered, closing my eyes in disgust at myself. "Please."

"Again."

"Please," I begged.

I waited for him to say something—to say I could have my dog back—but he just stood there, holding me by my hair.

He just stood there.

Was this what he wanted to see? Me degraded? Me scared?

He loved me scared. It got him excited.

I actually thought I liked it, too, once.

And as the seconds passed, and he held me there as my heart thumped in my chest, it was like we were teenagers again for a moment.

When I liked the games he played with me. Before I realized I was the toy.

The terror and the dread. But the exhilaration and the safety I felt in his arms.

How I'd never hated anyone as much as I hated him, but how I loved what I felt with him more than I loved anything I felt with anyone else, either. I was so stupid.

His fingers started to move, caressing me so softly as his breathing turned heavy and strained. "Winter..."

My clit throbbed once, and I broke, silently crying as shame heated my cheeks.

What the hell had he done to me?

He pulled me up, pushing my hair behind my shoulder and his voice suddenly normal.

"Good girl," he told me. "Of course, you can have your dog. Did you think I was a monster?"

I jerked away from his hands. "It hardly matters. You already ruined my life. Long ago."

"In the treehouse when you were eight," he finished my thought for me. "I remember that party. It's funny, though. That's all you do remember, isn't it?"

"What are you talking about?"

"The fountain," he pointed out. "Do you remember what happened in the fountain before we went to the treehouse that day?"

The fountain? I searched my brain through my confusion, not coming up with anything that stood out as out of the ordinary. I was eight, so I couldn't remember every detail after all this time. Just that he was hurt, and I'd tried to help. The events after the fountain were what mattered.

"Nothing happened," I told him.

I wasn't letting him take what happened that day and turn it around on me. I was nice to him. Nothing I did or said deserved what happened after. Neither did anything I did or said years later in high school deserve what else he took from me.

Part of me was still curious about what he was getting at, though, and I thought he might elaborate, but he didn't. He left me in the dark.

He sighed. "I'm out of my own control, Winter," he said, not explaining any further. "There are no choices. We are who we are, and we do what we do. It's nature. Like game pieces, I will play my part, because I can't resist. I can't be what I'm not."

I frowned. He sounded resolute. Like this was the end for me.

"I hope you won't disappoint," he finished.

So, this was it, then? He was going forward with whatever ugly desires that simmered inside his twisted brain, because he was determined to not understand the pain he caused and that crimes have consequences? He'd gotten what he deserved.

I won once. I'd do it again.

"Just pick new tactics," I told him. "I don't appreciate you ambushing me in the bathroom like some pervert."

"I don't know what you're talking about."

"Bridge Bay Theater," I prompted. "I was alone in the bathroom today. You came in and messed with me. I thought you would've learned how to up your game in prison."

He laughed once, took a drag of his cigarette, and exhaled.

"I have no idea what fantasy you were concocting in your dreams, but I was in New York all day," he said. "I just got back an hour ago."

"Yeah, of course you were."

"Why would I lie?"

I paused, realizing he might have a point. He had no motive to deny it. It was no secret he had it out for me and my family. And there was probably no proof he was there, and even if he was, an alibi could be forged to say he was elsewhere.

With just us, here in this room alone, he'd take pleasure in doing and saying whatever he wanted with no one else to hear.

He stepped up to me, and I could smell the tobacco on him, as well as the fragrance of his clothes, the expensive fabric and the leather of his shoes.

"I'm better than that," he nearly whispered down on me, and I could feel the ice on his cool breath from the drink he'd just had. "Why would I corner someone in a public space when anyone could walk in and interrupt me? I would need privacy."

His fingers brushed my hair off my cheek, and I jerked away.

"Like a big house?" he told me. "With miles of empty forest outside and no neighbors. No traffic. Nothing." I heard the sick smile in his voice and didn't miss his meaning at all.

He already had it all planned out.

"Everyone else is gone, leaving her alone," he continued. "No one to help. No one to hear her. No one to stop me. A whole night. Just the two of us." He whispered now, his breath on my lips. "In the house together. So much space to run, and only so many places to hide."

I curled my fingers into fists, and if I didn't know it before, I knew it now. He had changed, after all.

He'd gotten worse.

And in his head, he did the time, so may as well do the crime.

Dread curdled my stomach as he brushed past me.

"Goodnight, Winter," he said.

And I didn't mistake the hint of excitement in his voice.

CHAPTER 7

Damon

SEVEN YEARS AGO

So according to Mr. Kincaid, given what happened so many years ago, Winter Ashby's parents deemed it necessary to request that I attempt no interaction with their daughter—or either daughter, for that matter—while they were enrolled at Thunder Bay Prep. And failure to abide by that request would force them to seek a restraining order against me.

Unless I wanted something like that on my record, then I should obey.

Or you would think I would obey. Anyone else would.

But hearing that only got the wheels in my head turning, and I dove into the alluring possibility of the danger and all the trouble I could cause.

I nearly laughed, remembering the conversation. *A restraining order?* Gimme a fucking break. What a pussy. We were children back then. Griffin Ashby was just pissed his wife had been screwing my father once upon a time, and if he couldn't get his puny, pasty little hands on a man like Gabriel Torrance, then he pumped up the size of his dick by taking a jab at me now and then.

Yeah, there was an accident when we were kids, and Ashby had clearly poisoned his daughter over the years to warp her memory of exactly how that all went down, but I hadn't meant to hurt her. It was a fucking fluke, and kids have accidents.

I stepped out of my car and slammed the door, hitting the button on the key fob and arming the alarm.

"Why didn't you want me to pick you up?" Michael yelled over at me, getting out of his G-Class.

"Because I might not leave when you do," I told him.

"Or he'll be done before everyone else," Will added with a chuckle as he flanked Michael's side with Kai on the other.

The three of them drove together, and I was usually with them, but sometimes we came on our own. If we anticipated separating at some point during the night, that was.

I didn't really have a plan, but who knew?

After Winter's and my conversation in the cafeteria earlier this week, and her clear fear of me when we ran into each other in the locker room, I was intrigued. What did she remember about that day in the fountain? She was young when it happened—like me—so her memory might not be as sharp.

When she'd wandered into the locker room—or was pushed in, I later discovered—seeing the scared but stubbornly defiant look on her face reminded me of Banks. She looked about two seconds from cracking, the blush of embarrassment all over her cheeks and her eyes glistening a little. But her jaw was flexed hard and her fists were balled up tight. She was freaking out on the inside, but definitely pissed, too.

It was kind of cute.

And I liked the hint of helplessness. It made me feel...

I don't know. Powerful, I guess.

The same way I felt with Banks and the basketball team, because there were things that only I could do for them.

Call it arrogance. All I knew was that I didn't like the taunts directed at her when the guys noticed her.

No, scratch that.

I didn't like *anyone else* taunting her.

And I really didn't like another man coming to her rescue, even if it was Will.

And fuck her dad. He wouldn't take out a restraining order on me. The alumni liked winning games, didn't they? Michael, Kai, Will, and me...We were given very long leashes as long we kept doing our jobs. He didn't have the guts.

We headed around the circular driveway, "Bad Company" by Five Finger Death Punch drifting up from the backyard as we walked past the dumbass marble fountain with four horses spitting water and fat cherubs posing up on the higher tier. It was the type of ugly shit Americans put on their property when they wanted to look European, but it just kind of came off looking like a trailer park bird bath, only bigger.

Griffin Ashby was a poser. And even if he could like me, I still wouldn't be able to stand him. Luckily, he was in Meridian City for the weekend, his wife having gone with him, and their eldest daughter Arion decided to have a pool party tonight. Hopefully Winter hadn't gone with her parents. I wanted to talk to her again. See how long it would exactly take to get inside her head and fuck shit up.

"Hey!" I heard Will bark as we walked. "Whoa, whoa, whoa, come here!"

I looked over, seeing him grab a kid by the shirt and stop him as he headed through the driveway, trying to leave.

I instantly recognized him. Misha, his little cousin. Grandson of a state senator but looked more like the prodigy of Sid and Nancy.

"What the hell are you doing here?" Will asked him. "You're like twelve."

"And?"

Smart-ass kid.

Will faltered a moment and then laughed under his breath. "Yeah, you're right. Never mind. Drink responsibly." And he pushed the kid back toward the party around the back of the house.

But Misha pulled out of his hold and whipped back around, walking toward the road instead. "I'm going home," he grumbled. "This is boring."

"You can't walk from here, you little shit!" Will argued. "It's miles."

"So leave the party and gimme a ride."

"Are you nuts?"

The laugh was lost in my throat as I turned around and started heading for the backyard again.

"That damn kid," Will said, jogging to catch up to us. "I don't know how he can be my blood."

We walked around the house—the text invite stressing that no one was allowed inside the home and to come directly around to the backyard—and stopped just as the sprawling lawn came into view.

People danced and played drinking games, commotion going on in every corner as the music blasted and a football coasted through the air.

I could smell the food laid out on tables as several people played or talked in the pool. Nearly every chair was occupied, and some students took up the chaise lounges by the pool house, steam billowing out of the showers behind the structure. A light layer of mist also lingered just above the surface of the water, making the pool look like a hot tub.

"Hand in your phones," someone called out.

I looked over to see a JV football player—whose name I didn't know—sitting at a card table, eyeing us with our names already on Post-Its, ready to confiscate our shit, so no evidence of the party leaked online.

"Fuck your mother," I muttered and looked back to the party, hearing Kai snort next to me.

All we needed were our phones getting stolen while in someone else's possession. Pictures, texts, videos, receipts... I didn't give mine up for anyone. It was safer with me, and if they wanted to kick us out for not following a rule, then good luck with that. People didn't stay at parties we weren't at.

The freshman didn't say another word—or even move—as we walked into the party. Girls ran around, some in bikini tops, even though it was in the sixties tonight. I knew the pool was heated, but it had to be chilly if you were out of it.

One of them glanced up at me as she scurried by with her friends, a suggestive little smile playing on the corner of her lips that told me she probably wouldn't take as much work as some if I were interested tonight.

But I like work.

I let my eyes trail around the backyard, shooting from corners to tables to the sporadic clusters of people.

But I knew who I was looking for. Even though I knew I shouldn't be. This might actually be crossing a line, even for me.

When we were eight and eleven, it didn't seem complicated to want to know each other, but now it was. People would read it wrong.

Michael let out a sigh, rolling his head and stretching out his neck. "Let's get a drink."

We nodded and moved into the party, getting beers and stopping here and there to talk to people.

Eventually, we found a table and I kicked off my shoes, pulling off my hoodie and throwing it down on a chair before grabbing my beer bottle and downing the rest of it.

Spotting one of our own basketball JV guys at the table, I shoved the empty bottle at him, which he took as he halted his conversation, pausing only a moment before he rose to get me another.

"All of us," I mumbled to him as he left. Will drank faster than I did, so he'd be empty soon if he wasn't already.

Kai sat down at the table, drinking and laughing at something someone said, while Michael walked off to talk to Diana Forester.

"Whoo-hoo!" Will cupped his hands around his mouth, howling in the middle of the party, over the loud music.

Everyone startled and turned just in time to see him run, shoes and shirt discarded, and leap into the deep end of the pool, somersaulting backward in mid-air before splashing into the water.

People laughed, hooting and hollering after him, and I walked over to the edge and stepped in, dropping into waist-deep water. I wore long, black swim shorts that fell to just above my knees, and I hadn't brought a change of clothes. Banks had begged to come with me tonight, and I ended up charging out of the house to get away from that pathetic look on her face, a little pissed and a whole lot distracted and forgetting my cigarettes in the process.

Will popped up through the water, laughing and exchanging a few splashes with others before he swam over to me. I planted my elbows on the deck behind me, leaning against the edge of the pool.

"Arion Ashby wants your ass bad, man," he said, standing up and pushing his hair over the top of his head. He jerked his chin off behind me, amused.

I glanced over my shoulder, seeing Winter's older sister standing with her friends and eyeing us. My gaze traveled down her body, long, slender limbs in a white, strapless bikini and a long, fluffy ponytail. Both of her legs were adorned with anklets, and a multi-strand gold necklace in varying lengths rested on her chest.

She'd be hotter with just the jewelry on.

I turned back to Will. "I have plans for her. Don't worry."

His eyes lit up. "I love your imagination. Do I get to come?"

I tilted my lips in a smile, not missing his double-meaning. "I have plans for you, too."

And then I let my eyes fall to the two hickeys on his neck, one of them damn nasty looking. I knew exactly where they had come from, too. The girl who'd dealt them probably had twice as many of her own.

"Some girls need to learn that sucking dick like a vacuum is a skill you don't waste on a man's neck," I told him, flicking water with my fingers as aggravation settled in my gut. "Maybe you should watch while I retrain the one who did that to you."

"Aw, jealous?" he teased.

But then a look passed between us, and I wasn't fucking laughing. His cocky smile started to fall, and he straightened up.

Will was my best friend, and what was mine was mine. He knew that.

An awkward silence passed, but then he noticed something behind me and jerked his chin. "Uh-oh."

I looked over, seeing Arion walking toward us through the water. She'd let down her hair and had her hands tucked behind her back. I had geared up all week to be in the mood for something far different tonight, and I wasn't sure I wanted to stay.

But my plans fell apart, I had nothing better to do, and if she wanted to play, maybe I could get my head in gear, after all. She was pretty enough, even though she had a set to her eyes that made her look a little mean and her jaw was more square, making her look too thin and giving her an air of hardness I didn't like. She wasn't sweet.

But whatever. I wasn't the one who would fuck her.

As she reached us, she pulled her fists out from behind her, eyeing us coyly, and opened the left, revealing a turquoise triangular pill and handed it to Will.

X.

"Hell yeah." He took the pill and washed it down with his beer.

She then looked at me, opened her right hand, but it was empty.

I darted my eyes up to meet hers, but she just smirked and then opened her mouth, revealing my pill already on her tongue.

She rose up, moved in for my lips, but I turned my head away.

"I don't need help to get crazy," I told her.

Plus, this wasn't middle school.

Her eyebrows rose with the challenge, and she took my beer out of my hand and took a drink, swallowing the pill herself.

Licking her lips, she plastered her body to mine, and I let her stay there. For the moment.

"Let's go upstairs," she whispered up at me. "I'd like to see your crazy."

I reached up, holding her chin between my thumb and fingers.

Would you?

It no longer worried me that there were things wrong with me. That over the years I developed different tastes than other people, or that I was harder to please than other men.

The only thing that worried me now was that it was getting harder to please those tastes. It was like I was developing an immunity to kink, and I constantly needed to up the dose.

I stroked her jaw once, trailing the sharp ridge with my finger. "I want you to go into the hedges," I told her in a low voice. "Over there."

I gestured to her right with my eyes where there was a hedge line around the property before it gave way to the forest, the cliffs, and the ocean beyond. There wouldn't be anyone back there.

Her eyes fell to my mouth, and she looked like she liked that idea. "And what are you going to do to me behind the hedges?" she asked.

"I'm going to watch you."

Will laughed quietly at my side, and while a sliver of guilt nipped at the back of my mind, making my gaze falter, I dug my fingers into her jaw a little tighter, feeling the heat I needed coursing through me all of a sudden.

"I'm going to watch someone touch you," I told her. "I want to watch someone have you."

She paused, her face falling a little as realization hit. Her gaze shifted, looking unsure, and she was probably wondering if this was a joke or if she should back out now. Surely, she'd heard the stories.

She probably just thought she was so hot that how could I not want to fuck her myself, right?

Her blue eyes flashed to Will. "Him?"

I shook my head once.

Her eyes then wandered hesitantly, landing on someone behind me.

"Kai?"

I shook my head once again.

Will shook his head, too, sounding amused as he finished his beer. "Jesus."

"Marko Bryson," I said, eyeing the guy on the patio behind her.

He stood with a group of people, no shirt on, and a half-full bottle of Fireball in his hand. Arion looked behind her, seeing him for herself, and turned back to me.

"He has a girlfriend," she said under her breath.

"That's what makes it hot."

I'd already watched plenty of people have sex in my short lifetime. All the men hanging around my father's house and the whores they kept. The secret lives of the mothers and fathers in this town. The girls who ruled the underworld of our decadent little school just as much as the guys did.

Yeah, I'd seen some shit.

But now... *Stronger, harder, more. Always more.*

"But I want you," she protested.

"And I want you to like what I like."

She stared up at me, the wheels turning in her head, but she closed her mouth and didn't argue further.

She could leave. She could say no. It wouldn't break my heart, and she knew that. But she also knew if she said no, that would be the end of it. I wouldn't want her otherwise, and I certainly wouldn't make her my first girlfriend if she didn't accept everything I was about. I wasn't going to change.

"Someone will find out," she finally said.

And I couldn't help but tilt my lips in a little smile. It was the last protest. Her final attempt to find an excuse out of it. Or a reason to give in.

"He won't say no to you," I told her.

It was always subtle, but I could see when it happened. The last argument dying in her eyes like it did with anyone I played with.

She started to open her mouth to agree, but then her eyes shot up, above me. "What?" she barked, and I realized there was someone standing behind me.

"Arion, can you help me find the snow village in the basement?"

Snow village? *That voice.*

I closed my eyes, the little hairs on my neck rising.

Winter. She was home, after all.

"What? Now?" Arion whined. "Have Mom help you when she gets back."

Get the fuck out of the pool and get her what she wants.

"I don't know why you want it." Arion took my beer again. "It's not even Halloween yet, and you can't see the damn thing anyway. What's the point?"

Bitch.

But even as my aggravation with Arion Ashby rose, the skin on my back warmed, knowing Winter was right there behind me.

And even if I tried, I couldn't think of anything else right now.

What was I about to do to her sister just to get that same, exact feeling?

How did she get out here anyway, and how did she find her sister? I wanted to turn around, but I just stayed planted, listening.

"It has music," Winter said, her tone growing defensive. "I like it, so what do you care?"

But Arion didn't answer, and after a moment, her gaze dropped back down to me. Winter must've walked off.

Now that I knew she was home, any lukewarm interest I was able to muster for Arion had all but disappeared.

It has music. I like it.

I didn't know if I felt responsible for the fact that she now only had four senses by which to experience the world, but it was a strange feeling to want to protect someone from others when I knew I'd be worse for her health than anyone.

I nudged Arion off and turned around, hopping out of the pool. Walking over to the table, I grabbed a fresh towel and glanced around, finding Winter near the pool house. Her hand was hooked around the arm of another girl about her age. That must've been how she made her way out here and found her sister.

Girls swarmed around her, and she looked overwhelmed but happy. Her mouth changed a lot, showing that she was a little nervous with all the commotion, the music, the people in her backyard... Folding her lips between her teeth, pursing it to one side, various hesitant but sweet smiles... She wasn't used to this at all.

What kind of parties did she have at her blind school in Canada? And why the fuck did he send her all the way to Canada, as if she'd needed to be buried behind the curtain of some foreign country, so everyone would just forget about their less-than-perfect daughter? A wealthy family like hers could afford tutors for her to stay home if they thought regular school was too much. And if not, there were schools in the city.

Hooking the towel around my neck, I sat down at the table, instantly patting my shorts out of habit.

"Fuck," I muttered.

I needed to find a cigarette.

"Get your sister a sweatshirt," I heard Kai say to someone. "Everyone can see through her shirt."

I shook my head, about to laugh.

"So don't look at her tits," Arion replied as she reached over the table to grab a towel. "She's a kid."

Sister.

Arion's sister. I looked over, seeing Winter nodding to something someone was saying as her eyes lingered, unfocused toward the mid-section of the person in front of her.

She was barefoot in jeans and a white, ribbed tank top, a little stretched out and worn like she just did not care, but her face was clean of makeup, lips a natural dark pink and the barest remnants of curl left in her blonde ponytail as it draped past her shoulders. She was perfect.

A smile pulled at my lips, but I stopped myself and took a deep breath.

And that's when I noticed the outline of her breasts through the fabric. The faint curves of the half-circles and then the points, more prominent with the chill in the air tonight. I darted my gaze left and right, noticing one group of guys looking over at her, speaking amongst themselves and laughing in unison at whatever was said.

Dumb fucks.

Kai picked his sweatshirt up off his chair and tossed it to Arion. "Do it now," he commanded.

And from the tone and the look on his face, he wouldn't allow her to disobey.

"Fine," she spat out and got up.

But I grabbed the sweatshirt and yanked it out of her hand, throwing it back on the table.

Kai glared at me.

"She's fine," I told him, more as an order rather than a statement.

He rose up out of his chair, the hint of disdain on his face as he picked up the hoodie. "Not every woman in this world will be for your personal amusement," he bit out, staring down at me. "Someday one of them will be your kid, and you're gonna damn well worry when she's drawing the wrong kind of attention."

"You teach your daughter to hide in everyone else's world," I shot back, "and I'll teach mine everyone else exists in hers. Go fuck yourself, and leave the kid alone."

I wasn't sure where the hell I was coming from, because if Banks walked out of our room like that, I'd lose my shit. But with Winter...

Nothing she did would be wrong. It was their fault for looking.

He straightened, breathing hard but not blinking.

And grabbing the sweatshirt again, he turned around and headed toward Winter.

Fucker.

Kai and I weren't friends. We were brothers. In every way except biological. Whether we liked each other or not, we were family, and we had each other's backs.

But that didn't mean we liked each other, either.

He was the noble one. The voice of reason in our little group, and while I sometimes envied his happy house, I knew there would be a time when he'd have two choices—and he wouldn't choose me.

Noticing Arion still next to me, I looked up at her. "What are you waiting for?"

Her lips tightened into a line, knowing I was referring to Marko Bryson, and finally, she walked off, either to get to work on him or tell me to piss off and to get back to her friends. Either way, I didn't care. I just wanted her gone.

I turned my eyes back on Kai, watching as he approached Winter and the girls around her parting to let him in.

Winter's smile faltered as he leaned in and she listened to whatever he was saying. She pulled back a little, her spine straightening and her head bowing in embarrassment.

My fingers closed into a fist.

Then he took her hand and held the sweatshirt up to it, so she could take it and put it on.

But much to my surprise, she shook her head and waved him off, adding a small smile for good measure. Instead, she reached out to touch the brick column of the pool house, using it to feel her way as she left.

He watched after her, threw a look at me, and I just shook my head at him. She wouldn't cover up, but now she was leaving the party good and humiliated. *Great job, asshole.*

He threw the sweatshirt back over to the table, and I turned my eyes over to her, watching her trail the perimeter with her hand grazing the hedge line. How long did it take her to map out a new place in her head? She seemed pretty self-sufficient. Even at school already. Of course, she'd be familiar with her home the most. If she followed the hedges around the corner, they would take her all the way back up to the house.

Standing up, I took Kai's hoodie and walked, making sure to go slowly as I slipped away from the party and down the small incline, away from the noise and eyes.

Winter walked along the line, rustling the green leaves as she brushed past them on her way back to the house, and I pulled on the sweatshirt, masking my scent as I dove through an opening in the line to the other side of the hedges.

I slowed to a walk, my heart suddenly hammering as I saw the white of her shirt through the leaves, not one foot away from me. I put out my hand, following hers where it grazed the leaves on the other side.

I closed my eyes for a moment, walking with her and following the path with my hand as I heard the blood pump in my ears. My head started to float a little, and the world seemed to tilt under my feet.

I opened my eyes, still walking with her although she didn't know.

It was annoying, the loss of equilibrium when I closed my eyes, but I was sure it was far scarier than I realized. I would never know what it was like to be her, because I could always open my eyes.

"Where is he?" someone breathed out. "He wanted to watch this, didn't he?"

"I don't know if—" Arion's voice turned muffled, like she was being kissed, and I darted my eyes up to see her and Marko ahead of us, between two trees.

He bent Arion over just slightly and squeezed her tits. On the other side of the hedges, Winter had stopped, her body unmoving as she no doubt heard what I heard.

"Take off your top," I heard Marko order, but I wasn't looking at him. I lingered back, finding a glimpse of Winter's face through the leaves and watching the unreadable look on her face.

It was a mixture of curiosity and fear, but I wasn't sure which one she felt more of. How long would she stay?

"So glad I didn't bring Abby tonight," Marko said. "I needed to get off on something new."

Arion whimpered and moans filled the air around us, and I saw Winter's mouth drop open a little like she was about to run for the hills or break out in a laugh.

"We have to hurry. I don't want to get caught."

"Lick me," Marko told her. "Get me hard, Ari."

Winter's eyes widened, probably realizing it was her sister, and then I heard a zipper...

"Ah, yeah," Marko groaned. "Fuck. Swallow that shit, baby. Nice and deep."

Winter's jaw clenched, and she stalked off a few steps and then broke into a run, back to the house.

I quirked a smile. *Well, well, well...*

I slipped through an opening in the hedges, pulled up my hood, and followed her slowly as she headed back up to the dark, empty house, away from the noise and crowd of the party.

She scared easily.

Oh, good.

CHAPTER 8

Winter

SEVEN YEARS AGO

I shivered, swallowing the bad taste in my mouth. *What the hell was she doing?*

I rushed up the hedge line to the bricks, turned right, my hand grazing the bushes at my thighs, and then turned left, running up to the back door. I twisted the handle, pushed through, and slammed it behind me, locking it.

Bile rose in my throat. Why would my sister do that? And at a party and in the woods? *Jesus.*

I didn't know she had a boyfriend. She hadn't mentioned him since I'd returned home. What the hell?

I brought my hand up to my mouth, still freaked out by what I'd heard.

Did that happen a lot? Would other people be going at it on our lawn all night? I gagged, a little grossed out.

Maybe if I'd been here the past five years, in an average environment, it wouldn't have been such a shock, but damn. Outside of movies and YouTube and the occasional late-night convo with my friends in our dorm in Montreal, I'd never witnessed anything close to that. It didn't sound very...like romantic or anything.

Hope she had the good sense to be safe, at least.

Walking through the kitchen, I trailed down the hall, around the bannister, and up the stairs. The music still pounded outside, but it was a distant and dull thrumming now, and while I had kind of wanted to stay at the party, I'd already decided to leave even before I'd heard Arion and her boyfriend going at it in the brush.

Embarrassment rose to my cheeks, remembering the guy that came up to me a few minutes ago. *You're a little visible through your shirt,* he'd stuttered in my ear.

He wasn't unkind about it, but it was still embarrassing.

I resisted the urge to fold my arms over my chest, but instead tried to be casual about it and act like it wasn't a big deal. I'd felt my nipples even through my bras from time to time. It couldn't always be helped.

It was nice how he'd offered me the sweatshirt, though. Sweet, really.

I found my way to my room and swung the door closed a little, just in case Arion came in with her boyfriend. I'd locked the doors downstairs to keep the party outside, but Arion knew where the key was hidden when she wanted in.

I tore off my tank top and pulled on a sports bra, putting my top back on when I was done. I almost always wore bras since I didn't have the genetics to be as small as some dancers, but I wasn't that big, either, given the diet and training I still put myself through.

And the one time I didn't, someone said something. *Awesome.*

I grabbed my pointe shoes on my bureau, but then stopped and put them back, deciding against them, and felt for my slippers instead. Opening my door, I left the room and pulled my phone out of my back pocket. Leaning just barely into the bannister for support as I walked, I tapped the top of my screen, the voice-over reading the time.

"Ten-thirty," it said in a computerized male voice.

Arion would be down at the pool for hours yet. Plenty of time.

I walked toward the stairs, but the floorboards somewhere behind me suddenly creaked, and I stopped, turning my head.

"Arion?" I asked.

I hadn't heard her come in.

"Arion, are you here?" I called out again, louder this time.

Did I hear that right?

But it was silent now. No response. No more creaks. My heart started to pump harder, though, and I listened for a moment, my brain going through every possible scenario of what that could've been.

We didn't have pets.

My parents were gone.

I was the only one in the house.

The wind, maybe?

I clutched my phone, my thumb nervously rubbing over the corner of the screen. "Phone," the voice-over said as I accidently hit the app there. I startled, picking up my foot.

As I did, though, the floor creaked again, and I hesitated a moment before putting my foot back down on the same spot.

The floor creaked under me once again. Right at the spot I was stepping.

Was that me then? I turned my head behind me, perking my ear for any sounds. I could've sworn the sound came from the floorboards behind me.

I put my foot down again, the old hardwood floors in our antique home creaking under my weight as I trailed down the stairs and into the mini ballroom.

It was fine. I just came inside, and all the doors were locked.

I walked into the large room, counting the strides and picturing it in my mind from my memories as a kid. A whole wall of large windows sat to my left, facing the front of the house, and it was adorned with long, cobalt blue drapes,

I remembered. The dark wood floor always flickered with the glow of the electric candles coming from the massive chandelier above, and I still remembered the white fireplace against the far wall where I got to decorate the mantel every Christmas.

Or my mom would let me decorate it, and then she'd come and "fix" everything how she wanted it when I wasn't looking.

I pulled on my ballet slippers, my feet too sore to put up with the pointe shoes tonight, and picked up the remote for the small stereo system I had set up by the wall.

Clicking to the second track, I found "Nothing Else Matters" by Apocalyptica and increased the volume to drown out the music outside before tossing the remote and my phone on the table.

I walked around the square dance floor, marked by my sandpaper stickers still there, worn and dulled, after years of holidays and visits home when I practiced. When my parents had large dinners, there would be tables and chairs brought in and placed around the dance floor, but the room was all but empty at the moment. I could probably make my rehearsal space larger, given that there was no furniture to bump into.

The music started, and I walked the perimeter, counting my steps and bobbing my head to the strum of the cello. The beat teased *one, two, three, four, and five,* and I matched my steps to it as the other instruments kicked in, and I vaulted up onto my toes and swung around in a circle.

My arms shot out, my wrists bent and my fingers splayed, as I bowed my head and moved, just going with it as I let the music crawl inside and take over.

Yes.

The familiar flip hit my stomach, and I spun and stepped, swayed and dipped around the dance floor, feeling the energy of the music course under my skin.

And I smiled.

What I was doing wasn't classical, and I probably would never perform it, but it was my fun time, and my parents weren't home. My dad hated loud music, so may as well have a party of my own up here while I could.

I moved around the floor, my back cooling with sweat and my ponytail flying in my face as I spun, and I let my hands glide down my face and neck, the blare of the music flooding my veins and making me want to go wild. I bit my bottom lip as I dipped my head back and moved and moved and moved, swinging my arms and raising them up before running my hand sexily over my head and pushing my hair over to the side.

My brow ached with how hard I squeezed my eyes shut and...

Do you have the reflex anymore to squeeze them shut? Like when you're in pain or...when you're excited?

I faltered in my step, Damon's words from the other day in the cafeteria coming back to me. *Son of a bitch.*

I pressed on, tossing him out of my head. I matched my body to the beat, and, as the song ended, I slowed my movements, breathing hard and feeling a trickle of sweat glide down my back.

Jerk.

I heaved breath after breath as I landed on my feet again and put my hands on my hips.

Why had he just popped in my head like that?

I'd actually been able to avoid him this week after our initial encounters the first day. That didn't mean I hadn't been aware of him, though. In every hallway I walked down. In the lunchroom where I knew he ate the same period as me. In the parking lot where I could hear the loud exhaust from the truck of Will Grayson III—his best friend, I'd learned.

I was very aware of him in such proximity at school. And when we weren't at school, my mind still drifted to him way more often than necessary. Rika and her friends had definitely filled me in on what an enigma Damon Torrance had become since we were kids. Popular with a really bad reputation. And not bad in a way people envied, either. It made people want to avoid him, but not want to be caught avoiding him.

But still, rumor had it, girls were enamored. They thought he was a challenge, and they thought they could tame him. So I was warned—*don't be stupid enough to put yourself in his path. He has no heart.*

Well, no one had to worry about that. He'd already done irreparable damage. The couple of hours I knew him as a kid wasn't worth any more harm he could do. I'd steer clear.

Using the remote, I clicked through the tracks, counting until I found number fifteen, and then I raised my arms over my head, straining the sore muscles in my back.

But after a moment, no music came from the stereo.

I picked up the remote and clicked *Play* again—and then again.

I waited and nothing.

"Come on," I mumbled a whine and headed over to the wall.

Hitting the door frame, I followed the wall to the left and scaled down to where the system was plugged in. But when my hand grazed over the socket, the cord wasn't there. I fumbled over the socket with both hands. *What?*

I dropped my hands to the floor and found the plug laying on the floor. How the hell did that happen?

I plugged it back in and stood up, puzzled, as I trained my ears on any sound. Was someone messing with me?

I turned around, my back to the wall. "Is there someone here? Hello?"

Something felt off.

Holding my hands out, I felt for the door and left the room, heading to the kitchen for a bottle of water. Maybe I should call Mr. Ferguson up here. He was one of the security guards who patrolled the community at night.

But my parents didn't know Ari was having a party, and they would definitely hear about it if I called security up.

Walking into the kitchen, I plucked a bottle of water out of the fridge and uncapped the bottle, taking a drink. I could ask my sister to come up and take a sweep around the house. It would piss her off, but she would come if I threatened to tell Mom and Dad about the party. Heading over to the back door, I reached for the handle, but as soon as I grabbed it, the door moved, and I realized it was already open.

My heart skipped a beat, and I instantly reared back. *Oh, shit.*

I'd locked it.

"Arion?" I shouted, suddenly alert. "Are you here?"

I pawed for the handle on the outside, finding the key we hid under a loose brick outside still inserted. It had to be my sister. Only our family knew where that key was.

"Arion!" I growled, losing my patience. "Knock it off and answer me!"

She seemed to get off on pranking me this week after the locker room incident she was probably the mastermind of.

I patted my pockets, realizing I'd left my phone in the ballroom.

And then I heard it. A few feet away, but I heard it.

Another creak in the floor.

I was paralyzed, frozen in place as my head swam with not knowing what to do. I tried to swallow but my throat had closed.

My mouth tried to form the words, but nothing came out.

The floor didn't move again, and I didn't even breathe as I listened.

Someone was there.

I felt it. The presence was heavy, and it was there.

It wasn't a sound I could describe, though. Their heartbeat? The slow, nearly silent intake of breath. A joint in their body shifting.

It's Arion. It's Arion. It's...

Bile burned my throat.

I finally forced the words out. "Who...who is that?" I stammered. "The...um..." I tried to swallow. My mouth was so dry. "The...the party stays down at the pool. You're not supposed to be in the house."

I should've bolted out the door, but if someone actually broke in, I wouldn't get anywhere. Not without being able to run the shortcut I was never able to take anymore without tripping over something in the yard.

I took a step left, inching back into the kitchen. Toward the cutlery.

Not that it gave me any better chance, but...

I took another step, feeling him—or her—watching me. Mere feet away.

They were there. Were they matching my steps, moving in as I moved backward? I tried to listen, but my pulse in my ears was too damn loud.

I took another step.

"This isn't funny." My voice shook. "You getting your kicks or something? Get out of my house."

Another step.

Who was it? I felt lightheaded, my mind and heart racing.

And as I fumbled for the drawer at my side with one hand and shot out my other to protect myself, a breath hit my ear from behind.

"Boo," he breathed out.

I gasped, crying out and running as I pushed off the island and bolted through the kitchen. I scrambled for the back door, but it was suddenly pushed closed just as I reached it, and I fell onto the floor, instantly scurrying in the other direction, back toward the foyer and the front door.

My phone. My fucking phone. I wouldn't have time to stop for it.

Seriously, if this was a fucking prank, I was going to kill my sister.

It was a clear shot to the front door, so I ran. My hands slammed into the door, I grabbed the handle and yanked it open, and raced through, taking a single step outside.

But just then, an arm circled my waist, catching me mid-step, and pulled me back in, shutting the door.

I cried out as the tall body behind me now fixed both arms around me, holding my arms down, and pressed me into the door to contain my struggles.

"Damon?" I choked out. "Damon, is that you?"

Even though I was sure there were several people who might get off on a good prank—especially at Arion's behest— he was the first one I thought of. It didn't even occur to me he'd be here tonight, especially with the order to stay away from me, but it was entirely possible he showed up for the party, right?

"This isn't funny!" I shouted.

I kicked at the door, trying to push off it and back into him, but he just picked me up and moved me away. He released me, and my hands shot up to touch the wall.

The corner. He put us in the corner, next to the ballroom.

I whipped around, now free, and veered around him to get away. But he was there, stepping in front of me again.

My chest rose and fell, working double-time, as I shot to the other side and tried to get out of there.

But again, he was there.

I backed up, shaking my head. "Who are you? What is this?"

Why wasn't he talking?

I inhaled a shaky breath through my nose, but I didn't smell the smoke on him I smelled on Damon the other day. Damon smoked all the time from what others said. Was it not him?

"What?" I bellowed. "What do you want?"

But he just stood there.

I bared my teeth, anger rising. And then I shoved at his chest.

He barely moved.

I growled and went ape shit, whipping my hands across his face and pounding my fists into his chest, but he didn't answer me, and he didn't try to stop me. I darted left again, trying to get out, but he slid in front of me, and when I veered right, it was the same. He wouldn't let me go. He was a wall.

My chin trembled. "Who...who are you?"

He didn't utter a word, though. All I heard were the breaths pouring into his lungs and exhaling, the sound deafening, because he was right fucking there in front of me. Like an animal, unable to communicate but could clearly eat and breathe.

God, who are you?

I shoved my whole body into him and opened my mouth and screamed as loud as I could. "Help! Help me!"

I grunted, trying to budge him as I shouted.

But then his whisper hit my ear. "They can't hear you."

And the softness of his voice was all the scarier, because the words came down like a verdict with an eerie calmness and resolution that made my stomach twist.

They can't hear you.

I couldn't help the tears that pooled. *Jesus Christ.*

"What do you want?" I cried.

I couldn't slow my breathing, dragging in more air and more air and the sound being the only thing I could hear in the room. He was so fucking calm. Was this entertaining?

"What do you want?!" I yelled.

I let my eyes fall closed, tears streaming and realizing it could be hours before Arion made it back up to the house, and no one at the party needed to come up here. There was the pool house with the bathroom, and it had a small kitchen that was stocked with all the snacks and drinks they'd need.

A golf ball rose in my throat, and I felt like I was going to vomit. I shook my head, my fight dead. "What do you want?"

I felt his hand touch my hair, and then the ribbon was pulled and all my hair fell from its ponytail.

"Oh, God." I start batting at him and trying to get his hands off me. "Just stop. Please stop."

I fell to a squat, partially to get away from him and partially because I felt sick. I clamped my hand over my mouth to try to sustain the rolling of my stomach.

"It's a joke," I said to myself, losing my fucking mind. "You're doing this as a joke. It's just a joke." I started shaking. "It's a joke."

I felt him squat down in front of me, his breath close again. "Then why aren't you laughing?" he whispered.

I snarled, getting angry again.

Why was he whispering? Did that mean I knew him? Was he afraid I'd recognize his voice?

I forced myself to calm down, finally able to pull in a long, deep breath.

"Are you...are you going to hurt me?" I asked.

"I don't know."

He doesn't know?

"Do you want to?" I pressed.

"Kind of."

His masked voice was like a breeze through the trees. "Why?"

"Because I'm sick," he answered.

What? No one was that self-aware. Especially psychopaths.

He took my upper arms, and I stiffened as he pulled me up, both of us standing again.

He moved in, his shirt brushing my arms. "Because I can't feel guilt, sadness, anger, or shame as strongly as I can feel fear anymore, and there's no stronger fear than when I scare myself." He brushed a tear off my face, and I jerked away. "I never know quite what I'll do," he finished.

Everything he said sounded like a threat, only worse. As if he had zero control over himself, and he was just as much a victim in this as me.

Fuck you.

I shoved his body again, and my nails caught his neck as I kicked and yelled for help.

But he grabbed my wrists and spun me around, circling me with his arms like a steel band. My own arms were pinned as his breath fell on my ear.

"Save your strength," he told me.

But it was gone. My knees buckled and he fell with me, both of us crouched on the floor on our knees, his hold keeping me from falling forward.

I put my hands on the wall, my head bowed as I tried to get my head clear.

But that's when I noticed the chill seeping through my jeans. And the faint scent of chlorine. His bottoms were damp from the pool.

"I smell the pool on you," I told him, my voice strengthening a little. "You were at the party. Lots of people. Lots of witnesses. They will find you."

He held me quietly for a moment, and then spoke low but clear. "My kind of fun has a price," he whispered. "Better enjoy myself while I can."

"Why me?"

I mean, really. Not that I wished him on anyone, but was it because I was blind? Because he thought I was an easy target?

"I don't know," he said, and I finally heard a clip of his deep voice, although it was still too low to recognize.

"Were you in the ballroom when I was dancing?"

"Yes."

"You watched me the whole time?"

"Yes."

"Why?" I asked.

Oh, my God. The initial creak in the floorboards I heard upstairs before, too. That was him. He was here the whole time. The idea of his eyes on me. Being in the room, lurking in a corner and watching me...toying with me.

Why would he just hang out and watch?

"Because it was pretty," he finally said.

Pretty?

"You asked me why you?" he said, holding me to him, my back pressed into his chest. "That's why. You're pure."

Pure? What...? Did he want to make me impure now or...?

"Your parents are bad," he explained. "Your sister lacks any depth to be interesting, and I hate my house. It's so dark there." He paused, then continued. "It all fucking disappeared when you were dancing, though. It made the world prettier. I liked it."

"So, what?" I argued. "You wanna lock me in your basement to dance for you on command? Is that it?"

But instead of the creepy, monotone, and calm response I'd been getting, his chest shook with a quiet laugh. "Can I hide there with you?" he asked.

I knitted my brow, taken off guard by the tone. Almost sincere.

I pushed my confusion away, though, and thought fast. Jerking my head back into him twice, I finally felt it hit his face, and I didn't waste a moment once his hold loosened. It was only a second, but I planted my foot on the wall and pushed against it, making him lose his footing and sending him falling backward. He took me with him, but it was enough to loosen his grip on me, and I scrambled away, across the floor.

My parents had a landline in their bedroom and bathroom. I could lock myself in and still have plenty of time to grab for some kind of a weapon. Hell, I could break the mirror for the shards if I needed to.

I scurried up the stairs and down the hall to my parents' room. My legs felt like rubber, my lungs hurt for air, and my hair stuck to my face and body, a light layer of sweat cooling my skin.

I threw open their double doors and raced for the bedside table, hitting my leg on the bed frame as I rushed past.

"Shit," I grunted, pain shooting through my shin. I fumbled for the phone, found it, and gripped the receiver.

But just then, he was at my back. A sob lodged in my throat as he wrapped his arm around my stomach, lifted me up, and yanked the phone out of my hand.

I breathed hard, my head falling back on his shoulder as he carried me away. My limbs were exhausted, and the fear had drained me. Everything felt like it weighed a thousand pounds.

He stopped, leaning against what I thought was the wall next to the closet, and I used what strength I had left to alternate between pushing at his arms around me, trying to get him off, and batting for his head behind me, barely able to hit much while facing the wrong way.

But then he took one of my hands, clutching my fingers tight, and held it steady, even as I continued to pull and tug at his grasp.

Even with my resistance, he pulled my hand over my shoulder and pressed my fingers into his neck, the pulse of his vein there throbbing wildly against my fingertips.

He dropped his head into the back of mine, breathing heavy. "You know what I have to do to myself to get it to pump like that?" he whispered.

He sounded spent.

It was beating hard, and I could feel the sweat on his neck under my fingers. But so what? *My pulse was pounding, too, you freak.* We just ran up the stairs. What the hell was he talking about?

"Don't worry," he finally said, releasing my hand. "I'm not going to hurt you. Not tonight."

I brought my hand down, grazing his collarbone, but there was no rosary there. And he didn't have Damon's scent.

His hold around me tightened for a moment, though, and I didn't trust a damn thing he had to say. Then, he let me down, my feet touching the carpet.

But he wouldn't loosen his hold.

"I wanna leave," I told him.

If he wasn't going to hurt me, then he could let me go. We had no cameras inside or outside the house, and no one else was here. No one would know who he was if he left now. I certainly couldn't place him.

But then came his cocky response. "Then leave."

"You're not letting me," I growled, trying to push against his arms.

"People aren't going to let you do a lot of things, Winter."

So he wanted me to *make him* let me go? What game was he playing?

I was done entertaining him.

"Please," I said.

"Don't walk away from me!" someone suddenly shouted down the hall.

I popped my head up, realizing someone else was in the house.

What?

My mom. She was home.

"Fuck," the boy whispered.

I opened my mouth to shout, but he clamped his hand down over my mouth, hauled me up again, and I heard doors behind us swing open and realized he was hiding us in the walk-in closet.

I kicked and screamed, but the doors swung closed again, and his hand muffled my cry.

I heard the bedroom doors on the other side slam shut and a switch next to me click. He must've cut the light in the closet as he hid us behind the wall.

"No, no, no," I heard my father argue. "Since you had to drag us back home tonight, I'm just trying to make sure we're behind closed doors so the girls don't have to witness your drunk-mother-tantrum."

The guy holding me turned me around to face him, his arm circling my body and holding me to him tightly as his other hand stayed pressed over my mouth.

"Mom!" I called out, but his hand was so hard over my words, it barely carried. I breathed hard through my nose.

"Oh, yes, by alllllll means," I heard my mother shout back. "Let's take them to the next company function where your latest twenty-year-old slut can suck the sweat out of you in the men's room with all of our friends outside!"

My ears perked, and for a moment I stopped fighting him.

"Is this one pregnant, too?" she went on. "Paying for another abortion and to keep her mouth shut about it is really going to nail home those good Catholic values we've tried to instill in the children. You're such a piece of shit."

"Say it again," my father dared her.

Pregnant? Abortion? What?

I shook my head, clearing it, and called out again. "Mom! Dad!"

He held me so tight, my teeth cut into the inside of my mouth.

"You work for nothing and spend, spend, spend, you lazy bitch," my dad continued, "so if I want a young piece of ass to bounce up and down on my cock once in a while, then I'd say I earned it!"

I winced. Young piece of ass? Oh, my God. What the hell were they doing?

"And you can smile and take out my credit card, go shopping, and shut the fuck up about it," he told her.

A slap pierced the air, and I startled.

"I hate you," my mother choked out. "I hate you!"

The springs in the bed squeaked, and it sounded like a struggle.

"We weren't always like this!" my mom cried. "You wanted me. You loved me."

"Yeah, I did. When you were a young piece of ass."

Fabric ripped, and my mother growled as they fought. I froze, not fighting anymore and tears pooling so heavy they threatened to spill over.

"But thanks to my money," Dad said, "you still have the tits."

She cried out, and I heard another slap, and then grunts and groans, and I shook my head, starting to cry. But before I could think of what to do, the hands left my mouth and waist, and instead came up and covered my ears as he pulled me close.

"Shhhh," he soothed, his mouth next to my temple.

I cried quietly, their voices dulled now, but I could still pick up pieces.

"Oh, God," my father groaned. "Yeah."

I shrunk.

"Get off of me," my mom demanded. "No!"

"Uh, come on." My dad's voice sounded labored. "I've still got her all over my dick. Your cunt will smell like hers. Sweet, like honey."

I brought my hand up to cover the sobs escaping, and that's when he brought me into his chest, still holding his hand over one ear, but pressing the other into his heart.

I breathed through my hand, and even though I wanted out of here, and I didn't give a damn if they knew I'd heard them, I was afraid of the consequences. Since my father hadn't actually wanted to bring me home from Montreal, he wouldn't need a good excuse to send me back.

So I stayed in here, the boy's heartbeat drumming in my ear, and after a few moments, everything had calmed. My tears stopped, my breathing got slower and more steady, and I couldn't hear my parents anymore.

Just his heart, pumping heavy and fast and in a constant, perfect pace like a metronome, unchanging.

At some point I dropped my hand from my mouth, my arms hanging limply at my sides, but he never let me go. And the beating in his chest lulled me until my eyes grew too heavy to keep open anymore.

Exhaustion took over, and before I knew it, I was lost in it.

In his warmth. In his arms. In the thunder of his heartbeat.

• • •

The next morning, I woke up, slowly blinking my eyes awake and my body feeling like it weighed a ton.

Why did—?

But then my eyes popped open wide, and I shot up in bed, remembering last night.

"Hello?" I called out. "Is there anyone there?"

There was no answer, and I reached over, hitting my alarm clock.

"Nine-thirty a.m.," the clock said.

It was morning. Late morning. I never slept this late.

I plastered my hands to my body, inventorying my clothes. I still wore my jeans and tank top, and I still had on my bra and my ballet slippers.

I darted my hand to my jeans zipper, wincing just in case.

But my jeans were buttoned and zipped, and my body, although tired, felt fine. I didn't think he'd touched me. At least not in that way.

Throwing off my covers, I swung my legs over the side and rubbed the sleep from my eyes. How did I get in bed? I wasn't sure which was the least mortifying option. Actually falling asleep after he'd scared me half to death and then him putting me to bed or my parents finding me passed out in the closet and discovering I'd been there the whole time. And them putting me to bed. I almost didn't want to leave the room to find out the answer.

But I needed to face the music.

Standing up, I walked alongside my bed, toward the door, but I accidently kicked something in my way and stopped.

I held out my hands, finding a cardboard box.

No, actually... Two cardboard boxes, stacked on top of each other.

I opened the top one and reached hesitantly inside, feeling wood, ceramic, glass, and clay. There were miniature trees, glitter-capped roofs, and models of houses, buildings, and a clock tower.

Then my hand knocked a model, and *Carol of the Bells* began playing, and I knew it was the ice rink adorned with little trees and ice skaters.

I almost smiled. It was the Christmas village. Two boxes of components.

How did...

Footsteps pounded down the hallway, and I heard my mother call down to Arion, sounding completely different than she did last night. I veered around the boxes and opened the door, peeking my head out.

"Ari, is that you?"

"I'm getting my shower," she said as she passed me.

"Did you get the snow village for me?" I inquired. I wanted to thank her if she did.

But she just barked back at me. "I said ask Mom. I have no idea where it is."

Okay. Wasn't her then. I ducked back into my room, scratching my head.

What the hell was going on?

"Hey, sweetie," my mom greeted, entering my room. "Did you have a good night?"

Jesus, no. My mind flashed to what I'd heard with her and my dad—how they both sounded like they were killing each other. God, the things my father said...

Growing up, I remembered them fighting, but I'd been gone a long time, it seemed.

"Are...are you okay?" I asked hesitantly as she moved about my room, probably making my bed, because she still thought I needed help. "Last night, I mean. I thought I heard—"

"Oh, did Ari get the village for you?" She cut me off. "That was nice of her. See, she does love you."

She pinched my chin, teasing me, and I jerked a little, not in the mood.

"Get dressed," she told me. "We have brunch in an hour."

She left the room as quickly as she'd come in, and I gathered she didn't want to know how much I'd heard last night.

But she didn't seem to know I was in the closet, at least. Thank goodness for that.

And Ari was acting completely normal. For Ari anyway.

Neither of them were responsible for the Christmas village in my room, either.

"What the hell?" I thought out loud, knitting my brow. "What the hell was that last night?"

Was it just some elaborate prank? Why would he threaten and scare me the way he did and then...and then shield me when my parents started fighting? He protected me and put me to bed and somehow knew I wanted the Christmas village that my sister wouldn't get for me.

I knew I should tell my parents about what happened, but...

I don't know. It could've been just a prank, right?

If I told them, it could get me sent back to Montreal where I was "safer and in my own element" like my father wanted. I really didn't want to bring any drama to his attention, because I'd be the one to get punished.

No. The boy didn't hurt me. Not yet, anyway.

In fact, he was kind of an angel at the end. An angel with really black batwings.

Psycho.

CHAPTER 9

Damon

PRESENT

"So this is Women, Gender, and Sexuality in Japan," I said, walking into Banks' classroom. "Part One."

I added the last part sarcastically, unsure as to why this class needed to exist in the first place, much less needed more than one part to it.

My sister turned her head, locking eyes on me over her shoulder. Slowly, she dropped her pen and twisted in her seat, a cautious but faint smile on her lips at seeing me. The 'I love him, but should I be worried he's here?' variety.

"Your course list is like a plate filled with every single food I refused to eat as a kid," I told her.

"I like my course list."

And then she broke into a full smile, and my heart skipped a beat. It was the same smile she gave me when we would do all the childish shit my friends were too cool to do with me in high school.

Sneaking into movies without paying.

Playing tag in the rain in the maze.

Midnight drives way over the speed limit on a school night, because we just needed to get out of the house.

She smiled less the older we got, but just now, it came so easily. I could tell already. She was different.

I descended the steps slowly, one at a time, the auditorium having emptied a few minutes earlier after her class was over. She always stayed, though, and graded the pop quizzes after every lesson for the professor.

Quite the little student now.

"It's a lot of politics, history, and sociology," I remarked on her course list. "Why those classes?"

She shrugged and dropped her eyes, looking thoughtful as she glanced back at the papers at her seat. She'd done most of my homework in high school, and it was always well above passing, so I knew she was smart and a quick learner. It gave me pause to hear she was in college, though. It never occurred to me she enjoyed it.

"The world was small growing up," she finally answered, looking up at me again. "Now, everything I learn makes it bigger. I want to know everything. Every person who walked before me. Every war fought. Every culture that breathes the same air. I can't explain it, I just..."

"You just did." I stopped a few steps up, aggravated even though I didn't want to be. I knew she meant me. Even though she didn't come to live at my house until she was twelve, I was part of the reason her world was so small growing up. I wanted her to be happy, but I hadn't outgrown that possessiveness. I still had a hard time being happy that she was happy, when the reason she was happy wasn't because of me.

And this—I looked around the room—it was one more thing taking her away from me. The bigger her world became, the farther away from me she got, and out of any emotion that I avoided, I hated loss the most.

"I'm glad you're in school," I told her. "I never imagined you like this. But it suits you."

She was beautiful.

And bright. Her dark brown hair hung down her back in loose curls, her jeans and short-sleeved black blouse fit a lot better than my clothes ever did, she wore lipstick and mascara, and the light caught the small ruby encrusted with diamonds on her left hand. Kai must've gotten her a proper ring after their quick nuptials.

Fucking Kai. He'd clearly treated her how she deserved.

But was she his now? Truly?

I sighed, looking around. "I hated college."

"You hated being away from your family," she corrected. "And I don't mean Gabriel and me."

I clenched my jaw. *Yeah.*

The year and two months I spent at college sucked, and even now, I look back on it as though time had been suspended as I existed without Michael, Will, and Kai.

And her.

"You were the only loner I knew who hated being alone," she mused, gathering up her books and papers.

"So what will you do?" I asked, changing the subject. "With your education, I mean?"

"She's already doing it." A voice trailed down from the top of the stairs, and I glanced over my shoulder enough to see a skinny body with brown hair trot down.

Alex.

"She, Rika, and I are designing a curriculum for young women," she said, stopping just above me. "Self-defense, survival, situational awareness, decision-making... We're hoping to roll it out next summer, starting at Sensou."

Sensou. The dojo Kai, Rika, Will, and Michael owned together. Not with me.

Self-defense, survival, situational awareness... People don't need classes in that. You push someone in a pool, they learn how to swim quick enough.

Banks stood up, bringing her satchel—weighed down and bulging with books and who knew what else with her. She looked up at me, explaining, "I want to empower people. That's all I know for now."

"Ready for lunch?" Alex asked behind me, but I knew she wasn't talking to me. They were probably meeting Rika, too, since they all went to school here at Trinity College.

My sister walked past me, and I caught a little bow of her head, almost like an apology. It was subtle, and I hadn't seen it in forever, but she used to do it all the time, didn't she? Always little looks or gestures like that to handle me and my temper or keep me on an even keel.

I inhaled a deep breath.

I needed her. I needed an anchor.

"Banks," I said, and turned around slowly.

She stopped and paused, standing there but not turning around. She didn't want to deal with me, and she wasn't going to have to. I was her big brother. I took care of her, not the other way around.

"I'll catch up," she finally told Alex.

Alex shot me a look, and I cocked an eyebrow, reminding her that she really didn't like me upset.

Her lips formed a tight line and she nodded at Banks, leaving the auditorium.

Banks turned around, but she still wouldn't look at me.

We were only a few feet from each other, but all of a sudden, it felt like miles.

I'd nearly killed my friend.

I'd destroyed Kai's business.

I'd threatened her, had her guarded, and kept her practically caged.

I was sorry for some things, not for others.

I swallowed. "The way...the way I was with you..." I started, "I—"

"You raised me," she said, raising her eyes. "And who knows what would've happened to me if I'd stayed with my mother."

I waited for her to continue, not sure if she was just trying to make me feel better or if she really thought her life with me was worth it all.

"I like who I am," she told me. "I don't hate you for anything."

And despite my slow, steady breaths and unwavering gaze on her, a little relief started to seep through my bones.

I watched her leave the auditorium, looking a little less unsure than when I walked in.

She didn't trust me, and she might not choose me.

But she was still with me. Even just a bit.

That was something.

• • •

I arrived back at the Ashby house—technically now my house—just after six and fucking starving. I had barely eaten all day, and even though I'd rather wait until late to come in, so I'd have to deal with Arion as little as possible, I wanted to see her. I wanted Winter at my dinner table tonight.

"Hello, sir," Crane said, opening the door for me.

I walked into the house, hearing the driver pull off behind me, and charged immediately up the stairs as the wind outside whistled through the old wood and any cracks in window panes it had found.

But there was no music or footsteps, and the upstairs was dark.

I stopped, slipping my hand into my suit pocket.

"Is anyone home?" I peered over my shoulder down to Crane.

He cleared his throat. "Mrs. Ashby and Mrs. Torrance are on their way back from the city—shopping," he clarified. "They'll be here in time for dinner."

Mrs. Torrance. Jesus, fuck you.

I pinched the bridge of my nose, letting out a breath and waiting.

"And..." he continued. "*Miss* Ashby is in the backyard."

I stopped breathing for just a moment. *The backyard.* I hated the way knowing that she was so close could give me pause.

I locked my jaw and continued up the stairs.

"She's not alone, sir," he called after me. "Mr. Grayson is here."

I halted. *Will?*

"Please let me know if I shouldn't have admitted him," Crane rushed to add. "You only said—"

"It's fine," I bit out.

Continuing up the stairs, I barreled into my bedroom, throwing open the door so hard, the knob slammed into the wall. Charging over to the windows, I pulled back the gossamer curtain and peered down into the backyard, the view from the second floor spanning the terrace, pool, pool house, and wooded area beyond. I locked my gaze on them in the pool.

"What the fuck?" I growled low.

He had her in a headlock, her hair in her face, and a huge fucking smile on his. She struggled and fought, trying to reach him behind her, and while I was trying to decide if I was angrier that he was touching my shit or if he was really hurting her or just playing with her, he let her go, pushed her forward, and splashed her, both of them laughing and answering my question.

I gripped the window frame, scowling down at them. They stood waist deep, his chest naked, tattoos blaring, and she in some halter bikini top. Over the next several minutes he worked with her on different holds and how to get out of them. His lips moved, talking her through what to do as he grabbed or yanked her or backed her into the edge of the pool.

I almost snorted. *Fucking Rika.*

This was her idea. I'd bet any piece of ass she sent Will over here to teach Winter some self-defense moves to fend me off. Nice move, kid, but this was chess, not checkers. Remember?

Winter shot out her hands, planting them on Will's chest, and I breathed hard and deep, my eyes burning with a glare.

She doesn't touch him.

And he doesn't touch her.

Releasing the curtain, I spun around and walked out of the bedroom and down the stairs.

I liked that Will was here. I wanted him here. I wanted him with me.

But he was not her fucking lifeline. Period.

I rounded the bannister and made my way to the back of the house and through the back door. Walking to the edge of the terrace, I stopped and looked down at them as they talked and played.

It made sense now why he took her into the pool. Without her sight, it helped her maintain balance and cushioned any falls during their training. *Thank you for that, Will.* I wanted her in perfect condition.

Sprinkles of rain hit my shoulders, and Winter fluttered her eyelashes as she turned her face to the sky and held out her hands, palms up. Drops hit the water, clouding the still surface, and the fire pit crackled near the pool house, an inviting glow under the darkening sky.

Will smoothed his wet hair over the top of his head and finally looked up, spotting me. He stood there, still and unwavering, his fucking juniper eyes always twisting a goddamn hole through my head like a screwdriver, and for a moment, it was high school, we were side by side, and Winter wasn't standing between us.

In that moment, I wanted to grab him and her and Banks and put us all on an island, because they would never not belong to me.

Lightning shot through the sky, thunder cracked, and Will and Winter exchanged words before she hopped out of the pool. He followed, helping her find her towel.

Once she was dried off, she wrapped the towel around her body, but when he tried to take her hand, she waved him off. He said a few more words to her, she nodded, and then turned around.

Putting out her right hand, she made her way back up to the house, toward me, and I locked eyes with Will.

The corner of his mouth tilted in a challenge, and I shook my head as Winter made her way in my direction. Walking right past me, she paused, turning her head my way, and I looked down at her, knowing she knew I was here, mere inches away.

My eyes fell down her face, neck, and shoulders, touching her the only way I'd allow myself just yet.

Stupid girl. He only taught you to fend off one attacker. What if there were more?

She dropped her head, her lips tightening, and she walked on, back into the house.

Soon.

Will dried off and walked over to the fire pit, holding out his hands to warm up. I descended the brick steps, making my way over to him.

"I got your letter," he said, staring at the fire.

I quirked a smile, remembering the note I sent him a while back. Challenging him to find me. To face who he really was, and it wasn't as Michael and Kai's third wheel. Fuck them.

"You think you can stop me?" I stared at him over the fire. Is that why he was here? Doing Rika's bidding and trying to arm Winter against me?

But his eyes danced with mischief even though he still wasn't looking at me. "You didn't think that beating I gave you was the end of it, did you?"

My smile froze, remembering the beating I let him give me last year, because I knew I deserved it. I'd knelt there, letting him hit me again and again, because I wanted to feel worse on the outside than I did on the inside, and for so many moments, I just wanted him to kill me. *Just kill me, because I can't take it back, and I can't move on.*

I'd almost killed him. And I wanted him to hate me so hard he would fucking murder me, and then maybe, after his anger was spent, he'd love me again. Whether I lived or died, he needed to forgive me for standing by and letting Michael's brother do what he did on that yacht that night.

But I wasn't the only one to blame for all that shit that went down two years ago after we got out of prison, either. I took my punishment for my part, but I wasn't taking it lying down again.

And if at least a small part of him wasn't willing to forgive me, he wouldn't be here now. He wanted to be here. He hadn't let it go, which meant he hadn't let me go. Not completely.

"You missed me," I said in a low voice.

He moved behind the flames, circling the fire slowly, and I did the same, following him.

"Didn't you?" I taunted.

His wet jeans clung to his legs, and I noticed he'd added some more ink to his chest and arms since I last saw him.

But some things hadn't changed. He was still dwelling on shit and still getting drunk and high all the time. He needed me.

A small chuckle escaped him as I caught his eyes again. "You were my heroin once upon a time," he said, and his eyes disappeared behind the flames again.

I stepped again, moving around the fire and locking eyes with him again. "And you still like your drugs from what I hear."

He shook his head, knowing full well where I got that information. "Fucking Rika."

"Fucking Rika." I nodded.

He moved again, disappearing, and I advanced, seeking him. His eyes on me when he dropped out of sight and still on me when he reappeared. His lips twitched and his gaze was charged with fury, rage, excitement, the blacks of his eyes small and sober, because he didn't need that shit when he had me.

"Winter likes you," I said, taking another slow step. "She seems to trust you. Why?"

"I have a way...with women," he teased.

"I remember." I licked my lips. "You were fun to watch."

173

His breathing turned shallow, and I knew he was remembering all the shit we got up to back in the day. We had some fun.

Even without girls.

"You want to see me with her?" he asked. "Is that it?"

I laughed under my breath and cocked my head. "Not exactly."

I shot off, catching him off guard, darted around the fire and slammed my palms into his chest, pushing him backward into the wall of the pool house. He grunted, hitting the brick with his bare back.

The rain started pummeling the awning overhead, and I raced up to him, ready to throw him down on the ground, but he bent over and barreled into my stomach, sending us both falling to the concrete deck.

I bared my teeth, seething and throwing my fist across the side of his head while he punched my stomach. I tightened every muscle in my gut against his attack, and I didn't know if I was really angry or just desperate to engage him in anything, because I'd fucking missed this, but either way, I was having fun.

I threw him over onto his back, and he kept rolling, trying to get away, but I caught him. I landed on his back, pressing him into the ground and driving my arm into the back of his neck to keep him in place.

"Oh, I remember this," I taunted in his ear, every inch of my chest pressed against his back and both us very aware of my groin on his ass. "This is what you really missed, isn't it?"

He jerked his head back, trying to head butt me. "Don't fucking talk about that," he growled. "I was drunk."

"All three times?" I teased, smiling. "Michael and Kai don't know how close we got, do they?"

I lowered my mouth to his ear, ready to revive his memory of how there were moments when I was the only one who would give him what he needed. When no one else was there for him, and we had everything money could buy but all we really wanted were things that didn't have a price.

When we were young and already drained and rotting from the inside out, and for a few nights here and there we just wanted to touch someone who got it. Who understood.

I could make him remember. I could push forward and not think and make him not think and just go and take and feel and...

Reaching around, I grabbed the front of his throat and buried my face in his fucking neck, but he thrashed, jerking his head back once again, breaking free from my hold, and slamming me in the bottom lip.

I squeezed my eyes shut as the corner of my mouth dug into my teeth, and I growled, distracted long enough for him to throw me off.

Heat coursed under my skin, and my heart picked up pace as I laughed and licked the cut, tasting the blood on my mouth.

You fucking little shit. Will was nice...until he wasn't. Winter shouldn't trust him too much.

I stood up as he rose to his feet, as well.

"You know," he started, a condescending little smirk on his face. "I was never turned on by Winter growing up. Too pale. Too pure."

He bent over, swiping my cigarettes off the ground and pulled one out. He tossed the pack back to me, and I caught it, glaring at him as he bent down to the fire, lighting the end.

"She was pretty, but I like my meat hot." He blew out a stream of smoke, his gaze locked on the flames as he drifted off in thought for a moment. "Sexy with chocolate-colored hair and olive skin. Fat lips and dark eyes taunting me behind some seductive, librarian glasses."

He trailed off, lost in the images in his mind, and I knew exactly who he was thinking of. But after a moment, he shook his head, coming back. "I never really knew why you were drawn to Winter. Michael and Kai thought she was just a one-night stand to you, but I knew better." He raised his eyes, meeting mine. "They didn't see the way you would look at her at school, during lunch and in passing in the hallways. And how no one—no one," he re-emphasized the words, "fucked with her behind her back after what you did to any guy who disrespected her, like making an obscene gesture right next to her that she couldn't see."

He circled the fire again, and I did the same, not taking my eyes off him for a moment.

"But about a year ago," he said, "I checked in on your girl. Watched her rehearse at the theater with a fellow dancer. Some guy."

My teeth slowly ground together.

"Though they weren't doing much rehearsing," he taunted, and I could see the images playing behind his eyes. "He had her pinned against a wall, her long hair spilling around her and her skin flushed with sweat and heat from dancing... His hands were all over her, and his tongue halfway down her little throat."

I held back the snarl that pulled at my lips, but I couldn't help the images that flooded my mind. Of a time when I had her in very much the same fucking position. Her naked breasts, her arms around my neck and hugging me to her, us in a tangle so tight you couldn't tell what was me and what was her...

Slut. I hoped he was telling the truth.

"She stopped it when he tried to undress her," Will told me. "But one thing I noticed for certain. That girl is ready to be used like a woman." A heated look crossed his eyes. "And she may not have liked it with you, but she just might love it with me."

I balled my fists.

"Yeah," he mused, his tone trying to get under my skin. "She's damn-well turning me on now. She felt really good in the pool, and I can just see her lily-white ass backing up into my cock, her hair bouncing against her back—"

I kicked the fire pit, and it went tumbling into the pool, extinguishing, and I lunged for him, but he made no move to get away. With one hand on the front of his neck and the other hand on his back, I whipped him around and threw him into the wall of the pool house.

"I almost killed you once," I gritted through my teeth and getting in his face. "I could do it again."

"Then do it," he fired back. "Do it, because I got nothin' to lose, D. Nothing."

He gasped out the last, desperation suddenly rippling off of him, and it was familiar, because I felt it, too. I stared at him, his eyes searching mine.

"I can't stop going down this road I'm on," he nearly whispered, his eyes watering. "My family is done with me. Michael has Rika. Kai has Banks. You were a lie." He faltered, dropping his gaze. "*She* was a lie."

She.

She was next. After I was done with Winter, I'd do it for him.

"I'm not afraid of you," he said, even though his voice was laced with defeat. "I'm not afraid of anything anymore. If you don't kill me, I'll keep pushing you until you have to. And I will fuck you over any way I can." He bared his teeth, growling. "In ways she's gonna love."

I slammed him into the wall again, but he still didn't fight me.

"You wanna watch?" he egged me on. "Come on. She won't even know you're in the room. You can see if she likes it with me. See if she responds to me better than she responded to you."

Stop it.

"See how hard I make her sweat and moan and how fast I can make her come on my dick," he sneered.

PENELOPE DOUGLAS

I glowered at him, my fingers digging into his neck. She wouldn't want him. And so help her God if she did.

"So do it then," he urged, finally shoving his palms into my chest and pushing me back. "Kill me before I can fuck her, because I won't stop."

He pushed me again, and I stumbled back, my fingers tightening into fists.

No. Stop, just stop.

"Because I have a passion for self-destruction, and you always knew it, and you always knew we would end badly." His voice cracked. "This won't end any other way."

Was he right? Did I think our friendship would survive our future?

Be with me. Just be with me. Not against me.

But he shoved at me again. "I'll take her from you."

"Don't," I choked out.

The walls were closing in. I couldn't breathe.

But he pushed me again, and I winced, my chest now aching. "And she'll take me away from you, and then you'll be all alone. Like you always should've been."

My stomach churned, and I seethed, and then he hit me, fire spreading across my cheek and sending my head jerking to one side.

"You're gonna deal with me!" he yelled and then hit me again, sending me stumbling. "Kill me. Fucking finish the job and kill me, because I'm fucked, and I hate you, and if you don't take me out, I'll take you out, because it's fucking over!"

He shoved me again and again, and I was losing it. I shot out my hands to stop him, "Don't. Stop."

A tear streamed down his face, but he wiped it away, growling. "Do it," he bit out. "Snap my neck, rip out my throat, or strangle me, you sick fuck! Just do it!"

He punched me across the jaw, pain shot through my head, and I clenched my fists so tight my nails dug into my palms.

"Will..." I breathed out, unable to catch my breath. "Don't."

"I'll never stop." He shook his head, coming in again. "Never."

He pushed me. "Kill me."

Stop.

His hands slammed into me again. "I'm going to take her away from you, so kill me."

You can't have her. I'll...

"Kill me, so I'm out of your way!" he bellowed. "If you did it right last time I'd be at the bottom of the fucking ocean, so finish the job, and then you can have her!"

An image of him sinking below the deep, black surface of the sea crawled into my head, and I squeezed my eyes shut, trying to get rid of it.

He would've been gone forever.

"Fucking kill me," he said, his voice even and suddenly calm.

"No."

"Kill me. You're going to have to."

I shook my head.

He grabbed me by the collar, screaming, "Do it!"

And I grabbed his neck in my hands, ramming him into the wall of the pool house. "I can't!"

He grunted, breathing hard, and I dropped my forehead to his, unable to swallow the fucking needles in my throat.

"Fuck, I can't," I whispered. "Please, stop. Please."

"I can't," he mouthed, and tears streamed down his face. "I can't."

I moved my hands to his face, just holding him, and ready to say so much, because I never had to hide anything from him. He never saw weakness when he looked at me. I wanted to tell him things.

I wanted to tell him that I never would've hurt him. That I didn't know what Trevor was doing, and it wasn't supposed to go down like that, because out of all three of my friends, Will was the one I would always save first. That my pride and anger wouldn't let me retreat, and that if he had been pulled to the ocean's bottom, out of my reach, I would've followed him.

I would've fucking followed him and rotted down there, close to wherever he was, because nothing I would've acquired after that—my inheritance or my vengeance on Winter—would've been worthwhile without him.

His breath fell on my mouth, and his wet hair behind his head grew warm under my fingers. *He needed me.* I dug my fingers into his scalp. *He had to realize he needed me.* No one was going to hold him up like I would.

No one.

I dove in, catching his bottom lip between my teeth and pushing us both through the pool house door.

He stumbled back, snarling and ready to fight me, but I rushed in, sinking my mouth into his and pushing him down onto the couch. I covered his lips with mine, gripping his throat with one hand and holding myself up with the other.

"Fuck you," he sneered, pulling his mouth away.

I grinned and flicked his lip with my tongue. "Only if you want to."

Releasing his neck, I yanked his jeans open and slid my hand down inside as he grabbed at my hand, trying to stop me, but I gripped his fucking cock, feeling it was already a little stiff.

"What is she wearing?" I started, stroking him, not giving him time to think. "What is she fucking wearing for you, huh?"

He stopped breathing, closed his eyes, and tipped his head back, letting out a groan. "Damon, stop."

I hovered my mouth over his, stroking him a little faster as I nudged my knee between his legs, parting them. "What is she wearing?"

He grew full and hard, and I traced my tongue along his bottom lip. "She wants you in her mouth." I tightened my grip on his cock. "She wants this in her mouth."

"Yeah."

And I had him.

"What the fuck is she wearing?" I stroked him again and again, his skin smooth and hot in my hand.

"She sleeps..." He paused, gasping at what I was doing to him.

"Yes?"

His body shook. "She sleeps in these...in these sweet, little panties," he said, his eyes still closed and imagining the object of his obsession. "There's the smallest triangle of fabric in the front, just covering her."

"Red?" I bit his lip again.

But he shook his head. "Blue. And a T-shirt. She sleeps on her stomach, and her hips move in her sleep. God, her ass..."

"Mmmm..." I felt a little cum drip out of him. "She's grinding that cunt into the bed, huh? Her pussy must be nice and warm."

"Fuck, it's hot." He grabbed the back of my neck, our mouths centimeters away from each other. "Harder."

"And wet?" I teased him, jerking him faster and harder how he wanted. "Is it wet?"

He nodded, his breathing growing heavier.

"And tight?"

"Yeah."

"Lick her, Will," I told him, giving him what that bitch never did. "She loves you in the dark. She lets Will Grayson III, star of the basketball team, come over to her house, climb into her room at night, and come inside her whenever he wants."

His abs contracted, he got lost in the images in his head, bared his teeth, dug his fingers into the back of my neck, and then...released, spilling into my hand and down his long cock.

He moaned, sweat glistening across his neck and chest, and he kept his eyes closed, because he knew once he opened them the spell would be broken. It wasn't her on top of him. It was me.

After a moment, his breathing had calmed, and he opened his eyes slowly. His shoulders were relaxed, and he was done fighting.

I climbed off him and stood up, yanking a pool towel out of the wardrobe. I finished with it and tossed it down to him.

"That's all you can do, isn't it?" he said, cleaning and zipping up. "You can only fuck people or fuck with them. That's the only way you can connect."

He threw the towel down, calmer than before but still... still not with me.

"Thinking back now," he mused solemnly, "I wonder if anything I got from you was real."

I didn't know if he was right, and I didn't care. I maneuvered, he maneuvered, and I moved again, always with my win in sight. I did what I had to.

The trouble was, I didn't want to annihilate Will, and if I won whatever game we were playing, would I destroy him in the process? Was what he said true? Was it impossible for us to end any other way?

"If you hurt Winter, you'll deal with me," he said.

I righted my clothes, swiping the rain off my lapels. But I didn't respond. He knew I wouldn't heed his warning. I let him dole it out anyway.

"And Michael," he added. "And Kai."

"And Rika and Banks?" I threw in.

"And Alex." He shot me a sinister little grin, meeting my challenge. "Our army is bigger. You have no one."

"All I need is me. One person willing to do what none of you will." I paused and added, "You don't have the stomach for this, Will. Don't doubt that I will do whatever I have to to keep what's mine. That little girl belongs to me."

He hesitated, looking me up and down and then meeting my eyes with resolution. "She doesn't want to belong to you, Damon."

I planted my hand on the gray-tiled wall, letting the hot, rainfall shower water cascade down my neck and back.

She doesn't want to belong to you.

She doesn't want to belong to you.

Oh, I knew. And I was going to take great pleasure in delivering lots of what she didn't want.

But every muscle in my body tightened and knotted anyway, unable to let go.

She doesn't want to belong to you.

I closed my eyes, hearing the words echo in my ears.

"You belong to me," my mother says. "You belong to me, and I belong to you."

She lays beside me, slipping an arm underneath my head, looking down at me as she holds me close. "We'll always be each other's, Damon. Mommy will be yours no matter what. For the rest of your life. I'm yours, baby."

I nod, but absently, I close my fists, the sheets of her bed bunching in my hands. I sleep with my mom a lot. She likes to keep me close, but I don't tell anyone. I've been to other peoples' houses—other kids my age—and I know this isn't how they do things in their homes.

My mother's silk nightgown caresses my chest, and her black hair tickles my arm. She gazes down at me with a small smile.

"I don't belong to your father," she says. "Not the way I belong to you. I was only thirteen when he first saw me. Did he ever tell you that? I was only a couple of years older than you are now."

She dives in and tickles my neck, and I let out a little laugh before turning my head and pushing her hand away.

"He came to see my ballet troupe perform," she goes on. "He came a lot, and I would see him watching me from the audience. All the other girls were so jealous, because I

got flowers and presents, and I never did before. He called me his little princess, and I would dream he was going to take me home and make me his little girl and take care of me, so I didn't have to live in that cold theater anymore with so little to eat."

She looks off for a moment, her smile falling. I know my mother was young when she married my father. I hear people whisper when they find out she has an eleven-year-old son.

"And then one night," she continues, "a big, black car came to get me. I was told to dress in my prettiest costume, they did my hair and makeup, and I left the theater. I was taken to his house, outside of Moscow, and he asked me to dance for him." Her face lights up again, and she dives in, whispering as if it's some secret. "And I did. I twirled and leaped and danced under the chandeliers on the marble floors of the hall, feeling like I was in a dream. He let me eat cake and drink champagne."

One finger of her hand trails down the center of my torso, and then all of her fingers fan out across my stomach, making the little hairs on my body stand up. That feels good.

"And when I fell asleep," she says, watching her hand caress me, "I couldn't remember how I'd gotten to the bed. To his bed." She stares off, lost in the memory. "I'm not sure when I woke up. Maybe I'd only been asleep for a moment, but when I opened my eyes, he was pulling my costume down... baring my little body...and ripping off my tights and slippers."

I freeze, listening to her and surprised but not surprised, either. I haven't heard this before.

But my father does awful things.

"I started to cry," she tells me, "scared and screaming when he kissed me all over and bit my body so hard, and when he pulled down my panties and shoved himself inside me, I..." She breathes hard, still locked on the images in her head. "I liked it, Damon. I liked it."

I know what she's talking about. What he was doing to her. I've seen it before.

But she was thirteen. Her ballet studio in town had girls who were thirteen. I can't imagine any of them...

"I liked being ravaged by him," she continues. "I was a big girl now and he was so much rougher than the men I'd seen taking some of the other dancers when I would peek in the rooms of the theater. This is what men do. They ravage. They're strong and they ravage, Damon."

She looks down at me, and that's when I snap out of it and realize her fingertips are trailing down the front of my sleep pants.

"And it's time you start practicing," she says.

She reaches inside my pants and takes me in her hand, rubbing it.

I shake my head, squirming as I try to inch away from her.

"Shhh, it's okay," she croons, kissing the corner of my mouth and moving her hand faster on me. "Do you feel that, baby? It's getting hard. That means you like it. You like what Mommy's doing."

No, I don't. She's not supposed to do that. She's not...

I still, closing my eyes as it pumps with blood and sticks up straight.

No, no, no, no.... I don't want this. I want to leave. I want to leave.

"Enjoy it, baby. Just enjoy it." She leaves little kisses all over my mouth and face as she strokes. "You're a strong man and strong men get as many women as they want to make them feel good."

I don't want.... I don't want...

I squeeze my eyes shut and let out a groan. No, no, no...

I grabbed the soap from the dish and lathered it up, washing my chest and stomach again before soaping up my cock and getting it clean. Cleaner.

That was the first fucking time my mother ever touched me like that. The first episode of what turned into years of her on me.

My throat swelled with the vomit rising, and my shoulders slumped as I tried to turn inward, making myself as small as possible. It was an old feeling, but one I knew well. It made me hide in the fountain. In the maze. In showers and in closets, because if no one saw me, they wouldn't see the shame.

She's gone, I told myself. *She'll never take from me again. No one does.*

But looking back over the years, I realized now it started long before that night. She took me into the shower with her long after I was able to take them on my own. She washed me and dried me and stayed in the room when I dressed and undressed.

And after months of doing everything she could with her hands and mouth, she finally came to my room one night and...

I used to brag I had my first woman at twelve, reveling in how other guys either thought I was lying or I was so lucky, because of all the whores my father kept around the house. But I always told the truth.

My father had to know what was going on. In his head, though, it made me a man.

And it wasn't like he was against raping children, either. Considering how young my mother had been when they met.

I rinsed and shut off the water, grabbing a towel and drying off. I wrapped it around my waist and stepped out of the shower, walking to the mirror and wiping the condensation off.

I stared at my dark eyes, a little darker than hers, and the same black hair. A shadow lay on my jaw, and I picked up my straight razor, running it under the faucet to make sure it was clean.

What did Winter feel when she thought about me? Was the anger so thick that was all there was?

He asked her to dance for him.

He asked her to dance like I'd asked Winter to dance for me.

He watched my mother as I watched Winter.

Was that it then? Did I do to Winter in high school what my father did to my mother? Did I groom her?

I looked up, meeting my own black eyes in the mirror.

The secret of life that everyone knew and everyone forgot was that we weren't alone. We thought we were unique. We thought we were the first.

No one has been through what I've been through.

No one else is feeling this.

No one knows what it's like to be me.

This is the first time anyone has endured what I've endured, right?

They're lies we tell ourselves, because we think we're special. Because it would lessen the entitlement to suffer to know what we're going through is not uncommon. It was a secret I never forgot and was able to use to keep things in perspective, so I could get through the shit in my head, but now...

Now I wished I could forget it. I wanted to be alone.

I didn't want to know that I was like him or he was like me or that life followed patterns and history repeated itself. I wasn't him, and Winter wasn't my mother, and no one has been where we were.

This is special.

It's different.

It's unique and all mine.

She and I...we're alone in the universe. No one was us.

And unlike my mother at thirteen, Winter fucking deserved everything that would happen to her.

I shaved and finished in front of the sink, knowing any doubts I had wouldn't make me feel any better than being right where I was.

So I would stay the course. My mother was right about one thing. I liked everything when it was hard.

Walking into the bedroom, I spotted Arion right away, sitting on the bed with another girl, but I didn't slow as I walked to the table with the bowl and dug out my watch.

"Did you bring me something, Arion?" I fastened the watch to my wrist, not looking at either one of them.

She wasn't supposed to be in here, and she fucking knew it. The master bedroom was split into two rooms, conjoined by a walk-in closet in the middle. She had her space, I had mine. Maybe I'd invite her in one of these nights, but that was my call.

"A present," she answered. "Just a little one."

I spared a glance to the bed again, seeing her sitting behind the young, black woman, her arm draped over the girl's shoulder and both of them looking at me like they were here for my feeding. I couldn't see what Arion was wearing, but a strap of silk fell down her arm, while her other hand reached around, caressing the girl's bare stomach.

"How old is she?" I picked up my cigarettes and shook one out.

"However old you want me to be," I heard the girl answer for Arion.

I lit the cigarette and pinched the bridge of my nose, blowing out smoke. *Jesus, fuck.* Will would run into that bed, already hard and ready to fuck.

I didn't like being fed. I needed to hunt.

"Her pussy's dripping," Arion cooed. "Young, tight, and hot. So hot."

My cock started to throb a little, diving into my head and envisioning the feel of her.

"Really tight," the girl taunted. "My foster daddy used to say I'm tighter than his hand when he would do me."

Smoke poured out of my mouth as I laughed under my breath. *Jesus, honey, you're barking up a tall tree with that shit. Whatever little taboo story Arion fed you to get me hard is clearly too tame. My version of naughty is off most peoples' grid.*

"Fuck her bare," Arion said. "Look how wide she spreads."

Despite the games they played, I couldn't help but look over. The young woman sat at the edge of the bed, her wide open pussy bare, and her tits peeking out of the bottom of a little half-shirt.

Scenarios popped in my head, instinctively searching for what I needed to make this work.

A threesome. Girl on girl. Tying them up. A gag.

Yeah. A gag.

I took another drag, not taking my eyes off them as the pictures played in my head.

"Fuck her bare," Arion said again. "Fuck her as hard as you want, and make me watch. When it's time to come, come inside me."

And there it was. What she really wanted from me.

CHAPTER 10

Winter

PRESENT

"Where are you taking me tonight?" I asked, leading Isabella and Jade up to my room, so I could finish getting ready.

"It's a surprise."

"I'm blind," I shot back, heading to my closet and running my fingertips over the braille on the markers to find the black shirts. "Broken glass on a floor can be a surprise for me. I'm not game unless you get specific."

"It's Halloween-y," Jade offered.

But Isa hurried to shut her up. "Shhh…"

Great. It was almost Halloween—and worse, Devil's Night—but my house already felt like a Fear Fest. I wasn't in the mood.

And I wasn't sure I'd be allowed to leave.

"You need a girls' night," Jade chimed in again. "Especially with that freak show sleeping right down the hall. Let's have some fun."

I forced a small laugh, Damon immediately coming to mind, but I knew she meant my sister. All the dancers at the studio I grew up with—including Isabella and Jade—had plenty of Ari's antics over the years as she waited on me at lessons or sat through recitals and performances.

I sifted through my black clothing, not finding the black, leather pants with zippers down the legs. Where were they? I hadn't worn them since last winter.

A phone rang, and someone moved on my bed. "I have to take this," Jade said. "I'll be in the bathroom."

I continued searching for my pants, diving into the white, blue, and every other section of clothing.

"So, how are you?" Isabella asked.

I almost turned around, but I was afraid my face would give me away. "I don't know."

Damon was here. I caught a whiff of his cigarettes outside when I was working out with Will, but I hadn't heard anyone leave, so he was probably still in the house.

Did he give Will a hard time when he saw him here?

I smiled a little, thinking of Will. I couldn't believe he'd shown up. I remembered hearing a lot about him in high school, and I knew he was Damon's best friend.

Was.

But all of a sudden, he was at the door, and I didn't have to say much for him to understand what was going on here. I got the impression the rest of Damon's old crew was behind Will's visit, too, and before I knew it, he had me in the pool, working on moves. Like it would do any good, but I'd try. Plus, he made me laugh.

I should've used the opportunity to ask so many things. Anything to get the upper hand with Damon and learn something useful. Especially when I found out Erika Fane was now engaged to Michael Crist, another one of Damon's old friends.

"You know, you can come stay with me, right?" Isa said.

I turned my head, offering her a half-smile. I couldn't come and stay with her, but it was comforting that she offered. She had no idea what he could do. As much as I wanted to take her up on the offer, I wouldn't.

I let out a sigh, not finding my leather slacks anywhere. *Dammit, Arion.*

"Come with me for a sec," I told Isa.

Running my hand over Mikhail's head on the way, I left the room, still hearing Jade in the bathroom and chatting on the phone as we passed. I followed the wall, down the long hallway, past my father's bedroom door and down to my mother's. Or what used to be my mother's.

I entered Arion's new bedroom—not hearing any shrieks as I barged into her space, so she must not be in here—and veered right, into the dressing room my mother and father used to share.

"Search for black, leather skinny pants," I told Isa and got to work going around the room, touching fabrics on their hangers for the familiar feel of my favorite thing in the world to wear.

"Where's the light?" Isabella asked.

But before I could answer, voices carried in from the other room.

"Did you bring me something, Arion?" Damon said, and I stilled.

"Shh," I whispered Isa.

"A present," I heard my sister say. "A little one."

I felt my way over to the door on the other side of the closet leading to my father's old room. I hovered behind it as it hung open a little, Isabella damn-near knocking me over as she hid in back of me.

"How old is she?" he asked.

"However old you want me to be."

That wasn't my sister's voice.

"Oh, my God, is that him?" Isa asked in a hushed tone. "They don't sleep in the same room?"

I waved my hand at her to shut up. I didn't want to be found here.

"Her pussy's dripping," Arion taunted, all sensual and gross. "Young, tight, and hot."

"Really tight," the girl added. "My foster daddy used to say I'm tighter than his hand when he would do me."

I winced. Oh, my God.

Isa moved around me to where the door was cracked, and I guess she was peeking through.

"Don't let them see you," I mouthed, barely a whisper.

"Fuck her bare," my sister went on. "Look how wide she spreads."

I held my breath, waiting for his answer and dreading it, but I didn't know why. My sister had another woman in there. She was trying to get him into bed with them. Was he going to do it?

"He has a tattoo?" Isabella asked me. "I didn't know that. It's under his arm. Can't make it out, though."

A tattoo? *I don't know. I don't care...*

"Fuck her bare," Arion urged him. "Fuck her as hard as you want, and make me watch. When it's time to come, come inside me."

I instantly took a step back. "I don't want to hear any more."

It was disgusting. I didn't...want to hear that crap. Their sordid behavior. This only confirmed what I already knew. He was twisted and mean and used people for his enjoyment, like he would use my sister and that girl. He never cared about me all those years ago.

I started to leave, but Isa stopped me. "Wait," she said. "Why is Arion doing this? I've heard about swingers, but this is..."

"We want you," Arion said, interrupting our conversation.

"I know you do," Damon replied. "But you have no clue what I want. Or what I like."

"I know you like to watch." My sister's voice stayed playful. "Wanna watch us?"

I remained still, trying to hear his answer.

"He hasn't slept with her yet," Isabella whispered to me. "Who?"

"Your sister," she clarified. "She's trying to entice *him*. She's trying to get him into bed."

"Obviously."

"He doesn't want her," Isabella told me. "My sister told me about him. They were in school together, too. Damon had a really bad reputation. And I mean, bad. People were genuinely afraid of him."

"I don't care," I fired back, keeping my voice low. "I don't want to hear about his sex life."

"Girls hated him," she went on as if I'd said nothing. "Man, they hated him with a passion."

"Didn't stop them from going after him, like it was going to be some big surprise when he screwed them and then ditched them," I pointed out.

I mean, honestly, in all fairness, I wasn't sure why he was hated more than the other horseman. They did the same thing. They all slept around.

"That's not what he did, though," Isabella explained. "Didn't anyone tell you how he was? I mean, with other girls. Not you."

The reminder that she knew—that everyone knew and saw the video of Damon and me and how he was with me—sobered me for a moment, making me forget what was happening in the other room.

"I think that's part of the reason you had to leave school after that video," she pointed out. "They hated you."

"Who?"

"All the girls he wouldn't sleep with," she replied. "Rumor has it, Damon's appetite is not always fun to satisfy."

All the girls he wouldn't sleep with. So he didn't sleep around? Sure.

And then I remembered what my sister just said a moment ago, and how I met him when I was a teenager, and I paused.

"He likes to watch," I said, finally understanding.

"No," Isa corrected me. "He likes to fuck with heads and then watch."

Seemed about right.

"Sex doesn't turn him on," my friend continued. "Deviance is what he likes. Stories abounded, so I don't know what's true, but there were rumors that he got Abigail Clijsters' sister to screw her older sister's boyfriend. Another story about a gang of guy students at a young teacher's house one night. Will Grayson and some hotel maid. A couple of football players getting drunk and going at it in a car in the woods…"

She trailed off, and I didn't know for sure if anything she said was true, but…a small part of me wanted to believe it was. Maybe it made me less his victim to know he was the fucked-up one and not me for falling for his lie.

"He would take girls out," she went on, "let them think he was interested, and he was, but his pleasure was harder earned, let's just say. After he got them to do whatever he wanted them to do, sometimes he'd get off on them and sometimes he wouldn't."

"And if he didn't, they felt like even bigger shit afterwards," I added.

"Used," she agreed. "They degraded themselves for him and got nothing in return. He coerced but never forced. He kept you to himself, though. I wonder why."

The voices in the next room were barely audible as I thought about her question. She was one of the few people who saw that video and didn't see me asking for it. She knew he committed a crime. The other girls resented me after his arrest, because in their eyes, I got what they wanted.

Well, they could have him. I—

"Huh?" I heard my sister blurt out, sounding suddenly upset.

Her soft, sexy voice had changed. What happened?

"Get out," Damon said.

"What is your problem?" I heard her demand, but I wasn't staying to get caught here if he was kicking them out.

I pushed at Isa, backing away and signaling we needed to leave.

"Out," Damon shouted as we left the closet, and we dashed into the hallway as I heard the closet door swing open and my sister come flying through.

"Told you," Isa shot in my ear as we dove into my bedroom.

Strange appetite, indeed.

Whatever. I was just glad whatever my sister was trying to make happen failed miserably. I blamed her as much as him for our current situation, and I hoped she was unhappy with her new husband.

Her husband.

I shook my head clear, feeling something hit my body. I reached up and caught it.

"I got your pants," Isabella said. "Get dressed, and let's go."

Go where?

Although I no longer cared as long as it was out of this house.

I had no idea what she and Jade had planned for tonight as long as I didn't think about him.

Or her.

• • •

"Do you want me to read it to you?" Jade asked.

"Just paraphrase."

She put a pen in my hand and led me to the wooden makeshift counter, placing the tip on the line where I was supposed to sign.

"It's a disclaimer," she explained, "talking about how the haunted house is a 4D experience, and the actors will engage with you and touch you. They're not responsible or liable for any health problems. If you feel like anything is too much or you want it to stop, simply yell "quarter" and they will stop and offer assistance if you want to leave."

My hand started to shake as I pressed the pen to the paper and signed my name. I laughed at myself. You would think I'd be used to being scared by now, but the idea of mad doctors, ax murderers, and chainsaws was even freakier when you couldn't see them.

Quarter. Like as in 'forgiveness' or 'safe haven'? Well, at least they had a safe word.

"Stay close," Isa told me as we headed toward the entrance. "Hang onto my belt loop or arm, and let me know if you want to leave, okay?"

"Oh, you'll run before I do," I joked.

"Probably right," Jade chuckled.

I heard Isabella's tsk but didn't give her any more crap. The sun had set a couple hours ago, and I wished I'd brought a coat as we shuffled through the fallen leaves toward the warehouse and conglomeration of various-sized sheds that made up the haunted house.

The chill in the air seeped through my oversized black sweater, my exposed shoulder already feeling like I had an ice cube sitting in that one spot, but my legs were nice and toasty in the leather pants. Thank goodness I wore my Vans, since I was sure I'd be stumbling and scurrying a lot tonight.

"Welcome to Coldfield," a dark, deep voice suddenly said right next to me and I jumped a little.

Shit. I chuckled and took a step away, hearing my friends' laughter, as well.

"Nice blood," Jade commented, and I guessed he must be one of the actors sent to greet everyone in line. *Blood, huh?* I imagined prop blood on his face and clothes. Maybe a hacksaw in his hand with a really dull blade, if any, of course, to keep it safe.

Something brushed my arm, and then I heard his voice right next to me again. Did he move in closer when I moved away?

"Did you girls sign the waiver?" he asked.

"Yes," Isa answered, followed by a little giggle.

"Do you know the safe word?" he pressed.

"Yes," she said again.

"Good." I could damn-near feel his breath on me, and I almost forgot to breathe. "Don't use it. I don't like to stop my fun."

They laughed again, comfortable in their knowledge that they were indeed safe, but all I could do was stand there, déjà vu weighing me down like an anchor. The fear factor, the taunting, his threatening promises... So much for getting away from the house, everyone in it, and clearing my head tonight. This guy was Damon. Or like the point-five version.

And then I felt it.

His breath was on my cheek as he spoke. "I'll see you inside," he whispered.

My body went cold and my chest caved. God, he was like him. The tone. The taunt.

"He likes you," Jade teased. "Watch your back inside, Winter."

I barely breathed.

My kind of fun has a price. Better enjoy myself while I can.

My blood pumped hot, and all of a sudden, I wasn't cold anymore.

I knew this guy wasn't him. He didn't sound like him or smell like him or feel like him, but I lost all semblance of thought or reason as the line moved, Isa moved, and took me with her. Maybe I should be afraid of walking in here and remembering the terror Damon caused, but I went anyway, unable to resist wanting to test myself. To feel whatever was inside again. Even if just to see if I would handle myself any differently.

The air turned thick and musty as we stepped over the threshold and drafts hit me, like there was fake fog. My friends immediately started laughing and making surprised sounds, but since I couldn't see what they were seeing, I had to rely on everything else to get a picture of the atmosphere in my head.

I absorbed the scent of water on rocks, like a cave, and the echoes of muffled screams, howls, and cries in the distance. Some of it was sound effects, but others clearly weren't.

And somewhere, far off, the merry, child-like tune of a carousel pierced the windy night.

Something touched the top of my head, and I ducked, my heart leaping in my chest as I laughed. They had people in the rafters.

Coldfield was a Halloween attraction that popped up a couple of years ago, and no one knew who owned it, but everyone seemed to love it. Overnight—every September thirtieth—the old warehouse on the outskirts of town was finally put to use and transformed, now attached to an array of sheds, nooks, and outbuildings. Some people missed the parties they had out here on Devil's Night, but most loved the new haunted theme park, especially with The Cove—the old amusement park up the coast a few miles—now shut down and abandoned.

"Pray fooooor the dead, and the dead will pray for youuuuuuu," a creepy-ass voice said, and I felt a plastic bag blow into my body with a breeze. "They will pray for you and they will prey on you."

A cackling laugh followed, and I pushed the huge plastic sheet away from me, but as my hand dipped into the plastic, it hit something solid, and then...a male growl followed, the plastic was all over us, and arms and legs attacked through the sheet.

"Ah! Ah!" the girls screamed, scrambling away as I tightened my grip on Isa's arm.

My stomach flipped, and I breathed out a small laugh.

I inched toward the far wall to get away from the huge guy behind the tarp and felt a hand poking out of the wall. I jumped back, but it grabbed for me, and we all were laughing as a dozen or more hands reached for us out of both sides of the hallway now.

We moved from room to room, some of it—like the evil operating room—going over my head, because there weren't many sounds or screams or anything to give away what was actually going on, but I liked the juggernaut and his sledgehammer, pounding the floor ahead of us and chasing us into one room after another. My heart beat so hard, but it was thrilling to be chased, because I knew I was safe. I wasn't as scared as the other two when people came out of the portraits, because obviously, I couldn't see them following us with their eyes.

The spiral staircase almost made me pee my pants, though, single file and being chased up the tiny and steep incline by Jason Vorhees. You didn't want to be taking up the rear in a situation like that, and of course, I always did, because I had to follow instead of lead.

It was fun, though. And I was too distracted to be worried about the shitstorm at my house.

"Oh, shit!" Isabella shouted.

"What?" Jade asked.

"There! When the light flashes again, look."

I gripped Isa with both hands, huddling behind her and waiting for whatever was coming.

"Oh, shit!" Jade yelled.

What? What was going on?

They laughed. "He's getting closer every time the light flashes!" Jade squealed.

And then I heard it.

The fucking chainsaw.

I groaned, my knees shaking. I hated Leatherface.

Laughter and shrieks, and then we all stumbled as several chainsaws raced in, chomping at our legs with their harmless, chainless saws. I hopped from one leg to the next, trying to keep hold of Isabella as we all struggled to tear away from our attackers. She grappled for my hand, but all of a sudden, the wall behind me gave way, I fell through, losing my grip on her arm, and freefell backward onto the hard cement before I heard a door close, and all the screams and chainsaws faded away.

I was suddenly in silence.

I pushed off the cold floor, held out my hands, and walked back in the direction from where I fell. What the hell?

At least, I thought it was the direction. I might've gotten spun around as I fell into the room.

"Isabella!" I called out, my hands landing on a wooden wall. I patted around for a door knob or hinges—anything to tell me where I was at or how to get out.

"Jade!" I bellowed.

But everything sounded distant. The cries and yelps. The music beyond the walls and down other hallways.

"Hello?" I said. "How...how do I get out?"

I only fell a few feet. Where the hell was I? My friends were right on the other side of one of these walls.

"Hello!" I shouted. "Help!"

Was I alone in here? I trailed down the walls, feeling for a way out. *God, I hope so.* I wanted my friends, but I didn't want anyone else. I was having a blast a minute ago, but now... This changed things. How would I get away? Or find my frickin' way out?

A clink pierced the silence behind me, and I froze.

"Hello?"

Was I alone? That sounded like a chain.

I shuffled down the wall, searching for the door—if it even was a real door and not a trap door—and a chill crawled up my shoulder. I pulled up my sweater to cover the bare skin, but it just fell down again.

I sucked in a deep breath, belting out, "Isa! Jade!"

But then, behind me, a chain clanked with another like there was wind, but I didn't feel a draft.

I whipped around, shooting out my hands.

"Hello?" I demanded. "Who's there?"

Are you going to hurt me?

I don't know.

Do you want to?

Kind of.

A silvery sting throbbed between my legs, and I clenched my thighs to get control of myself. *Fuck.*

Safe word. What was the safe word?

Quarter. I let out a breath, relieved I'd remembered it. *Thank God.*

I took a few steps into the room. Maybe there was a hallway, and it connected to another part of the haunted house. There was a whole line of people outside. Isabella, Jade, and I weren't the only customers in here.

But then I brushed cool metal, and I jerked back on reflex, hearing the chain chime as it hit another one. Hesitantly, I waved my hands in front of me again, sending several chains swinging. They were hanging from the ceiling?

I let out a little laugh. Maybe it was just a draft, after all.

But then I heard chains clink again, and my smile fell. It was a lot of them, and not a little tinkling that comes with a breeze. It was ...purposeful.

I opened my mouth, but my voice was barely working. "Hello?"

Boo, I heard Damon that night in my head. I'd known someone was there.

And I knew I wasn't alone now. There was someone in here.

"Qu...w..." Bile burned my throat, and my mind raced. *It's not real. It's just a game.*

Except the last time this happened, I said the same thing and I'd been wrong.

I pawed the air in front of me, brushing chains but stilling them to keep from making noise, so I could hear the room.

But it was complete silence.

My pulse thundered in my ears, and sweat cooled my neck as my breath blew a strand of hair hanging in my face that I was too afraid to budge an inch to move.

I could hear him breathing.

I knew he was there.

I closed my eyes, opened my mouth, but instead of uttering the safe word, I drew in a breath, feeling his eyes on me. Every inch of my skin became sensitive and aware of my clothes suddenly chafing my skin. My lacy bra and sweater irritated the points of my breasts, and the skin of my thighs stuck to the leather pants, my belly quaking and heat settling between my legs, making me throb.

My heart filled my throat, and I was so scared, but I...I wanted to yank my sweater down and be rid of it. It was hot, and it was like every hair on my body vibrated. What the hell?

All of a sudden, a gang of chains shook and swooped, there was a loud, deep growl, and someone started charging. I opened my mouth to cry out, but he clenched my neck in his fist and shoved me into the wall, jabbing something into my stomach several times. It didn't hurt, though. It was probably one of those prop knives that retracted, but the fear of the moment still overtook me, and I screamed as I was thrown down on the ground, landing on something soft.

I didn't have time to guess what it was before he was on top of me, forcing my arms over my head with one hand. I gasped and opened my mouth to cry out again, but then he shot his knife up to my neck, pressing on the skin as he breathed down on me, and I stopped, aware of the skin of my nipples, burning under the itchy fabric of my sweater and his weight on me. He felt like fire on my skin.

"I'm hungry," he whispered down on me.

I smelled a wood fire on him, and cinnamon wafted off his breath. I smelled cigarettes, too, but they weren't like Damon's.

Music pounded somewhere, shaking the foundation, and I guessed I was lying on a mattress, another creepy prop that I was glad I couldn't see.

"Give me your tongue," he growled softly. "I want to eat it."

I shook my head slowly. Was I taunting him?

Why wasn't I screaming?

The prop knife left my neck and dug into my side, retracting on impact. I sucked in a breath, the blood there throbbing instantly, but I was safe. I knew I was safe.

And somewhere, deep inside my head where I felt the burn of shame, but no one else could see or read me, I'd missed this. I'd missed my mind racing, my heart trying to jump out of my chest, and someone not handling me like I was a glass ball. Where, in the inch of space between him and me, I reveled in the dirt on my skin and the terror of his words.

Why wasn't I using the safe word?

The actor's weight eased off mine as he pulled up a little. "Are you okay?"

His voice was soft now. Normal.

"Yes," replied.

"You know the safe word, right?"

I nodded. "Yeah."

"You don't want to use it?"

I swallowed and shifted my leg, pulling it out from under him, but then I realized now he was between my legs. He settled in, slowly lowering his body on top of me again.

"Last chance," he whispered the same low growl as before.

I breathed hard, the heat pooling between us, and I tipped my head back, taking his wrist and putting the knife on my neck again.

"Keep it there," I told him.

God, I didn't care. I liked the illusion. I liked that feeling again, and I didn't fucking care—here and in the dark where this dude would never see me again, because I would never come back here—that I needed this. *He* did this to me. I hated it and hated him, but I wanted to see. Needed to see. See if I liked it or to prove to myself that he, and what he did to me, didn't mean anything and that I didn't want it.

"Or maybe I'm hungry for something else, Little Girl," he threatened.

Pressing the knife into my throat, he thrusted between my legs, and we both sucked in a breath as our bodies moved in unison. My eyes rolled back, his cock already hard through his jeans as it rolled over my clit. I could feel the wet heat in my panties, and I closed my eyes, diving into the black.

He humped me over and over again, sucking air between his teeth and getting rougher as his narrow hips rolled again and again. He dug the knife's blade under my chin, and my orgasm crested, starting to roll through me.

"Holy shit," he said, breaking character. "God, this is fucking awesome."

And I lost it. The orgasm drifted away, hanging on by a tether until it snapped and disappeared.

Tears sprang to my eyes, and I cracked.

Jesus Christ.

Pushing him away, I stopped him and crawled out from under him.

What the hell was I doing?

Music poured into the room with screams and laughter, and I knew others had fallen through the trap door, too. I followed their voices, scurrying past them and out the door.

"Wait, come back!" the guy yelled after me. "I didn't mean anything. Are you okay?"

No. I wasn't okay. I'd lost my fucking mind.

"Winter!" I heard Jade call. "Oh, my God. Thank God. We've been looking for you everywhere. You freaked us out. Are you okay?"

"Let's just get out of here."

The lost orgasm still lingered, keeping me hot and my head buzzing. I still needed the release.

They led me back to the entrance, and I sucked in lungfuls of air as we stepped outside into the welcome chill.

"Whew," Isa giggled. "We have to come back. That was fun."

I chewed my lip, not wanting to think about it. I wasn't about to tell them what just happened, even though I knew they'd eat it up.

I didn't hate that I enjoyed it. I hated that it reminded me of him, and that was why I enjoyed it. I still wanted to come. He'd changed my palette.

I didn't want to understand Damon, but sometimes, I couldn't help thinking of all the times he watched me but never touched me—confusing me and intriguing me. And how he hadn't really changed so much.

Thirteen years ago he was hiding from his mother in a fountain, and after what happened in his room tonight and what Isa had told me, he was still hiding. Trying to feel everything through everyone else as he stood back and watched.

But bottom lines never changed. He still took what I never would've given him.

They all thought he was different with me, not realizing that I was just a different kind of kink to him. Something to get him off. He fucked with my head just like he did everyone's, and coerce is still a way to force.

He was as guilty as sin.

No one knew the real tragedy, though. It wasn't a matter of why he was different with me, but rather, now... I was different because of him.

CHAPTER 11

Winter

SEVEN YEARS AGO

"Ugh, I hate this!" I whisper-yelled, yanking out my earbuds, tossing them onto my bed, and stopping the audio-text.

No one used algebra.

No one.

I'd have to sign up for tutoring or something. I needed to keep my grades up or my father would pull me out of Thunder Bay and send me back to Montreal.

Why was I having such a hard time with this? All my other classes—no problem. I mean, math had always been hard, but the teacher... She talked fast and relied a lot on her Smartboard, projector, and all the other little gadgets that were of no use to me.

And it was pretty clear she didn't want to change what worked for twenty other kids for the sake of one. I thought my mom could talk to her—help her get a clue—but I didn't want my father to find out. He hated me being an inconvenience as much as I did.

I pushed my laptop, calculator, and braille keyboard away and crashed back onto the bed, taking my earbuds with me. I plugged them into my phone, found my music app, and clicked on one of my playlists. "Is Your Love Strong

Enough?" started playing, and I closed my eyes, my mind immediately going to the choreography I always envisioned myself dancing to for every song I listened to. I loved dancing so much, and if my mom wasn't asleep, I would blast some music downstairs and get to it.

When I danced and all I heard in my ears was the music, that was where I wanted to live forever.

I laid there, moving my head in a little figure eight motion to the music, and without thinking, my hands and arms started moving a little, too.

What if he was watching me right now? He could be in my room, feet away, at this very moment.

But, no. It had been a week, and I hadn't heard anything from him. He was probably at my sister's party, and it was probably just a prank. A one-time thing and some kind of joke he regularly pulled. I wanted to ask someone about him—tell them what happened—but I had no idea how to start that conversation, and other than the smell of the pool on him, I didn't have much to go by. He'd whispered and hadn't said anything personal. Like where he lived, his family, his friends, his age... He was tall, though, and his whisper was deep. He was undoubtedly older than me, if even just a couple years.

I hadn't told my parents, either, and I knew how irresponsible it was not to, but... I knew the consequences if my family thought I was in danger.

And he hadn't hurt me, so...

That didn't mean he wouldn't, but I didn't know. If I told, he wouldn't be able to come back.

And I wasn't sure I didn't want him to.

Stupid girl. The guy terrorized me over the course of a half hour, and instead of running for cover, I was drinking the Kool-Aid.

I was always stupid. I still thought I was going to be a dancer, I ignored the pain my father caused, because this house was my anchor, and I kept my intruder a little secret, because it excited me. Because I never had a secret, and it made me feel like... I didn't know. A teenager, maybe?

The song ended and the calm whir of the next one began to play, but in the moment of silence between, I noticed the smallest, barest vibration underneath my bed. The same one I felt when the garage door opened or the landscapers brought in their equipment to work on the yard and trim the trees.

I pulled out my earbuds and propped myself up on my elbows, training my ears for what it was I felt.

Arion had left hours ago for Devil's Night, some weird tradition of youth mischief the night before Halloween most of the world had forgotten about except our little town, and my father never came home, probably spending the night in the city again.

I remembered my mother's words about a mistress he kept, but I pushed the thought away and stood up. Other than me, my mom was the only one in the house, and she went to bed with an Ambien an hour ago.

Walking to my door, I pulled it open a sliver and listened. Maybe my mom got up or Arion brought friends home.

But now I could tell the vibration I'd felt was a slow whine, but constant and melodic. Up and down, long and slow.

Music. Someone was playing music.

I crept into the hallway, the pulse under my foot growing strong the closer I got to the sound. My heart beat harder, and I descended the stairs, finally recognizing the song set at a really low volume. A Bush song from my playlist in the ballroom.

I pulled my bottom lip in between my teeth, trying to stifle the fear and excitement raging through me. I should call for my mom. I should wake her up.

But I ignored that voice in my head and pushed through the ballroom doors. The song played from my system next to the wall at a low volume, and I didn't know if it was the monsters we all feel when we're scared or some sixth sense I didn't believe in, but I could feel someone in the room.

I walked to the dance floor and stopped on the marker in the middle, twisting in a slow circle.

"Are you there?" I asked.

The music suddenly cut off, and my breath caught in my throat as my heart jumped.

"Yes," a whisper far off in front of me said.

I licked my lips, every limb trembling, but the way his voice washed over me... My blood flowed electric.

I had to swallow a couple times to get my throat wet. "You found the snow village for me?"

He didn't answer. I knew it was him, but hearing him confirm it would have at least confirmed he was at the party—and near my sister—to hear me ask her for it. It might've been possible to pin down who he was then.

"Why did you come back?" I asked, keeping my voice low.

"Maybe I never left."

His whispering was haunting but there was something soft and playful in it.

And the fact that he kept whispering meant I might have heard his voice, and he was afraid of being recognized. Or maybe he just wanted to scare me.

"Who are you?"

"A ghost."

I shook my head, a slight smile playing on my lips. "I don't believe in ghosts."

"Why aren't you screaming?" he inquired, changing the subject. "Or calling for help?"

I fell quiet, wishing I could answer his question. For my own sake. I might be in danger. At the very least a strange man was in my home uninvited, and he'd been here before, threatening me.

Run. Scream.

"I don't know," I answered instead.

I still could scream. I wasn't ready just yet.

"Why did you come back?" I asked.

"I wanted to see if you'd dance again."

"How did you know I'd be alone?"

"I don't give a fuck if you're alone," he said. "Just as long as I have you to myself."

My heart skipped a beat, and I breathed faster and shallower.

I wanted to be like him. *Bold.*

"I have your shoes," he whispered.

My shoes?

Oh, my pointe shoes. I'd left them near the stereo when I rehearsed this morning before school.

Dance for him...

I could. As long as I didn't blast it, the music wouldn't wake my mother.

What would happen after I danced, though?

What was wrong with me that I liked that he was here?

He liked my dancing. He came to see if I would dance.

It made the world prettier.

I quickly hid the smile that tried to peek out.

I held out my hand. "Shoes?"

He set them in my hand, using both of his hands to make sure I had them.

I dropped to the floor and slipped the shoes on, lacing up the ribbons as I heard him walk away, probably to give me room.

Once the slippers were fastened tightly, I stood up and walked to the center of the dance floor, finding my X, and turned out into second position. Bending my knees in a quick demi-plié to find my balance, I rose up to en pointe onto my toes and back down again.

I should have had more of a warm up, but I was suddenly nervous. Maybe because the last time he saw me dance I didn't know he was watching or because I still wasn't sure if he was going to slit my throat or not.

"Track seven," I called out, my voice shaking a little. "Could you find it, please?"

I heard him move across the room as he did what I asked, and I wished I was dressed. The situation being what it was, I couldn't believe I was worried about that, but I only had on my sleep shorts, a tank top, and no damn bra.

Ellie Goulding's sonorous humming and chanting finally started, low and faint at first, but grew stronger, and I walked slowly around the dance floor, making a casual circle and getting a feel. I had only played around with choreography on this track once, and I couldn't remember it, so I guessed I was winging it.

The music built, haunting and crawling inside my skin, and then her voice gave in to lyrics, echoing and layered with chants as the drums started.

My pulse started to beat harder, and I closed my eyes, marking the tape on the floor in my head as I grazed over it and started moving. I hit the beat, rolling my head, shooting up on my toes, and twirling in a circle, feeling the music.

I forgot about him, and all of my teachers who complained about my technique, and just slipped into my own world where I craved the feel of my body slicing through the air and my hands in my hair and on my neck.

My back arched as I swung into an attitude, and I felt my heart leap in my chest when I twirled and posed in an arabesque. I smiled, biting down on my bottom lip to stifle the laugh I wanted to let loose. I spun and bent and dipped and slithered through whatever I wanted to do, just letting the music tell me.

When it ended, the air felt cold all of a sudden, and I breathed hard, remembering I wasn't alone.

"Are you...are you still there?" I asked, my mouth parched.

He didn't say anything for a moment, but when he did, his voice was calm. "The way you move, it's...different."

"Different than what?" I stilled, breathing hard.

But he didn't answer. I'd gathered my teachers were sometimes frustrated with me over years because I improvised. A lot. I appreciated the classical education I'd received, but I didn't want to do the same things that had already been done to death. I kind of just went on impulse, because it made me happy. Did he not like it?

I found my way to the chair again and sat down, removing my pointe shoes. "Are you still thinking you might hurt me?" I broached.

"I'm not in a hurry."

I almost laughed. It was a pointless question to ask, because I didn't expect him to tell me the truth, but somehow, I liked his answer. There was humor in it.

"Why don't you call the police?" he whispered, and I could tell his voice had gotten closer. He was approaching me.

I bent over, slipping the first shoe off and stretching out the ache in my foot. "Did you like the dance?" I asked instead.

"I won't stop you if you call for help," he explained. "Not tonight. Go ahead."

"It wasn't choreographed. I just improvised."

"I could kill you," he pointed out. "It would be over before you realized what was happening."

"I want you to like the dance," I continued, ignoring his one-sided conversation, because it would mean I would have to have answers for things I didn't have answers for yet. "My parents think the idea of a blind ballet dancer is ridiculous, but it's all I've ever wanted to do. It can be done."

"You could die tonight," he went on as if he hadn't heard me.

I unlaced the other shoe and slid it off, letting it drop to the floor. "I could die ten times on any given day. I could've died when I lost my sight when I was eight."

I was used to feeling endangered. Every step I took could lead me off the side of a building for all I knew. Maybe that was why I wasn't as scared of him.

"What happened that day?" he asked.

When I lost my sight?

"I fell," replied. "From a treehouse. I hit my head twice on the way down. Optic nerve damage. Irreparable."

"Were you pushed?"

I closed my right fist, still remembering the terrible feeling of the boy's hand slowly slipping out of it and knowing that was all that was standing between me and the ground far below.

I wasn't pushed. Not exactly.

"I shouldn't have been up there." My voice had lowered to a mumble. "I wish I'd never met him. I wish I'd never gone up there with him. I..." How very different my life would be if I could change that one day and never step foot in that fountain. "I miss seeing things. Movies and the sea." I paused before continuing. "Your face."

Not being able to gauge his body language or expressions left me at a disadvantage.

I heard a chair scrape against the floor and then it was placed in front of me before I heard his weight sit down on it. He took my hand, but I jerked back, sitting up steel rod straight in my chair and suddenly alert.

He took it again, squeezing my fingers a little tighter. "Stand up."

I guessed what he was doing, and I'd gone this far, so... Hesitantly, I stood up from my chair, every muscle still rigid and ready to run if I had to.

His hand was a bit bigger than mine, and his fingers were long and sculpted but so chilled. So cold. He took both of my hands and led me to him. To his face.

"What do you see?" he asked, placing my hands on him and releasing me.

My fingers splayed across both sides of his face, and I stood still for a moment, afraid to move my fingers, because he would feel how much I was shaking. Every inch of my skin that touched his buzzed underneath the surface, and I almost pulled away because it tickled so bad.

"You're tall," I said, clearing my throat. "When you're standing, I mean. Aren't you?"

I remembered the feel of his body pressed into mine last time, and even sitting now, the top of his head reached just above my breasts.

Moving my hands over his face, I took in the smooth skin, gently brushing his forehead, temples, cheekbones and brow with my fingertips.

"Young," I continued, painting a picture in my head. "Oval face but a hard jaw. Sharp nose." I lightly pinched where the bone met the cartilage, smoothing my fingers down the length. "How did you break it?"

It was just a faint curve the naked eye probably wouldn't catch, but I could feel how it bent just slightly in that centimeter.

"I fell," he answered.

I cocked my head, reading between the lines. I'd gotten pretty good at figuring out what people didn't say.

"Yeah, my mom falls a lot, too," I told him.

He was clearly punched and didn't want to elaborate. Which meant he was either still pissed about it or... embarrassed and ashamed.

Moving on, I ran my fingers over his straight eyebrows, the cold, smooth ridge of his ears and lobes, and his thick hair that fell over his forehead and in his eyes a little. He was probably dark-haired, since fair people like me often had thinner hair.

I trailed my hands down to his chin, my heart pounding as my fingers danced around his mouth, but then I brought them up and traced the lines of his lips.

His hot breath fell across my fingers, and my whole body warmed. Was he looking at my face, too? Into my eyes? What was he thinking?

"I wish I could see you for real," I told him. "I want to know what you look like when you look at me."

He remained silent, and embarrassment burned across my skin. I shook it off, moving on.

"No piercings," I added. "On your head anyway."

His upper lip tilted up, and I half-smiled. "And he smirks," I teased.

Of course, I didn't need to feel his mischievous smile to know he was a bad boy, but it comforted me to know he had a sense of humor.

"Your neck..." I grazed my fingertips down his smooth skin and throat.

"What about it?"

I leaned in, surprising myself as I pressed my cheek into the skin there. He didn't move a muscle.

"It's warm," I remarked. "Smooth."

And the house was cold.

I inhaled, smelling his soap and shampoo, far too fragrant to be hours old.

"You just showered," I guessed.

Pulling up, I took a step closer, holding his head right in front of me and sliding my fingers back into his hair.

"Tall, dark, young," I commented on what I knew about so far. "Good personal hygiene, likes to fight, long eyelashes, kind of a pretty boy, I'm thinking..."

He snorted, and I smiled, too, but then my fingers grazed something on his scalp but before I could figure out what it was, I felt another one. My face fell, contemplating the raised pieces of skin. As I examined the rest of his scalp, I found several others. All about a quarter inch long.

Scars.

"I fell," he said again, not waiting for me to ask the question.

I clenched my teeth for a moment. "That's a lot of falls," I said. "Do you have those anywhere else?"

"You wanna check the rest of my body?" he asked, sounding cocky.

I dropped my hand, trying not to roll my eyes. *Thanks for the offer.*

"How old are you?" I asked.

But his guard stayed up when he replied, "Older than you."

What was he doing here? Really? Was he just a prankster, pulling another joke for Devil's Night, or did he actually have more sinister intentions when he broke in a week ago, before he saw me dance and got suddenly smitten? What would happen if I refused to dance again? What did he really want?

"What's one thing you'll never be able to do but really want to?" he asked.

I nearly laughed. One thing?

"Are you kidding?" I shot back. "I have a whole list."

"Just tell me one."

I pondered it for a moment, thinking about how I missed all the things I would never see again. Films, plays, mountains, trees, waterfalls, dresses, shoes, the faces of my family and friends... I didn't know what it was like to leave the house alone or do simple things like go hiking or for a stroll in the woods by myself. I would never be able to escape, run away, or experience the freedom of a spontaneous getaway all by myself without anyone knowing or being there to help me.

"Drive," I finally answered him. "My dad used to have this old stock car in the barn at our ski lodge in Vermont, and I would sit in it and shift the gears, pretending I was racing. I'd love to be able to drive."

He was quiet for a moment, and then finally, he rose, and I could feel him right in front of me.

"Would you really?" he asked.

There was a sneaky smile in his voice that made my heart skip a beat.

"Let's get out of here then." And he grabbed my hand and pulled me along.

"Huh?" I stumbled, perplexed but letting him take me even though I had no idea what was going on. "And go where? I can't leave!"

I remembered my mother upstairs and closed my mouth, shutting up immediately.

"I can take you if I want," he said, pulling me into the foyer toward the front door. "Or you can scream now and the fun has to end."

"Who says I'm having any fun?"

"You're about to." He stopped but kept hold of my fingers. "Or, if you want, I can put you to bed and go have fun with someone else."

I rolled my eyes. *Please.* Like I'd be jealous or something?

"You're the one I want to play with, though," he whispered, leaning in.

Yeah, I'm sure. A psycho with a penchant for blind girls who can't pick him out of a line-up. Was I out of my mind?

"People and music and fires and beer," he taunted. "Let's go, Winter. The world awaits."

I shook my head at myself. I *was* out of my mind.

"You'll bring me home?" I asked.

"Of course."

"Alive and... untouched?"

And he laughed, and it was the first time I'd heard his voice. Deep and smooth and very much humored at my expense. "Tonight. Sure."

My expression fell, and I hesitated only a moment before I pulled out of his grasp and inched my way over to the closet, feeling for one of my hoodies that was bound to be in there.

Finding one, I pulled it out and slipped it on, digging out a pair of sneakers, too. I wanted my phone. I should bring it.

I turned back toward the stairs, but then stopped, remembering the GPS on it my parents used to track me with an app.

If my mom woke up or my dad came home, would I want them to be able to find me with a boy whose name I didn't even know, doing something I shouldn't be doing, and use it as an excuse to send me away again?

But then again, if I needed them to find me, I was going to be damn glad I had the phone, wasn't I?

Decisions, decisions.

Screw it.

I inhaled a breath, turned around, and reached for his hand.

He took it and opened the door.

• • •

"Why don't you use a stick?" he asked, leading me down the driveway. "Or a guide dog or something?"

Believe me, I'd love to. It would allow me a little more freedom.

"If I need to go anywhere, someone helps me," I told him. "My parents don't like me to draw attention to myself."

They thought people would stare at me. I wasn't the only visually impaired person in town, but I was pretty sure I was the only full-on blind one, and I knew their fears without even asking. And they were right. It made people uncomfortable. I'd been through enough awkward conversations to know when someone just wanted to be away from me, because they didn't know how to act around me.

The part they were wrong about was that they thought the world was still the same for me, and I should learn how to navigate it the same way I did before. I couldn't. People might be uncomfortable, but they would get used to it. They would change. It was a source of resentment that my parents thought that no one should be inconvenienced, and it was *my* responsibility not to be a burden to others.

It was my world, too.

"You could never not draw attention," he finally said. "And it has nothing to do with you being blind."

The way he said it—gentle and thoughtful—made heat rise to my cheeks, and I didn't know if he meant my dancing or if I was pretty, but I smiled to myself, suddenly warm all over.

I didn't have time to ask him to clarify, though, because the next thing I knew he was in front of me, reaching back, grabbing my thighs, and hefting me up onto his back. I sucked in a breath, my feet lifting off the ground, and I hurriedly circled my arms around his neck so I wouldn't fall.

"I can walk faster," I told him. "I can. I didn't mean—"

"Shut up and hold me tight."

Okayyyy. I locked my arms around his neck.

"Tighter," he bit out. "Like in the closet the other night."

I smirked but he couldn't see it. I tightened my arms around his neck, tucking my head close with my cheek next to his. I'd tried not to think about my parents' fight that night, but I couldn't not think about him. How his arms, heat, and pulse in my ear made it all go away. How sometimes you have to get the worst to feel the best. It was a nice memory.

He carried me down the driveway, and when his shoes hit rocks, I knew we were outside my walls.

He stopped and set me down, my leg brushing a body of metal. I put out my hands, rubbing them over steel, glass, and a door handle.

I smiled.

Of course, he wouldn't have pulled up right in front of my house. He'd parked outside the open gates.

I trailed the length of the car, feeling the smooth surface, but not glossy like glass. It was a matte paint, the long, clean lines and grill narrow, sophisticated, and sleek. Definitely foreign.

"I like your car," I told him and then teased, "What's its name?"

He breathed out a laugh and then I felt him behind me, his whisper hitting my ear. "My pets all have pulses."

The hair on the back of my neck stood up, and every inch of my skin sparked to life. How did he do that?

Taking my hand, he led me around to the driver's side, opened the door, and climbed in, and I heard the seat slide, but I wasn't sure if he was moving it forward or backward. Something else shifted, too. The steering wheel?

My heart pumped harder, and apprehension made me retreat a step. *I don't think…*

"Come here," he said.

Uh, no. Maybe this isn't a great idea.

His fingers took mine, and he tugged. "Get in this car right now."

My stomach sank to my feet as I hesitated, and I felt a little sick.

I could go back to the house right now. I could go to bed with my music and audiobooks and my quiet house while the world continued to spin around me, and the next time I was given a chance to do something wild, stupid, and scary, it would be even easier to turn tail and run… Every day just as predictable as the last.

This was stupid. And illegal.

But he was fun. I didn't want it to be over.

I closed my eyes and let my shoulders slump a little, defeated.

Fine. I slid a leg into the car, ducking my head as he guided me into his lap, fitting my legs between his long ones. I leaned back a little, so I wasn't right up on the steering wheel, my back pressed against his chest.

Placing my hands on the wheel, he wrapped my fingers around it. "It's like a clock," he instructed. "You're at ten o'clock and two o'clock right now."

His fists tightened around mine, emphasizing my position.

I nodded, my belly still somersaulting like crazy.

"I'll handle the pedals and the stick shift," he told me. "You just steer."

"Steer how?" I blurted out, tears of frustration springing to my eyes already. "We're going to die."

He snorted. "It's an empty road," he told me. "And at this hour, sure to be deserted. Relax."

I shook my head, still unsure.

"Hey." He nudged my chin, turning me to face him. "All you have to do is trust me, kid. You understand?"

I paused, feeling his eyes on me and his body behind me.

But the fear melted away. He was in charge, and he could do anything. I did trust him.

I nodded and then took a deep breath and turned my head forward again.

His legs shifted under me, his hand reached underneath mine, and suddenly, the car purred to life as he started the engine.

His right hand settled on the gear shift, moving it into position, and his breath fell on my neck as my fists grinded the steering wheel.

"You're going to pull up onto the street, just to the left," he explained. "When you feel all four tires on the smooth pavement, straighten out."

I swallowed, nodding again. "Not too much gas at first, okay?"

All I heard was another laugh, though. Okay, so maybe I didn't trust him.

"Giving it some gas," he warned me, and the engine revved.

I shook the steering wheel side to side, nervous, but he hadn't taken his foot off the brake...or the clutch or whatever yet, so we weren't moving, and I relaxed again, feeling stupid.

He didn't laugh at me, though.

A little more gas, and I felt the tires crunch the rocks underneath. I gripped the wheel so hard I was sure my hands would need to be pried off. The left front tire climbed over a bump, and I turned the wheel in that direction until I felt the right wheel join the other on the pavement.

I smiled, a combination between a laugh and a gasp pouring out of me, and as soon as I registered the rear tires climb onto the road, I twisted the wheel back to the right to make sure I stayed in my lane.

But then the car quickly fell off the road again, back onto the same rocks and grass I just drove away from, bouncing over the bump where the pavement ended.

"Oh, shit!" I turned the wheel left, taking us back onto the road. But I was afraid I would drive into the other lane and shot right again, both tires on the right side, falling off the side of the damn road again.

I can't do this.

I shook my head, breathing hard as I tried to right myself. "I'm sorry. I'm sorry..."

"Shhh," he soothed, his left hand resting on my hip. "We've got all the time in the world."

My chin trembled, because I was embarrassed and frustrated, and I didn't want to do this, because I would just make a fool out of myself. I was just going to fail! Why was he trying to embarrass me?

Tears pooled, the car slowed to a crawl, and I closed my eyes, breathing in and out to get my head straight again.

It's okay. We've got all the time in the world.

We've got all the time in the world.

I blew out a long, slow breath.

It's okay.

It's okay.

He wasn't rushing me. He wasn't mocking me. He wasn't hurrying me.

It was okay if I learned things a little slower. It was okay.

I sniffled, and even though he couldn't see my face, he probably knew I was crying, but I stretched my fingers and gripped the wheel again.

"Okay," I said.

He gave it some gas, and I pulled back onto the road, moving the steering wheel smaller this time, swerving the car side to side to find the edges of my lane, kind of like I do when I dance. Gauging the perimeter and counting time to feel for my mark.

The left tires ran over little bumps every few feet, and I realized they were reflectors in the middle of the road, so drivers could see their lanes at night.

That was my mark. How I could tell when I left my lane.

My shoulders relaxed just a little, and I sat up straighter. *Okay.*

I kept the wheel positioned in my lane, feeling when the right side would dip a little as it did right before it gave way to grass, and feeling the reflectors on the left, keeping me from veering into the opposing lane. My wheel wasn't always straight, but we were going slow enough I could tell when the road curved just slightly in order to stay between my markers.

"You did it," he whispered.

I broke out in a smile, my eyes still wet, but feeling a lot better than I did a few minutes ago. He didn't teach me, either. He didn't tell me about the reflectors or how to move the wheel or anything. He just waited for me to learn it on my own. It was a nice change and took the pressure off. It was nice not to feel hurried.

"We're gonna go faster," he told me.

Faster? And there went the relaxation and confidence I'd just been basking in.

"I'll let you know which way to move the wheel, okay?"

"Okay," I replied. It made sense. We'd be going faster, so I'd have less time to correct myself.

His legs moved under me, he shifted gears, and the car picked up pace, making my body jerk against him. Instinctively, I gripped the wheel harder and didn't blink for a second as I tried to concentrate.

The engine roared, and I could feel the acceleration vibrate under my thighs as we barreled into the night where anything could come out at me too fast for two minds to react in sync. An animal, another car, a person... *Jesus.* Too fast. Too fast. The car rumbled under my feet, making my heart leap in my chest.

"The wheel is at noon," he said. "When I say 'go', slowly and softly veer to the left, to about ten o'clock."

I couldn't swallow or speak, so I just nodded, curling my toes in fear. *Shit.*

"Go," he said.

As he instructed, I gently turned the wheel a few inches, feeling the tires run over the reflectors, but instead of swerving in the other direction to correct myself, I found them with the very edge of my left tires and stayed on them. It would probably freak out oncoming traffic with my hugging the middle of the road like this, but I was able to manage the curves of the road all by myself.

"Okay, it's gonna curve right in—"

"Shh," I snapped, shutting him up.

I needed to listen.

And then, as he warned, the reflectors twisted right, and I needed to correct the wheel to follow it, surprisingly not going off the road like I half-expected.

"Jesus Christ," he laughed, sounding impressed. "Okay, I'll just take a nap. You have fun."

"Don't you dare!" I scolded.

We'd eventually come to an intersection, a street light, or a pedestrian. Plus, he worked the gas.

"Can we go faster?" I asked.

I'd been tensing and concentrating so hard, I wanted to be thrilled.

He shifted and accelerated, and if my count was right, we were in fourth or fifth gear.

"It's pretty straight for the next couple of minutes," he told me. "You want some music?"

I thought about it, realizing I could feel us running over the reflectors, and I didn't necessarily need to hear them.

"Okay."

He turned on his stereo, "Go to Hell" playing, and I relaxed back into him, my heart beating hard with the speed but still studying every little bump underneath us to keep us on the road.

An engine started to rumble from farther off, and the ground under me shook a little harder. What was that?

I turned my head to check with him, but all of a sudden, the wind whipped past us and a loud horn blared as a truck, I thought, zoomed right past us.

I gasped, feeling the car shake with the draft, and my hands shook on the wheel, feeling the reflectors underneath the right tires again. "Holy shit!"

I laughed, and I felt his body shake with his own laughter behind me.

"Why didn't you tell me?" I barked but smiled. "We could've died!"

"Fun, huh?"

Asshole jerk.

And yes, it was fun.

"Ready for more?" he taunted.

"Yes." I bit my bottom lip, butterflies still swarming my stomach, but I couldn't stop.

"In a minute, you're going to jerk the wheel to nine-o'clock," he explained. "I'm not going to slow down."

"What?"

"In three...two..."

"Wait, you said I had 'a minute'!" I yelped.

"One!" he shouted in my ear. "Go!"

"Fuck..." I cried out, jerking the wheel left to nine o'clock and gasping. "You!"

The car skidded, bouncing and barreling over the pavement and onto a gravel road, and I felt his hand cover the top of my head as our bodies were thrown side to side, my skull damn near hitting the roof.

"Oh, my God, oh, my God..."

He down shifted. "Straighten out," he told me.

I did, breathing faster than a bullet as he shifted again and sped up, both of us charging into the night, down an unlit gravel road, to whatever tree we were going to wrap this car around.

But holy shit. Everything on me was warm. Hot. My blood raced, and my arms felt strong enough to make me fly.

I turned up the music, found the window buttons on the door, and rolled down the window, the much-needed cool air whipping through my hair as the music pounded.

I turned my head toward him, his breath on the corner of my mouth. "Can we go faster?"

He didn't say anything. He didn't budge other than to press the clutch, shift gears, and punch the gas.

We charged down the road, and I was having so much fun now. But I wasn't the one who was losing control. My pulse and breathing had calmed. His, on the other hand…

I felt his chest rise and fall against my back as his breath hit my cheek, shallow and labored.

I curled my lips in a little smile. *My turn.*

"Tell me when," I said.

"When what?"

"I want to turn again."

I felt his head shake side to side. "We're going too fast for that now, Little Devil."

I held onto the wheel and lifted up my foot, putting it on top of his and pressing it into the pedal, so he didn't let off the gas. "Please?"

His voice shook. "Winter…"

I nudged the steering wheel side to side, playing. "Left or right? You choose or I will."

He breathed hard through his teeth, gripping my hips with both hands now. "No."

"I'm gonna do it."

"No," he growled in a loud whisper. "You do what you're told."

I jammed down on his foot, accelerating the car a little more.

"Left or right?" I asked, my nose brushing his. "Tell me."

He panted, digging his fingers into my skin through my sweatshirt.

"Three," I threatened, counting down. "Two..."

"Okay, okay, okay," he said. "Wait. Just wait."

I leaned my forehead into his. "One."

"Okay, three o'clock! Now!" he hissed.

I faced forward, rotated the wheel right, both of us slamming into the door as the car sprung over the dips and uneven earth on the new gravel road.

"No, four!" he shouted, realizing three wasn't enough. "Four o'clock! Shit!"

I turned it more, but we knew it was a lost cause. I lost the wheel as the car skidded and spun out, and my body coiled up on reflex to protect itself. His arms went around me, covering my head, and I screamed as the car tipped onto one side, balancing for a moment and threatening to flip over, but then fell back onto all four tires again.

The car stilled, the engine died, and I stayed like that, cradled in his lap, taking a mental inventory of my body.

Other than banging my knee on the steering wheel when I brought it up, and an ache in my shoulder from hitting the car door, I was fine. I popped my head up, bringing my hands to his face.

"Did I kill you?" I asked.

But he didn't laugh or say anything for a moment. Just breathed.

"My heart..." he said. "Shit."

I remembered what he said last week at my house. *Do you know what I have to do to get it to beat like that?*

"I scared you."

"Not an emotion I'm used to being on the receiving end of," he mused.

And then his fingers found the pulse on my neck and pressed down. I followed suit, placing my three fingers on his neck, on the side of his throat, and finding his pulse, as well. We sat there for a moment, each of us with one hand on our own neck and another on the other person's.

It was fast like mine, and I liked that I did that to him.

"What color is your car?" I asked, pulling my hands down from his neck and mine.

"Black."

Of course.

"When I remember the colors in my head," I remarked, "I get a feeling sometimes. Pink is how I feel now. My stomach doing somersaults and laughing. Giddy. Squirrelly..." I slid off him and into the passenger side seat. "I don't know what I feel when I picture black, though. Nothing, really, I guess."

"That sounds like a challenge."

I smiled to myself. "You scared me, I scared you, now it's your turn again."

He started the car and shifted into gear. "Pull your hood up and put your seatbelt on."

"Why?"

"Because I told you to," he muttered, trying to sound commanding, but it just came off as playful.

I pulled my seatbelt on, fastened it, and pulled up the hood of my sweatshirt, my hair spilling out the sides.

We drove in silence, which was fine by me, because he blasted the stereo, and the only time I got to enjoy loud music in the car was with my sister, but she hardly ever had to chauffeur me anywhere, so those times were rare.

Turning my face toward the window, I zoned out, thinking about everything that had happened the past hour. Dancing for him, touching him, the way he was patient with me but also pushed me, to see what I was made of.

And how I wasn't entirely sure if it was for my benefit or for his pleasure.

His body moved next to me, shifting gears and putting pedal to the metal, but every once in a while, I felt his eyes on me. My heartbeat started to pick up pace, and I was glad I couldn't see him with my eyes. Glad I would never be able to see him.

He would be the picture he was in my head. A faceless boy with dark hair and fire in his eyes, just how I wanted it.

Forever.

We drove into town—he started curbing his speed, and I think we stopped at a traffic light—and after a few turns, he pulled the car to a stop and turned off the engine.

"I'll be right back," he said, taking his keys. "Keep your hood up."

I didn't respond, and he didn't wait for confirmation that I'd heard. Opening the car door, he climbed out, slammed the door shut, and I heard the click of the lock right before everything went silent. Of course, I could still open my door. I could get out. He was keeping anyone else from getting in.

I felt a little traffic farther away, and I could hear the subterranean droning of music coming from the building to my left, but other than that, the village was quiet. I had no idea what time it was.

Why did I need to cover myself? Maybe he was planning on slicing and dicing me, after all, and didn't want witnesses tracking my whereabouts after the fact?

I almost laughed. I was pretty sure he had no malicious intent at this point.

But then something occurred to me. What if he didn't want his friends to see me? What if he had a girlfriend?

Nope. Don't do it. He came to me. He found me. He brought me out. I wasn't going to look for excuses to end the night.

In no time at all, the door opened, but this time it was my door.

"Let's go," he said, taking my hand.

"Where?" I climbed out, following him.

"To see black."

See black? I loved his imagination.

Confused but intrigued, I remained quiet as I followed him down the street, hearing the sizzling sound of a neon sign with the smell of pizza damn near making me moan with hunger. *Sticks.* We were across from the park in the town square right in front of a local hangout. A bar that admitted minors, because it had bands and pool tables, so really, people of all ages could be found there. Is that where he ran to a moment ago?

He held something up to me, and I took it, turning it around in my hands and finally realizing it was a helmet.

A helmet?

I heard something move, a key being inserted, and I hesitated a moment, because I was in sleep shorts, and if we fell, I'd have no clothing protecting my legs, my most prized possessions on which I trusted my future in dance.

I groaned to myself. As long as he didn't expect me to drive, I guess...

Fastening the strap of the half helmet under my chin, I held onto his arm as he helped me climb on behind him. It was a little chilly, and the wind might be too brisk. I brushed the back of his head with my hand, feeling that he wasn't wearing a helmet at all.

"Whose bike is this?" I asked.

"A friend."

I put my hands on his waist, but his body shot up and then came down hard, sparking the motor to life, and I didn't need him to tell me what to do. I wrapped my arms around him, and put my head down behind his back, but I was nervous as hell. I'd never ridden on a motorcycle before.

"Don't let go," he ordered me.

Yeah, like, duh.

I tucked my feet up on the footrests and squeezed him tight as we shot off, kicking up gears and picking up pace.

I whimpered, but I didn't think he heard it.

This was faster than the car. Or maybe it was because I could feel the wind.

He veered left, turning around the square, and the bike leaned so far, I thought we'd tip over.

"Can you slow down a little bit?" I yelled. "Please?"

But once we rounded the corner, he sped off, shooting to warp speed, and I yelped, locking my arms around his body and squeezing him between my thighs.

"I don't feel..." I laughed for good measure, "Like really secure. Slow down!"

But he didn't. He veered right, then left, then right again, the weight of our bodies feeling like too much as we tipped from side to side.

There was a dip, my stomach vaulted up and down, and we shot up a steep hill, and I gasped, holding him tighter.

We raced over the top of the hill, leaving the ground and picking up air as we flew over the hump and to the ground again. My heart leapt into my throat, and I felt like I was on a ride I couldn't control and didn't have time to think, and even if I could, I couldn't stop what was happening. My body rushed with heat and energy, terror swelled in my throat, and I couldn't figure out if I wanted to laugh, puke, or scream.

He sped around a bend, we leaned, and I could almost feel the ground an inch under my leg. I couldn't stop myself. "I'm gonna fall!" I cried out. "Stop, please!"

And he did. He slowed and halted, and as if by magic, everything was quiet again.

I didn't let him go.

"This is black," he said. "Fear, falling, release. Excitement, risk, danger."

I sat there, hugging him and trying to figure out if I liked it or not. It scared me just like he did when he broke into the house last week. I hated that, but... I didn't really hate it anymore. Probably because I wasn't as scared of him anymore. It was fear in a controlled environment. The motorcycle wasn't.

Or maybe I just needed to try it again.

"I won't let you go ag—" He stopped and evened out his voice. "I won't let you go," he said. "Hold on."

I inhaled a shaky breath and readied myself for another go. And when the bike shot off again, I lifted my head, making myself not hide from it.

He won't let me go. He won't let me go.

The wind cut my face, and I closed my eyes to keep them from watering. After a moment, I found my body molded to his and moved with it as he turned and leaned, sped and broke, and it was like we were one rider.

When he leaned, and I thought we were going to fall, I squeezed my eyes shut and stopped breathing, letting him handle the bike and me and carrying us around in one piece.

When it happened again, I eased my muscles a little more, trusting him and letting him do it. I tipped my head back, feeling the wind and my body move with his, no longer needing to squeeze him so tightly.

I wanted to go all night now, because for the first time in forever, I was seeing things again. And just because I'd lost my sight didn't mean that I needed to fear getting lost.

Just maybe, it was exactly what I'd been dying for.

The rumble of the motor shook my tummy, and I smiled, hoping for a thousand more nights like this.

He slowed to a stop and put his feet down on the ground. "Fear, falling, release," he said again. "Excitement, risk, danger."

"And at any moment, death," I mused, still with my smile toward the sky.

"Freedom," he added.

I laid my head on his back again, and he put the stand down and took out the key.

"We're done," he told me, sounding a little amused when I wouldn't let him go.

"I'm cold." I nuzzled closer.

He chuckled under his breath, and the smell of Sticks pizza wafted through my nostrils again. "Can you show me red?" I asked.

I didn't want the night to end.

He paused for a moment and then whispered over his shoulder. "Someday."

"Are you still going to hurt me?" I joked.

But he paused again, his whisper barely audible. "Someday," he said.

CHAPTER 12

Damon

PRESENT

I was glad Michael and Rika weren't having their engagement party at St. Killian's. I refused to step foot in the nightmare they no doubt made of one of our favorite high school haunts.

St. Killian's was an old, abandoned cathedral we all explored as kids, precious hours spent away from parents and left to our own devices, and when we became teenagers, the catacombs underneath were our obsession. I could still smell the earth and stone and hear the water trickling down the walls. It was decadent and indulgent, and my domain.

We ran and hid, scared each other, drank, and had all kinds of hot fun down there growing up. It was our pathetic little empire, but it was freedom.

And they just had to douche it up by buying it and renovating it into their new, lovely home, probably taking away everything that was wild and primitive about it.

God, please, someone fuck me in the ass. Where the hell did the kids at Thunder Bay Prep go now on Devil's Night? Did anyone keep up the tradition after we'd left? Was everything we did pointless and dead now, lost in vague memories that wouldn't outlive anyone who knew us?

I tipped my head to the side, hearing my neck crack, and took a drink of the Stoli in my glass. I said I would stay at this party for three minutes. It had been eight.

They got engaged two years ago, and they were finally celebrating it? Maybe Rika had wanted to finish school first or Michael's schedule had been too busy. Whatever.

Pods of people loitered around the art museum, dressed in their best and here to wish Michael and his little monster a happy little life. But really, it was just a precaution. Michael and Rika were American royalty and would inherit a lot of power, eventually. Best to pay your respects in hopes of earning a seat at their table one day.

Glasses clinked, chatter melted together, sounding like a flock of birds, and everyone was smiling, except me. They all avoided me. Even though two of my friends went to prison with me, I was the only real criminal here. I was the rapist. The sexual deviant. The sick one. Lock up your daughters, wives, sisters, and moms. Hell, lock up Grandma, too.

I caught their sideways looks at me, and then they'd freak out when I looked back, and they hurriedly turned their heads. I laughed to myself and emptied my glass. *Jesus Christ.*

Crane, my head of security, approached my side, and I set the empty glass on a passing tray, picking up a new one.

"Where did she disappear to the other night?" I asked him.

"Coldfield," he reported low for only me to hear. "The new haunted house. With her friends. No men with them."

I scanned the room slowly, looking for Winter but not finding her. "Did she like it?"

I didn't know why I cared. Maybe it would tell me if I needed to up my game when the time came.

"I think so," he said. "I lost track of her for several minutes. Her friends did, as well."

I spotted Arion and her mother talking to a group of older ladies. Vicious cunts like the rest of the matriarchs in this town.

"Was she meeting someone?" I suggested. She was blind. She would've been careful not to get lost by accident. Was it on purpose then?

"I don't think so," he answered. "When she reappeared, she looked shaken. Flushed. I think she just got lost."

I laughed under my breath. She always did scare easily.

"And the attorney?" I asked about the rest of his list of duties I'd given him.

"Yes, the appointment's set up."

I locked eyes on Rika on the dance floor with some guy I didn't know. His hand sat too low on her hip, his fingers brushing the top of her ass, and I narrowed my eyes on them, taking another sip. "And the council?"

Crane chuckled. "Yeah, it's done," he said. "If your father finds out how much of his money you've thrown around town..."

"Oh, he will," I mused. "When it's too late, of course. But I need all my ducks in a row first."

And then I spotted Michael Crist, my old-friend-now-enemy, heading straight for me. Oh, great.

"Quack, quack," Crane mumbled, probably seeing him approach, too.

I grinned at his joke as he walked away and squared my shoulders as Michael approached.

"Do you think I won't kick you out?" he sneered. "The women don't protect you."

"Maybe not my women."

He thought I thought I could be here, because the Ashbys were invited, but my insinuation was clear. Both his fiancée and Kai's wife held less of a grudge. They may not hate me being here.

"Speaking of which..." I gestured to Erika on the dance floor. "Have you noticed the paws someone's putting all over yours?"

"She is none of your concern."

"Do something about it, or I'll make it my concern."

Why did I even care? I didn't know. I spent a lot of time resenting Rika and her influence over the guys that I didn't really realize...she belonged. Maybe I kind of liked her.

"Michael? Everything okay?" Kai walked over, and I rolled my eyes so far back in my head I almost saw my brain.

Two peas in a pod.

I glanced over to Rika again, noticing by just the guy's look and smile that he was flirting. And Michael had his back turned, fucking oblivious.

"You know," I said, stepping forward into Michael's space, "when the alpha in a pack gets old or sick—weak—the other dogs can sense it." I narrowed my eyes on him. "And they stop backing down."

He stepped up to me, too, both of us nose to nose, him gauging how far he wanted to take this at his own engagement party and me not giving a shit. My family had money and connections, too, and I was done vying for a place among them. I was stronger. While Will and Kai took a plea deal on their assault and battery charges, I never gave in. I was in prison longer, and I'd been alone enough. This was my fucking town, too, and if I had to tear everything down and rebuild it to make some of it mine, I would do it.

Kai stepped in as he always did, trying to diffuse the situation.

"Damon, if you're not enjoying yourself, you can leave," he said.

"Nonsense," I taunted, taking in the string quartet, champagne, and servers with trays of shit-colored canapés. "I like your party. It's so...tasteful." I laughed, taking a sip of my drink. "I remember when you had an imagination."

"And I remember when you had a prayer," Michael shot back, inching in. "I have my own bank account, Damon, with my own money, credit cards, and an education. I have connections outside of my father, friends, respect, standing, a fucking credit score, and the door is open to me at any restaurant, bank, or country club I want to do business with in the world." He grinned. "Tried to get into Hunter-Bailey lately?"

Prick. He'd had me banned from the men's club two years ago.

"I can fuck my beautiful fiancée any time I want," he went on, "and she looks really amazing dressed only in that quarter-of-a-million-dollar necklace around her neck right now. A necklace I bought without asking my daddy for the money."

"And how about fun?" I retorted. "Are you having any of that without me?"

This was not the party it should've been. My sister didn't get the party she should've had, either. God, they were pathetic. We would've laughed at this polite, bland, and pretentious snooze-fest back in the day, and then grabbed the girls and taken them for an all-night ride through our underworld. What a shitshow.

Kai looked at me, his dark eyes only a shade lighter than mine. "Banks loves you," he said. "And we would never disinvite the Ashbys. Those are the only reasons you're here. You burned down my dojo, you tried to kill us, and you're not to be trusted around Rika. We're not friends, so when we run into each other, we'll keep it brief and civil for the women's sake, but I'm not ready to pretend anything is okay."

"Everything okay?" Arion popped up in front of us, asking.

I snorted, the little speech he thought would have me shaking in my boots ruined now.

The whole group arrived—Will and Alex, Margot, Arion and Winter, along with that little shit-stain Ethan Belmont. He was next on Crane's list of duties.

But I guessed they had to invite everyone to get the pretentious part right. Rika was circulating now, and my sister was AWOL. I imagined these things made her as uncomfortable as me.

"Peachy," Michael replied and then leaned over to Margot, kissing her on the cheek. "Thank you for coming."

"Thank you for inviting us," she said and then joked. "Even if your mother made you."

"Please." He chuckled. "Rika and I run our own show now. The misfits stick together."

She smiled at him, and I knew Michael's mother and Winter's mother were friendly, both of them probably finding common ground in their family drama.

He offered her an arm and led her off to the dance floor, Kai faded away, and Arion sidled up to me, taking a sip of my drink. I cast her a glance, able to appreciate how beautiful she actually was in her skin-tight gold dress, long golden hair, and every inch of visible skin glowing and soft.

But she was cold, shallow, and boring. Someday someone might be able to get inside her head and reach her, but it wouldn't be me. I'd already been there with someone else and never again.

"Wanna dance?" I heard Ethan say.

I looked over to see Belmont with his arm around Winter, and I let my eyes fall down her body, noticing she had changed clothes. Her gown was gone, replaced with a thin, black fabric that draped over a black bodysuit—or leotard—with the gauze twisted into straps over her shoulders and fitted around her breasts. The sheer fabric draped past her ass, down her legs, and not quite to her ankles which were laced with matching black ballet slippers. No tights. Her bare legs were completely visible through the dress, which slit up the middle, giving her free rein to move.

"I was just about to," she answered. "Rika and Michael asked me."

Asked you? To dance?

"Sweet," he replied.

But I cocked an eyebrow. "Why the hell would they do that?"

Was this Rika's way of keeping an eye on Winter? Installing herself in her life again?

Winter's chin lifted a hair and she set her jaw. "Because I'm good," she stated.

"Well, this should be entertaining," Arion mumbled with a smirk.

I didn't know if I agreed. Winter would dance. For me. I didn't like they'd gone behind my back to arrange this with her.

"Oh, Winter, this is Alex, by the way," Will said and then eyed me. "My new best friend."

My lips twitched with a smile. Touché.

Alex reached out with both hands, taking Winter's and shaking it. "Hi, nice to meet you."

"You, too."

"Alex goes to school with Rika in the city," Will explained to Winter.

She nodded, and I chuckled to myself. Yeah, Will, that was how we knew her. Sure.

I lifted my drink to my mouth. "Is Alex for hire tonight?" I asked, gazing down her body, the caramel-colored gown perfectly accenting her deep brown hair.

Will turned his glare on me. "Fuck you."

"I'm completely serious," I maintained, turning to my wife. "Do you like her?"

I mean, she was all ready to bring another woman into our bed—or my bed—days ago, right? And this was Alex's job. As an escort, she should appreciate the business.

Arion remained quiet, her eyes falling and looking uncomfortable. "Damon, it's not the place."

"Do you like her?" I pressed, gazing down into her eyes and threading my finger under her necklace, gently pulling her mouth up to mine. "I like her. Tits for days and big eyes. I'd love to see those big eyes on me when she fucks you."

"Jesus," I heard someone mumble.

Another person sighed their aggravation.

But Winter remained silent. I could feel her, though. She was all I felt. I wanted her to hate this. To feel hurt that her eyes would never be on anyone, and she would never be as enjoyable or as sexy as Alex or Arion, because they could taunt with a single look.

She was pathetic, and less, and without. *Like I could've ever enjoyed you like a real woman. Is that what you thought, Winter?*

Arion kept her eyes down, not wanting what she was willing to do in the privacy of our bedroom displayed in public and in front of others.

Her lips pursed, but she finally answered. "You're in charge."

I quirked a smile, hating that she was so pliable, but glad Winter heard that. I didn't need her. I could get what I wanted from anyone. Let her sit on that in bed tonight.

Even if I didn't want it from just anyone.

I dropped my hand, peering over at Alex. "Is it still full price if I just watch?" I teased. "And if we do like a punch card, can you blow me on the eighth visit?"

Arion growled and spun around, walking away, while Ethan grabbed Winter's hand and left.

"Fucking piece of shit," Will said, turning to Alex. "Let's go."

I laughed, watching him walk away and thinking his little escort was following. Instead, Alex shook her head and sauntered over to stand at my side.

She crossed her arms, observing the party with me. "It is an art how quickly you can make everyone want to kill you."

I shrugged, hearing the smile in her voice. "I just can't help myself."

I took another drink, kind of wanting to kill myself for a second, too. The shit that came out of my mouth. All for Winter's sake, because she was my sole motivation in everything I did, and I was kind of fucking ashamed she had that power.

I didn't have to explain myself to Alex, though. She knew what I was doing. I respected her, because she was no nonsense and made no excuse to do what she needed to do to get what she wanted. The world respected people who didn't crave approval.

"How's the job going?" I inquired, glancing down at her.

Her brow shot up, looking dissatisfied. "It's almost not worth what you're paying me. That old fuck is agonizingly boring, Damon," she told me. "And pompous."

"I know."

Michael's father had information I needed, and I doubted he'd care that I put Alex into bed with him to get it. It was for a good cause.

"Are you getting close?"

She pulled a flash drive out of her bodice and held it up to me. "I was able to grab this. But there's more," she pointed out. "Gimme a few days."

I took it, hoping lots of good things were on it. For all our sakes. Her computer science minor was definitely a perk for this job.

"Make it two," I told her, "and you get a bonus."

I held up the flash drive, looking at it and pleased that everything was coming together. All the ducks. "Quack, quack," I mumbled, feeling fucking great all of a sudden.

Someone bumped into me, knocking my shoulder, and the flash drive fell to the ground.

"Oh, excuse me," a blonde woman dressed in a gray gown said.

She dove down and plucked the flash drive off the floor, and then stood up, raising her hand to give it back to me.

But she froze, meeting my eyes. Her face fell, and she didn't move except to breathe.

Christiane Fane. Rika's mother.

And even though she had a full-grown daughter and spent years on pills and alcohol, she was still incredibly beautiful. Her hair was loosely pinned back, strands framing her face, and her skin shimmered in the candlelight. Jewels hung from her ears, and her eyes flaunted several shades of blue that made them look exotic.

I wondered why my father never pursued her after her husband died. My mother had left by then, and Christiane was the wealthiest woman in town. She was gorgeous, still young enough to have more kids, and kind of stupid. I'd never understand how anyone remained that weak their entire lives, but here she was.

Why the fuck was she staring at me?

"Like what you see?" I smarted off, snatching the flash drive from her hand.

Jesus, go away.

She blinked, snapping out of it, and then dropped her head and walked away. Was she drunk or something? I thought Michael got her to kick that shit.

Whatever.

"So you going tell me what you're doing exactly?" Alex asked once she'd left.

I tucked the drive into my pocket, letting out a deep breath. "Getting my family back. I—"

But I didn't have a chance to finish. The string quartet stopped playing, and everyone exited the dance floor as I was sure a speech was about to start.

But it was Winter's voice I heard.

"I have a special gift for Michael and Erika," she said, and I moved a few steps to the right to get a view of her standing in the middle of the dance floor. "Something I hope they'll find entertaining. But..." she smiled, looking beautiful with her hair piled on top her head. "I hope the lovely couple doesn't mind—I'm dedicating this to my sister's new husband."

What?

And then she moved her head around the room. "Damon?" she called out, making everyone turn their heads in my direction.

"I worked very hard," she told me. "I hope you like it. You know how much I love Christmas."

Christmas? The village she wanted out of the basement when she was in high school sprung to mind, and I remembered that she decorated for the holiday the day after Halloween. Which would be soon.

My eyes didn't leave her as I took a step closer and placed my glass on a tray as the server passed.

She wouldn't dance for me. Not willingly anyway.

Finding her mark already placed on the dance floor, she settled into a traditional pose, one foot turned out, the other laying behind her, and her arms positioned down, forming a circle.

She never started like that. She always came in already moving, natural and unsophisticated. That was how she danced. Uncivilized. It was what I loved.

The music started, a slow, jazzy guitar sound, the beats all poised and separate. With each string, she moved. Controlled, routine, and trite, a new pose for every chord. Arm out, toe out. Arms up, feet moving from one elementary position to the next. There was no flow. It was like a warm-up.

But then the lyrics started, a deep and raw voice coming out of the sound system, and she popped up on her toes, stepping one foot in front of the other, her body all of a sudden coming to life and slinking from one move to the other.

And that's when the song registered. *You're a Mean One, Mr. Grinch.*

But it was a cover—some bluesy, rock variation—sexy, slow, and taunting.

I clenched my jaw.

Her shoulders rolled, one after the other, and her hips swayed to the music, her eyes closing and her neck bending like a seduction.

The drums kicked in, building up the song, and she jerked her body with every beat. Then she threw her head back, moved her arms, spun around, and rolled her head, pulling the pin holding her hair up, and it all came spilling down around her as the music let go and the singer's voice cried out its raw rendition.

"Whoo-hoo!" Shouts went off around the room as people started to lose control, and I balled my fists, watching her.

That wasn't fucking ballet. She may as well be taking her clothes off.

"Oh, hell yeah," some guy cheered.

"Shit, that's hot," another one chimed in.

Motherfucker.

She twirled and stepped, moving like sex and running her hands all over her body, the muscles of her toned thighs visible through the sheer skirt all the way up to her crotch. The leotard left nothing to the imagination. Her hair whipped around, falling in her face, and her lips parted, making her look hot and breathless. My cock warmed with the rush of blood, and I wanted nothing more than to give her the spanking she damn-well deserved out in the car right now.

God.

"Whoo!"

Michael's fucking basketball player buddies were going wild, and the song choice was not lost on me at all.

You're a Mean One, Mr. Grinch.

A Christmas song, indeed. And dedicated to me with its nasty lyrics meant to describe me, too.

Clever.

I shot my eyes over to Michael and Kai standing next to each other, both of them laughing and sharing words, enjoying this too much. Michael looked up at me, grinning like he won something, and Kai followed his gaze, laughing again. Winter publicly slighted me, and everyone was loving it.

She continued dancing, working every inch of the song and feeding off the crowd, and I buttoned my jacket, using every ounce of control to not lose my cool here.

Someone appeared, and I shifted my gaze away from the dance floor as Michael approached.

"You know what?" he said, laughing and patting me on both arms. "I'm feeling generous tonight. Forget what I said. You can stay as long as you like. Eat, drink…" He tossed a glance behind him to the dance floor and then turned back to me. "Because it looks like you have your hands full enough at home. Ouch."

I steeled myself, letting him walk away, but the air pouring out of my nose was damn near steam.

The song ended, the crowd cheered, and I saw Crane approach my side again as I watched Winter smile on the dance floor and soak up all that love at my expense.

"She needs to be disciplined," I said.

• • •

"Did you have fun?" I asked, hearing the front door close.

Headlights shone through the drapes, and I pushed my chair back and rose from the dining room table, Winter's dog popping his head up from my lap to let me up.

I knew she'd come home. Good girl.

And at one a.m., no less.

The headlights outside died, and I stalked into the dark foyer, seeing Winter still dressed in her costume from the party. I put my hand on her abdomen and walked into her, forcing her back against the door.

She sucked in a breath, planting her hands on my chest.

"Four hours," I scolded. "When I think of all the trouble you could've gotten up to in four hours…"

After her dance, she disappeared, and it only took Crane a few minutes to find out she'd left with Ethan Belmont, escaping while she could. I sent someone to his house, but no one was home.

Hopefully that was him who just dropped her off, too.

"I'm an adult," she shot back. "You have no power."

But just then protests and struggles rang out loud and clear as people entered the house.

"Get your hands off me!" Ethan shouted as Crane dragged him into the room from the side door in the dining room.

I kept my eyes on Winter, though, a smirk curling my lips.

Perfect timing.

A puzzled look crossed her face when she heard his voice. "Wha—what are you doing? Leave him alone."

I moved my hand to her jaw, holding it in one hand. "I think he touched you," I told her. "He kept you out after curfew."

She clutched my hand with both of hers, breathing hard.

"He's been dying to get you into bed. Judging from the naked pictures of you all over his bedroom wall, anyway."

"What?" she blurted out. "Stop it, Damon."

Belmont struggled against Crane's hold to my right.

"He's been photographing you," I told her, reporting what Crane found when he went to Belmont's house earlier. "I really hope you didn't know."

"It wasn't like that!" he yelled. "I just... Winter, they're not bad pictures. I promise."

I kept my stare on her. "They're bad to me," I bit out. "She's in her bathing suit, her shorts, bending over... All without her knowledge from the looks of it, am I right?"

"Spare me your concern about what happens without her knowledge!" he fired back. "You only care when it's not you taking advantage!"

I ground my teeth together. He wasn't lying exactly. But still...

"Winter?" he pleaded when she didn't say anything. "Winter, I just... It's not as bad as it sounds, okay?"

She shook, still trying to pry my hand off, but not trying as hard as she could. She didn't know who to trust, and she was struggling to figure out what to do or who to turn to. I just took away one of her only friends.

"They were candids," he explained. "You were so beautiful, I..." He stopped and then shouted at me, "You broke into my house?"

"Did you mess with her?" I demanded.

When he didn't answer, I shot in, whispering against Winter's lips. "If he touched you, I'll know," I told her. "Your skin will be red and flushed. Your lips will be swollen. His stink will be all over you."

She panted against me, and for a moment, I was reminded of our times together back in the day. When I whispered to hide my voice, but she was mine and I was hers, and she was in my lap, driving my car. Did she ever think about that?

I jerked my chin at Crane, and he spun Belmont around and landed a punch right into his stomach. The pipsqueak dropped like a ton of bricks, crumbling to his knees, coughing, and gasping.

"Again," I said.

But Winter piped up. "No!" she answered quickly. "He didn't touch me!"

"I didn't touch her," he said, wheezing and still coughing. "I would never hurt her."

I released Winter but kept my body on her, so she didn't move.

"Get him out of here," I said.

Crane picked up the kid on the floor, and after a moment, they were gone through the side door again. Headlights streamed through the window, there were shouts, and eventually doors slammed, and two engines drove off. He was probably worried about leaving Winter here with me, but Crane would make sure he got home, even if he had to give his car a little push with the SUV.

"You thought you were so fucking cute tonight with that little performance, didn't you?" I taunted. "Now, I like it when you misbehave, just do it in private where we both can take some pleasure in your punishment. You make me wait, it gets less fun for you."

"I hate you."

I pressed her back into the door again, and she sucked in a breath as my body molded to hers. She wouldn't look at me as I leaned down, smelling the remnants of her lip gloss still on her mouth. Where had the rest gone? Did he taste it tonight?

Or maybe she wore it because she knew I liked it.

Her little face turned away, so defiant. But she wasn't moving, either.

"Are you sure you hate me?" I asked in a low voice.

And I slipped a hand between her legs, swiping my fingers over the fabric of her leotard, and feeling what I knew would be there. She was seeping through. She was wet.

I brought my fingers up. "If he didn't touch you, then is this for me?"

She slammed me in the chest, and I stumbled back, letting her out.

"You're a monster. You're no better than him," she growled. "You played with me. You took advantage of me not being able to see, just like he did, and got exactly what you wanted. You abused me."

"Yeah." I nodded, getting back up in her face. "Yeah, I did. I got you any way I could. I..."

I stopped, finding myself losing control. I couldn't say too much.

"You wanted to be powerful," she said. "You wanted to win. You wanted revenge on my family and to cause pain, and you did. You humiliated me. You *wanted* to humiliate me. You wanted what you wanted, and you didn't care about me!"

I stared at her, knowing I would never explain myself.

She thought she knew everything. She thought it was black and white.

She thought I'd wanted to hurt her. She thought I'd meant for people to see that video. She thought I wanted to trick her.

The only motive I had was to be around her, and if I had to lie to get it...

I wasn't taking responsibility for everything. She liked it.

"I think I love you," I said, repeating her words to me all those years ago. "Don't stop. Please don't stop. I want you to be my first. It's okay. Touch me." I stepped up to her, invading her space and throwing all of her shame back at her. "You'll be the first to kiss me here." I flicked her ear. "And here." I touched her neck. "And here." I brushed her nipple with my thumb. "I want to feel your body on mine. Am I okay? Am I doing it right? It feels good. Don't stop. Oh, God. Oh, God. Don't walk away. Please, I want this. You don't have to protect me. You want it, too. I'm okay. I want it. I want to feel you so bad."

I threaded my hand through the back of her hair and fisted it, holding her still. "And then you spread those pretty legs for me."

"I thought you were someone else!"

"I was," I challenged. "I was someone you kinda liked."

She shook her head, more denying herself than me as tears welled in her eyes. "You were a lie," she said. "And all you are now is pathetic. You didn't earn a cent of the money you throw around, and those men don't guard you because you're Damon Torrance. They guard you because you're Gabriel's son. You're nothing!"

I shook her. *Bitch.*

"I was proof that people change," I told her.

"The only thing you're proof of is that not all males grow up to be men."

I released her, slamming my hand into the wall behind her. She shoved me away and darted around me, holding out her hands to find the bannister and scurrying up the stairs.

I hesitated for a moment before I ran after her, charging up the stairs.

I caught her and spun her around, holding her in my arms and crushing her to me. "Arion thinks I'm a man," I told her, keeping my voice low and taunting. "She'll touch me like I'm a man. She'll ride me in my bed and swallow me, because she wants what she thinks was yours."

Her jaw tightened, and she didn't move other than to breathe.

Do you want her to touch me? Do you even care?

"And she thinks she can do me better and erase you from my memory," I said.

"I don't care."

Her expression was flat, and her voice was mechanical.

I nodded, ignoring the needles in my throat. "Good," I said, feeling her breath on my mouth. "Because when you hear us tonight, I want you to know it's because I don't care, either. There's nothing of you for her to erase." I gripped the back of her head again, pressing her forehead into mine. "And in your bed tonight, when it's late and dark, and the rest of the house is quiet, except for my wife's moans down the hall and you're pissed and angry, because you think you hate me, but you slip a hand under the covers anyway, because no one will be the wiser if you indulge yourself in the memory of me, I just want you to also know..." I lowered my voice to a whisper, "that's what red feels like. Anger and fury and heat and need so strong you're a fucking animal, Winter. It's primal."

A tear spilled out of the corner of her eyes, and I could feel her fucking heart pounding in her chest.

I released her, pushing her away and backing up toward my bedroom. "I'll fuck her and make you come, too."

CHAPTER 13

Winter

SEVEN YEARS AGO

"I can always tell when they arrive," I remarked, sticking a nugget to the end of my fork. "You all get so quiet."

A few laughs go off around the lunch table as Noah, Rika, and the other girls check out the horsemen, whom I've also become aware of in my short time here. It was easy to notice when one or all of them entered a room. The chatter changed, there would be a whisper or two, and while I'd love to get caught up in the intrigues of Thunder Bay Prep, it was probably best I couldn't see how hot they reportedly were. We were freshman, and they were seniors and completely out of our league.

I already had a crush anyway. My insides tingled every time I thought about our escapades in the car and motorcycle last night. I was more than ready for my first kiss, and while I wasn't sure what his interest in me was, he clearly wasn't reading my deep-seated, teenage desire for some heat. Maybe he didn't see me like that at all.

After the motorcycle ride, we got into his car, he took me home, and I went to bed, no one in my family the wiser that I'd even been gone. I thought we would talk more, or I'd get some kind of idea if he'd be back and when, but he didn't say anything, and neither did I. That wasn't the last time I'd talk to him, right? I mean, that was no way to say goodbye.

I dreamt of him last night and woke up concocting a hot little fantasy in my head of him finding me years down the road and doing passionate things to me. I ached when I remembered I didn't want to wait that long to be with him again, though. If ever.

The only bright side I could find in possibly never feeling him again was that your first love was a learning experience. Or so my mom said. They're not the ones you marry, she told me. They're the ones who break you, so you can rebuild yourself better. Stronger.

But I didn't care. I wanted him to come back. I wanted him to hurt me. Just as long as he came back.

"What are they like?" I asked, breaking the silence and trying to change the subject. "The horsemen? Besides Damon, I mean?"

I already had an idea of the tool he'd turned into. I couldn't believe I'd suspected him to be my ghost. My guy was out of this world. And he didn't smoke, thank goodness.

"Well, Kai's the nicest," Rika's friend, Claudia, said.

"He's bad in all the right places, though," someone else teased.

"He and Damon look a lot alike," Claudia continued. "Both dark hair and eyes, but Kai's more...manicured, I guess you could say. Damon always looks like he just shifted back to his human form after being a wolf all night." She laughed. "His hair and clothes are never in order..."

"And Will?" I asked, trying to get the focus off Damon.

"Will's nice, too," Rika chimed in, "but he's not as sincere as Kai is, I think. He's good-looking and even better for a laugh. He treats girls better than Damon or Michael do, but...I don't know." She trailed off, pensive. "He's never serious. I don't think he's ever had a serious girlfriend like Kai has, has he?"

"Maybe his heart already belongs to someone he can't have," Claudia said.

"Aw."

"Yeah, like Damon," Noah chuckled. "They're very close. Like *really* close, I hear. He keeps Will on a leash. Figuratively speaking."

"And Michael?" I pressed.

"Michael."

"Michael."

"Michael."

They all sounded off around the table, and I heard Rika heave a sigh to my left.

"Rika knows all about him," Noah teased.

"Shut up, you guys," Rika scolded, sounding embarrassed.

After a moment, she spoke up, answering my question. "He's kind of the leader," she explained. "Probably on his way to the pros eventually. Light brown hair, golden skin, hazel eyes. Polar opposite of Will. He's very serious."

"Hazel eyes. Bedroom eyes," Claudia taunted. "Rika's slept in his bed. Did she tell you that?"

Slept in his bed? He had to be eighteen. Or almost anyway.

"I was thirteen," she explained, "and he put me there. It's not like he slept there, too. I told you guys that."

And then she spoke to me. "I grew up around him. Our families are close, so I'm at his house a lot."

"That's code for 'she loves him, will have his babies, and keep your damn paws off'," Noah told me.

I nodded once, heeding the warning. "Gotcha."

All of a sudden, music poured out of the speakers and commotion went off around us. People laughed and hooted, and I trained my ears, trying to figure out what was happening.

Was that seriously a Bobby Brown song?

"Oh, my God," someone said and laughed.

"What?" I asked. "What's going on?"

"Will Grayson is dancing," Rika answered, sounding like she was embarrassed for him. "Oh, my God, he's on a table."

Everyone in our area broke into laughter, and whatever he was doing must've been entertaining.

"My Prerogative" blared, and I couldn't help but smile and bob my head a little bit. It was a fun choice of music. I'd probably like Will.

"Such a lover, not a fighter," someone said.

"He's so hot," Claudia added.

"If you ever fall for one of them, make it Will or Kai, got it?" Noah said over the table, and I guessed it was to me. "They'll at least hold you for ten seconds after it's over."

I let out a nervous laugh and picked at my food. Okay, maybe I wouldn't like any of them, after all.

"Guys, be quiet," Rika said and then to me, "They're just joking with you."

Got it. And no worries. I'd steer clear of spoiled seniors. Although, I wondered what my ghost would do if someone liked me. Would he care? Would he know? He could be in the room right now? Hell, he could be Noah.

But I got rid of that notion. I'd held Noah's arm on the way to Music Appreciation. It wasn't like *his* body. Not as tall, not as strong. My insides didn't do pirouettes when I touched him.

As the music played, though, and everyone was lost in the distraction of Will Grayson's exhibition, everything started to fade way—the laughter, music, and noise becoming distant as it fell to the background and echoed from somewhere far away.

I wanted to feel him again.

I felt him again. Like I was in his lap, driving. Or huddled behind him, warm but freezing in the night air on the motorcycle. Or wrapped tightly in his arms, hidden in a closet, a world within a world.

I wished he was close. I wished he was watching me. Always watching me. I tucked my hair behind my ear, turning my head toward the direction where I would imagine he was, and reveled in the feeling of his eyes being on me.

"Are you okay?" Rika asked.

The music cut off, and I heard a teacher scolding someone—probably Will—and I nodded. "Yeah." I dropped my plastic fork and wiped my fingers on a napkin. "When you're done, would you mind pointing me to the library? I'm going to hang out and listen to some of the readings until class. I'll have the librarian's assistant help me to the next class."

"Yeah," she said. "I'm done now. Let's go."

We picked up our bags, tossed out our lunches, and headed for the doors. But as we went, I smiled to myself, the feeling of him still in my head and his eyes watching me, following me and never leaving me as I exited the cafeteria.

• • •

"How about right here?" Rika asked me. "It's empty and quiet."

I nodded, reaching the third floor of the library and feeling for the chairs nearby. I found a cushy couch instead and dropped my bag, taking a seat and digging out my phone and earbuds.

"I need to run to the office and get some fliers printed for the Math Club," she explained. "I can swing by as soon as I'm done and get you for English."

"Oh, no, it's fine," I told her, plugging in my earbuds and relaxing into the corner of the couch. "I'll find someone. Or...maybe I'll go wild and find class myself."

"Don't do that," she scolded.

I smiled, half-joking and half not. English One was the first door across the hall from the stairwell upstairs, and the stairwell was right outside the library to the left. I was sure

I could make it. And after driving an actual car last night, I kind of wanted to try. It would be the extent of my fun for the day.

But I put her at ease anyway, knowing she still felt guilty about me getting shoved into the locker room. "I'm kidding," I told her. "I'll be fine. Someone will help me. I promise."

"Okay," she acquiesced. "I'll see you in class."

I gave a little wave and stuck in my earbuds, starting the audiobook chapter on Native American tribes and early colonization. I made sure not to put the volume too high, though, so I could hear the first bell alerting me that lunch was over, and I had five minutes to get to class.

I leaned my head back, closed my eyes, and listened to the woman's voice go over tribes of eastern America and Canada and trade with European settlers. Out of all the audiobooks for my classes, I enjoyed this one the most. Her voice was sweet and soft with lots of inflection like she was telling a bedtime story.

Except for Algebra, which was always hard and I had little care for, since I knew I wouldn't have a career where it would be useful, all my classes were going surprisingly well. My teachers were helpful, and it was getting less awkward to have conversations with them and be open about what I needed. I mean, schools accommodated for learning disabilities, poverty, illness, and severe behavioral problems. By comparison, I couldn't be that great of a burden, right?

My parents—and Arion—had really done a number on me. While it was the psycho-stalker-sicko who made me smile and gave me confidence. Go figure.

Life was weird.

I needed to ask him questions when I met him again. If I met him again. He wouldn't answer just because I wanted him to, though. I'd have to pry it out of him, like dancing the entire *Nutcracker* Suite in exchange for his frickin' name.

I snorted but quickly got rid of my smile just in case anyone was watching me and wondered what my deal was.

And then I noticed it. A sound piercing the air, loud and cutting the quiet with a sharp ring that made me wince.

"What the hell?" I said to myself.

I yanked out my earbuds, finally realizing what it must be.

Was that...?

A fire alarm sliced into my ears like nails across a chalkboard tenfold, and I sat up, trying to listen for voices to hear if this was real or a drill or what.

"Don't run!" the librarian, I would assume, called out. "Walk and exit the building like you've been taught." And then a shout. "No running!"

"Wait," I said, clutching my phone and gathering up my backpack. "Wait!"

I knew how to get to the stairwell, but I wasn't sure about the exit. It was one floor down, but after that, I thought it was down the hall and to the right at the end of the lockers? Maybe?

I heard the heavy library doors open and close repeatedly, and I yelled, "Wait!"

Hugging my backpack to me, I grabbed hold of the railing and barreled down the stairs as fast as I could, but the earbud cord dangling from my phone caught under my step, and it was yanked out of my hand, pummeling to the end of the first landing. It tumbled off somewhere, and I fell to my knees, dropping my bag as I pawed the ceramic tile, trying to look for it.

There wasn't a real fire, right? It was just a drill.

Waving my hands all over, I found the cord and yanked it to me, but the phone wasn't attached anymore. I slammed my palm onto my thigh in frustration. "Dammit."

Screw it. It was replaceable, and if anyone found it, it had a lock code, so they couldn't get in.

I left my shit on the floor and made my way down the rest of the stairs, the alarm still blaringly loud.

But I didn't hear anything else. There were no voices, no movement, no doors being slammed... Was everyone already gone?

My heart started to thump harder. *What do I do? Shit!*

Half the school was in the lunchroom. They would've just gotten out through the exit in there. The rest of the school—everyone in classes or the auditorium—wouldn't be gone yet. Right?

"Hello?" I called out.

I waved my hands in front of me, trying to veer in the direction the doors were in, but I walked right into something hard and hissed at the pain in my shin. I grabbed hold of a wooden chair that had been left untucked from the table in the rush to get out.

My hands finally found the wall, and I scaled them down until I found the doors that led into the rest of the school. Opening one, I stepped through.

"Hello!" I shouted again. "Can someone help me? I don't know my way out!"

The alarm pinged again and again down the hallway, and I inhaled through my nose, smelling smoke.

No. I paused. *Not smoke.*

It was a cigarette.

Had someone been smoking in the school?

But then my face fell as I breathed in the faint scent that reminded me of the last time I smelled that.

My heart started to race, and not in a good way.

Finding the stairwell, I descended one flight and found my way through the entrance to the main floor.

"Hey!" I called out again. "Anyone?"

I inched to the right side of the hall, the locker doors clanking against their frames as I moved from one to the other.

Even if it was a real fire, firefighters would be here soon. I couldn't be completely alone.

"Hello?" I demanded. "Hello! Anybody there? I need help!"

I followed the path of the lockers, trailing down the right side of the hallway. When I came to the end, I rounded the corner and pawed the wall until another row of lockers began.

Okay, okay, okay... If I followed this, and kept going straight, it should lead me to the doors leading to the front of the school.

"Hello?" I called again.

My hands shook.

I should've told Rika to come back for me. Why was I so stubborn? Even if she was forced to exit the building by the teachers, she would've known to tell them that I was in the library waiting for her, and they would've sent someone to get me.

"Hello?"

Then, all of a sudden, there was a pounding on the lockers ahead.

I paused for a split-second, listening.

"Hey," I said to whoever was down there. "Can you help me? Is everyone outside? Can you help me get out?"

But there was no answer.

The sound happened again. *Bang, bang, bang...* on the lockers, and I narrowed my eyes, confused.

"Can you help me?" I shot out, trailing down the lockers faster. "Please, can you..."

My hands landed on a tall body with a broad chest in a collared shirt, and I jerked back.

It was a man, but I thought I felt a tie hanging around his neck. A student?

"Is there a fire?" I asked him. "What's going on?"

But whoever it was didn't say anything. *Were we the only ones in the building?*

I opened my mouth to speak, but his hand came up, tucking my hair behind my ear.

There was no way I'd be the victim of two weird guys in such a short time.

I cocked my head. "Is that you?" I demanded.

My ghost who liked to scare me?

I lost my patience. "So help me God, I'm going to—"

He slipped his arms underneath mine, wrapping them around me, and picked me up off my feet.

"Going to what?" he asked.

And I stopped breathing. It wasn't the whisper I was used to hearing but the deep, loaded, and menacing tone I never wanted to be alone with again.

Ever.

I gulped, feeling Damon's arms tighten around me. "You're not him."

"Him who?"

"L—Let me go," I stammered but didn't have time to scream.

He whipped us around, carrying me away, and I pushed at his body to get away.

A door opened, then closed, and I was forced back into the room, my combat boot hitting something on wheels. A bucket, I think. We must be in a closet.

My mind raced. The bucket would have a mop. That was a weapon.

"You did this?" I asked, realization finally hitting me. The alarm. He and I alone in the school. Did he see Rika leave me alone in the library?

"What do you want?" I yelled and then shouted at the top of my lungs, "Help!" I sucked in another breath. "Help!"

His hand found my throat, and I was pinned to the wall. I grabbed his wrist, fighting to pull it off.

"What do you want?" I struggled to speak, rage coursing through my veins.

His body came in close as he spoke down to me. "Are you scared?"

I shifted on my feet, struggling with his hand on my neck. "No," I gritted out.

"Liar."

"Fuck you!" I fired back. "Let me out!"

I kicked at his leg, but he didn't budge. I kicked him again, harder, and twisted my body out of his grasp, finally feeling him lose his hold. I ran for it, but he grabbed hold of my necktie and yanked me back to him.

My body slammed into his. "Let me out!" I screamed again. "My sister is ready for you. Always ready for you. Why don't you bring her in here?"

He picked me up again, this time wrapping his arms around me like a steel band, my arms pinned to my body under his tight hold.

"Why bother with her when there's you?" he taunted. "I like you."

I shook my head at him. He was horrible. And disgusting and sick, and I hated that I had his attention. I wished he'd never laid eyes on me. Was this it then? Was he going to hurt me again? It wouldn't be like last time. I was old enough to know how men hurt women now.

"You know, a lot of girls would love to be in your position right now," he told me.

"Yeah, I'm guessing you didn't almost kill them once upon a time."

"Do you want me to apologize?"

I hesitated, because his tone actually gave the impression he would apologize if I asked him to. "No," I finally answered.

"Why?"

"Because I won't forgive you anyway," I said.

No need to waste your time.

He held me, his chest moving with mine, and I could feel his eyes on my face. He didn't speak for several seconds.

When he did, it sounded almost sad. "Winter..."

But whatever he wanted to say, he didn't finish, and I didn't care. I wasn't going to spend another six years recovering from anything he did to me. Another scratch, and I'd kill him to make sure he never touched me again.

"Aren't you worried I'll hurt you?" he asked, his tone threatening again.

I replied calmly. "No."

"Why?"

"Because black."

"Black?" he pressed.

I inched in, getting in his face. "Because I'm in the black right now, and here... I think I enjoy myself," I said, remembering last night and the freedom of risking and fighting and meeting your match. I wanted that life. "The only part of me anyone can ever hurt is my heart, and there's no one on the planet my heart is more out of reach from than you," I growled.

He jostled me in his arms, and I could hear him breathing through his teeth.

"Big words for such a little girl," he said.

"Same old, same old, from the same, scared little boy," I shot back. "Still climbing into fountains to hide from Mommy?"

"Mommy?" he repeated. "I killed that bitch last night."

I faltered, unnerved he would say something so odd. Of course, he was just talking shit. I'd heard his mother, Madame Delova, left Thunder Bay a few years ago and never returned.

What the hell was the matter with him? Did he want my father putting a restraining order on him? I hated Damon Torrance, but even I didn't want that. It would just make my parents worry to learn I was having problems with him at school, and Thunder Bay would be like being in a frying pan if I got one of the school's star players in trouble. Everyone would see it as my fault.

"Let me go," I told him. "Let me go or I'll bite."

"Exactly what I had in mind."

What? Why would he want me to bite him?

"Let me go," I said.

He didn't budge.

"Let. Me. Go."

Nothing.

Diving in, I sank my teeth into his jaw, hearing him let out a chuckle, and bit down harder to shut him the hell up.

Asshole.

I couldn't reach much, given my position, otherwise I'd go for his ear and tear it off, but I clamped down on his bone, my teeth digging into the skin.

Harder. I increased the pressure. *Harder.*

He froze, just standing there, and when his breathing became raspy, I knew he was about to tap out and let me go. It had to hurt.

But instead of freeing me, he stuttered, "Har—Harder."

Rage twisted my face, and I bit down as hard as I could, my teeth aching in my jaw, and I heard him pant and gasp, and then his arms fell, and I was free. I fell to the ground and pushed him away, knocking him in the nose.

He grunted and stumbled, because I heard the shuffle of buckets and brooms.

"Next time, I'll be armed. And I'll kill you," I told him.

I began to walk away, and I heard his voice behind me. "You might have to."

I stopped for a second, feeling defeated. Why? Why would I have to? Would he not stop? What did he want?

"Would you have forgiven me..." he asked, "if I'd gone over the side of the treehouse with you that day?"

I stood there, tears burning the backs of my eyes.

I didn't know how to answer. I searched my brain. Why did that question strike me like it did? It seemed almost vulnerable. It was the first moment since I'd started school here that he hadn't acted like an asshole.

Would I have forgiven him if he'd been hurt, too? I could've died that day. I could've been hurt a lot worse than I was now. My neck could've broke. I could've wound up in a coma for the rest of my life.

And he could've gone over with me and been hurt and killed, too. What would be my thoughts about him now if that had happened? Would I be more forgiving?

Maybe.

I thought about it.

Yes. I would've said 'kids are kids' and 'bad things happen'. Children weren't mature enough to control themselves. I would've tried to understand.

But even if I didn't hate what he'd done to me all those years ago, I still hated him because of who he was now. Boys grew up. He hadn't.

"I should've known it was you," someone suddenly growled and I finally registered that the door to the closet had swung open.

I sucked in a breath and straightened as people barreled in, someone taking my hand and leading me out.

Five minutes later we were in the dean's office, a loud slap piercing the air.

"She is a freshman!" Dean Kincaid bellowed at Damon. "Do you have any shame?"

I stood there, my hands locked behind my back as Damon and I stood a few feet apart in front of Kincaid's desk.

Damon coughed and sniffled next to me. "I think she hurt me more than I hurt her," he said, his breathing labored. "I'm bleeding like a stuck pig. You might just be my type, girl."

He laughed, and I ground my teeth together. I hadn't realized I'd bit his jaw *that* hard. Or maybe it was from when I hit his nose.

Either way, good.

"You're expelled," Kincaid bit out, his tone clipped. "I don't care what your father threatens me with. We're going to end up on the goddamn national news because of you!"

"Expel me?" Damon challenged. "The alumni will love that. And perfect timing, too. Your contract is up for review. Wait till they hear you don't like winning basketball games."

Something slammed on the desktop in front of us, and I jumped.

I closed my eyes, exasperated. *Oh, my God.* He was a piece of work. And he was going to win, too. Kincaid wasn't going to expel him. Not with wealthy, connected alumni caring more about athletics than they did education.

Wait until Damon actually grew up and realized the whole world wasn't going to bend over for him forever.

It was only a matter of time for me, though. Before he'd be too much to take, and something would have to be done. Dealing with all the anger and attitude in the school for getting him expelled or taking myself and going back to Montreal. I didn't want to leave. That would be a sure way never to see him again. The ghost. Whoever he was.

But life here would be intolerable if Damon backed me into a corner and I had to fight back. No one would be on my side.

I swallowed the bitter taste in my mouth. "Don't bother, Mr. Kincaid," I muttered. "I'm leaving the school."

"The fuck you are," Damon growled. And then to Mr. Kincaid, "It was just a disagreement. I'll leave her alone. You have my word."

"Your word..." he mocked.

"I don't lie," Damon said, anger hardening his voice. "She'll be fine. I swear. I won't even look at her for the rest of the year, as long as I'm at this school and under your care. I promise." He evened out his tone. "The basketball team goes on, she can stay, and we'll pretend this never happened. Her father doesn't have to know." And then to me, "Right?"

I hardened my jaw, standing there and not giving him an ounce of my attention. Was he telling the truth? Could he stay out of my way?

Because I was desperate to stay.

"I will leave her alone," Damon reiterated again when the dean remained silent.

"Sir," a woman called behind us.

"Don't move," Kincaid told us, and I heard him walk past us and step onto the stones of the main office. The door stayed open, and I could hear voices out there.

And then I felt him next to me, his warm breath just above my ear.

"Enjoy your freedom while it lasts, Winter Ashby, because we're not done," Damon warned in a low voice that snaked through my ear, taunting me. "Grow up, learn things, and have fun in high school, but don't change the little girl who loves it 'in the black', because I like you there, too. And I will be back for what's mine when you're old enough for bigger things."

I turned my face away, breathing harder.

"And be good," he told me. "If I hear anyone touched you, I will crack his fucking skull."

My mouth went dry, my stomach rolling as the voices outside grew closer, and then his heat was gone as he put space between us and Kincaid walked back into the room.

Damn him.

The meeting ended, Kincaid doling out harsh words for Damon but accepting his terms and promising to hold him to it. The dean didn't trust him or like him, but the politics of Thunder Bay society would win over a man who feared for his job and position. He was an educator second and an employee of every parent in this town first.

Someone from the office got me and guided me to my next class, everyone now back inside after the false alarm, and as I walked out of the main office, turning right as Damon went left, I wondered how long I had and how many notches up he would take his behavior when we met again.

Because it wasn't over.

He was just waiting.

Chapter 14

Winter

Present

I blinked my eyes, waking up, and immediately winced as I rolled off my side and onto my back. *Shit.* Pain shot through the left side of my neck, and I bent it, trying to stretch it out. I didn't think I moved all night. My whole body was kinked up. I never slept that deep.

Sitting up, I slid my legs over the side of the bed, rolling my neck and ankles before stretching my toes to a point.

"Ugh," I groaned.

I was exhausted. I rubbed my eyes, feeling that they were a little swollen and achy.

Then it came back to me. The dance at Michael and Erika's engagement party last night. Damon and me. Damon trying to taunt me with what he was going to enjoy with my sister.

I'd cried. A lot.

I'd come to bed, locked my door, and sobbed into my pillow, because I couldn't stop myself, and I didn't want to be heard.

I hated him. I hated his vile words and his cigarettes and his arrogance and insanity in thinking he wasn't responsible for anything. I hated how he grabbed and threatened and wouldn't let me go. He had no right.

And I hated that I'd missed him. I hated that so fucking much.

How I still felt the parts about him I loved when I didn't know it was him I was with. How his arms around me still felt protective and how his whispers reminded me of when I loved the feel of them all over my neck.

I shook my head. It was an act. It had all been an act. He'd used me.

I stood up and closed my eyes, stretching my arms over my head to wake up my body.

A light rain tapped my window, and I inhaled, smelling it seeping into the house as I tried to clear my head. Coffee first.

A creak sounded above me, and I tipped my head back, training my ears on the sound. Who would be in the attic? No one went up there except servants, and we no longer had any of those. Full time ones, anyway.

Stepping over to my chaise, I picked up the sweater laying on it and pulled it on, rubbing my arms against the chill. I pulled my hair up into a ponytail and removed my chair lodged under my doorknob before unlocking my bedroom door and swinging it open. Not that anything would stop Damon from getting into this room if he wanted, but at least it would take more than one kick and give me a warning bell of sorts when I was dead asleep at night.

I stepped into the hallway, the cool wood under my feet creaking as I yawned.

So quiet.

I stood there, hearing the rain outside create a shield of white noise around the house, and somewhere, deep in the house, a breeze whistled through a cracked window or wall. A chickadee sang in the distance, every little sound amplified, because there was nothing else drowning them out. No noise.

No television. No hair dryer. No shower running.

No footsteps or dishes clattering or doors opening and closing.

"Hey, Google," I called back into my room. "What time is it?"

"The time is seven-oh-three a.m."

We were early risers. My mom and Arion worked out in the morning, while I got plenty of exercise dancing.

But we'd been to a party last night. Maybe they were sleeping in?

Or maybe not. Something felt off.

Why hadn't they intervened in my fight with Damon last night? They had to have heard it.

"Mom?" I called out over the railing. She was normally already up and moving around the house when I woke up. "Mom, are you up?"

Nothing.

Grazing the railing, I trailed down the hall and into my mother's room first, cracking open the door. "Mom?" I said lightly, afraid to startle her out of her sleep.

There was no response.

I inched into the room and found my way to her bed, running my hands across the smooth, cold comforter. The bed was still made. Or had she already made it up after rising?

Walking over to where her vanity sat, I found the lamp and touched the bulb, tapping it and then holding it when I realized it was cold.

The only time this lamp was off was at night or when she wasn't home.

My pulse quickened.

I left her room and made my way down to Arion's in the master suite, calling her name as I entered, too. "Arion?" I said. "Are you here?"

I checked her bed and her lamps, her room in the same untouched state as my mother's. I walked over to the closet she shared with Damon, not going in, though.

"Ari?" I called. She could be in his room.

His room.

My teeth ached, and I unclenched my jaw, leaving the room and heading back to mine.

Grabbing my phone off the bedside table, I searched my apps, finding Uber, and ordered a car using VoiceOver to help me navigate. I forwent typing "assist" in the promotional code to let the driver know I had a disability. I was in a hurry, and no one in this town didn't not know me, so we'd muddle through.

I slipped on some jeans, a T-shirt and jacket, and pulled on a baseball cap. After I got my shoes and socks on, I stuffed some cash from my stash into my wallet and stuck it into my pocket with my phone.

Heading downstairs, I called for my dog. "Mikhail!"

I pulled out my phone, checking the driver's location.

"Four minutes," VoiceOver read.

"Mikhail!" I shouted again, pulling his leash out of the drawer in the foyer table.

Something creaked above me again, and I shook my head, going breathless.

Something was wrong. That wouldn't be my family. I called their names. They didn't answer. Where were they?

Damon, what have you done?

I heard a noise, like the refrigerator closing, and maybe...

"Mom!" I yelled.

What was that? Where was my dog?

Racing into the kitchen, I halted, facing the direction of the refrigerator. "Hello? Who's there?"

No answer.

Shit. I lunged, swinging open the back door. "Mikhail!"

Rain pattered the terrace and awnings, and I couldn't hear him. He would come in if it was raining, and it he didn't, he'd be huddled right outside this door. No jingling leash telling me he was running for me or whining to get out of the water. Where did he go?

Two footfalls hit the floor above me, and I stopped breathing.

Damn you. The fear of that night seven years ago when he first messed with me came flooding back, only this time, I doubted my dancing could get me out of this.

I slipped my hand in my pocket, finding the house keys already there, and fitting two between my fingers as a weapon. I closed the door, hearing my phone ding, probably with the notification that my ride was here. I gripped the leash in one hand, the keys in the other, and backed up a step.

The floor whined to my right as someone stepped, and I tried to inhale but couldn't. Then something clicked from somewhere in the house, a door softly closing.

Weight settled on one of the stairs, and I heard the rings on a curtain slide along a rod. Closing.

More movement in the attic, and in my head, I'd already run.

Go. I forced every ounce of energy to pool in my legs as I gripped my weapons, spun around, and bolted out of the kitchen, taking the straight shot all the way to the front door.

I grabbed the handle, whipped it open, and flew outside into the rain and cool morning air. I slammed right into a car and fumbled with the door handle, finally opening it.

"Jesse?" I said the driver's name I got from the app.

"Yeah, you okay?"

I scurried inside, barely registering the cackling I heard coming from inside my house since I'd left the door open.

Asshole.

My heart was trying to jump out of my goddamn chest.

And it still didn't answer where my family was. Or my dog.

"Lock the doors," I told him.

He did and took off, rounding the fountain and heading for St. Killian's, the address I'd already entered into the app.

I put my head back, still gripping the leash in my hand. *Mikhail.* God, he wouldn't hurt him, would he? The dog was coming to me less and less. I didn't know if he was warming to Damon or hiding in fear.

Rain spattered the windshield, and the driver stayed quiet as he drove, probably noticing that I was out of sorts.

It was a short drive. St. Killian's wasn't too far from my house if you were in a car. I'd learned from Will that Michael and Rika had an apartment in Meridian City, but they spent almost as much time in Thunder Bay now in their newly renovated home. An old, abandoned cathedral that overlooked the sea.

In no time, the driver turned off the highway, and I expected to feel the gravel I remembered from years ago when I came out here, but there was no crunch of rock underneath the car. It was paved now, and I imagined they'd also manicured the land around the church. Italian cypresses lining the driveway, maybe. A fountain or statue or maybe flowery display in front of the house.

He stopped and put the car in *Park*, and I grabbed the door handle, ready to get out, since the ride had already been charged to my card on file.

"Would you mind guiding me to the front door?" I asked.

"Yeah, sure."

He got out of his side, and I climbed out of the car, meeting him as he came around. I didn't know him, but it wasn't a big town. He probably knew I was blind.

I took his arm and he led me across the driveway and up to the house.

"There's stairs," he warned.

"Gotcha," I replied, finding the first step. "And the door is directly at the top?"

"Yep."

"Okay, I got it from here," I told him.

"You sure?"

"Yeah, thank you."

Rika told me to come over today to hang out, so I knew she'd be home. It was early, though.

The driver left me and walked back to his car, and I wanted him to wait for me, but they didn't work like a taxi. I would just have to order another ride later.

I reached the top of the stairs and searched for a doorbell but didn't find one. Locating a knocker, though, I rapped it twice and waited.

Please be home. Please be awake.

Damon's friends—former friends, I'd learned—were the only people he could threaten all day and never hurt. They were just as powerful, if not more. He could be stopped.

I rapped the knocker again, three times this time, and waited, the rain growing a little heavier now as thunder cracked overhead.

"Hello?" I called, knowing it was useless. If they hadn't heard the massive piece of iron hitting the door...

I grabbed the door handle, a heavy metal ring in keeping with the medieval style I knew the cathedral sported, and twisted, the door magically giving way and opening.

That meant they were up, at least.

"Hello, anybody home?" I called. "It's Winter Ashby."

I stepped inside and closed the door, inhaling the most amazing scent. A mixture of coffee, vanilla, and stone. I could feel the air above me and knew the ceiling was sky high. It smelled spacious with lots of fresh air. This place would be a nightmare to heat, though.

"Hello?" I said.

Still no answer. I dug out my phone.

"Dial Erika Fane," I said.

My phone chimed, and after a moment I heard my line start to ring, and then I heard her phone receive the call somewhere in the house. Her ringtone played "Fire Breather" by LAUREL above me, and I smiled, following the sound. I didn't want to invade her home, but I really didn't have time to lose.

"Hello?" I sing-songed again.

They had to be here. I got closer to the ring, my foot hitting a step, and I climbed it, finding her phone a few stairs up. I picked it up just as it stopped ringing and went to voicemail. I ended my call.

I took another step, but this time, it brushed something, and I bent down, picking up a long and full mess of fabric. A dress.

"Keep the necklace on," I heard Michael say. "Just the necklace."

Huh?

I took another step but heard a moan and halted.

"You're the most beautiful woman I've ever seen," he said, his breathing labored. "You were always the sweetest little thing."

"Michael," Rika gasped.

Oh, shit. I dropped the dress and shot my hand to my mouth, scared they would hear my breathing. They must've just gotten home. Wonder what they did last night after the party.

I took a slow and careful step back down the stairs.

"But you are keeping things from me," he told her.

And I stopped.

"I like it when you have your secrets," he went on, his voice hot and threatening. "It drives me insane in all the best ways. And maybe I have secrets, too."

"You want me to be suspicious of you?" she challenged.

But then she let out a breathy groan, and I took another step down, the wooden stair whining under my weight.

Fuck! I stopped, my face etched in pain. They hadn't heard that, had they? *Please, please, please...* Did they even have wooden stairs in the original cathedral? Wouldn't they have been stone? Stone doesn't make noise.

"You're not suspicious?" he asked. "I spend a lot of time out of town, Rika. I can get whatever I want from anyone I want."

She whimpered. "Yeah, you can, but you don't."

"How do you know?"

The bed creaked, moans and breathing followed, and I shook my head, wishing I was deaf instead.

They were fighting.

While they were having sex.

It was weird.

"Because you're not stupid," she threw back at him. "No one will feel like me on your body."

The headboard banged into the wall faster and faster, and my head filled with their grunts and moaning, their panting picking up pace.

"Rika," he breathed out.

"You would never risk losing this," she taunted.

"No," he agreed. "I don't want anything but this. Fuck, baby."

"I love you, Michael," she whispered loudly as they got caught up in what they were doing. "I've always loved you."

And I stood there, no longer wincing or dreading my invasion of their privacy but feeling everything they were feeling and wanting more.

The skin touching skin. My body on fire and alive with him. His breath. His tongue. His mouth and hands. His teeth nipping at my stomach and thighs.

That feeling of wanting nothing else, and I would rather never eat again than not have him.

I don't want to...make you dirty.

"I will find out what you're keeping from me," Michael growled as the bed rocked.

"You can try."

"I should pull out right now and fucking leave you like this."

"No, please," she whimpered.

"Or maybe I'll just have lots of fun getting the answer out of you. Flip over."

Weight shifted, her body turning over maybe, and I knew the position they were in. I hadn't done that yet, but I wanted to. Someday.

You won't make me dirty. There is no you. There is no me. This is us. Us.

My eyes burned, and my chin trembled. I didn't want to do those things with just anyone, though.

A body pressed into my back and I blinked, swallowing the tears in my throat.

"I was supposed to come to you for our next appointment," Will teased, resting his head on my shoulder.

Upstairs, Rika and Michael went at it, growing louder and harder.

"Don't worry," he said, and I could hear the smirk in his voice. "I won't tell them you were eavesdropping."

I turned around, but he wouldn't let me leave. I smelled liquor on his breath. Had he not been to bed yet, either?

"You have this look on your face," he told me, keeping his voice low and intimate. "Are you wishing someone would do that to you or are you *remembering* when someone did that to you?"

That. Meaning Michael and Rika's fucking.

I pushed past him and descended the stairs, finding my way through the great room and to the front door again.

"Need a ride home?" he asked.

"You're drunk." I pulled the door open. "I'll call someone."

I slammed the door, not caring if Michael and Rika heard me at that point, and walked down the stairs, rain pummeling my hat and shoulders.

The door behind me opened again, and before I knew it, I was swung around, engulfed in strong arms, with a mouth on mine and tongue inside me.

I grunted, trying to push him away as I tasted the faint remnants of whiskey, his tongue brushing mine and playing with me. Forced up on my toes, Will devoured me, gripping the back of my neck, his breath and heat filtering through my body like syrup, down to my toes. Every inch of me suddenly starving.

He pulled away from my mouth, but kept me in his arms. "You need to get fucked and bad," he told me. "If you don't want him to do it, I will." Then he leaned in, whispering over my mouth. "And I would make that offer sober."

He let me go, and I inhaled shallow breaths, the cool rain welcome on my hot skin.

"See you soon, Winter," he taunted and went back into the house.

I stood there for a moment, waiting to get my shaking under control before I ordered another ride.

He might be right. I was twenty-one, plenty old enough to have a healthy, active sex life, but when it did happen again, I wanted it to be like it was for Erika and Michael. They seemed to like to play games, but it was passionate, and it was love.

The love was what felt good. Unfortunately, it had been one-sided in my past experience. I could be tempted to take Will up on his offer to let off some steam, but he wouldn't be more than that. I wanted him as a friend.

The real question was, was he on Damon's side or mine?

• • •

I pulled the leash out of my pocket, letting the heavy, metal clip at the end dangle at my side.

Where the hell was my dog?

"I'm not sure what you heard, Miss Ashby," Crane told me, as he walked back into the foyer from the rear of the house. "But no one was home except you this morning. Damon left for the city before you were even awake, I was taking care of some errands, and there was no one else here."

I stood just inside the open door to my house, the rain pouring in fat drops on the driveway behind me.

"And my family?"

"They left last night after the party." I heard him open a drawer on one of the tables and pull out keys. "I took them to the airport myself."

"Left?" I blurted out. "What do you mean?"

My mother and Ari were gone? Without me?

"Yes, the Maldives for the honeymoon," he informed me as if he were reminding me. "Damon sent Mrs. Ashby and Mrs. Torrance on ahead without him. He's supposed to join them in a few days."

"Wait, so they were already gone when I came home last night?"

I felt dizzy, my head like a balloon floating away from my body. The confrontation with Damon played in slow motion in my mind, reprocessing everything we said and the threats he made, and all the while, they weren't even in the house. His taunts about what he and Ari were going to do had been empty, and I'd gone to bed under this roof, alone in the house with him, with absolutely no security that my family was close.

"Yes, ma'am," Crane finally answered.

I pulled off my baseball cap and fisted the top of my hair, closing my eyes. *Fuck.*

I didn't just imagine it this morning. There was someone in the house with me. Several someones, to be exact. All those noises and movements happening simultaneously in different parts of the house? I wasn't just scared and overly alert of every little creak. I knew what I heard, dammit.

And then someone messing with me in the theater bathroom that night? Damon claimed it wasn't him. This all had to be him.

"I've searched the house, top to bottom," he said. "There's nothing here."

"Like I would trust you," I snapped.

He worked for that monster. He was paid to fall in line and protect Damon's interests, not mine.

And Damon had a very long history of loving to scare me.

Crane didn't argue, though. He just bowed out. "Excuse me, ma'am."

He walked past me, his keys jingling, so I assumed he was leaving, and I called out, keeping my voice stern. "My dog is missing," I told him. "Would you please take a look around the property before you leave?"

"Yes, Miss Ashby."

"And my friend?" I inquired. "He got home safely last night?"

"Yes, ma'am."

I couldn't talk to Ethan after what I'd learned, but I didn't want him lying in a ditch somewhere, either.

"And you will not hurt him or involve him—or anyone else—any further," I stated rather than questioned.

"Mr. Torrance would say you're the one to answer that question, ma'am."

Oh, I'm sure he would.

If I ran, if I complained, if I embarrassed him or misbehaved in any way, he would hurt me by hurting those close to me. It was almost impressive what a strategist he was. People could endure a lot, and he knew I'd have no problem risking myself to fight him, but risking others was a heavier burden.

Crane left, closing the door behind him, and I locked it, going around the rest of the downstairs to check all the entrances, windows, and close the doors to rooms I wouldn't use. Finding one or more open later would give me a clue someone was in the house.

I took off my jacket and took out my phone, turning it on to call my mother.

Or trying to call my mother.

The phone wouldn't fire up.

And then I remembered that I'd forgotten to plug it in last night to charge. I exhaled a breath, fighting the urge to cry.

Yanking open the drawer on the foyer table, I pulled out a charger and plugged in the phone, but I thought better of leaving it out in the open. Instead, I threaded the cord through the back of the drawer and hid the phone inside while it charged. He'd get it away from me if he really wanted to, but hopefully I'd get it charged enough to make some calls first.

How could my mother leave me like that? He got them packed, changed and out of the house in a matter of a few hours before I got home last night, and he or Crane hadn't relayed a message, I hadn't gotten any calls—that I knew of yet, but I'd check my phone as soon as it had a charge—and no one else had contacted me to let me know my mother was concerned or trying to reach me.

She hadn't just left me. Arion would have, but not my mom. What threat or lie did he feed her to get her out of the house? Did he even handle it himself or did he use some of his dad's hired muscle?

And were they really in the Maldives? Like all the way in fucking Asia? Ari always wanted to go. He would've agreed to anything to get rid of her.

But he wasn't joining them.

He wasn't going anywhere. Even I knew that.

Walking into the kitchen, I took a glass from the cupboard and filled it with bottled water, hooking the tip of my finger over the edge of the glass to feel when the water reached close to the top. Taking a long drink, I closed my eyes and listened to the house. To the wind and the rain and the floors, absorbing the hum of the refrigerator, the heater warming the water, and the silence.

Too much silence.

My blood coursed under my skin, and my hair stood up on my arms.

I still felt it. The same thing I felt this morning.

No creaks. No footsteps. No music.

No Mikhail.

But it was still there. The heaviness in the air.

And I knew.

I just knew.

I set out a bowl of food for Mikhail in the mud room and freshened up his water, just in case he was outside somewhere. I knew he wasn't. He would've come back by now. But just in case...

And then I took my water and headed upstairs, into the bathroom, my eyelids trying to close like I hadn't slept all night.

I set my water down, it clinking against the granite countertop, and walked over to the tub, sitting on the edge as I turned on the water. Making it as hot as I could stand, I sat there running my hand under the water, the steam wafting up to my face.

I closed my eyes, feeling my pulse thunder inside as everything else was so quiet.

I feel you.

I feel you everywhere.

The cloves on his clothes, the fountain on his skin.

The words on his tongue, the breath on his lips.

The hand on my neck, the sharp in his silence.

Down the hall. Sitting in the study. Outside in the rain.

At the open bathroom door.

Or right in the corner of the room.

Right here. Watching me.

He was always coming.

Or...

Maybe I never left. His words came back to me.

When he was in prison, he was here. When I wanted to want other men, he was here. When I danced, when I cried, whenever I was alone, and when I was quiet in a room full of people and thinking about him, he was here.

The truth was, I'd had what Michael and Rika had. I thought I had anyway. Those days were when I was the happiest. Even though it was a lie, it was the best I'd ever felt.

Damon.

It was useless to close the door. My fight wasn't enough. He couldn't be contained. I had to let go.

I stood up, kicked off my shoes, and pulled my T-shirt over my head, letting it drop to the floor. I didn't lick my lips even though they were dry or barely breathed even though I was starved to.

Calm and slow, as if my brain was floating high above my head, and I was watching myself from above, I removed my bra and unbuttoned my jeans, letting both fall, as well, and hooked my fingers under the hem of my panties, pausing.

No creaks. No footsteps. No door opening or closing.

But I felt him.

The cool October air caressed my skin, making the flesh of my nipples pebble and harden, and I only hesitated another moment before I pushed them down my legs.

Stepping into the water, I lowered myself, an inch of water underneath me and immediately making chills spread across my skin with the utter warmth. I almost groaned.

Closing my eyes again, I hugged my knees to me as the water ran, steam billowed around me, and my toes curled in the water.

The heat coursed through my body, settling my muscles and nerves, and making my limbs feel like anchors. I didn't want to move, and I didn't have the will to care right now.

Hurt me. You still won't win.

No creaks. No footsteps. No doors.

Nothing.

What did he see when he watched me?

His enemy? Or something he wanted?

Was I someone to torment or something to play with? Did he know the difference?

Did he want me to like it?

What did he see?

I spaced off, feeling the hairs on my arms stand up and my skin harden like armor as I felt him, and anger and violence swirled in my gut, because I wanted to tear at him and hurt him and prove to him that I wasn't scared yet.

That I was going fucking mad, but I wasn't a baby.

What would he see when he looked at me right now?

My watery eyes, trembling hands, and huddled form?

Or did he see that I was alone? That I was naked, wet, and alone for so long?

So long.

I took the sponge and soaked it with water, squeezing it down over my bent knees and letting it fall down my legs over and over again. Then I did the same thing to my neck, moving my hair to one side and letting hot water run down my back.

Moving the sponge to the front of my neck, I tipped my head back, straightened my spine, and sat up tall, squeezing the water out, while letting my legs fall cross-legged and away from my body so the water could cascade down over my breasts and stomach. It caressed me, the warmth feeling so good, and I panted as I did it over and over again, rubbing the sponge down my neck.

And in your bed tonight, when it's late and dark, and the rest of the house is quiet...you're pissed and angry, because you think you hate me, but you slip a hand under the covers anyway, because no one will be the wiser if you indulge yourself in the memory of me...

I laid back, still only an inch of water under me, because I hadn't plugged the tub yet, and slowly ran the sponge down my torso, between my breasts, and down my tummy, nearly reaching my panty line.

Tears sprang up behind my closed lids, but I wasn't sad. Every inch of my skin buzzed with heat—with wanting something to happen, anything to happen—as long as I could get rid of what was winding through my brain and stomach like a goddamn screwdriver and pooling between my legs.

Anger and fury and heat and need so strong you're a fucking animal, Winter. It's primal.

Primal.

There was no sense, but it was strong. It was need.

My chest rose and fell harder and harder, the sponge rubbing down the inside of my thigh, and I gripped it, seeing him watching me in my mind. Making him watch what he'd never do to me, and what I could get on my own.

I grabbed a breast, feeling its round, perfect shape and squeezing it, then tearing my hand away and making it bounce.

Dropping the sponge, I cupped myself between my legs and rolled my head, slipping a finger inside me and moaning.

What did he see when he looked at me? Did he want it? Did he want his mouth on me and his hands on my eager skin, sweaty in my sheets as he fucked me with my sister out of town?

Or did he want his little dancer to perform for him? To make him come but never get me dirty.

Growling under my breath, I slid my body up, hooked my legs over the end of the tub, and adjusted the nob, making the thick stream of water a slow dribble and less hot.

The little flow of water fell down out of the faucet above, hitting my clit positioned below, and I let out a whimper, my body immediately convulsing with pleasure.

I didn't have any control here, though. I wanted to fuck. Gripping both sides of the tub, I pulled myself up onto the rim, my legs still dangling over the side as I got closer to the stream, positioning myself right under it.

The water hit me, pounding my little clit, and I opened my mouth, letting out a groan as I rolled my hips into it. The air tickled my skin as I jutted out my breasts and rode it harder and faster, getting tapped and teased by the little stream.

The flesh of my nipples grew taut, and I wanted a mouth. I wanted to be kissed and sucked, and I needed exactly what Will said I needed.

I spread my legs wider, baring my pussy as I strained the muscles in my legs and arm, masturbating myself on the water.

He watched me. Did he like it?

I whimpered and moaned, feeling the pressure rise inside me as my body begged to be filled. Moving my ass faster, I grabbed the fishhook faucet like it was his head, fucking harder and breathing in and out, deeper and louder.

"You're not the boss," I gasped, taunting him. "Not the boss of me. Little sister does anything she wants. *Whoever* she wants. You're not my daddy."

My orgasm crested, I shook and jerked harder, and then I threw my head back, heat coming out of my pores and pleasure wracking through my whole body like sparks.

"Ah, fuck," I cried out. "Fuck."

Every muscle tightened as it coursed through my body, and even though I burned with the strain of my position, I'd come so good I wanted to cry.

I stayed like that for almost a minute, letting myself calm down, before I lowered myself back into the tub.

I hated him. He was everything bad that happened to me.

But he was the only time—other than dancing—that I felt alive, too.

Being with him was like dancing. Dancing with death.

After a few more moments and the room had fallen quiet again, I hugged my knees to my chest again.

"I know you're there," I told him to wherever he was standing in the room. Where I always knew he was standing, because the house was heavy, it was too quiet, and I could smell the cloves on his clothes, the fountain on his skin, and the hot on his breath.

"And now you know..." I said, "I always close my eyes when I come."

In high school, he'd asked if I closed my eyes in pleasure, and now he had his answer.

He didn't move, and neither did I. I no longer cared. I was tired of wondering what he'd do. Now he was wondering what I could do.

This was a game to him, and that was fine.

He just wasn't the only one playing anymore.

CHAPTER 15

Damon

PRESENT

I leaned over the bathtub, my hands gripping the sides and hovering less than a foot from her mouth as I watched her masturbate.

Jesus Christ. She was beautiful.

And mine. All mine whether she fucking liked it or not. She'd do this for me. Only for me from now on.

A lock of hair spilled down her face, getting sucked between her lips and back out again every time she panted.

Mine. This was why I tolerated Arion. Because her little sister was my favorite little cunt. *God, look at her.*

Her body waving and hips rolling, her tits bouncing, her legs spread wide and hanging over the rim of the tub... The trickle of water teased her little clit, and I ran my tongue across the backside of my teeth, wanting to be the water and taste what it tasted and do to her what it was doing.

She danced even when she wasn't on her feet.

She rode it out, fucking and coming as she threw her head back and moaned, and I dropped my eyes down her body, remembering all that I had touched and taking in the new in all the years that had passed. The same taut tummy and toned thighs. The same tight, round ass and tits, nipples poking straight out and built to be sucked.

But her hair was longer now, a few more muscles in her stomach and legs, and her pussy… The tightest thing I'd ever been inside of. She was a woman. I wouldn't have to be gentle with her this time.

I raised my eyes to her face again, cocking my head and watching her eyebrows etched in pleasure and pain and wanting to kiss her so I could taste the sweat above her top lip.

Did she think about me? Did she do this a lot? Was she dying for it that badly? Did it feel as good as having a man between her legs?

It had been so long since I was spent like she looked now.

She lowered herself back into the tub, tucking her knees up to her chest again, and calmed her breathing.

No, do it again. My dick was so hard, and if I slid it inside her right now, how wet would she be? God, what was she doing to me? *Do it again.*

"I know you're there," she said.

And I shot my eyes up to her eyes, seeing her stare off at nothing, serene and resolute.

"And now you know…" she went on. "I always close my eyes when I come."

I remained there, the fire in my body a moment ago now turning to ice. She knew I was here. She'd known from the start. I thought it was odd she left the door open. I just assumed she thought she was alone in the house. Can't fault me for watching what happens in plain sight.

But she planned this.

And I raised my hand, bringing it to her face, claws bent and starving to grab her pretty little neck, but…I drew back. Provoking me was her goal, and that was not how you were going to wind up in my bed, little Winter.

She thought she was strong. She thought she could play with me.

She could try. *I had you once. I'll have you again.*

I rose silently and stood there as she finally got out of the tub, wrapping herself in a towel, and left the bathroom. I quietly followed, stopping just outside the bathroom door and watching as she trailed down the hallway, no turn of the head to hear if anyone was behind her and no fear that anything was at her back, and entered her bedroom, closing the door behind her.

I inhaled a deep breath, feeling the silence of the house and anticipation for the long nights ahead. Ari and her mother were gone.

Her father was gone.

All the ducks in a row.

Walking into my room, I shut the door, seeing Mikhail's head pop from where he'd been asleep on the bed. He jumped to his feet, wagging his tail and tongue hanging out of his mouth.

I couldn't help but quirk a smile as I dug into my pocket for a treat. He gobbled it out of my hand, and I petted him with the other, stroking his blond head. Amazing how some animals knew not to bite the hand that fed them while others couldn't deny their nature to be what they were.

"I can't sleep, boy," I told him, smoothing both hands over his head now. "It's not so complicated for an animal, is it? Why can't the things I need be basic?"

Or physical?

I wanted to fuck. I wanted it slow, feeling her fear, her desire, and her mouth giving back what I gave to her.

But I needed her mind.

"It's all in my head," I muttered.

The control. The memories. The knowledge that our bodies betray us, and it was the brain that was the prize. That the mind knew what we really wanted, not the body.

"Wake up!" I whisper, shaking Banks. "Get up!"

She lifts her head, still half-asleep. "What? Huh?"

I rip the covers off her and grab her wrist, pulling her

out of my bed. It's like dragging a five-year-old. My sister is fourteen, but she's still so lanky and skinny compared to me, and I'm only a year older than her. My boxers and T-shirt hang on her like drapes.

Footfalls hit the stairs outside my bedroom, and I'd forgotten to lock the door.

I shove Banks into the closet, and she sits down, knowing the drill. I put my headphones on her, metal music playing. "Don't come out until I get you," I tell her.

And I shut the door just as my bedroom door creaks open.

My mother, barefoot and dressed in a deep purple slip and robe, enters my room, a surprised look on her face when she sees me still awake.

She smiles and locks my bedroom door before heading across the room to me.

"You're still up?" she asks, the musical tone to her voice making me wince.

It sounds surreal, because it has no place in what happened in this room. Nothing is happy or innocent.

She approaches, putting her hands on my face and patting my skin to feel for a temperature or some shit, but the touch turns intimate. A languorous drag of her fingertips. How her hand softly falls down my neck. How she stands close enough her breasts graze my bare chest through her nightie.

"Trouble sleeping?" she asks. And then smiles, teasing me. "Someone needs their sleeping pill."

My sleeping pill. *Because it's medicinal for growing boys to have their dicks milked by their mothers.*

She caresses my face and shoulders, looking up at me like I'm still eleven and always her boy.

"I can take care of anything my son needs." She smiles and comes in, wrapping her arms around my neck. "Such a beautiful boy. You're going to be a powerful man someday."

She presses her body into mine, and I close my eyes, trying to go to that place I always go. Where I can pretend she's someone else. A girl at school. Some chick in my class.

My mother is still young, only sixteen when she had me, so her skin is still tight from youth and years of dancing, her black hair is long and soft, she smells good...

I've had sex with others. Girls around town. Women my father keeps. I can do this.

And if I want it to stop, who will I tell anyway? My father won't care. No one will, and telling will make him angry and make people laugh at me. I'd be weak and an embarrassment to him.

I can't tell.

This isn't a big deal. My mother isn't unusual. Men look at Banks the same way my mother looks at me. That's why I hide my sister. So they won't go after her.

I see so much shit, and I don't know if it's wrong, but it never ends, and I've gotten used to everything that happens in the late hours. Maybe it happens everywhere and nobody talks about it.

But she rubs her hand over my dick through my jeans, and I just can't.

"No, stop," I growl, stumbling back. "I don't want to."

I don't fucking want to. I won't tell, but I'm not doing shit I don't want to do anymore.

But she protests, "Damon."

She advances on me but stops, and looks down at the floor. Picking up her foot, she inspects the smears staining the wood. "Is that... blood?" she asks me and reaches down, lifting the ankle of my jeans and seeing the blood soaked into the hem. "Oh, my God, what have you done?"

Not enough, apparently. I'd completely forgotten about the cuts once she walked in, because the broken skin wasn't enough pain to mask the shit she brought with her.

Taking my hand, she drags me into the bathroom adjoining my bedroom and pushes me back against the countertop, lifting up my foot.

"Are these cuts?" she exclaims.

Like you're shocked. *She knows what I've been doing for years now. The cuts I hide under my feet. The scars under my arms and hair. The slices, pricks, and burns that are covered under my boxers until they heal and then I do it all over again. I'd gotten creative in hiding the shit I did to release pain.*

She wets a washcloth and pushes me back more, so I sit on the counter, and lifts my foot.

But I jerk away. "I can do it!"

She slaps me, and my head jerks to the side, the sting of her hand burning across my face like fire and ice. I close my eyes, grateful for it. A cool sweat breaks out all over me.

"There, there, now," *she soothes like I'm five.* "You don't need to talk. Remember what we said? You don't need to talk. I always know what you need."

She wipes up the blood, applies Band-Aids to the five slices I made, and checks the other foot, sighing in relief that it wasn't injured.

"You need to be careful," *she tells me.* "The basketball team needs you. You can't hurt your feet like that."

That was why I did it. It didn't hurt my game at all. If anything, I played harder and faster, so the pain of running on that court would exhaust me, so I couldn't think or fight when I came home.

"Better?" *she asks.*

She doesn't wait for my answer, though. Coming in, she wraps her arms around me again, kissing my cheek and trailing more over my jaw and mouth.

"Such a good boy," *she whispers.* "So much energy. So physical." *Her hands move over my body as her kisses get wetter and longer.* "So much endurance and muscle. So much power." *And then her hand reaches between my legs, massaging my cock.* "Such a good, growing boy."

I grip the back of her hair, and she moans as my fingers dig into her scalp and I stare at my reflection in the glass shower door.

Bitch.

Slut.

Pussy.

Nothing but a fuck.

"Rachel Kensington's mother called me," she says, licking, kissing, and panting against my neck. "She said she found you and her daughter half naked on their couch last night."

I take her waist in my other hand, kneading the flesh through the silk, never blinking as I stare at myself and letting all the emotions rip through me.

Anger.

Shame.

Fear.

Violence.

Pain.

Sadness.

Helplessness.

They float through, jumbling together until I can't identify one from the other, and it's not even me in the reflection anymore. Everything in my brain leaves, my mind turns off, and my hands stop shaking. I'm just a body.

This is me.

I am me.

"She was glad nothing serious had happened," my mother goes on.

Rachel who?

"Oh, sweetie," she coos. "I understand. Boys will be boys, and she teased you, didn't she? She wouldn't let you have it."

I dig my fingers into her skull, squeezing her hip tighter.

"Shhh," she says, trying to pull away from my hold. *"Little girls just don't understand what boys need. It's okay. I'm here."* Her lips trailed a line across my jaw, mewling as she tries to get my grip off her hair.

"You can pretend I'm her," she tells me, my dick growing hard and hot with blood. *"Show me what you were going to do to her. Show me how you wanted to fuck that silly little girl."*

No, no, no...

"Show me," she urges. *"Fuck me."*

No...

"Take what's yours," she growls. *"Give that girl what she deserves."*

I suck in a breath, tears springing to my eyes, and I jump off the counter, swing around, grab her by the back of the neck, and bend her over the counter.

She spreads her legs and pulls up her nightie for me, bites her bottom lip. "That's my boy."

I hold her head right in front of the mirror, staring at her as she challenges me back.

"Do it, baby," she whispers. *"Come all inside me. Come on, come on, come on..."*

And I glare at her, tighten my hold on her hair and neck, press her into the counter, and pull her head up—

She gasps, ready to get it.

And I shove her head into the mirror as hard as I can, splintering the glass, and she screams.

"Damon!" she cries out, but I can't stop.

A wave of euphoria washes over me, and I don't know why my cheeks are wet, but my muscles are charged, and I just want her to fucking die.

I growl, bringing her head down again and again, blood covering the mirror, and then I haul her up, her body limp and blood pouring down her face, and I hit her, sending her flying to the floor.

She coughs and sputters, and tears stream down my face, but in that moment, I knew.

It would never happen again.

This never had to happen again. I'd kill her if I had to.

Seeing something out of the corner of my eye, I look over my shoulder, seeing Banks standing there with my headphones in her hand.

She looks from my mother on the floor—bloody and weak—to me, her eyes scared.

I rush over, grab her hand, and run from the room. She doesn't ask questions as I pull her down the stairs, through the house, and out the back doors, into the backyard.

The moon casts a glow over the hedge maze, and we dive in, knowing our way well and finding the fountain immediately.

We climb in and settle behind the water, just like I had done a thousand times before, only once with a girl other than my sister. Banks doesn't ask me what happened or what I'm going to do. She knows not to talk in here.

Reaching under the groove of the bowl above us, I dig out the silver barrette with pink crystals I hide there, and wrap my fist around it, remembering Winter Ashby's words from so long ago in that fountain.

Your body can only feel one pain at a time.

She was right. I've found that to be true.

But instead of hurting myself to mask pain with more pain, tonight I learned something else.

Hurting others is just as effective.

My mother left after that beating. An hour later, Banks and I had gone back to my room to find her gone, and we fell asleep on the bed, leaving the door unlocked, because we knew. We couldn't stop the world from happening to us. We could only react.

By morning, my mother was gone, and I never asked where. And as time passed, my father made no effort to bring her home again. I didn't see her until a couple of years later.

And I dealt with it for good that night.

Just like I was going to deal with Winter and the false hope she nearly destroyed me with.

"I want her to want it," I told Mikhail, his brown eyes looking up at me expectantly. "I want her to want me, to give me her heart, and be my soft, sweet, smiling Little Devil, clutching at me and unable to stop herself." My heart quickened. "And then I want her to hate herself for it. To turn against herself and hate that she likes it, so she knows she's weak and pathetic and no different than any other bitch. That she wasn't special."

Once I see her as just like everyone else, I'll have destroyed her and killed my obsession with her. I would've killed her power over me, just like Natalya's.

"And I think she wants to play this game with me," I joked with the animal.

A knock sounded on the door.

"Come," I called.

The door opened and closed, and then I heard Crane's voice behind me.

"She's inquiring about the dog, sir."

"Tell her the truth," I said, smoothing the animal's fur. "She doesn't have one anymore."

"She says there were sounds in the house this morning, too," he pointed out. "Man-made sounds after you left. She got scared, ran, and went to St. Killian's."

"How'd she do that?"

"Uber," he answered.

I scoffed. *Jesus.* I never thought of that. Woman was certainly self-sufficient.

But I remembered the first part he said. Noises?

"You think she's overreacting?" I asked him.

"I don't know. She seemed very sure," he explained. "I can install cameras and an alarm system."

"No," I told him. "Take on more men. Two details of four each."

"Yes, sir. She'll be safe."

"From everyone but me," I clarified.

"Yes, sir."

She was probably just overly alert. Thanks to me.

But she also mentioned a visitor at Bridge Bay Theater days ago. Someone who came into the bathroom and scared her. She thought it was me.

It wasn't.

This house should have better security, but I didn't like cameras or video. I'd learned the hard way to not leave evidence.

And given our affluent neighborhood and the low crime rate, Winter's father never saw fit to arm the house with an alarm system, at the very least. Maybe I'd add one eventually. Right now, I liked coming and going quickly.

"And, sir?" Crane prodded.

"What is it?"

"Her phone's been ringing downstairs," he told me, approaching my side. "Would you like me to give it her or...?"

I glanced to where he held it out for me, amused at his coy attempt to give me her phone but still remain innocent in the matter.

I took it.

He left, and I turned it on, seeing it was armed with a pattern passcode. I couldn't get into it, but there were several notifications visible just on her lock screen.

Mostly from Rika.

An article in the town paper about Winter's performance last night.

Talk on social media and some videos. Lots of shares and comments as the video spread outside of our town.

I squeezed the phone. She didn't think she was getting out of here, did she?

And then I expanded a text from Rika. It was a screenshot of a Twitter comment on the video of Winter dancing:

This girl should be everywhere! Why isn't she touring?

Rika texted below the image:

What she said! Need some sponsors? I might know a few. Let's talk.

I gritted my teeth together, barking at the dog. "Komyen ya!"

He scurried to my side as I left the room, and I carried the phone downstairs and dropped it on the foyer table. I whipped open the front door, charging out of the house.

Fuckin' Rika.

"Stay," I told Crane who stood in the driveway, washing the other car. "She doesn't leave."

He nodded, and I jumped in my car, the dog taking the passenger seat. I sped off, kicking it into high gear in less than five seconds.

Goddamn her.

My ex-friends were the only people who could protect those in Winter's life I threatened, and that's why I needed Rika on my side. Seemed she was tired of waiting for me to keep my end of the bargain, though, so she was trying to undo hers.

She gave me Winter. Now she was trying to take her away.

• • •

I stepped into the large hall, hanging back in the shadows as lots of activity happened around the room. I'd missed this place. Hunter-Bailey was a nice club to relax because it was geared for men and didn't allow women.

Other than one.

After some digging, I'd found out Rika had installed two bouting nights per week at Hunter-Bailey for fencing, and one of them was tonight. It had always been a hobby of hers, as well as collecting swords and various kinds of daggers, and while no other woman was permitted on the premises, Rika could come and go as she pleased as long as she was covert about it. The perks of having a star athlete fiancé for the Meridian City Storm, and a future father-in-law who owned a large fraction of the city.

Boxers went at it in a ring to the left, some worked out, and others lounged on chairs with drinks, chatting it up. I followed the sound of foils clanging together and veered to the other room off to the right and entered, seeing more chairs occupied, a full bar, and members in the middle of the room dueling it out, dressed in their white protective gear and helmets.

I spotted Rika right away. Her body was unmistakable in the tight pants.

She lunged for her opponent, landing her point right in his heart, and I heard him growl and back away before setting himself up again.

I wanted to go over there and drag her off now, but I wasn't supposed to be in here, Michael having had them cancel my membership two years ago. I was barely able to sneak in at all.

I watched the way she stepped and retreated, rolling her wrists and swinging her arm. Like choreography. Methodical. It was like chess with strategy, but also like a dance. Graceful and statuesque.

I wasn't sure how long I stood there, leaning against the wall and watching her, but she finished, and I didn't even know if she'd won. Keeping her mask on, she put up her foil, and walked to the other side of the room, ascending the stairs.

I followed.

They didn't have a female locker room here—or they didn't the last time I was here—so I imagined she changed in a private room.

I climbed the two flights of stairs, and once at the third floor, I stepped quietly down the hallway. Doors lined both sides and I was unsure of where she went.

There were offices, a library, a few bedrooms, and on the right, I passed a billiards room, the door open and Rika leaning on the pool table with her back to me. I stopped, seeing her staring at a collection of weapons hung on the wall.

"Michael didn't want me to come tonight," she said.

I smiled to myself. Couldn't sneak up on her anymore.

"He knew you knew my routine," she continued. "But lately, and with as happy as I am with so much in my life, the bouts are the only time I feel like I'm sure of what I'm doing anymore. The only time my strike is sure. I couldn't miss it."

She stood up and turned around, still dressed in her fencing gear minus the helmet. Her hair was up in a ponytail, and she looked down at the pool table, absently rolling the pink ball back and forth.

"You know, after our meeting at the club that night," she told me, "I started reading up on chess. I mean, I knew how to play. My father made sure of it. But I wasn't very clever with it."

I approached the table, listening.

"I thought each piece's power increased based on its proximity to the king, but that's not true." She looked up at me. "Other than the queen, the most powerful player is—"

"The rook," I said.

She nodded. "Yes."

"So you're finally ready to begin?" I asked, pouring myself a glass of bourbon.

But she just turned around, looking back at the wall of weapons. "The game has already begun."

My pulse throbbed harder in my neck as I carried my drink to the table. I lived for this shit.

But while I liked my games, intrigue, and going wild, I didn't like doing it alone. I wanted someone on my side. I wanted *her* on my side.

"All of this is mine," she said, gesturing to the wall of weapons and turning her head to meet my eyes. "It's only taken me a few months to gather it. Some purchased, some traded, and some borrowed from private collections."

She turned back around, studying it again, and I stared at the back of her head as I took a swig of the alcohol.

"The curator of the Menkin Museum would love to have this for her weapons exhibit next summer," she explained. "And I'm prepared to let her have it in exchange for a favor from her husband, whenever I choose to call it in."

A favor? Who was her husband?

She paused and then clarified, "Her soon-to-be *police commissioner* husband, *Martin Scott.*"

I blinked long and hard, anger winding its way through my stomach.

Martin Scott.

As in Emory Scott.

The girl with the abusive—police officer—older brother whom Kai and Will were sent to prison for assaulting as payback for beating up on his little sister.

The little sister who wasn't little anymore and who Will was still obsessed with.

He hated us, and was now more powerful than ever.

Rika shot up, grabbed a sword off the wall, and whipped around, holding it at her side and pinning me with a stare. "And guess where he plays billiards every Friday night?" she taunted.

Goddammit. My hand tightened around the glass.

"See, the thing I always wondered about was," she said, circling the table, and I did the same, glass in hand. "Kai and Will served time for assaulting Martin Scott, but..." She eyed me. "They weren't the only ones there. Someone was filming."

You little shit.

"And that's like... aiding and abetting, right?" she asked.

The glass shattered in my fist, and I felt the sting of a cut as the liquid spilled and the shards fell to the ground.

She just smirked at me, a glint in her blue eyes. "Queen takes rook."

You fucking bitch.

"Fucking little monster," I muttered, breathing lava out of my nose.

"Kai and Will protected you," she stated, fighting not to smile. "That charge along with the statutory rape charge? You would still be in prison. If Martin Scott were to find out...

"There's no proof."

"There's Kai and Will," she fired back. "And they're mad at you right now."

Goddamn her. Martin Scott knew it was me filming his much-deserved beat-down, but without a reason for Will and Kai to be silent about my part in it anymore, all I had was Rika. She pulled the strings.

She circled the table, held up the sword, and pointed it at me. "You will not force her," she ordered her terms. "You will not threaten, torture, or coerce her into your bed. You will not touch her."

I shot out my hands, planting them on the pool table and leaning over it to look her in the eyes. "And if she *wants* me to touch her?"

"It's good to dream big, Damon."

I almost snorted, but I couldn't contain my smile. "God, you're like a female version of me," I said. "It's turning me on."

"Makes sense. You love yourself best."

I stood upright again, brushing off my hands. She was exquisite, and if she weren't working against me, I'd think she was brilliant.

Smart. Tough. Clever.

And cold when she needed to be.

Cold.

"The queen," I mused, rolling a ball on the table as a memory came to mind. "The snow queen."

She thinned her eyes, probably confused.

"Years ago," I explained, "when your father brought his young bride here from South Africa, I'm told my father was quite enamored of her. She reminded him of the beautiful snow queen from the *Nutcracker* ballet." I tipped my chin down, casting her a knowing look. "And that's what he called her. His *little* snow queen."

She growled and lunged, and I shot backward just as she slammed the sword on the table. Leaping onto the table, she forwent charging around it to chase me, and hopped off, going straight for me.

Did she not like me insinuating my father got inside her mother's panties?

She swung for my legs, but I stomped my foot on the sword, knocking it out of her hand, and threw her down on the floor, pressing her shoulders into the wood.

Her face was red with fury.

"The queen is the most valuable player," I told her, "but to win, she's not the last one standing. Her job..." I paused, arching an eyebrow, "is to protect the king."

She pulled out a knife from somewhere and pressed the side of the blade into my neck.

Jesus. She must be fun in bed.

I grinned. "You won't hurt me."

"And why not?"

"Because we're friends."

"You don't know the meaning of the word!" she snapped. "You don't care about me!"

"I would kill for you," I shot back, getting in her face.

The incredulous look on her face, like she didn't know if she should be touched or laughing, mimicked exactly what was happening in my head right now.

Yes.

It kind of just came out, but I thought it was true. At one time, I would've killed for Michael, Kai, and Will. I might still.

But I'd definitely kill for Erika and Banks. They may not like me a whole lot, but they understood me.

I pushed her knife off my neck and looked down at her.

"Now I'm impressed, but you're on the wrong side," I told her.

And then I reached into my breast pocket and pulled out the flash drive with the information Alex had retrieved. The proof I said I would get in exchange for the information on Winter's father Rika got for me.

She looked at me, realization crossing her eyes and all the anger leaving her face as she took it from my hand.

Getting off her, I sat down next to her. "There's more coming. Gimme a few days."

"It's bad?" she asked, turning her head to look at me.

"It's exactly what I told you last year," I said. "I told you I don't lie. Evans Crist—and my father—had yours killed."

It was something I'd picked up over years of accidently overhearing conversations in my house, and I'd had Alex working Evans Crist—Michael's father—and gathering security cam footage and bank statements that I knew he kept just in case, so he could hold it over my father if he ever needed to.

"Your father was involved?" Rika asked. "Why yours?"

It was a good question, and one I wasn't sure how to answer yet. It was obvious why Evans wanted to get rid of Schraeder Fane. They were friends, and Evans had power of attorney over his friend's estate in case anything happened. And Evans saw his chance. He wanted to marry Rika off to his son Trevor when she grew up, so the Fane fortune would be theirs. He knew Schraeder had no plans to allow his daughter to marry too young, though, and he knew Rika's mother was much more pliable.

As for my father helping, I had no idea why. He wasn't getting anything out of it. Maybe just a favor?

"I don't know that yet," I told her.

She sat up, and I watched her stare at the drive as she fingered the scar on her neck. The one she got when she was thirteen in the car accident that killed her father because his brakes had been cut. Gabriel and Evans didn't expect her to be in the car that day, but thank goodness she lived.

Because I needed her and we had shit to do.

CHAPTER 16

Winter

FIVE YEARS AGO

"All set?" Sara Dahlberg asked as she walked into the ticket booth.

I pooled all the nickels into my hand, dumped them back into the tray, and recorded the sum on a notepad, fingering the indentations of my pen marks to find where I needed to write the total. "Yep."

"I'll count your bills." She pulled the tray over to her side, and I heard the shuffle of money as she counted the rest of my bank.

"Thanks."

I shut down my computer and switched off the marquee outside, the constant buzz of the lighting above finally dying. I'd only been working here about eight weeks, but already that sound was killing me. I would've rather worked concessions inside, but the theater manager was concerned about how I would manage behind the counter with the chaos of other employees moving about. I had ideas, but she had a system that worked, so...

I didn't really expect much more from her, though. She didn't think I should do a lot of things. She only gave me this job right before my junior year started several weeks ago to shut me up about dancing with the company, since the theater not only showed movies but held plays, symphonies, and ballets.

I'd started looking for a job when the last school year ended to stay busy and enjoy some independence, but I'd had rotten luck, so it was either this or stay home to revel in Arion's constant self-importance and listen to my parents fight.

"'Okay," Sara said. "Here you go."

I held out my arms, and she placed the tray with the count on a piece of paper in my hold, and held the door open for me as I left the little room. I tucked the tray under my arm, propped up on my hip, and held out my free hand to walk the path to the manager's office. I'd gotten used to navigating it over the past two months, counting my steps and feeling my way.

Two months.

Two months since I'd started working an actual job.

Two months until Christmas and the only time Arion and I got along.

Two months plus one until I was seventeen.

And less than two years until I graduated, and two years since I'd spoken to him.

Two whole years.

The night of the car ride and motorcycle ride was the last time he paid me a visit. Why hadn't he come back?

Scenarios and fears raced through my mind over time.

He'd been arrested.

He'd moved.

He'd died.

All of those were agonizing possibilities, but not nearly as painful as facing the most likely one.

He'd lost interest.

He'd had his fun, moved on, and was happy and laughing with someone else, while I sat around and missed him.

I thought that was why it was a good idea to get a job. *If you can't keep your head on straight, then at least keep busy.*

I was still constantly aware of him, though. Living my life as if he were watching me. Curling my hair, asking Ari for makeup advice—which she loved and was actually really nice about helping with—and dancing. Dancing late at night after everyone had gone to bed in hopes that he was there and would know it was safe to come out.

Two strange but fascinating visits two years ago, and I still walked around like he was watching me.

Because, I swore, sometimes I thought he was. After that Devil's Night and he disappeared, I could be at a party or a basketball game or sitting on the terrace under the awning in a summer rain and listening to my audiobook, and then...I'd feel it. The heat of his eyes.

I guessed he could've still been watching, but why cut off contact?

Probably just my mind playing tricks on me, but it made it hard to forget him. He'd definitely succeeded at making an impression, hadn't he?

And in all the time since I'd last spoken to him, I hadn't told anyone about him. I'd joined the dance club at school, made some new friends, and even though I felt a lot more comfortable there now, it was the one place that was drama free for me. I could only imagine how the story of my mysterious interlude with a dark stranger would suddenly turn into a story of how I was forced to dance for a psycho serial killer who wanted to dress me up in pigtails and keep my feet as souvenirs. *No, thank you.* I wouldn't let anyone ruin it.

Not to mention, telling others risked my parents finding out, and that would be bad.

Carrying the tray up the stairwell, I walked into the manager's office and set it down on her desk.

"Thank you, Winter," she said. "How are you? You seem to be doing well down there."

Yeah. "A nine-year-old could do that job."

"Winter..." she scolded.

321

I wasn't really joking, though. It was the truth. A typical teenage job. While I didn't need the money, it was nice to earn my own cash and have something low-stress, so it didn't distract from school, but it was also a job *she* thought I could do. She'd picked it for me.

And I wanted to do more.

I stood there, hovering, and she must've seen the look on my face, because she stopped counting the money.

"You nearly broke an arm," she reminded me, sighing.

I fell practicing over a year ago. Dancers fell and broke bones all the time.

"You can't dance with the corps," she went on. "You learn slower than we can work with. The wrong fall could kill you. I mean...do you know what you're asking of us, honey?"

My jaw locked, because she was tired of this conversation, and I had no new arguments. I danced on that stage downstairs many times when I was little. I danced at home with no accidents. Yes, it took me longer to learn my stage, and I would make everyone's job just a little bit harder and that sucked, but it wasn't impossible. I'd gone over it in my head a thousand times, mapping the choreography—mine and the other dancers'. I just wanted a shot.

She rose from her chair, the wheels squeaking underneath, and she pinched my chin lightly between her fingers.

"Challenges find us so we can become who we're meant to be," she told me. "God has taken you on an exciting new path. Trust his judgment and see where it leads."

What the hell?

"I bought a first-class ticket," I told her. "I'm not taking the bus."

And I spun around, heading back down the stairwell.

People were priceless. The things we told ourselves to justify giving up and falling in line like we had to accept anything less than what we wanted. Like fighting for your dream was a bad thing.

I would tour, and people would pay to watch me.

Heading into the ticket booth, I gathered up my school bag and phone, and switched off the light, heading back into the lobby and out the front doors. I called my driver to check if she was almost here, but there was no answer, so I left a voicemail. Since Arion was away studying abroad this semester for college, and my parents had schedules to keep, my mother arranged a car service in town to pick me up and drop me off to and from work. It probably cost more than I was making, but since our town didn't have a public transportation system, I couldn't manage any other way. I tried to give them my paychecks to cover the cost, but my mom wouldn't take it.

I stood out on the town sidewalk, hearing the cars drive by and music coming from Sticks across the square, but I stayed close to the theater doors, just to be on the safe side, until my ride showed. The concession staff was still in there cleaning, so I had help if I needed it.

"Hey, Winter," someone said across the street. "Want a ride?"

Sara. She'd worked the booth with me tonight, and trained me when I started the job. She must just be leaving, too.

"Oh, no, I'm okay," I told her. "My driver should be here soon."

"My driver..." someone repeated, chuckling.

I didn't recognize the voice. Did I just sound pretentious?

"I can't leave you standing there," Sara joked. "Come on. Cancel your car. We'll take you."

We?

I pondered for a moment, not really having a good reason to say no. The driver wouldn't care. She'd still get paid *and* get in bed earlier tonight.

"Okay," I said. "Thanks."

Car doors slammed, an engine started, and tires skidded, the car coming around to my side of the street.

Sara got out and took my hand, leading me to the car. I gently pulled my hand out and placed it on her arm.

"Do you know Astrid Colby?" she asked, holding the back door open for me. "And her boyfriend, Miles Anderson? They're both seniors. This is his car." And then, "You guys, this is Winter Ashby."

I stopped. "Oh, I don't want to cause any inconvenience." I thought she was driving. "I have a ride coming. It's fine."

I didn't know Astrid and Miles, but I knew of them. I definitely got the impression they were trouble.

"Relax." Sara nudged me. "We'll have you home in no time."

Fine. As long as she was here, it should be okay, I guess.

I pulled my bag off and climbed into the car, smelling cigarette smoke and sucking in a breath as the cold leather seats hit the backs of my thighs. I still wore my theater uniform—pleated skirt, button down, and bow tie—but as soon as I was settled, I sent a message to the driver.

After Sara got in and shut the door, we sped off. I felt the car turning, so I assumed we were rounding the square, and next probably cutting through the neighborhood toward the highway.

Judging from the deep rumble of the engine, the leather bench seat I sat on, and the heavy sound of the door closing a moment ago, it was an old car. Classic American muscle, maybe? I didn't want to be a traitor or anything, because the spaciousness was nice, but I preferred the sound and feel of another car. His car. The only car I'd ever driven and probably would ever drive. Agile, fast, quick to respond.... It drove like slicing butter.

And him underneath me. That might've had something to do with my loyalty to that car, too.

I thought it was a BMW. My sister got one for graduation, and I sat in it, damn near falling into a trance when I felt the exact same circular emblem in the middle of the steering wheel as he had in his car.

"Turn off your brights, asshole," the guy driving said.

"He's like right on our ass, too," Astrid commented.

"Yeah, you're being followed, Miles," Sara added, teasing. "It's almost Devil's Night. Let the pranks begin."

I heard him scoff and another whiff of smoke hit me.

That's right. Devil's Night was tomorrow.

"You guys getting up to anything?" Sara asked them. "It's so boring without the horsemen around."

"Fuck them," Miles said. "We can stir up our own shit."

I ran my fingers through my hair, flipping it to one side as I turned toward the window. Miles was the only person I'd heard of who didn't worship at the horsemen altar. Wonder why?

The energy at school since they left, though, was in the dumps. The basketball team was suffering, and there was no excitement anymore. Everyone was caught in suspended animation.

Miles swerved the car to the right and slammed on the brakes, pulling the car to a sudden stop. I shot out my hand to the back of his seat to stop myself from lunging forward.

"Get out, bitch," Astrid said.

Huh?

The door on Sara's side opened, and she shifted next to me. "Thanks for the ride, guys," she chirped.

I froze, every muscle tense. What?

"You know where Winter lives, right?" Sara questioned them.

Wait, they were dropping her off first? I held in my groan. *Shit.* Thanks a lot. Why would she leave me with people I didn't know?

"Don't worry," Astrid told her. "We'll get her home."

"It's fine," I rushed out, gathering my bag and phone. "I'll get out here and call my driver."

"Don't be a bitch, bitch," Astrid shot back but with a teasing tone.

"Have a good night, Winter," Sara said, and then she slammed the door.

I exhaled. *It's fine. It would be fine.*

Miles shifted into gear and took off, and I hit the back of my seat, gripping my phone.

I needed to learn how to be rude. I should've just said 'no' to the ride.

We drove in silence for a few minutes, and I gauged from the straight line he was going that we were hopefully on the highway, heading to my house.

"Is that car still behind us?" I heard Astrid ask.

"Yep," he said in a clipped tone.

My heart picked up pace. Someone was following them? If something was going to happen, I wanted to be out of here before it did.

"So," Astrid spoke again, "what do you see exactly?"

There was silence, and I straightened, coming to attention. "You're talking to me?"

"Yes." She laughed.

I shook my head. "I don't see anything."

"Well, I know, but is it like black or white or what?" she pressed. "Like when I close my eyes, sometimes I see a kaleidoscope of colors and sometimes it's just dark."

"Nothing," I said again. "I don't see. The sense doesn't exist."

"Psychedelic," she cooed her approval.

I chuckled. It was hard for people to wrap their heads around it. When seeing people couldn't see, it was because their eyes were covered. That's what they assumed it was like for me. My eyes were just closed to them.

Whereas in reality, I didn't have eyes at all. But my body did still perform the same involuntary actions: blinking, crying...

"That's a mighty cute uniform you got on," Miles said as he drove.

Astrid didn't respond, so I guessed he was talking to me.

"Thanks," I muttered.

His tone was loaded, and instinctively, I pulled down my skirt as far as it would reach, suddenly feeling like it was too short.

"You know where I live, right?"

She didn't say anything, and he just laughed quietly.

I clutched my phone in my hand, thumbing the power button.

Cool metal touched my hand, and I jerked.

"Try some," Astrid said, handing me something.

I took it, turning the palm-sized object in my hand and hearing the liquid inside swish.

"No, thanks." I handed it back at her.

I could still hear my mother's words when I was like twelve. She educated me really early. *Don't ever drink an alcoholic drink you didn't make or open yourself.*

She told Ari the same thing, but she knew I was at a bigger risk of being victimized. Someone could slip anything in my drink, and do it right in front of me, without my knowing.

But Astrid just took the flask back, whining, "Party pooper."

I was about to say 'thank you anyway', but we turned and gravel crunched underneath the tires. I immediately narrowed my eyes, on alert. There were no gravel roads on the way to my house.

"Where are we going?" I asked.

But neither of them answered.

Suspicion twisted in my gut. I couldn't be thrown into a locker room out here, but they could find lots of ways to prank me.

"Is that car still following?" Astrid asked.

"They turned off just as we did. Some road behind us," he answered.

"Cool."

"What's going on?" I demanded.

"We want to show you something," Astrid replied.

"I just want to go home."

The car jostled on the pot holes, and I bounced, hitting my head on the roof.

"Ouch," I hissed.

Goddammit, this wasn't funny. It was already after ten, and I didn't know these people. Why would they think they could just drag me wherever they wanted?

"I want to go home," I said again.

"Hold your horses," Miles chided me. "We need you for something."

"What?"

"Climb up here, and sit in the middle," he instructed.

"Why?"

"Come on!" Astrid yanked at my arm. "I need you to hold my legs."

"Hold your legs?"

Air rushed into the car suddenly, blowing my hair, and a scream sounded from outside the car. My breathing turned shallow. Was she sticking her head out the window?

"Come on, please?" she begged, tugging at my arm again. "We'll take you home in a few."

I twisted my lips to the side. *Fine*.

Taking off my jacket, I left my phone and satchel in the back and scooted up, swinging a leg over the front seat. Wind blew under my skirt and my hair into my face, so I moved quickly, sitting down between Miles and Astrid, the hair on the back of my neck rising with fear and a little excitement. Déjà vu hit me, and for a second, it was like he was here, taking me on another adventure.

"Okay, I'm popping up," Astrid said. "Grab my legs and hold on."

"Wait..."

But she was already moving. The car charged down the backroad, barreling and bouncing over the uneven terrain, and I reached out, wrapping my arms around her jean-clad legs as she sat up on the door through the open window.

Howling filled the chilly, night air, and the weight of her body pulled at me as it hung over the side of the car. I fumbled with my hands, unsure if I had a good enough hold of her.

She was going to fall. I couldn't keep hold. What the hell was she doing?

Whatever it was, she seemed to be loving it, though. She laughed and screamed, and Miles just went faster.

He jerked the steering wheel, and I felt Astrid's body get thrown a little with it. I tightened my hold so hard, my muscles ached.

"Damn, baby," Miles said, and I hoped he was talking to her.

It lasted for about another minute, and then Astrid slid back in through the window, cackling and filled with excitement as she rolled her window back up.

"That was hot, babe," she told him.

The car slowed down, and I slid back over to the middle, wiping at the sweat on the back of my neck.

"You should do it," she said, knocking me in the arm.

"I'm fine." I laughed a little.

Not that I wouldn't try it ever, but I'd want to be with people I trusted. I didn't know these two well enough.

The engine started to grow quiet as the car slowed down more, and I rubbed my hands down my thighs, drying my sweaty palms.

Can we please get out of here now?

But instead of driving farther or turning the car around to head to my house, Miles veered to the side, taking the car into some grass, and crawled to a stop.

Why were we stopping?

He left the car idling, put it in *Park*, and everyone sat there for a moment, the music droning on a low volume. I swallowed through the dryness in my throat.

He wasn't explaining why he'd stopped, and she didn't ask. As if they already had a plan and knew what was about to happen.

Astrid turned toward me on my right, her voice low. "You're really pretty," she said.

Something about her tone was...intimate. My mouth was so dry.

"Thank you," I replied, but it came out as a whisper.

I could feel his eyes on me, too.

"We see you around school," she said. "You seem scared to live it up sometimes. As if you don't belong."

I fisted the hem of my skirt. "It's complicated," I told her.

I just wanted to go home.

"We like to have fun," Miles chimed in. "We live it up."

And then Astrid's whisper brushed my ear, "And we want to take you with us."

I lost my breath and jerked away.

But she didn't stop. "We'll show you so much fun," she taunted. And then she flicked my ear with her tongue and trailed her fingers up the inside of my thigh.

Oh, God.

I slapped her away, gritting out, "Get away from me!"

"You'll like us," Miles told me in a hard voice as he gripped the back of my neck and forced me to face him. "Once you try us."

"No!" And I slapped at him, hitting him right in the face.

Asshole.

He jostled me, angry. "You little b—"

But he stopped, something seeming to catch his attention.

"Did you hear that?" he asked.

"What?" Astrid inquired.

I tried to push away from him, thankful he was distracted by something. I hoped it was a cop or people or anyone I could get out of this car and run to.

And then I heard it, too. Howls.

Yelps and barks. Hoots and yells.

"What is that?" Miles said more to himself.

Did we have wolves in our area? I didn't think so, but I would rather take my chances with wild animals than these two.

The sounds disappeared, and Miles and Astrid barely breathed as they remained completely still and listened for a few more moments.

The branches of the trees whined in the wind above us, and I thought I heard leaves shuffling around the car, but I couldn't be certain with the music still on.

"There's something out there," Astrid muttered.

And I remembered how they thought they were being followed earlier.

I felt Miles move next to me. "I don't—"

But something heavy hit the windshield, and he cut off, Astrid gasping next to me.

"What the...?" he barked.

The same force hit Astrid's side, too, suddenly, then the rear window and Miles' side, as well.

"Is that...paint?" Astrid asked. "Someone's splattering paint on the windows."

"Son of a bitch!" he growled.

Releasing me, he opened the door, but there was a pounding sound coming from the outside, and he howled with pain, falling over on me.

Did someone just try to shut the door on him?

I didn't know what was happening, but I felt the car shake under me and vibrations come from the rear area, like someone was back there doing something.

"The windows are covered in black paint!" Astrid exclaimed. "Someone's out there. Just drive!"

My mind raced, debating on whether to try to get out or if the danger was greater out there. Before I had a chance to make a decision, though, Miles shifted into gear and put his foot on the gas.

But we didn't move. He gave it more gas, revving the engine, but the car simply turned its wheels, squeaking underneath us as they spun, but didn't take us anywhere.

"Do you smell gas?" Astrid asked.

I inhaled, feeling a burn hit the back of my throat.

"Oh, shit," Miles suddenly said.

What? Dammit, what was going on?

"Look," he told Astrid.

"They wouldn't," she replied, breathless.

What were they seeing?

And the next thing I knew, the doors opened, and they scurried out of the car, leaving me in the front seat alone.

What the hell?

I didn't know why they ran, but they saw something that scared them, so was the car not safe then? I didn't know what to do, if I should run, who I should be scared of, but they were gone, and I debated for about half a second before I lunged over to the driver's side door and pulled it close, hitting the lock, and doing the same thing to Astrid's door. I might not be out of the woods, but at least I was safe from them.

The key was still in the ignition, and it was probably a bad idea, but I'd get out of here if I had to. I'd just follow the gravel road.

If I could get the car moving, which Miles hadn't been able to do for some reason.

I sat there for a moment, not hearing any sounds outside anymore, just the rumble of the engine and some White Stripes remix on the radio.

My phone. I'd call my mom and have her track my phone to find me. I had no idea where I was.

But just then, I heard his breathing.

Right behind me, in the back seat.

I stilled, not moving a muscle as dread wracked through my body, and my imagination went wild, trying to figure out who or what was behind me.

It was faint but constant, and pain sliced its way through my jaw and neck as a scream filled my throat.

Tears welled, and I couldn't believe I'd been so stupid.

I'd forgotten to lock the back doors.

I opened my mouth, getting ready to cry out and lunge for the door, but then his voice was in my ear.

"Hey, Little Devil," he whispered.

I gasped, the nickname and his hushed tone registering in one powerful, overwhelming blow, and I almost sobbed with happiness.

Are you kidding me?

All of a sudden, he reached forward and took me in his arms, hauling me into the back seat. I shot my hands behind me, touching his face—the sharp nose and angular jaw—grazing the scars on his scalp, and burying my nose in his neck. Freshly showered. As always.

"Oh, my God." I pressed my forehead into his cheek, holding him close. "Where have you been?"

He didn't answer, just held me in his lap, in his arms.

I closed my eyes and exhaled, feeling like I was letting out two years of breath. He was here. He was alive and hadn't forgotten about me.

But...

I sat up and turned around, straddling him in the backseat and grabbing him by the collar of his hoodie.

"You scared the shit out me," I told him.

"Yeah, I do that."

Yeah, lots of people liked to do that in this town.

I wanted to be mad, but a laugh escaped, and I couldn't be angry. He was here, and he got rid of Miles and Astrid.

Keeping hold of him, I dipped my forehead to his, reveling in the feel of him.

He took my upper arms in his hands and held me. "What were you doing with them?" he asked sternly.

I stayed right where I was, our lips an inch away. "You were the one following them?"

He nodded. "I show up to see you again, and when I do, I see you getting in a car with another man."

"Yeah, that's a good stretch," I said, smarting off. "There were two other girls in the car, too. I thought I was safe."

Releasing his collar, I glided my hands around his neck, feeling the same warm, smooth skin. He remained still, almost rigid, as I stayed there, holding him and breathing him in.

Slowly, his hands left my arms, his touch drifting down, to my waist, digging his fingers in just slightly. Heat settled between my legs, and I bit my lip to keep my breathing under control.

"Did you do something I'm going to make you regret?" he whispered.

Make *me* regret?

"Jealous?" I teased.

But Miles and Astrid were far away now. Barely a concern. Tomorrow, I'd tell my mom what happened, but right now, I had all I wanted in this car.

I touched his neck, trailing my fingers to his collarbone, and hovered over his mouth, playing with the tiny space of breath between us.

"Winter..." He was almost growling.

I moved around his face, caressing him with my nose, forehead, and hands, my tongue dying to reach beyond my lips and taste him.

"You've been gone two years," I said. "That's a long time."

"Did they touch you?"

"And if they did?" I taunted. "I'm grown up now."

"You're not," he said, sounding like a warning but breathing harder himself.

I pressed my chest into his, squeezing him between my thighs. "I'm old enough for things."

He gripped my waist harder, pressing my body into his. "You're old enough when I say."

I smiled, tipping my head back and feeling his lips trail a line up my throat. His mouth said one thing and was doing another.

My body started to move, taunting him. Teasing him. Rubbing on him.

I wanted to whisper his name, but I couldn't.

I took his hands and pulled them away from my body, sliding them up my thighs, just under my skirt. I wasn't shy around him. I knew he wanted me, but he kept doing things—being bossy and overprotective—that reminded me of an older brother. It needed to stop. I wasn't a child. I was ready.

"So what do you say?" I asked, inviting him to touch me.

He curled his fingers against my skin.

"Stop it," he ordered me.

"I'm sixteen, and I've never been kissed." I put my hands on his chest, feeling my breasts grazing his body. "I waited for you."

"Winter..."

"I waited for you," I repeated, panting and brushing his lips with mine. "But I won't wait forever."

I layered my lips with his and dipped my tongue out, flicking his lip as I rolled my hips on him. The unmistakably hard ridge of his cock rubbed against my panties through his jeans, and I moaned.

He grabbed me under my arms, holding me up to his face. "That better not be a threat," he bit out.

And then he took my face in one hand and snatched up my lips, biting my bottom one, almost chewing it like he was starving.

He groaned, I whimpered, and we both gave in, holding each other in our arms, our mouths melting together.

I was fast and clumsy, and I couldn't keep up with his kisses and tongue in my mouth, but I loved every second.

He nibbled and bit and took with force, gripping the back of my hair to tip my head back and eat at my neck. He moved from my throat to my chin to my jaw and then back to my mouth, and I clutched at his shoulders, tugging on his sweatshirt as I dry-humped him. God, I couldn't stop myself. He felt so good. It was like an itch that I needed to scratch more and harder.

I tugged at my bow tie, unable to breathe.

Pulling it loose, I unbuttoned my top button, finally feeling freer and diving in, hugging him to where he was sucking on my neck.

My hips moved back and forth, grinding into him

"Winter..." he groaned, pulling back. "I don't want to..."

I picked up pace, and he grabbed my ass, helping me move.

"Don't want to what?" I gasped out.

"Make you dirty."

I slowed, touching his mouth with mine and kissing him softly.

Why would he think that?

"You won't." I shook my head, touching his face. "We won't go all the way. We'll just play."

He breathed out a laugh.

I kissed him, and he dug his fingers in again, making my body explode and every inch of skin come alive. God, I loved it when he did that.

"Hey, man, what are we doing?" someone shouted outside. "You want us to wait or what?"

I startled, taking a moment to register he had friends with him. I threaded my fingers into his hair, going for his mouth again.

Don't leave.

"Dude!" the guy barked again. "Girls your own age, right out here! What the fuck?"

A breathy laugh rumbled from his chest. "I don't think I can wait for her to be legal, man," he whispered to his friend but only loud enough for me to hear.

I nibbled his mouth, playing. "Sixteen is the legal age of consent in thirty-three states," I teased. "Just not ours. It's a technicality."

"Researched it, have you?"

I started to grin, but the guy outside grew impatient. "Man, come on!"

But the boy in my arms shot out his fist, slamming it into the window to shut his friend up, and I heard the glass crack and splinter under his fist.

"Ah, Jesus," the guy whined, and I heard more laughter from others. "Let's give them some room, guys."

Their voices drifted off, and he slowed down, touching me, devouring my neck, and getting to know my body. His hands drifted up my skirt, teasing the line but never crossing it, and I slid my hands under his sweatshirt and T-shirt, feeling his hot skin, taut body, and narrow waist.

I brushed across raised pieces of skin under his arms, and paused, noticing they reminded me of what I'd felt under his hair two years ago. I rubbed over them with my thumb several times.

"Why were you upset earlier?" he asked. "When you left work?"

That's right. He saw me leave the theater. I looked upset?

I guess I kind of whipped the door closed rather vehemently.

"Did someone else do something to you?" He pulled back to look at me as he buttoned my top button and retied my bow tie.

Normally, I hated when people handled me like a kid and assumed they should do things for me, but I got the impression it was more for him. About putting me 'right' again.

"Just a bad night all around," I told him.

"What happened?"

"Nothing important."

He finished and settled his hands on my waist, waiting.

I laughed quietly, giving in. "I think I quit my job tonight," I told him. "I've been working the ticket booth at Bridge Bay Theater. They'd asked me not to dance on the premises anymore, and I..." I paused, searching for a way to explain so I didn't sound pathetic, "did whatever I could

337

to stay involved there, maybe change their minds. But she won't budge."

I drew in a deep breath and exhaled, reiterating my boss's words. "It's unsafe, and I could hurt myself," I told him, getting angry all over again and starting to tear up. "My boss said something like, 'God has a path, and I need to go where life leads me.'"

"What the fuck?"

"Right?" I said, my voice thick with tears. "I just wanted to, like...burn the whole place down."

He snorted, shaking with laughter, and after a moment, I started laughing, too. He kissed me, reminding me that no matter how the night started, it was ending very well. I wanted to stay with him, but he had friends with him, and I wasn't sure if he already had plans.

"So..." I said, changing the subject. "You have friends."

It was kind of weird, confirming that he was a regular guy with an everyday life. And here I thought he was a vampire, rising only when the sun set.

"Can I meet them?" I asked.

"No."

"Why?"

"Because they're mine, not yours," he warned, moving his mouth under my ear. "And you're mine, not theirs."

"Well that narrows down your identity," I replied. "An only child, because you never learned to share."

I'd figure it out eventually. Or find a way to make him tell me. After all, I was keeping him a secret from others, too.

But, it occurred to me, I wasn't a secret to him. While he was one to me.

Why?

I didn't feel guilty about hiding him from others, but he was hiding himself from me. There was a reason for that.

Was he old? Attached? Psychotic?

Or maybe...embarrassed by me?

But he suddenly spoke up, breaking me out of my thoughts. "Where does your boss live?" he asked.

My boss?

I narrowed my eyes. "Why?"

CHAPTER 17

Damon

FIVE YEARS AGO

We left Anderson's car where it was and climbed in mine, the guys having already moved on, as I drove her back through town and to her boss's house.

"What are you going to do?" she asked me.

I pulled up, parking along the curb, across the street from the theater manager's house, a craftsman-style home with a large wraparound porch and several gables. The yard was green and pristine and only a single light shone from outside the front door.

I wasn't sure yet. But I always came up with something.

Emory Scott lived in this neighborhood. It was nice and clean but boasted none of the mansions the seaside area of town did. I actually preferred it here. Houses close together, neighbors...it would've been a nice place to grow up.

I put the car in *Neutral* and pulled up the e-brake. "What do you want me to do?"

I looked over at her, her hands clasped in her lap, looking kind of nervous, and I smiled. Her mouth twisted, and I could see the apprehension all over her face. So scared of getting into trouble.

But I was sorry. No one told her what she could and could not do.

Except maybe me.

"I don't know," she muttered, looking uncertain. "Let's just leave."

"You want to dance?" I prodded. "I'll get you anything you want."

"How are you going to do that?"

"I *get* anything I want," I stated quite plainly.

She laughed under her breath, probably thinking I was joking, and I went weak for a moment, the light in her eyes the most beautiful thing I'd seen in a long time.

But she shook her head. "No."

Jesus. Is this how she wanted it? Me taking care of shit that hurt her or pissed her off behind her back because she was too timid? Because that's what would happen. I didn't let things slide.

"No one denies you," I said.

"But not like this," she told me. "I won't like how it feels if I don't earn it honestly."

Yeah, I got it. I'd probably feel the same way about basketball.

But...

"She deserves to cry like she made you cry, at least," I pointed out. "At the very least, a pout."

Telling Winter to give up dancing—encouraging anyone to not do what they wanted to do—was arrogant, presumptive, and smug. I wanted to shut her up.

"I can probably have her fired," I said.

But Winter just laughed.

I frowned. "Can I at least flood her yard and do donuts?"

"Nothing destructive," she ordered me. "Nothing mean. It's got to be funny. And like...easy to clean up. You know? Something elegant."

"Something middle school," I corrected her snidely.

She rolled her eyes and sat back in her seat again, smiling to herself.

I relaxed into the headrest, pondering what I had in my trunk. My buddies and I had all been summoned back to town from college to host Devil's Night tomorrow night, and as soon as we got back today, we'd gone supply shopping. I had bottles of liquor in my trunk, but Winter didn't want to start any fires. There was plaster, glue, flashlights, and the guys had some other shit, like rope, smoke bombs, and sledge hammers. Most of this stuff we probably wouldn't use tomorrow, but we'd been so into it after having not taken part in the Thunder Bay night of mischief for a couple years, we lost our heads and got excited.

Something non-destructive, though.

We didn't do anything non-destructive.

And then I remembered. I also had some air horns and duct tape in my trunk.

Jesus. Well, that was it then. I knew what we had to do.

I couldn't believe I was sinking this low, for Christ's sake.

"Buckle up," I told her, shaking my head at myself. "I know what we're going to do."

· · ·

She held the back of my sweatshirt, following me as I jogged down the pathway, around the corner, and past the elevators. I'd been forced to come to Bridge Bay Theater dozens of times growing up to see performances my parents sponsored or to visit my mother when she deigned to perform as if the town should be so grateful to have a genuine Bolshoi ballerina in their midst. Really, it was just an ego boost for her, since she hadn't performed on a grand scale since she was fifteen. My father married her, brought her to America, and that was that.

I knew this place like the back of my hand, even though I hadn't been here in years. Luckily, the basement window still didn't lock.

"You've done this before?" Winter asked me.

I held the door open, pulling her into the ladies' bathroom and turning on the lights and my flashlight off.

"My sister and I did it at our house and once again at the pizza parlor," I told her.

We were like fourteen, but I remember it being pretty funny.

Oh, how times had changed and what made me smile.

"Here, hop up on the counter," I told her.

She did, and I dumped my duffel bag in the sink, digging out some air horns, wooden sticks, and duct tape.

Diving into one of the stalls, I measured the stick's length from underneath the toilet seat to the button on the horn, seeing how it fit.

Perfect.

Good.

I came back to her at the sinks and put the bottle in her hand, fitting her fist around the can and the stick, to hold it in place.

"Hold that right there," I instructed. "Hold it tight."

She nodded, and I got busy making the can, wrapping tape to keep the stick in place on the button, so when someone put weight on it, like sitting on the toilet seat, for example, it would sound off, creating an ear-splitting cry loud enough to shake the foundations of this whole fucking place.

And make every single person inside choke on their coffee.

"So you have a sister," she inquired, continuing our conversation.

"Yep. *Not* an only child," I corrected her and her assumption about my lack of manners in sharing.

"How old is she?"

"A year younger than me."

The roll of tape screeched as I wrapped it around the bottle and then set it down, grabbing another can and stick and putting them in her hand to do the same thing.

"And how old are you?" she asked, playing for information.

"Older than you."

She laughed. "You're not like sixty, are you?"

Sixty? Did I feel sixty when she touched me?

I stopped what I was doing and got down in her face. "Old enough to vote, not old enough to buy liquor," I told her. "But I can still get liquor. If you want."

She just grinned and let it go.

It was amazing she hadn't figured it out yet, but I was careful to take off the rosary when I met her, and I always showered before I came. I thought it would be tough, not smoking to give myself away, but when I was around her, I just wanted to stay around her. My nic fit wasn't worth leaving her until I was damn good and ready.

I'd also never worn my mask, because then she would know I was a horseman.

But if I told her I was nineteen, she'd figure out which class I graduated, and with my lurking and scaring her just like Damon did in the janitor's closet and in the lunchroom, she'd eventually have to face the reality of who I really was, and for now... I liked that she liked me.

I wasn't trying to get her into bed. I wasn't trying to prove how tough I was. I wasn't angry or weighed down or tired of my stupid, fucking life. I was the only place I wanted to be.

Everything was new to her. She was an escape. I could feel anything and feel things again for the first time in her words, her body's reaction, and her face.

It had been hard to stay away, but I knew I had to. The closer we got, the sooner I'd hurt her or she'd find out, and then it would be over.

It only occurred to me tonight, though, when I saw her get into Anderson's fucking car, that she was old enough for things, and it was only a matter of time. I'd wanted to wait until I showed myself again. Wait until she got older, but I just needed to get her out of that prick's car.

I didn't know if I was ever going to take her to bed, but I definitely knew he wasn't going to.

I finished up, making seven cans, and I took one into a stall, affixing it to the floor with the wooden stick underneath the seat, which lifted it up just a hair. I secured everything with tape and came back out, pulling her off the counter.

Lifting her up into my arms, I guided her legs around me and held her there, looking up at her.

"You been good?" I asked her.

Mischief pulled at the corners of her lips, and I stared at them, drawn in to the supple skin and how she'd tasted earlier. She tasted like watermelon. It must've been a lip gloss. Her cheekbones were more pronounced than two years ago, and her blue eyes more piercing with the mascara she'd started wearing.

She circled her arms around my neck, whispering, "Yeah."

"You gonna keep being good?"

Her chest rose and fell against mine, our lips inches from each other.

But she didn't say anything.

"Answer me." I jostled her. "Tell me you'll be good."

She swallowed, but still didn't answer. Instead, she whispered, "What will you do to me if I'm not good?"

Oh, Jesus. She sounded almost hopeful, and my cock swelled as I stared at her dark pink mouth, her parted lips, and I wanted to take them in mine and taste those fucking crazy words on her breath.

What wouldn't I do to her...

"What will I do?" I repeated, brushing her mouth with mine as I carried her into the stall. "I'm going to throw you down..." I lowered us, leaning forward as she held onto me, breathless. "And give you..." Lower, lower. "A big..." Lower. "Fat..." Lower... "Spanking."

And I dropped her ass on the toilet seat, the blaring, banshee cry of the air horn ripping through the theater, splitting my ears.

She screamed and scrambled off the toilet, grabbing onto me and bursting into laughter.

"Oh, my God!" Her face shined, and she looked fucking delighted.

I rolled my eyes, hoping no one heard that out on the street, so they wouldn't find out my shame.

She lowered herself to the seat again, the horn blasted its shrill cry, and she startled, breaking out in laughter again.

I shook my head, pulling her off the seat. "You're so gay."

"Tame compared to what you're used to?" she teased.

"Yes."

God, if the guys found out about this... I needed to get her home before she made me T.P. a house tonight.

Maybe someday I'd take her on a real adventure.

Working quickly, I taped up all the horns, including the one in her boss's office, so when the dancers, employees, and she came in tomorrow, they had a nice little scare.

I packed up all our gear, grabbed Winter, and turned off the lights and my flashlight on, leaving the building.

Once outside, I dumped everything back in the trunk, and moved to open the door.

"Wait," Winter called out.

I looked up, seeing her head turn as if hearing something.

"The fountain," she said, moving around to my side of the car. "In the square. Can you take me to it?"

I listened, faintly hearing it, too. I'd forgotten about it. As a kid, I remembered I'd wanted to play in it, but of course, it wasn't allowed.

Looking around, I noticed the village wasn't that busy and the traffic was nearly dead. It had to be after midnight by now, and since everyone was saving their energy for tomorrow night, it was pretty quiet. Still, though, I had no idea where the guys were, and there was some noise coming from Sticks. I didn't want anyone seeing me and calling my name or seeing *her* with me.

Fuck.

I pulled up my hood and took her hand, leading up the hill to where the small pond with a bridge sat, a large fountain in a garden, and a witch's hat gazebo off to the right. It was a nice, elevated little oasis from the busy village center.

The water spilling into the fountain grew louder, and she let go of my hand, approaching it. She held out her palms, feeling the spray and smiling, and I wanted to take her and climb in with her right now.

Digging into the pocket of her jacket, she pulled something out, turned with her back to the fountain, closed her eyes, and then tossed the coin over her shoulder and into the water.

"Wanna do one?" she asked me, pulling another coin out of her pocket.

I walked up to her, taking in her little bow tie, her hair, almost white with strands of gold, parted and falling on one side, and her lips, the color of bubble gum. Unable to tear my eyes away, I took the coin and flung it over her shoulder and into the water, never taking my gaze off her face.

Using my shoulder to keep herself steady, she slipped off her flats and hopped up on the rim of the fountain and then let me go, having some fun doing ballet moves and balancing herself.

Her phone rang, though, and she stopped, pulling it out and turning it off without answering it.

"Parents calling?" I asked.

"Yeah."

She must've had a particular ringtone to identify them.

Watching her move, twirl, bend, and dip, I followed her around the fountain as she pointed her toes and flexed the muscles in her legs.

What would happen when she grew up? Who would have her? Where would she move? How would this all change?

And all I knew in that moment was that I would fight for nothing more than to keep her like this. Innocent and happy and pure.

Dancing in fountains.

Wobbling, she suddenly reached out for me, and I stepped up to her, catching her before she fell.

She laughed, putting her hands on my shoulders.

"Training hard?" I asked, lifting up her foot to look at the bruises and redness from her toenails cutting into her skin.

"Always," she replied.

These were a dancer's feet.

"Does it hurt?"

She shrugged. "I'm used to it."

Then she wrapped her arms around me and jumped into my hold, forcing me to circle her waist to catch her. She smiled at me, and I held her like that, refusing to put her down as we just stayed there.

But then, tightening her hold, she slowly brought herself in and hugged me.

My chest swelled, aching like shit, and everything washed over me at once. Her smell, her warmth, her hair and body... My lungs caved, and I didn't know why, but it felt so fucking good. I wrapped my arms around her like a steel band, almost feeling relief at holding something—or someone—for the first time in forever.

When was the last time this happened? I never gave fucking hugs, except when Banks needed to talk me down, and that was more like hanging on to something than...

Than actual affection. Than someone actually liking me.

I wasn't weak. I didn't need this shit.

But God, she felt good.

"You dance?" she said in my ear.

"No."

"You are right now," she pointed out.

And I stopped, realizing we'd been turning in a slow circle.

"I think I like this dancing even more than ballet," she told me.

And the corners of my lips turned up in a smile. If only Kincaid could see me now...

But then I saw people approach the other side of the pond, walking up the incline, looking at us.

"We have to get out of here," I told her.

No one could see her with me.

We got back to the car and sped off, and I drove her home, knowing her father would be calling the police station soon if he hadn't already. She was probably supposed to be home over two hours ago.

"They're probably pretty mad," she said as I slowed the engine outside the hedges of her property.

I killed the lights and crawled down the driveway—the gates open—and rounding the hideous fucking fountain to her front door.

I braked, pressing in the clutch, and put the car in first again, sitting there. She hadn't needed help to the door that night I took her out driving, so I assumed she was okay.

But she just sat there, her face turned down a little.

"When will I see you again?" she asked in a timid voice.

I didn't know how to answer that. I was busy tomorrow night, and I'd be going back to school a couple days after that.

I would see her again.

Or...

Maybe. I didn't know.

Jesus, why was she asking? Were we in a relationship or something? Was this a date?

I knew this would happen. She'd have expectations.

Yes, I wanted to see her again. She was mine. In our secluded, secret little world, she was mine.

I wanted to watch her dance, and I wanted to steal her away a thousand more times to feel her excitement and fear and live through how vulnerable and sweet she was, but...

I wanted to keep her happy, pure, and innocent, too. I didn't want to ruin her.

The more time we spent together, and the older she got, the more this would turn into something else. We'd eventually fuck, and she'd make demands I couldn't fulfill.

When she found out who I was, she'd run.

"Is it because I'm blind?" she asked, her voice cracking. "Is that why you hide yourself from me?"

I glared over at her, resenting the shimmer of tears in her eyes as she tried so hard to hold back the little tremble of her chin. So sweet. So sad.

"She was right, wasn't she?" she mused, her tone with a strange resoluteness to it. "I may still want what I want, but I have no control over people who don't want me to have it."

She was talking about that boss of hers who tried to tell her she couldn't have everything she wanted. She wanted me, and while we could fight for what we wanted, people couldn't always be won. Or, that was what she thought. She thought I was embarrassed by her. That I didn't want to take her out or be with her during the light of day.

Her face cracked as she smoothed her skirt over her thighs, and she folded her lips between her teeth to keep from crying, but the tears spilled anyway.

I told you I was going to hurt you someday.

She pulled her house keys from her bag, and removed one key from the ring, dropping it in the cupholder.

"Just keep it," she said. "I like thinking you might come back some day."

And then she climbed out of the car and found her way into the lit-up house, closing the door behind her.

I dropped my eyes, gripping the steering wheel and staring at the key like it was a goddamn drug. I wanted it. I knew I would use it.

I wanted to use it this second.

Goddamn her.

I drove off, careful to keep my speed low and my lights off, and as I turned onto the highway, I turned up the music, kicked the car into third gear and then punched into fifth.

But then I blinked, shook my head, and immediately swerved off to the side of the road, and skidded to a fucking halt.

Damn her. Shit!

What the fuck?

What was she doing to me?

Where was my head?

I'd rolled through the past two years, watching her from a distance, knowing that she would be my heroin and knowing that my obsession was a no-win situation when I got to her again.

I wanted to be with her. I wanted to touch her. I wanted to keep playing games with her.

But I wanted to keep her fourteen forever, too. Young and beautiful and innocent and the one place in my life that wasn't dirty.

She wasn't fourteen anymore, though.

She was growing into something men would want.

Something I wanted.

I looked down at the key, gold and sharp, sitting there in my console, screaming at me louder than the music coming out of my speakers, and I... I just...

I didn't want to leave yet.

I wanted to hide somewhere dark and quiet, feeling her whispers on my lips and smelling the mint in her hair.

Fuck it.

Swinging the car around, the tires screeching on the pavement, I drove back to the entrance of the driveway and parked outside it.

Grabbing her house key, I plucked my phone out of the console and turned it on to text the guys I'd be in for the rest of the night, but I noticed it was dead. I pulled our group phone off the charger—the one we used to record our pranks for Devil's Night—and tossed the guys a text with that one, telling them not to expect me the rest of the evening, and stuffed it into my pocket as I plugged in mine to charge. I locked my car, jogging into the property and keeping out of sight as I veered into the backyard, noticing the downstairs lights were off but a few upstairs remained on.

Walking into the backyard, I dug out the key she gave me and paused, remembering they didn't have an alarm system last time I was here. Hopefully that hadn't changed.

Sliding the key in, I twisted the lock, turned the handle, and opened the door, finding complete silence as I stepped into the dark kitchen.

But not for long.

"Winter, I leave for the airport at five a.m.!" someone shouted upstairs. "You couldn't call?"

I looked around, scanning the kitchen and area, finding it empty. Quietly closing the door, I walked as softly as possible down the hall and into the foyer, staying close to the stairs for cover.

"I'm sorry," I heard Winter say.

They were upset because she was late and hadn't called.

"Have you been crying?" her mother asked, sounding exasperated.

But she didn't have a chance to answer before her father bellowed from down the hall, "You're lucky I didn't phone the station! If you can't handle some common courtesy, then you're quitting that job, or any job for that matter." And then he added, "It's utterly pointless anyway."

Motherfucker. No wonder she was desperate for a little freedom. They thought she was too stupid to handle any.

"I'll deal with this. Go to bed," his wife told him.

"Don't shut me up. She's just as much mine as yours."

She's not either of yours. They were nothing to her.

"And this is why Montreal is best for you," her father went on. "The school there can give you a community where you're safe and comfortable and help you find a college and part-time job if you want."

353

Winter didn't say anything, and I pictured her sitting on her bed, letting them talk, like she either thought it was pointless to argue or thought maybe they were right.

It was neither.

They were so boring. She was incredible.

"All right," her mother interjected, "as long as you're okay. We'll talk about this when I get home next week. I need at least a few hours of sleep tonight. I have to get to bed."

I waited there for several minutes as footsteps pounded above, lights turned off, and doors closed, and after another minute, I swung around the bannister and slowly crept up the stairs, keeping an eye out for anyone still up.

Winter walked across the landing and headed into the bathroom, and as she started the shower and her music, I flew up the steps, dove in after her, and closed the door, grabbing her as she whipped around and sucked in a breath.

I kissed her, cutting off her cry, her protest fading away when she realized it was me.

I hauled her up, wrapped her legs around me, and I ate up her full lips, dragging out the bottom one between my teeth and tasting the tears still on her cheeks.

"What are you doing?" she asked, probably worried I'd be caught.

But I just shook my head, keeping my voice low in case her parents were still awake. "I don't know, baby," I told her. "Just don't let me go, okay?"

She broke down, more tears spilling from her eyes as she kissed and held me so tight.

The lights were off, but the moon lit up the floor, and I slipped my hand under her skirt, letting her know I wanted her. My shit had nothing to do with the fact that she couldn't see me. I wasn't shallow, and this was so much more complicated than she would ever know. Hopefully ever know.

We deserved one night. A few minutes or a few hours, just a little longer.

I knew this was bad. I knew I was fucked.

She hated me. Her family hated me.

She was one of the few people I didn't *want* to hurt.

I was nineteen, and she was too young.

But her mouth. Her damn mouth, leaving little kisses on the corner of mine, her tongue teasing me, the taste of her skin...

I wanted to swallow her up.

"Something I Can Never Have" played, the shower ran, and it was like we were in the fountain as kids again. Everything was pure and sweet, just for that short amount of time, and this was how it was supposed to happen. It was always going to happen with us.

I wanted to feel her on me. Her skin on mine. I wanted every inch of her.

Carrying her to the sink, I set her down and she pulled up my sweatshirt and T-shirt, helping me get them off. I dropped them to the floor and held her face, kissing her again and again, my tongue meeting hers and our heat and breath mixing together.

I pulled back, looking at her eyes as I slipped the bow tie off and unbuttoned her blouse. She ran her hands down my chest all the way to my stomach, fingering the grooves and dips, and I groaned at how good her fingers felt.

This was the only way she could see me, and even though it made my blood race in the most unbearable way, I tried to be patient and let her explore.

Fingers splayed over my collarbone, across my shoulders, down my arms, tracing the lines and muscles on my chest and stomach, and then she slipped her fingers under the waist of my jeans, filling my groin with heat.

"Winter..." I barely whispered.

I wished she knew my name. I wanted to hear her say it.

Why did she feel so different than anyone else?

She slipped out of her shirt, but when she reached around to unclasp her bra, I stopped her, pulling the

PENELOPE DOUGLAS

straps off her shoulders instead and kissing a path up her collarbone to her neck.

Wrapping my arm around her, I brought her body against mine, my groin rubbing between her legs, aching painfully as I kissed her forehead.

"I want you to be my first," she whispered.

I closed my eyes.

"I want it to be you," she continued, "even if you're going to disappear on me again, I want it to be you."

I dug my fingers into her young thighs, wanting to fuck her on this sink right now and kiss her until I couldn't move anymore.

I wanted her first time.

"I..." Fuck, I needed to leave. "I..."

"You. I want you." She peppered my neck with kisses. "I love how the world looks when I'm with you. I want it to be you."

She sucked on my neck, gently sinking her teeth in, and my body exploded with a charge of electric current, my dick begging to get out of these jeans, and I slipped my hand into her hair, holding her mouth to my body. "Fuck."

"Do you have your phone?" she asked against my skin.

"Yeah, why?"

"Take a picture of me doing this," she whispered. "If you disappear, I want you to remember me."

Baby, I've never disappeared. I've always been here. This past summer when you were lying on the beach, I was there. When you went into the shop with your mom for a coffee, I was right there.

She never knew how close I always was.

I dug out my phone and turned it on, remembering I had the group phone. It didn't matter. I'd transfer it later.

"A video, okay?" I breathed out. "I want to have everything."

The way she moved, the sounds she made... I wanted to remember this when I couldn't have her anymore.

Starting a recording, I focused on us and closed my eyes, saving the sounds and images of her pretty face kissing me forever.

"Keep going," I begged.

She licked and nibbled my neck, and I tipped my head back, gripping the back of hers. She took my mouth, sinking her tongue inside mine, and I went fucking weak. The phone spilled out of my hand, and I took her in my arms, holding her tight.

"Goddammit, Winter," I said low. "You're killing me."

She trailed her mouth down my chest and back up again, and my muscles charged with desire so strong I couldn't wait anymore. I pinned her hands behind her back and took over, kissing and biting her with her at my mercy.

She gasped. "I love..." But she stopped herself, realizing what she was about to say.

I hovered over her lips, anger and happiness mixing in with my desire.

Love me? *You love me?* We've met three times, and she didn't even know my name.

But she was quick to recover. "I hate you," she said instead. "I hate you so much."

I gripped her hands, feeling the passion rise, a little smile pulling at my lips. "Yeah, I hate you, too," I told her, hefting her up into my arms and carrying her to the shower. "I just want a hot piece of ass."

"Yeah?" she egged me on.

I dropped her to her feet, not taking my eyes off her face and I yanked her bra down to her stomach, pulling that and her skirt down her legs and off her body.

She brought up her arms, immediately covering her chest as she stood there in her white panties.

I stripped off the rest of my clothes and slid my hands into the back of her underwear, gripping her ass and pulling her into me.

"Take your arms away," I muttered over her lips.

She hesitated, our chests rising and falling in shallow breaths, completely in sync.

"I want to see," I told her.

Slowly, she let her arms fall away, and I felt her nipple and flesh brush my chest, but I couldn't take my eyes off her beautiful face.

I didn't want her first time. I wanted every time.

But I didn't want to love her, either. I didn't want it to feel like this. It couldn't feel like this.

When she found out I lied, she'd hate me.

This had no future.

It was just sex.

Peeling her panties down her legs, I kissed her stomach, feeling her tremble under my mouth, and then I backed her into the shower, closing the frosted door before I pinned her against the black marble wall.

Steam filled the air in a cloud, the hot spray sending chills all over my body as I leaned down and dove into her mouth.

"Your parents are bad," I said, repeating my words from the first time I scared her. "Your sister lacks any depth to be interesting. I told you I was going to hurt you. Didn't I?"

She nodded. "You promised."

My cock twitched, immediately nudging her between her legs.

"I did," I said. "I told you someday I'd hurt you."

She whimpered, rolling her beautiful body into mine, wanting my dick inside her.

I gripped her jaw, planting kisses on her mouth. "I'm gonna fuck your daddy's little girl," I taunted, trying to work myself up.

"Yeah," she panted.

"You want me?" I asked, lifting her up and spreading her legs for me. "Because I want to fuck you, little sweet."

She tried to ride me a little, rubbing herself on me.

"So pretty," I taunted. "Daddy's Little Girl, right?"

She nodded, tipping her head back for me.

"Good girl." I dipped down, sucking on a breast. "Doing what good girls are supposed to do for men. He's gonna have a fuckin' fit when he sees what I did to you. What I did to his little baby."

She threaded her hands into my hair, but I nudged her off. "Take your hands off me," I gritted out, diving deep into my head where it was just action and no fucking thoughts. "If I want to be touched, I'll tell you where. Understand?"

She opened her eyes, looking a little confused, but I didn't care. I wasn't in love with her. This wasn't love.

"Daddy's Little Girl," I said again, an ache wracking through my chest. "Daddy's little slut that fucks guys she doesn't even know when her parents are in bed, huh?"

Pain crossed her face and she stilled, her body going rigid.

"You wanna fuck?" I nipped at her breast, sucking it hard and trying not to feel the nausea roll through me. "Spread your legs and give me a piece of that cunt."

She sucked in a breath, fighting a sudden sob as her eyes welled with tears. "Pl—please," she stuttered, upset. "Please don't talk like that anymore."

And I stopped, my forehead in her chest, the sound of her hurt voice making the bile swell in my throat.

I couldn't do this.

She deserved better.

Even if it was just this one time, I could do it right.

It could mean more. Just with her.

"Can you be gentle?" she asked, tears in her throat.

I shook my head, still not looking at her. "I don't do gentle," I said. "But God, baby, you are tearing me apart right now."

She threaded her fingers through my hair.

"The less special I make this, the less you'll be hurt," I offered.

I knew she didn't know what I was talking about. But the only thing she said was, "You promised to hurt me. Don't stop now."

"I'm afraid to..." I couldn't catch my breath all of a sudden. "I'm afraid I'll make you—"

"I'm not dirty," she rushed, remembering what I said earlier in the car and knowing what I was trying to say. "You're not making me dirty. There is no you. There's no me. This is us. Just us."

And that was all I needed to hear to carry her over to the marble bench and lay her down. Coming down on top her, I kissed her hard, and she parted her legs, bending her knees up and out, letting me settle in.

I groaned, the warmth of her seeping into my groin as I pulsed and ached with need to be inside of her tight body.

I hovered over her, staring down at her face and running my hand over her body. Her slender neck and smooth chest. Her round, pointed breasts and taut stomach. Her thighs and around to her ass.

I positioned myself, seeing her body pump with heavy breaths, and I pushed inside her, every muscle in her body going still as she cried out.

I came down, putting my hand over her mouth as I sank the rest of the way inside her, burying myself deep.

Her whimpers vibrated against my hand as she panted, and I didn't move, waiting for the pain to subside.

A mixture of pleasure and anger coursed through, knowing it was done, and I'd ruined her now, but everything feeling so goddamn good that I knew I'd do this all over again if I had a chance to go back.

Her body squeezed me tightly in heat, and my cock throbbed with the need to start pumping.

I removed my hand. "Does it still hurt?"

She paused but then started to relax, her thighs falling wide again and her nails retracting from my shoulders. "No." She swallowed. "Not really anymore."

I slid my hand under her ass, grabbing hold, and with my gaze on her face, I pulled out of her and thrust right back in.

She made the sweetest little sound, her face twisted up in pain and pleasure as she adjusted to me, and when she started to arch her back and roll her hips to meet me, I knew I didn't have to hold back anymore.

I pumped my cock, seeing her breasts shake with the movement and her throat bare and open for my mouth as she threw her head back.

Her moans grew louder, and I put my mouth over hers, flicking her with my tongue and nibbling her lips. "Shhhh," I teased. "You're going to get me in trouble."

She smiled, biting her lip. "It feels so good."

Yeah, but this wasn't going to last long. It was taking everything I had to hold back. My dick was charged and ready, and I wanted to go harder.

"Touch yourself," I told her.

I needed her to help me get her off before I came.

She did what she was told and reached down, rubbing herself as I thrust inside her faster and deeper.

She arched up and kissed me, raising her knees higher, knowing what I needed to sink farther into her. She was so wet, and I sucked the water off her breasts, neck, and jaw as her hand worked herself between us.

She got faster and faster, started moaning, and then sank her claws into my shoulder again as she stopped touching herself and let me ride her to orgasm.

I put my hand over her mouth as she came, her muscles contracting around my cock, squeezing me like a vise grip, and the sweetest little whimpers coming out of her mouth.

"Did you like that?" I asked, leaving kisses on her lips.

She nodded, and I pumped harder, going at her with free rein now and not holding back.

My dick swelled, and my insides drove with a need so fucking good, and I couldn't hold it anymore.

"I'm going to pull out, okay?" I told her.

She was quiet for a second. "Like on me?"

"Yeah, baby."

It probably took her a minute to figure out what I meant, but then she nodded. We weren't using any protection, after all. I doubted she was on the pill.

I thrust a few more times, unable to hold it anymore, and pulled out, stroking myself until I came and spilled onto her stomach. The orgasm wracked through me, and my head floated away from me as I closed my eyes and savored the feel of her and what she did to me.

The wave spread through my entire body, and I stayed there, pretty fucking sure nothing compared to her.

She was incredible.

Why did that feel so different?

I opened my eyes, seeing a little smile pull at her mouth as she reached out a finger, trying to feel what I left on her stomach.

But I stopped her, pulling her hand away. "No, don't touch it," I said. "I'll... Just wait." I climbed off her. "Don't move."

I left the shower, finding a washcloth and came back in, wetting it under the spray. Ringing out the water, I cleaned up the mess on her stomach, shaking my head at myself.

What the fuck? I came on her?

Jesus.

Once she was clean again, I rinsed the cloth, soaking it with warm water, and then folded it before laying it down against her skin between her legs.

I had no clue how she felt, but I'd gone at her pretty hard, and it was her first time.

"That feels good," she said.

"Just hold it there."

She laid there, doing as I said, and I stood under the spray rinsing myself off and wetting my hair.

I tried not to look at her, but I couldn't stop myself. She was wet and naked and beautiful, and the only pure thing I'd ever had.

And, of course, I messed her all up.

"Why are you smiling?" I asked, noticing the curl to her lips.

"Shouldn't I be smiling?"

Yeah, okay.

"This feels like the time I sat in a fountain once," she told me. "The water spilled around us, shielding us. Hiding us. It was like a world within a world. One of my worst memories but also one of my best."

I smoothed my wet hair over my head over and over again, that day like yesterday in my memory. If only she knew the boy she was with in the fountain was the boy who just fucked her.

Did she still hate him?

"Us?" I prodded.

I wanted to hear her talk about me. See what was still in her head. If time had healed anything.

But she just stayed quiet, not elaborating any further.

"So was that red?" she asked, changing the subject.

Red?

Oh, right. The night of the motorcycle ride. She wanted to know what red felt like.

I scoffed. "Maybe like orange."

"Orange?" She looked appalled. "Can it at least be purple?"

I laughed under my breath, walking over to her and taking the wash cloth off of her. "Purple then."

I helped her to her feet, so we could get her clean, and she found her way under the water wetting her hair.

"When can I see red?" she asked.

And I planted my hand on the wall, holding her face with the other one, as I stared down at her and saw all the shit that was going to eventually hit the fucking fan.

When you find out who just fucked you, you're gonna see plenty of red then.

CHAPTER 18

Winter

PRESENT

"Mikhail?" I called, trailing down the hallway. I'd woken up, hearing his nails clicking on the hardwood floor.

Music played in the house, and I could hear some people downstairs, moving freely, as well as cars driving up to the house. What was going on?

After the bath, I'd locked my door, slipped on some clothes, dried my hair, and repacked my escape bag, counting my money again and making a mental list of where I could go, just in case. I knew I wouldn't run, because that would put others at risk, but I needed something to keep myself occupied.

And then stupidly, I'd fallen asleep, the worry, the fright from this morning, and the bathtub making me crawl into a ball on my bed and sink far away.

I needed another plan. One, I thought, that involved Damon's old friends. They could stop him.

They would stop him for me.

"Mikhail?" I said louder.

My phone was still downstairs—hopefully fully charged, given that it was almost eight at night—but I heard a whine and veered into my father's room, instead.

367

I heard the faucet run in the master bath, but I didn't give a shit if Damon was in there or not.

"Mikhail."

My dog's wet nose hit my leg, and he breathed happily, licking my fingers.

I knelt down, smiling and relieved. "Hey." I petted and hugged him, the dreariness of the last couple of days gone all of a sudden.

Thank you, thank you, thank you...

I'd been pretty sure Damon wouldn't have taken him out and had him shot, but tears sprang to my eyes, so happy he wasn't gone for good.

"Why were you in here?" I scolded in a playful tone, taking his collar in my hand and standing up. "Stay away from him, boy."

"Ke nighg-ya," an order came from the bathroom, Russian again.

Mikhail pulled out of my grasp and ran away, the nails of his paws tapping against the bathroom tiles.

"Mikhail?" I said sterner.

"The dog was a mistake," Damon said. "He won't protect you from me. I know how to handle him. I know how to get things to obey me."

"Give him to me."

"Sure," he chirped. "Take him. If you can."

"Mikhail," I demanded, tapping my leg. "Mikhail, come here!"

But my dog didn't move, not a single jingle from his leash or sound of his nails.

My chin trembled, but I refused to cry.

But before I got a chance to spin around and walk away, Damon grabbed my wrist and pulled me into the bathroom. I resisted, trying to pull away and noticing he was only in a towel as he pressed me against the sink and shoved a long piece of metal in my hands.

"What is this?" I asked as he wrapped his fist around mine, forcing me to hold it.

The scent of shaving cream filled the space, and the steam of his shower crawled into my pores.

"Do you want to know how I control him?" Damon asked.

I didn't give a shit...

"Food," he explained. "Most animals, including humans, can be controlled by a system of consequences and rewards."

Something hit the ground, I heard Mikhail move, and his jaws yapped as he ate whatever Damon tossed him.

"We want to eat, so we do what we need to in order to be fed," he said. "And all animals have that in common. They can't synthesize their own nourishment, so they easily become subject to whoever provides it. It's how animals are domesticated. How humans can be enslaved in soul-draining jobs and relationships." He leaned in, his breath wafting over my face. "We all need to eat, Winter."

I jerked my head, trying to pull away from him again.

"And humans are complex," he went on. "More than just our stomachs need to be fed."

He raised my hand, and whatever was in it, to his face, and even though I gritted my teeth, trying to pull away, he forced it against his skin and glided it up his neck to his jaw. He forced my hand, and I stopped fighting as it grated against his stubble. Then he lowered my hand to the sink behind me, rinsing it clean.

A razor. A straight razor. I brought up my other hand, carefully feeling the object in my hand. Cool and metal, the blade was smooth and sharp, while the handle featured filigree etchings, making for an easier grip. Was it an antique? No one used these anymore.

He lifted me up and planted my ass on the counter, his hand on both sides of me.

"Keep going," he said in a low voice.

Keep going? Did he want to die today? Or did he think I wouldn't use this on him?

"Why?" I asked him. "So you can prove how well I can do what I'm told? Like a dog?" I put my free hand on his chest, trying to keep him from getting too close. "I don't need you to feed me."

"Maybe I need you to feed me."

What did that mean?

"Do it," he urged.

I held the blade, liking how easily the handle fit in my fist, and loving how he was right in front of me, putting a weapon in my hand, and this could all end now.

Did he trust me? Or did he think he could stop me in time?

He was definitely testing me. Seeing how much I did or didn't hate him.

And he was willing to put himself in danger to find out.

All of a sudden, I felt like I did the night I drove his car all those years ago.

Like I was dangerous.

"I'll cut you," I warned him.

"Yeah."

"And if I slit your throat?"

He breathed a laugh. "My kind of fun has a price, remember?"

I stopped breathing for a moment, remembering those words. Remembering that he was him. My ghost. The one I kissed and made love to.

At first those words had filled me with dread, because it meant he'd had no limit. Then they excited me, because I wanted adventures with the boy I thought I loved.

I brought my free hand up and gripped his face, tipping it back and keeping it still. Then I drifted my fingers down his neck, feeling where the skin was smooth and already shaven and where the shaving cream still sat.

"Come in, closer," I told him.

He did, forcing me to spread my legs as his fingers brushed the outside of my thighs, bare in my sleep shorts. I ignored the goosebumps that spread over my skin.

Bringing the blade up slowly, I felt his chest start to rise and cave with shallow breaths, and I damn near smiled, because, if even just a little, he was nervous.

Finding the position with my thumb, I put the blade to his skin and pressed, increasing the pressure just a little more than I should have and feeling him suck in a breath.

It was his turn to be scared.

I let it sit there for a moment, feeling the air grow thick between us as he waited for what I was going to do with the blade pressed to his neck. Were his eyes cast down on me, watching me? Was he waiting for it? Was he ready for it?

I held it there for another moment and then...glided the blade up his neck, shaving it.

He held his breath for a moment and then exhaled softly as the blade left his neck.

Running my fingers over the strip I just shaved, I felt smooth skin. Skin I'd had my lips on when I'd thought he was someone else.

Rinsing off the blade, I took his face again, shoving it back to where I had it, because he'd dropped it again—probably to watch me.

He stood there silently as I slowly dragged the blade up his throat, the grainy sound filling the room and everything in the distance fading away. My hand shook with the knowledge that at any moment I could cut him.

Deep.

He would deserve it. After what he did to me...

After being everything I craved and needed, he made me fall in love with him, but come to find out, I'd fallen for a lie. A boy who treated me badly and found out how easy it was to hide right under my nose and get me to fuck him. Did he laugh about it after with his friends? Did he have fun?

My eyes pooled with tears as I shaved another strip, the tension in my hand making it ache as I gripped the razor so tightly.

How could he lie like that? The way he was... The words, the kissing, the shower, the way he held me and acted so sad sometimes, the desperation in his body when he took mine over and we were lost in the heat and the need to feel each other.... How could he lie so well? Young girls weren't hard-hearted. He had to know how easily I would fall. Did he think it would be funny when he got my hopes up and played with me like that? Did he laugh at how pathetic the little blind girl was to think he loved her?

He sucked in a short breath, and I stopped, my tears threatening to spill over as I realized I'd cut him.

He didn't say anything, though, and he didn't move. I sat there, my hand in mid-air under his chin as I waited. I actually hadn't meant to do that. Was it bad?

I heard him swallow and then he said, "Keep going." But it came out as a whisper.

I blinked away the tears and loosened my grip, trying to relax.

"What's all the noise downstairs?" I asked him.

"Extra security."

"To keep me locked in?"

"To keep you safe," he corrected in a coy tone.

I was sure the disdain was visible on my face. But then I remembered how he denied being in the theater bathroom and Crane denied that anyone was in the house this morning when I ran to St. Killian's. They had no reason to lie. Was I in more danger than I thought? Was someone else after me? Enemies my father made or something?

I quieted, almost afraid of his answer when I asked, "Is my family really in the Maldives?"

"Yes," he said.

Pain pricked at the back of my throat.

And while it was unusual my mother was on his honeymoon and not him, I knew why. He had no interest in the Maldives. Everything that interested him was here.

"Why would my mother leave me with you?"

"Because she's a cunt."

My hand shook a little, part of me angry and part of me wanting to cry. She left me. She actually left me. Did she fight? Sob? Have to be forced out the door at least? Did he offer her anything? Was she supposed to be back soon?

Why did she let him convince her to leave?

Because she's a cunt.

My chin trembled for a moment, almost appreciating the genuine anger in his voice. He'd done this. He'd sent them away.

But even though he did what he thought he had to do to get what he wanted, he still didn't have any respect for my mother for giving in to him. What kind of parent...

"Where do you go when you're not here?" I pried, changing the subject. "Are you really going into the city? Or New York? Where?"

Or were you close? Always close.

He was gone a lot, and it hadn't escaped my notice that he barely stayed here at night. Where the hell was he sleeping?

Maybe he had another woman. Another woman other than my sister, I meant.

He hissed again, and I knew I'd cut him again.

Shit.

But he still didn't move or speak, just breathed, exhaling slow, almost like a sigh of relief.

"Keep going," he whispered, sounding breathless and raspy this time.

Heat rolled off him, and I could feel his chest under my hand, the slow, steady breaths almost sounding calm and spent, like he enjoyed it.

He liked being cut?

Or he liked the fear?

Again, I was reminded of the night driving his car. I'd loved how he didn't get mad at my mistakes and waited for me to do things at my pace. Just like now. He wasn't mad I cut him.

But maybe there was something in it for him, too. He enjoyed toying with death. Fear made us feel alive.

I finished with his neck and rinsed off the blade. "Bend forward a little," I told him. "I can't reach your face."

He came in as close as he could, pressing between my legs, and tipped his head down at me, our bodies chest to chest. His warmth spread across my face with him only inches away, and I felt self-conscious. "Don't stare at me."

I could feel his shitty little smile.

Finding my position, I slid the blade up the side of his face, going with the grain, because my father did it that way, and Damon didn't say to do it differently. I shaved one cheek and moved the other, grazing my fingers over his skin to feel for any missed spots.

His warm breath hit my forehead, the heat of his body everywhere, and I knew he was looking down at me, but I suddenly didn't want to tell him to stop, because for a split second, I remembered how good his arms and hands felt. Even if it was a lie, I let myself enjoy the intimacy I'd been starved for. For just a moment.

I ran the blade down his skin, shaving everywhere I felt stubble. His cheeks, his chin, above his top lip, and below his bottom one, and I dragged my fingers over every inch of jawline to feel for anything I'd missed, and after seconds of my hand on him, I was drawn back to the ballroom seven years ago when he let me look at him with my hands.

Nothing had changed.

I set the blade down and brought both hands up to cup his face. "Just need to check," I told him, but it came out so soft I wasn't sure he heard me.

I touched him, grazing my fingertips across his cheekbones, down to his jaw, up his neck, and over the hollows of his cheeks. He moved into it, meeting my touch by cocking his head and turning it, giving me complete access as I checked my work, and then his words came back to me from all that time ago.

Want to check the rest of my body?

Absently, my fingers fell down his neck, and I dug my fingers in just a little, because I wanted to touch more, and I hated myself for it.

His breathing turned labored, and he pressed his hands into the grooves of my thighs where they met my hips, kneading them.

He leaned down, his nose brushing mine as he pressed his chest into me and growled in a whisper, "Winter..."

I gripped his shoulders, feeling the ridge of his hard cock nudge me between my legs as heat pooled in my groin. My heart pounded. I wanted to run away.

And I wanted him to rip off my clothes, too.

I hate you.

I hate you.

I hate you.

He fell into me, pushing me back against the mirror, and I rolled myself into him, my clit throbbing with the tease of his muscle through his towel.

And I knew...even with as good as he felt and how lonely I'd been, because I couldn't trust anyone or myself after the humiliation of that video, once it was done, I'd hate myself. I'd hate myself for letting him have a piece of me again.

I turned away from him, pushing at his body to get free. "Get off me."

But he stayed there a moment, breathing hard.

"Why?" he finally asked. "You seem to like me."

"Get off me!" I snapped. "You're not getting that from me."

I shoved at him, putting all of my strength against his chest, but he just rumbled with a laugh.

"I've already had *that*," he said, his voice sharp and threatening. "Now I want your sanity. Just a little turn of the screw..."

I scrambled out from underneath him, stood up, and slammed him in the chest.

He stumbled back, laughing again. "All in good—"

"Yo, Winter!" a shout damn near shook the house from downstairs. "We're here!"

Huh?

"Who is that?" Damon demanded. "That sounds like Will."

But he didn't give me a chance to answer. He shot past me, and I let out a breath, relief washing over me as I remembered my talk with Will last night.

Coldfield.

I'd been talking to Will and his friend, Alex, at the party, telling them how fun the new haunted house park was and how I wanted to go back before it closed for the season.

Since I'd kind of left abruptly last time and hadn't gotten around to everything.

They hadn't gone yet, and so we said we'd go tonight.

I'd completely forgotten.

After the past twenty-four hours, I wasn't in the mood for haunted houses tonight, but anywhere was better than here.

I walked out of the bathroom and master bedroom, across the landing and to the railing, showing myself to wherever they were in the foyer below.

"Why are you two here?" Damon asked them, and I startled, realizing I'd stopped next to him.

Great. I was in my pajamas, he was in a towel, and we both just came out of his bedroom. Perfect.

"None of your business," Will told him. And then to me, "Winter, show Alex to your room. She's going to help you get ready."

I then heard footfalls on the stairs, getting closer.

Ready? I was capable of getting dressed on my own.

"Why do you have your mask?" I heard Damon ask Will, I would assume.

The way he said 'your mask' sounded like Damon had one, too. All the horsemen did, I'd heard.

"Fucker, no one's talking to you," Will barked back.

I snorted, and I could feel Damon fume next to me.

Will was fun. I think I liked him.

Damon didn't have a chance to question me, though, because a cool, slender hand took my arm, and I led Alex down the hall to my bedroom, a little more excited for the night out than I was a moment ago.

I wanted a fun outfit, a drink, and some chills and thrills. As long as none of them came from Damon Torrance.

• • •

It wasn't just any night on the Coldfield calendar of events. It was 18 & Over Night, which meant no minors allowed, hard liquor and cocktails served, and clothing didn't have to leave much to the imagination. Costumes encouraged.

We walked through the entrance, brandishing our All Access wristbands, and I pulled my skirt taut as much as I could, feeling a little shy. *Fun outfit, indeed.* Alex was interesting, and to think she got nearly everything I was wearing from my own closet.

After we'd disappeared into my bedroom, she got busy, making short work of my hair and makeup and doing my face up like some clown. Or a sexy clown, as she'd said. She painted some designs on my forehead with tear drops under my eyes and finished it off with red paint on the tip of my nose and some black lipstick outlined with white around my lips.

While I'd been asleep, I'd received a voice text from my mother, letting me know she and Ari were okay and that I was going to be fine.

No calls. No further information.

They were okay, and I was going to be fine.

Cryptic and cruel, and I didn't understand it.

I'd tried calling both of them, but they didn't answer, and I wasn't sure I expected them to. What would they say, after all?

What had Damon told my mother?

Maybe he was a smooth talker and made her assurances? Maybe the financial arrangement was too good to pass up. Maybe she was just tired of fighting.

Just a little turn of the screw...

His taunt echoed in my mind again, and whatever he was planning wasn't something by force like I'd thought. He was trying to wind his way into my head.

Alex teased and fluffed my hair, the heaven I was in with all the grooming and being touched starting to relax me, but then she went to my closet, dug out some things, and with my permission, began ripping and cutting to make me a costume.

I wore my fluffy, black miniskirt with tulle layered underneath, a strappy, leather bra she'd had with her, and the tutu torn off one of my ballet costumes from when I was little wrapped around my neck in a big collar. She dressed up my wrists with whatever I had in my armoire and sprayed some body glitter on my stomach, legs, and arms.

She tried to put heels on me but quickly realized that would be a mistake—as I'd told her it would be—and I slipped into my black Chucks instead.

But before we left the room, she remembered one last thing.

Fangs.

Sharp, smooth, and acrylic, she took out her extra set, mixed up the plaster, filled the grooves inside the two fangs, and asked me if I wanted them on my canines or incisors.

Blade or True Blood?

Blade.

Canines, it was. She fastened them on top on my real teeth, and I held them for a couple of minutes, letting the plaster dry and getting used to the feeling. The points brushed against the inside of my bottom lip, but otherwise they felt pretty functional.

I was ready.

I wasn't sure how I looked, but Will let out a whistle when I came down, and Damon let me leave with no problem. In fact, he was unusually pleasant about the whole thing. About me going out with his friends half-naked.

It kind of gave me pause.

Have fun, he'd said in a tone more loaded than I could figure out.

Whatever. I was sure I'd deal with him later tonight.

"Drinks!" Alex called out, ordering our first stop of the evening.

People swarmed the park, squeals and screams going off around me as others ran or chased, one bumping into me, and "Bloodletting" by Concrete Blonde played from somewhere in the distance while spooky, haunted sounds of creaking doors and evil laughter drifted from the speakers around us. I inhaled, the smell of the earth hitting the back of my throat, and the kerosene from the torches going straight to my head.

I held onto Will's arm as we made our way through a throng of people over to the liquor and food stands I smelled last time that we didn't get a chance to try out.

"What'll you have?" he said as we stopped. "Looks like they can do mixed drinks, shots, draft and bottled beer, wine..."

He reached into his back pocket, so I let his arm go to let him move.

"Um, beer," I answered. "Any lager is fine. Bottle. Unopened, please."

"Good girl."

Yeah. And not really what I was in the mood for, but it was the only thing I was sure wouldn't be tampered with. In a setting like this, with all these people and madness around...

"Oh, wait, I have money." I slipped my fingers through the straps of my bra under the clown collar where I concealed my money clip and phone.

But he just laughed. "Yeah, so do I. Don't worry about it."

I pulled my hand back out. "Thanks."

Really, how was he Damon's best friend back in the day? He was so different. Did he like abuse or something?

I couldn't picture him having Damon's dark side.

Taking our drinks, I twisted off the top of the aluminum bottle, the condensation wetting my hand, and took a drink, followed by a few more. Even just the taste got me in the mood for this, and I started to relax.

Sound effects of howls and screams filled the air, and Alex offered me her arm as we walked to our first experience, *The Tunnel of Terror.*

I heard a track and the clank of bars as we waited in line, and it sounded like a ride with cars that carried us along a path. I gripped Alex's arm a little tighter, the adrenaline already warming my heart.

So this would be something where we're locked in, unable to run.

The line moved, and we climbed in a car, Alex first, and I followed. Will squeezed in next to me, and I raised my hands to let the belt-bar come down on us, but I accidentally knocked his mask, and I winced.

"Shit, I'm sorry," I laughed.

I patted the hard plastic in a sympathetic gesture, feeling the grooves of the skull paintball mask and what felt like scars designed across it.

"Why do you think I wore the mask?" he joked.

Oh, shut up.

The ride shot off, my head bouncing against the back of the car and then veered right, swinging us around the bend so hard, we both fell over into Will. Alex squealed, and I didn't know if the squeaks of the wheels on the track were just a sound effect or actually real, but it felt seedy and cheap—kind of corrupting—and I rubbed my thighs together, sort of liking it. We pushed through the double doors, and I felt the fog thick in the air and heard blocks of metal and chains clanking.

I felt Alex and Will both jump a couple times, followed by disgusted sounds from Alex, so there was more to see than to feel in the tunnels, but I expected it. I'd told them in the car on the way here not to narrate for me. We'd just all enjoy what we could.

A whiff of air hit my ear, followed by a bark, and I jerked, laughing.

"There's speakers and sensors in the back of the car," Will figured.

Other sounds drifted out—chainsaws, potions boiling, screams, and bat wings cutting through the air—and Alex inched into me, forcing me into Will. She pushed farther into my space, and I heard a whimper and guessed an actor was on her side of the car, taunting her. I laughed at her fright, feeling a little superior that I wasn't affected as easily.

We wound through more tunnels, both of them absorbing the darkness and creepy characters in bloody costumes or masks that I didn't see, but as soon as I'd relaxed, the car stopped.

"What is that?" Alex asked.

"I can't see anything," Will replied.

Okay. Guess I'd just wait.

We sat there, and I couldn't hear any other voices around us, so they must have considerable space between the cars.

"Will, what is that?" Alex blurted out. "Right there!"

And then, all of a sudden, I heard growling. Like a feral wolf, frothing at the mouth. Was that a sound effect?

"Ah!" Alex cried out, and I tensed.

Weight hit our car, jostling the front of it, I listened as the low growling got closer and closer.

And closer.

The deep rumble of an animal, and my toes curled and my body instinctively tried to crawl into a ball, but I couldn't with the bar over my lap.

The growling came closer and closer, the breath falling on my face, and I knew someone was standing on the front of our car and leaning down right into my face.

It was breathy and scary and vicious, and my heart pounded as he taunted me.

Alex and Will either whimpered or laughed, and if I could see him, I might've been scared out of my mind, but like this it was just...frightening enough. A tingle shot between my thighs, and I clenched them as I breathed hard.

The cars started moving again, and I felt him linger for a moment longer before jumping off.

"Oh, he liked you," Will teased.

My pulse still raced, and everything was warm. I rubbed my hands down my thighs and tongued one of my fangs, wondering what was wrong with me that it was kind of a turn on.

Did I like fear?

Or did I only like it because I knew I was safe?

The ride ended, and we left the car, taking our drinks with us. I uncapped my beer, taking a gulp to cool down and clear my throat, suddenly parched.

Tossing it in the trash, we headed for the maze next, and I took Will's arm this time, since Alex didn't want to lead, and I refused to take up the rear.

Actors reached through walls, grabbing at us, while others stood in the passageways, lurking still and quiet for some good jump scares. Hands grabbed at my arms, and I scurried to Will's other side, laughing, only to be attacked on that side, as well.

Of course, there were things I missed that made those two jump, but I could feel the tight space of the walls and low ceiling and smell the cold air and soil. It felt like we were underground, but I knew we weren't.

We rounded a corner, and Will halted, quickly backing up into me and stepping on my toe.

"Ouch!" I snapped.

But I didn't get a chance to find out what scared him. Alex screamed behind me, and Will took my hand, turning us both around to find out what was wrong.

"Hey!" he yelled. "That's mine! Give her back!"

Huh? I inched closer to him, holding on to his arm. What was happening?

Alex's squeals kept filling the corridor, but they started to fade, echoing from down the hall. My mouth fell open.

Did they take her? Where did she go?

Oh, my God.

"Shit, let's go," Will said, a laugh following.

He pulled me onto his back, and I hooked my arms around his neck, while he held me under my knees, and we ran back the way we came, going after Alex.

The actors—since they were allowed to touch us—must've grabbed her and carried her off.

Will bolted down the tunnel, and someone nipped at my back, growling and clawing. I cried out, squealing as I scrunched up my shoulders and hugged Will tightly. "Hurry," I gasped. "They're going to take me, too!"

He ran unbelievably well with someone on his back, and my heart raced a mile a minute, about to beat out of my chest in the excitement. He turned corners, listening for Alex's screams, and the muscles in my arms and legs burned as I tried to hold onto him.

Alex's cries sounded closer, and then I heard her.

She was laughing. "Will?" she shouted. "Oh, my God. He threw me over his shoulder like I was a feather. I thought I was going to get eaten."

We stopped and Will let me down. I kept hold of his arm as he bent over, maybe to help her up to wherever the actor had dropped her, but we barely had time to collect ourselves before growls and loud motors filled the air and we were swarmed by what felt like ten chainsaw murderers. They came at us, nipping at our legs with their bladeless chainsaws, and we all stumbled, scurried, and veered in any direction we could to get away.

"Winter, where are you?" I heard Will shout from farther away than I thought he was.

But then, all of a sudden, he was there, grabbing my hand and pulling me away.

I breathed a sigh of relief. He walked fast, dragging me as the air blowers shot at my legs, and I laughed as the hay sack tunics the slasher killers wore brushed my arms as we passed, telling me just how close I was to getting caught. Chills spread across my body, and my pulse went wild, unable to contain the frenzy of danger and the intoxication in my head it created. I was high from it.

We turned right and then right again, and as the noise fell away and no one came at us anymore, he slowed his walk, pulling me around walls and passageways in the maze.

I panted, still holding his hand but bringing my free one up to his mask and feeling it. "That's you, right?"

Just making sure.

I still laughed a little but relaxed when I felt the hard plastic skull with grooves.

"This is so much fun," I told him.

Silence filled the corridor now, except for the sound effects of wind howling, a heart beating, and clocks chiming drifting out of the speakers, his hand tightening around mine as we walked. I didn't mind. He wasn't doing it because I couldn't see. He probably did it, so I wouldn't get stolen like Alex.

Alex.

I turned my head left and right, listening for her footsteps.

"Where's Alex?" I asked.

She was with us, wasn't she? He only grabbed me for a quick escape.

But just then, I stepped in something wet, my foot sloshing in something on the ground.

"Oh, yuck." I stepped away, inching into him to get away from whatever the pool was on the ground. Smelled like vodka. Someone must've spilled their drink.

Wrapping his arm around my waist, he picked me up, and I circled my arms around his neck as he carried me over it.

"Thanks," I told him.

But he didn't put me down.

My legs dangled as he slowly walked, the sound of his breathing through his mask even, like a machine.

Awareness made the hairs rise on my skin, and I felt so dizzy all of a sudden. My voice barely registered above a whisper. "I can walk now."

He still didn't put me down, though. Instead, he hefted me up so my legs circled his waist, and the realization that the man in my arms wasn't Will washed over me in a panic so savory it sank down low in my belly, warming every inch of my body.

He carried me, his steps perfectly paced and heavy, echoing in the hallway like they were coming for me and knew exactly where I was hiding.

This wasn't Will.

I knew it even before I slipped my fingers into the back of his hair and felt the same little scars I'd come across years ago.

But in this moment, in the dark where I was someone else and he was someone else, I didn't pull away.

Why wasn't I pulling away?

God, he felt good.

In my arms. I'd almost forgotten.

For just a few minutes, he was my ghost back in the house.

Taunting me.

Playing with me.

Making me feel things I wanted to feel.

I'd missed this so much.

I locked my ankles behind his back and held my head in front of his, quiet and calm on the outside but every emotion I'd ever had raging on the inside. I wasn't sure if he could see

PENELOPE DOUGLAS

where he was walking, but it seemed like we both were on auto-pilot.

"Where are you taking me?" I asked him quietly.

But he just kept silent.

His heart beat against my chest, and I matched my breathing to his, fear and fantasy taking me over as the foggy air soaked into my skin and the sounds of the haunted carnival outside waged on without us. Heat pooled between my legs, and I barely noticed when an actor jumped out at us, trying to scare me.

They dug their fingers into my back, screeching, but I just kept holding on to him, wanting to stay like this, because this scared me more and I liked the fear.

What was he going to do to me?

We trailed down a long hall, another actor grabbing at us, but I just clutched him tighter, my forehead against the forehead of his mask as my fangs dug into my bottom lip and my pussy throbbed.

"Will you say anything?" I whispered.

Where was he taking me? Where were my friends?

But really, I didn't care. I just felt like I should.

He wasn't my enemy in here. He was my secret shame.

Marilyn Manson's "Cry Little Sister" played through the speakers outside, and he hefted me up again, his stomach pressed between my legs. I whimpered as his hands gripped my ass.

Oh, God.

My lips hovered over the mouth of his mask, and I dug my fingers into the back of his neck, aching with need and groaning under my breath.

The next thing I knew, we were through another door and then another, and I let him carry me into a quiet room that smelled of wet straw and flannel. He pulled me off him, sending me falling onto a pile of hay, and I sucked in a breath, a scream lodged in my throat and instinct kicking in as I scurried backward to get away from him.

The slow, gentleness from him a moment ago was now gone.

I crawled backward, hearing the noise and music outside, but he caught my ankle and pulled me back to him. My stomach somersaulted as he flipped me over, knocking the air out of me as he hauled me up on my knees.

My chest pumped with shallow breaths, and my fight kicked in as I scrambled to my feet and bolted.

But he caught me from behind, wrapping an arm around my waist and picking me up. My head fell back against his shoulder as he reached between us and undid the belt fastening Alex's bondage bra that I wore.

His rough hands, the partygoers outside on the other side of the wall, his silence, my costume, his mask... everything turned me on, and in this little room, we took hold of our little world where only the two of us lived and dared to sink deep, if only for a few minutes where no one would know.

Air hit my nipples as the bra fell away, and in the next moment, I was on my feet again, his hands pawing my breasts.

I gasped, my eyes closing at the pleasure of being touched there, but then I heard something hit the ground, and his teeth came in, sinking into my neck.

I cried out, unable to control the roll of my hips, because I needed him inside me as my legs nearly gave out under me. The heat of his mouth poured over my skin like hot syrup, and the pain was just enough to bring every other inch of my skin to full awareness. Everywhere he touched was sensitive, feeling like a flaming torch over my body. I couldn't think. I didn't want anything else.

I reached back, touching his face, now free of the mask, and he left my neck, gripping my hair and yanking my head back. I was completely immobile as he chewed at my lips, kneaded my breasts, and flicked one of my fangs with his tongue.

His breath almost sounded like a growl as he seethed, as completely lost as me.

Picking me up, he spun me around, bringing us both down onto the ground. I landed on my hands and knees, and tried to rise, but he pushed me back down.

I heard the jingle of his belt and then his zipper, and my arms shook under me, and I couldn't breathe. I'd never done it this way.

He knocked my knees wider, gripped my hips, and yanked me back to him, the hard flesh of his cock pressing into me.

A moan escaped me, and I could already feel how wet I was.

He grabbed hold of my panties and ripped them away, the fabric stretching and tearing off my body. He took hold of himself, crowned me, and before I could say anything, he slid inside me, burying himself deep and filling me so good my knees quaked.

"Ah," I whimpered, going rigid for a moment to adjust.

The spot he hit deep inside sent a wave of pleasure to the rest of my body, everything tingling and buzzing, and I heard his labored breaths behind me as he gave into it, too.

He didn't wait long, though. Squeezing my hips where they met my thighs, he started pumping, hard and fast, and I fumbled my hands on the hay-covered floor to keep myself on my knees.

All I could do was try not to fall as he thrust into me in short, quick attacks, filling me up with his size and warmth, and then pulling back out to do it again.

God, he felt so good. My body jerked, and he panted and grunted as he fucked me harder and harder, and I licked my parched lips, tasting the clown makeup I still wore.

After a moment, his hoodie was gone, and I wanted to turn around to feel him. To feel his chest against mine, but the deeper he hit, the stronger my orgasm built, and after less than a minute, my stomach started shaking, fireworks started to spark deep inside me, and I held my breath, letting the orgasm explode all over my body. I felt the skin of my nipples tighten and harden, and I cried out, but kept it under my breath, because I didn't know where we were or how secluded this place was.

Lost in a daze, I felt him grip my hair and pull my head back up, forcing my back to arch more and my ass to stick out farther for him. He drove violently, pumping me hard and fast until he, too, started to grunt, growing more strained as he started to come.

He jerked into me several more times, and then one final thrust as he spilled, breathing so loud and so spent, I was sure he might fall down on top of me.

But he didn't.

He stayed there, buried inside me for another minute, tightening and untightening his fist in my hair and calming his body. My scalp burned from where he pulled my hair, but I didn't even care, I was so tired.

And in the minute as things calmed and my desire and every other overwhelming emotion I'd just felt left, I couldn't help but think one thing.

I'd let it happen. Again.

With all the men in the world, why did I hate myself so much that he was the only one, in the heat of the moment, I wanted?

Pulling away from him, unwelcome cool air now filling where he'd just been, I scooted away and pulled a piece of the tulle off the inside of my skirt, trying to clean up best I could.

Tears stung the back of my throat, feeling the heat of his cum seeping out of me. I needed a bathroom.

I heard him move and refasten his jeans and belt and then the lid of a lighter opening and closing as he lit a cigarette.

"You came inside me," I told him.

He blew out smoke, not saying anything for a moment.

"And?" he finally answered, Damon's voice strong and sure.

"And the whole town knows all the beds you've been in," I spat out.

"Like yours, you mean?"

Yeah, years ago.

He let out a sigh and then my bra hit me in the chest as he tossed it. I grabbed it just before it fell. "My father wants his grandchildren, Winter."

My stomach sank, anger and shame burning my face. Oh, God, if I got pregnant...

I quickly went through the calendar in my head, remembering I'd just had my period last week. It should be okay.

As much as I wanted to be mad at him, though, I could've stopped him. I just didn't think about it.

I stood up and slipped my bra back on, but unable to fasten it. "I will never have your children," I told him.

It was Damon. It was my sister's husband. And I'd rather die than raise a family under his thumb. He'd be a terrible father.

But I felt him approach and stop just in front of me, his deep voice quiet but steady. "You're going to have lots of my children," he informed me.

And then he brushed past me, leaving the room, and I stood there, unable to move as his words lingered in the air.

I hated him. I hated who I turned into with him.

How could I have just done that? Why did I do it? He didn't force me. I could've run. I didn't even think to say no. I didn't want to say no. It was like we were animals, for Christ's sake.

Red.

Anger, fury, heat, and need so strong you're a fucking animal, Winter. It's primal.

So that was red. I'd wanted to do it. I loved the flames. I had dived in.

But now, the pain of the burns.

I hated him.

"Hey," I heard Alex as she closed the door. "We just saw Damon. He said you were in here." And then she touched my arm, and I could hear the ice jingle in her drink. "Baby, I'm so sorry we lost you. Are you okay? Shit."

Judging from her reaction, I must look a sight. My makeup was probably everywhere.

"It's okay," I mumbled. I couldn't explain it right now.

"Are you okay?" she prodded again, probably just wanting to know if I was hurt.

I just turned around. "Would you please refasten me?"

She let out a sigh, seeing clearly that my bra had been off. "Did he hurt you?"

She tugged at me as she pulled the belt of the clasp tight again, and I no longer had the energy to muster any tears.

"Not as much as I hurt myself," I told her.

CHAPTER 19

Damon

PRESENT

I brought the lighter to the tip of my cigarette, lighting the end and sucking in a puff of smoke. The taste and burn hit my tongue, filling my lungs, and I blew it back out, already relaxing.

People walked about as I stood around the side of one of the concession stands, keeping an eye across the way on the restroom door for Winter and Alex to come out, just to make sure they were still together.

I didn't give a shit if Winter was happy right now, but this place was sketchy as fuck. Perfect for me, really, but she didn't have a sign on her saying she was blind, and if one of these actors picked her up and carried her off, like I just did, she might be in trouble.

Will was doing a piss poor job watching out for her. Grabbing her was way too easy.

I took another drag, noticing a couple of girls in line watching me. I caught the eyes of one of them, and she smiled, giving me a little wave.

I blew out the smoke, flicking the ash off the cigarette, but it was ash that dried my mouth. Everyone in this town knew my history and women could either be really distant—which suited me just fine—or they were really into it, like

I was some dangerous animal, and it totally turned them on. While some were of the opinion that I took advantage of Winter, and judged the gossip they heard about my weird sexual appetite for watching others, no one saw that video and thought I forced her.

I was either the victim of a technicality or a deviant who messed with a girl they didn't know was far from a one-night stand.

Winter's age wasn't the problem to me. I didn't even see it.

The crime was, I couldn't tell her who I was.

And the crime was, she didn't love me back.

Her heart was so shallow she couldn't understand and know that I was real. Every moment with her, I was real. I would've been faithful, and I would've died protecting her.

As soon as she knew, though, she cut me out. It was over. That quickly, she hated me, her fickle heart abandoning me and completely forgetting it all.

I was going to take great pleasure in making sure she never stopped hating me.

And at twenty-one, there was no question she was old enough for what I just did to her. I'd wanted to fuck her like that since I moved into the house, and she had come downstairs in her skimpy little shorts and tank top that night looking for her dog. She didn't deserve better.

I tightened my fist, crushing the cigarette and closing my eyes through the burn being snuffed out on the inside of my palm.

And a smile curled my lips, thinking about what I should do next. Maybe Will or Alex—or both—would like to join me for the next round.

Winter seemed to like them, after all.

Opening my eyes, I saw her and Alex step out of the restroom, Winter's clothes and hair back in order, but her face tight, containing some anger I was totally responsible for. Alex smiled and waved, and I saw Rika approach and grab Alex in an excited hug.

What?

And then I noticed someone coming toward me out of the corner of my eye and turned my head to see Michael, Kai, and Will head straight for me.

"Oh, fucking great," I grumbled, throwing the cigarette away.

Michael came up right into my face, all of them dressed casually in jeans and T-shirts. "I want to talk to you in private," he said.

I straightened my spine, meeting him eye to eye. "Private?" I teased. "Like steam-room private? I'm game."

He folded his arms over his chest, his hazel eyes, piercing me. "Speaking of which, pay any visits to Hunter-Bailey recently?"

I laughed under my breath. "Ask Erika," I taunted him. "Or is she keeping things from you?"

His face was frozen, but I knew the storm that raged under his skin. I wasn't saying shit. I loved that his girl kept me a secret from him.

"I trust her," he said. "I don't trust you. What are you hanging over her head?"

Me? Oh, so that was it. The only way she'd give me the time of day was if I were blackmailing her?

"Believe it or not," I told him, "she's the one who has my neck in a noose. Quite the little dominant, your monster is. I'm kind of digging it. If you want to share." And then I shot my eyes to Kai. "With everyone, I mean."

"Jesus," Kai muttered.

Yeah, I was definitely pissed when I heard about the three of them. It was just another time the two of them made all the decisions and had all the fun. Will and I simply tagged along when we were permitted.

Alex and Banks made their way over, Will taking the beer Alex brought him.

"Where's Winter?" he asked.

"With Rika," she said.

Michael and I didn't blink.

"You're not the only one who knows how to deal with garbage," Michael said in a low voice as everyone stood silently by. "I didn't erase my brother to keep her safe, so you could come along and fuck with us, too. I went that far, and I'll do what I have to do again."

Maybe.

He killed one person, making that self-defense. Make it a habit, and that becomes risk. He had lots to lose now.

"Who is that?" I heard Will ask.

But Michael, Kai, and I were locked, barely hearing him.

"No one will miss you," Michael whispered, threatening me.

And I almost laughed. Bet his dick grew another fourth of an inch off that big boy threat.

"Michael," Will said.

But Michael still stared at me, simply pumping his chest. Rika would never tolerate me doing anything to hurt her. He knew that. If she and I had a meeting, it was because she wanted to be there, and he was jealous.

Fuck him.

"Who the fuck is that?" Will barked. "Michael!"

"What?" Michael jerked his head to Will.

"Seriously?" Will blurted out. "You're not watching this?"

Dragging my eyes away from Michael and Kai, we all turned our gazes on Will, following his line of sight to Rika, Winter, and some guy in black pants, a dark gray pullover, and leather shoes with his dark hair slicked back. Maybe five or six years older than us.

"That guy," Will pointed out, looking at us as we looked at them. "He had a mask on before. He walked up and put his hands on Rika like he was one of the actors. He grabbed her, picked her up, had his hands way too close to certain things..."

Will turned back to her as he spoke, and I narrowed my eyes, taking note that Winter was standing back as Rika and the guy talked. He looked familiar. Where have I seen him before?

"She got away from him when she realized it wasn't you," Will continued, "but now he has the mask off, and he's talking to her like they know each other. I don't think she knows it was the same guy that fondled her before."

I looked away, shaking my head.

They all just stood there. Michael, Kai, Will...

"It's one of her professors," Alex offered. "She's part of his research team at the college."

"He was not touching her very professionally when he was in disguise," Will replied sarcastically, taking a swig of his beer.

Looking back over to make sure he wasn't talking to Winter, I watched as he leaned in to Rika, tilting his head and touching her arm as they spoke. There were things guys did that told you they were flirting.

She turned to Winter for a moment, and once her back was turned, his eyes dropped, giving Rika a long once-over and licking his lips.

Yep.

Girls didn't always notice, because it was subtle, and we didn't always realize we were doing it, but he was interested. And he'd copped a feel while her fiancé was standing right here, too.

Was Michael doing anything? Of course not.

And that was the same guy I saw dancing with her at her engagement party, too. I finally recognized him, because he rubbed me the wrong way then, as well.

"He's flirting with her," Will told Michael the same thing I already knew.

"Does he know she's engaged?" Banks asked.

"He was at dinner at our fucking house," Michael growled under his breath as he glared at the professor.

"Aw, don't worry," I said. "Rika can handle her own shit, right?"

I dug out a cigarette, lighting it, a puff of smoke filtering into the air above our heads.

"It's kind of got me wondering, though," I went on. "She's got her own money, and she can take care of herself, because you don't coddle her, so...why does she need you exactly?"

I narrowed my eyes on Michael, amused. He always made Rika solve her own problems, because he didn't see her as a possession but rather an extension of himself.

He didn't want a puppy. He wanted a partner.

But there comes a point when you have to defend your house and take charge. And not just in the bedroom.

Which was all she needed him for.

I grinned. "I guess she does need to be serviced from time to time, doesn't she?"

He bared his teeth, grabbing the collar of my sweatshirt, but my feet didn't budge from the ground.

"Oh, please, go ahead," I dared him, holding his eyes. "It is long past due between you and me."

He stared into my eyes, probably taking in all the people around us, the security, the cameras, and while I didn't give a shit, he had a charmed life at risk now. A sports star, soon-to-be wife, business deals in the works...

Do it.

I actually didn't want either him or me getting arrested for a fight tonight, but I wanted to see some kind of life from him. Some remnant of the guy who was once my friend. Someone I remember very well, wanting to go to that edge and lead us all over it.

This is what happened when you fell in love. You lost your nerve, because you didn't want to lose what had become more important.

But instead of wimping out, he just smiled.

"You know what?" he said, releasing me. "You're right. My imagination is nothing compared to yours. Tell me, how would you handle him?"

How would I handle him? Need me to do your dirty work for you, or was this an invitation to play?

"Come on," Kai egged me on, smirking. "Show us what we're missing from the good old days. You're so fucking arrogant. You educate us."

My heart started pumping a little harder, and I stood there, pondering the challenge. Would they do what I suggested?

I wasn't even going to leave it up to them. They'd pussy out.

I locked eyes with my sister. "How fast can the butcher be here?"

She stared at me only a moment before realization dawned, and a smile spread across her face. She glanced at Kai who looked at his wife curiously and then back to me, digging out her cell. "For us?" she asked, looking excited. "Minutes."

And then she put the phone to her ear and walked away to make the call.

I glanced at Alex. "See if they have a first aid kit with smelling salts?"

She nodded, looking hesitant, but walked toward the service tent.

And then I taunted Kai. "Still able to knock someone out with a single kick?"

"Want a demonstration?" he shot back.

I laughed, putting the rest of the pieces together in my head.

"What are you going to do?" Michael asked, pulling back and suddenly interested.

"Me? Oh, this will take all of us," I told him. "You want it or not?"

He rolled his eyes but stood there, Will on his left, Kai on his right, and his pride telling him not to engage with me.

But then he looked over at Rika, and I didn't know about him, but I knew if her teacher was pulling shit like this in front of her fiancé, what was he thinking of trying one of these days when Michael wasn't around during one of their research meetings or an after-class discussion?

Of course, Rika could take care of herself, but he was disrespecting Michael, too. Michael needed to check that shit.

He met my eyes. "Fine. What are we doing?"

I quirked a smile and filled everyone in on their part, sending Banks to meet the butcher in the parking lot and Will to grab another prop from inside one of the haunted houses.

When Alex came back with the salts, I told her what she had to do, unfortunately the bulk of the work falling on her for this whole thing. She was the only chick here not spoken for, so that came in handy when she needed to lure him.

Banks arrived with a backpack, and she, Michael, and I made our way to the tree line behind the barn, shielding ourselves behind the trunks, while Kai and Will hid around the corner of the barn, waiting.

I stuffed my mask, still hooked onto my wrist, in the backpack, and not two minutes later, spotted Alex rounding the corner with the professor. She looked perfect. Short white dress, top hat, makeup. He didn't look as enamored as he did with Rika, but he was willing to indulge a little walk around the park with another beautiful student.

Kai looked over at me, twenty yards away, and I jerked my chin, alerting him it was time. He stepped back, giving himself room, got in his stance, and as soon as Alex came around the corner, Kai shot out, swung his leg around, and knocked the dude right in his temple. He didn't even have time to turn and see who was there.

His head jerked back, his knees gave out, and he fell forward, face planting on the dirt ground.

"Oh, shit!" Will shook with laughter. "He went down like a dead deer."

A snort sounded from either Michael or Banks, and Kai looked down at his victim, surveying his handiwork with pride.

"You didn't kill him, did you?" Banks whisper-yelled, looking worried as she crept over.

Michael and I followed.

She crouched down next to the guy, feeling for the pulse on his neck.

After a pause, she pulled away, sighing with relief. "Okay, good."

"Baby, please." Kai looked insulted.

"Grab his feet," I told Will as I flipped him over and took his hands. "Let's go."

We carried him back beyond the tree line, Alex, Michael, and Kai following, while Banks bent over, picking up the heavy backpack off the ground as we passed.

I cocked an eyebrow at Michael. "You gonna make my sister carry that?"

Or do we do all the work and you just watch?

He yanked the bag out of her hand, she made a face at him, and we all scurried deeper into the woods and out of sight.

Plopping the dead weight down, I grabbed Alex, pulled her over, and ripped open the bodice of her dress, exposing her skin from chest to abdomen, her breasts still covered, though.

She gasped, snarling at me. "Asshole!"

"Lie down," I told her.

"Why do I always have to do the dirty work?"

"Now." I gestured to the ground.

Frowning, she dropped to the cold earth, fallen leaves rustling under her as she carefully laid herself back.

"Knife," I asked Will, reminding him I needed the prop he stole from one of the haunted houses.

He slapped it in my hand, the harness from whatever actor or mannequin he got it off of attached and dangling from my fist.

Michael, Kai, and Will situated themselves off a short distance away, shielding themselves behind trees, while

Banks and I finished getting Alex all dressed up. We did this as teenagers to one of my father's security guards who kept patting Banks on the ass when he spoke to her.

I poured some of the shit she got from the butcher on the professor's clothes and then hauled him over and set him face down on top of Alex, between her legs.

"Ugh," she groaned, looking like she was about to gag with all the crap on her, including the professor.

Banks planted a quick kiss on her forehead as she scrambled around her, giving her arms and chest smears of blood. "Love you. Mean it," she chirped at Alex sarcastically and then looked up at me, smiling.

I couldn't help but give her one back.

Like old times.

We finished up, Banks gathered the backpack and everything in it, and ran to where the guys were hiding, while I pulled out the smelling salts.

"When you're ready," I said, handing it to Alex.

She took it, nodding.

I backed away, surveying my work, that fucking prick who thought he could put his hands on something of ours and get away with it passed out between her legs with his head resting on her chest.

Then I turned, joining everyone else where we could watch but not be seen.

Alex moved a little, lifting her head to check the placement of his hand on the knife and her position under him.

Will was laughing already, lifting his phone to record.

But Kai grabbed it out of his hand to stop him. "Fuck no."

Will's mouth dropped open, confused, but then the light dawned. "Oh, right."

Yeah. Not going down that road again. No videos.

Alex brought the salts to his nose, and I warned everyone, "Shhh," shutting them up.

She waved them under his nostrils, we waited and watched, and then suddenly...he jerked to life, and her arm and head fell back to the ground in position, the salts spilling off somewhere as she closed her eyes and hung her mouth open, playing dead.

A laugh rumbled in my chest.

He moved, trying to lift his head, but it just bobbed as he groaned.

He shifted on top of her body, and then hissed, putting his hand to his temple and feeling the ache of Kai's kick.

"Ah, what the hell?" he said in a raspy voice, rubbing his head.

But then he slowly came to, lifted his body up, and blinked his eyes open, finally seeing what was underneath him.

The body of a dead girl, covered in blood, and his fingers wrapped around the hilt of the prop knife buried in Alex's chest.

He just sat there, looking down at her, unsure if he truly knew what he was seeing.

Removing his hand from the knife, he nudged her on the jaw, sending her head flopping side to side, and then let out a shocked cry, falling over, and scrambling to get away and making us all struggle to hold in our laughter.

"Ah!" He crawled backward, just staring at her in utter horror.

Snorts went off around us, and I shook my head.

It was a prank you were never really too old for. I always dreamed of having this room in my house someday with splatters of red paint all over the walls and sheets, so I could dump drunk friends in there who would wake up in the light of day the next morning, shitting their pants at the massacre on the walls.

The small delights in life.

He stood up, pawing at the evidence all over his clothes and took in the blood spilling off the butcher knife buried in the chest of a young girl. He quickly looked around for anyone who might've seen, and we dove behind the trunks, making sure we weren't detected.

He was starting to freak out, his fear vibrating off him, and I could only imagine the thoughts racing through his mind right now.

"Oh, my God," he panted. "Oh, my God. What the fuck?"

Aw. Poor baby.

We peered back around to see him start running at top speed away from the body, whipping off his pullover and trying to wipe himself clean as he bolted back into the far-off crowd before he could be caught.

"Holy shit," Will chuckled, not holding back as we all came out from behind the trees and watched him disappear. "He didn't even try to take his murder weapon. What a pinhead."

Banks' head fell back as she and Kai laughed, and Michael couldn't help grinning as he dipped down, helping Alex up.

"I don't think he'll be at school on Monday," he remarked.

"Yeah, he should be three states over by then," Kai added.

"Or confessing to the police," Will snickered.

No one could stop laughing, all of us shaking with the amusement at the painful ride home he was going to have tonight and the sleep he wasn't gonna get for a few days until he realized it was a prank.

"And if he does it again," Alex snapped, aggravated with the mess all over her as she shot a look to Will, "we'll put him in a bed between *your* legs, surrounded by dildos and lube next time."

"Now that was an idea," Will chimed in, pointing to me with an excited look.

We all broke into laughter again, picturing the sight, and my head was light and my stomach unknotted for the first time in a long time. I hadn't laughed like this in a while.

My head fell back, exhausted from the day and night, but kind of happy.

Really happy, actually.

But then the chuckles died down.

They faded to smiles, which faded to nothing, and we all grew quiet, discomfort and awkwardness chilling the air as we remembered we hated each other.

Years ago, this was what it was like with us. Before we realized fun had a price, and anger clouded everything as we latched on to anyone to blame.

Especially me.

Tonight was a bittersweet reminder of everything I'd ruined, and they hadn't forgotten that it was mostly my fault.

We'd happily fallen back into the things that helped us find each other for a few minutes. The same needs, the same passion for thrills, and the same desire to break away from restraints.

But they couldn't forgive.

And this couldn't happen.

"Hey, where have you guys been?" Rika walked over to us with Winter in tow.

I looked at her, but her head was down and turned away, as if she were trying to be invisible.

Michael went over and pulled Rika into him, hefting her up into his arms. "We were doing manly things."

"Manly things?" she asked, not believing it for a second.

But he just slapped her on the ass, gripping her flesh through her dress. "Let's go to the car for a minute."

"Michael!" she scolded as he carried her away, what he wanted clear.

The rest of us stood there for about two seconds, the wait of their silence enough to kill the fun I'd just had.

I grabbed the backpack with my mask inside and looked at Will. "If she's not home by two," I gestured to Winter, "my security will bring her home. Don't test me."

I left, strolling past her and definitely wanting another piece of her soon, half-tempted to drag her home now, but

I wasn't giving in. I didn't want her to know I craved it. The sex would not become habit. It was a move in the game, and I needed to figure out my next one.

• • •

Later that night, I woke with a start. Two sharp pangs hit me, one on my neck, next my throat, and another on my side, between my ribs. I sucked in a breath, feeling the sting of broken skin.

"What is it about me that makes you so angry?" I heard Winter ask in a soft voice.

I raised my eyes, finally realizing she was straddling me on the bed, two blades dug into my skin.

Kitchen knives?

I spread my fingers where my arms laid at my side, itching to grab her and throw her off me. I knew I could do it before she stabbed me, but...

I'd been concerned with my next move instead of anticipating hers.

I remained still, the sheets cool and soft and the room silent and black.

"What about me makes you so angry?" she asked again, still just as calm.

"Three years," I said.

Three years in jail for doing something she wanted me to do.

"But it started before that," she prodded. "In high school. You terrorized me. Why? What did I do?"

I didn't terrorize her. I never hurt her. I just wanted what I wanted.

The points of the knives poked too hard, and my breathing trembled.

"I was a kid," she said, pain in her voice. "I thought I was in love. I was a naïve, stupid kid. Do you know what it's like to think someone loves you and then you find out you were nothing but meat?"

I curled my fists, taking the sheets with me as I shut out my own memories that tried to spring up.

"Yes," I whispered.

Yes, I did.

I knew what it was like to have horrible things being done to your body, and watch it betray you and make you think you're bad for liking it when you knew you didn't.

I shot out my hands, grabbing her hips and lifting my head as the blade threatened to sink into me. "And I killed her for it," I told her. "So do it then."

She breathed hard, and I could feel her grips shaking as she held her weapons.

"Because I won't stop," I said quietly, smelling her shampooed hair.

She'd showered, all the makeup and the costume now gone, replaced with silk sleep shorts and a white T-shirt with her hair still wet.

"Do it," I egged her on.

The sharp points burrowed, threatening me, and I loved the view of her like this. Taking control of me, her power painful but demanding, and I wanted her to demand anything she wanted from me right now.

My cock started to grow hard under her, drawn to her warmth as she sat on me, and I was very prepared to let this happen again tonight. Just for tonight.

She came to me, after all.

"You weren't lying," she finally said, looking thoughtful like a memory was playing in her mind.

I'd told her in the janitor's closet seven years ago that I killed my mother. She thought I was talking shit. Now she knew.

"When did it start?" she asked, her brain deciphering what happened.

But I wasn't going there. Never, ever again.

"In the fountain when you were eight and I was eleven," I told her.

"That's not what I meant."

"That's all that matters." And I dug my fingers into her ass as I lifted my hips and pressed my cock between her legs.

"Ah, yeah," I gasped, my rock-hard ridge soaking in her heat through her lacy, silk boxers.

I couldn't fucking think.

Breathing faster, I dove into it all, the demand of her questions and the threat of the knives ready to hurt me and end me right here, right now. Sweat cooled my skin, the rustle of my body in the sheets filled my ears, and every other sense heightened with awareness as I let go, wanting to feel this. To be filled with anything of her.

Moving one hand to where her neck met her shoulder, I took hold of her body and rode her from the bottom, her clothes still on and the torture making it all the more insane.

"Stop," she breathed out. "Damon, stop."

"Get off me then."

She was sitting on me. I had no control here.

"I may be married to Ari," I told her, dying to get inside her body again. "But her little sister is who I really wanted to play with." I yanked her down to me, the knives falling away as I whispered against her lips. "Always wanted to play with."

She trembled, and her eyes watered, and I thought she was going to pull away and run, but she was frozen.

"You're mine," I said, kissing her mouth once as I humped her. "Mine." I kissed her again. "Mine in that fountain. Mine in the locker room and in the janitor's closet. Mine in the dean's office." I took her jaw in my hand. "You'll have my kids and be my woman and fuck me, because that's what I want."

"No," she said, barely audible.

But then she locked her hand around my neck and whimpered, her body arching to meet my hips.

"You're different than them," I whispered, pulling off her shirt to feel her tits against my chest. "Different than my friends. Different than Ari. Different than my parents, my sister, and every woman. You see everything."

A sob escaped her, and I gripped the back of her hair, bending her head back to watch her face as I dry-fucked her, our bodies moving in perfect sync.

"Yeah, was that the line you fed my mother to get her to leave?" she spat out. "That I was *everything* to you?"

I flicked her lips with my tongue, so fucking hungry for her despite myself. "I told her the only way I could stay married to Ari for a year was if we were together as little as possible," I said, both of us mouth to mouth and panting.

"I told her that I wanted you," I went on. "That you loved me, because there was no faking what happened in that fucking video, and I told her that I loved you, too, and I was sorry for stealing you the way I did, but it was the only way I could get close to you."

Her breath shook as she sucked it in between her teeth.

"I told her that I never intended for anyone to see that video," I admitted, "and I needed time. Time to convince you that you were mine and that you wanted to be mine. We just needed to be left alone."

It was true. I told her mother all those things. Things she wanted to hear. Things she wanted to believe.

I married Ari to get into this house and because she was easy, but they all knew what I was really after.

"I told her you'd be set for life," I said, both of us rubbing on each other, "and I'd make all your dreams come true. You'll dance and no doors will be closed to you ever again."

Grunts and groans filled the room, while my other hand roamed, sliding down her back and feeling the light layer of sweat before I gripped her ass, helping her move.

Yeah, Ari left, because she did what she was told, and she wanted to believe I was joining them in a few days. Her mother left because she wanted to believe all the things I said to get her to go. That Winter and I were fucking in love, and we needed space to get through our shit.

My cock was so hard, and I wanted inside her, but just as I pulled her up, taking her nipple in my mouth, she came, rasping and shaking as I sucked on her.

And as she came down, quivering with her orgasm, I stopped moving and wrapped my arm around her, holding her to me as I licked and kissed her breast.

I wanted this. So much more of this. Her body in my arms, shivering and sweating, in a hundred different positions, no piece of her left untouched.

But as hard as I was and as much as I wanted to strip her down and take full advantage that I had the house all to myself with my sweet, new little sister-in-law... this bitch sent me to jail with no hesitation and no regret.

We weren't in love.

I pulled her head down to me, teasing her with little kisses she didn't return because she hated what she just let happen again.

"I love fucking you," I told her. "There's no struggle to connect in bed. No mystery with you."

Her thighs were so warm, and my dick ached, thinking about how hot and wet she probably was right now.

But I simply tightened my grip on her, brushing her nose with mine and taunting her. "It's comforting how it's always the same," I said. "How all you cunts turn into sluts once you've got a good dicking."

She grew still, a slight tilt to her lips that looked like she was trying not to cry, but everything else was calm and stoic.

As if she finally understood... I was here to hurt.

CHAPTER 20

Damon

FIVE YEARS AGO

I blew out smoke, staring at the back of Erika Fane's head as we drove through the neighborhood, having just left the village. It had been a long day—and it would probably be an even longer night—and I was both intrigued and pissed Michael let her tag along for Devil's Night tonight.

I'd been away at college, with my friends all at different schools, and it finally felt fucking good to be back where I was happiest, and now everyone had to guard themselves to not offend Michael's pet project.

But then again, maybe a distraction—something to take my mind off Winter and what happened last night in the shower—was exactly what I'd needed.

Perspective.

And closing my eyes, shutting off my head, and just charging on into whatever shit behavior I could, would tear my gut to shreds, so I couldn't feel her anymore.

So I could let her go before she found out.

Maybe years down the road, when I was out of college, and she was older and away from her parents...

No.

No, that wouldn't happen, either.

413

She'd still need to know the truth. About who I was and what I did to her these past few years. I didn't want her to ever know.

I was fucked. It had to end.

I just had to find a diversion. A nice, healthy, blonde diversion who looked a little like Winter Ashby and smelled just as good.

Rika sensed me staring and turned her eyes over her shoulder, meeting mine.

I stared back at her.

She had blue eyes. Just like Winter.

But unlike Winter, I could hate Rika and remind myself what women were for.

They were the same age, too. I wasn't sure if they hung out anymore, but maybe I could pretend the little Winter-lookalike was actually Winter to drown out the real one in my head.

Rika tipped her chin up and turned back around, and I laughed under my breath, taking another drag of my cigarette.

I always made her nervous, and I kind of liked it. As if there were a bigger game at play that we'd eventually get to someday, but neither of us knew what it was.

I saw Michael watching me in the rearview mirror, and I did a shitty job of hiding my grin.

Hey, if he didn't want anyone else noticing his little piece of ass, he shouldn't have brought her along in the first place. It was one thing to have your fun. It was another to do it in front of us.

Tonight was ours. She wasn't important enough to be here.

He pulled up in front of the Ashby house, outside the walls with two tall columns with lanterns on top and the gate closed. Hopefully that meant the parents were out, and she was alone.

Or, at least her father was out. The mother said something during the fight last night about having to catch a plane today.

And Arion was away from her college for a semester abroad, so Winter was the only other person in the house.

I climbed up from my seat, heading for Will's door to hop out. "I won't take long."

"Sooooo confident," Will teased. "Get a great angle for us, okay?"

He held up the group cell phone we used to record all our pranks, and I took it, remembering I had that shot of Winter on it from last night. If it recorded at all. I'd dropped the phone, but thankfully it hadn't broken.

Stuffing it in my back pocket, I flung open the door and hopped out, pulling up my hood.

"Got protection?" Will asked.

"Shut the fuck up."

I slammed the door shut, hearing his chuckle from inside, and scaled the tree outside the wall, making my way over it in seconds, because this was not the first time I'd done this.

Landing on my feet, I jogged across the lawn, seeing a few lights her father left on in the house, my gaze immediately locking on the windows of the ballroom and hearing the music from inside. I couldn't help but smile, knowing she was in there.

I dug out the key she gave me and pulled off my sweatshirt, tossing it behind some bushes, because it was covered in smoke.

Heading around to the backdoor, I unlocked it as quietly as possible and pushed it open, slipping into the dark kitchen and instantly hearing the music playing as loud as she wanted, because no one was home.

I crept down the hallway and through the foyer, veering right, toward the open ballroom doors with the music growing louder and drifting up to the ceiling.

It had a haunting, sad vibe, and my heart started thumping harder even before I entered.

She twirled around the floor, her head and arms all playing a part as her feet moved, creeping with the song, like someone possessed or lost in a dream. My throat swelled as I inched off to the side, in the shadows, not taking my eyes off her.

The chorus chanted, the drums like a pulse, and I watched her hair fly, and the muscles in her legs flex through her tight, black leggings. Slits cut across the back of her long-sleeve pink shirt, her sports bra and skin visible in the moonlight streaming in through the windows.

But I blinked
And the world was gone

The voice sang, the music coursing through her as if it were coming from her body, every movement perfectly timed. I scaled my eyes down her face and form as she spun and leaped, wishing I could be the air around her and feel her move.

My chest ached so badly it hurt to breathe.

There was no one in the world like her.

The music ended, and silence fell in the house as she fell back on her feet, breathing hard. She stayed there, unmoving and quiet.

And finally, her voice pierced the air. "Are you here?"

I didn't say anything.

"Were you watching?" she asked softly.

I wanted to bring her into my chest and just feel her relax, easing her mind and making her feel safe.

But she'd smell the smoke still on me, which I didn't hold back on tonight on purpose. I didn't want to be tempted to come see her.

I did anyway, though. I'd told the guys I was paying a hot, little visit to Mrs. Ashby, knowing they'd love that. None of us liked her husband.

But I just wanted to see Winter.

After what I did to her last night.

"I hate that you don't talk to me," she said, still rooted in the same spot but slowly turning in a circle, because she didn't know where I was. "Like *really* talk. But I guess it wouldn't have been like you to still be here this morning."

No, it wouldn't have been. After another half-hour in the shower, we'd dried, and I dressed, following her down to her room to lay with her for a while.

When she fell asleep, I stayed.

Still not sleeping.

Until about four a.m., then I snuck out.

And told myself that tonight I'd screw someone else.

And get Winter out of me.

"You are like a ghost," she mused. "Or a vampire. You're only alive for me at night."

She swallowed and inhaled a breath.

"It's okay. I was warned, wasn't I?" she said. "That you would hurt me?"

Yes.

"My father thinks it would be better for me back in Montreal," she told me. "He says that 'the community here can't accommodate my needs.'"

She repeated his words, feigning his deep, condescending voice, but fire coursed up my neck, and I was nervous.

Back to Montreal.

Away.

I'd never see her. What if she stayed there after high school?

If I didn't think we should see each other, then we wouldn't, but I didn't like the choice being taken from me.

"What he really means is that I can't afford to be a teenager," she explained. "He thinks I'll make mistakes and be hurt."

Like how she stayed out last night, past curfew, and made them worry. Doing things everyone does, but the rules for her were stricter, because they didn't think she could protect herself.

Had she ever made them worry before? Her father was using this as an excuse to send her away. With both daughters gone, he wouldn't have a reason to return home more frequently than necessary. For appearances' sake.

She grew quiet, dropping her head a little and pleading, "Don't let me go."

I closed my eyes for a moment, my insides knotting so tightly.

I didn't want to let her go.

"He's in the city tonight," she said. "And my mother flew to Spain today to visit Ari. I have the whole house to myself. All night."

Oh, Jesus. My chest caved.

What the fuck?

It was everything I wanted.

Don't do this to me.

She smirked. "Suddenly you have nothing to say?"

And I shook my head, more to myself than her.

She could be anyone.

I could get from anyone what I got from her.

I didn't want her in my head.

I don't want this. I wanted her to stay perfect.

She'd find out, and it would be over.

Don't stay, I told myself. *And don't come back.*

"We don't have to talk," she told me. "I'm going to go upstairs and take a shower. You might join me, and I'd want that. And afterward, I'm going to climb into my bed to sleep, and you might join me. I'd want that, too." She closed her eyes, looking like her heart was breaking. "I just want you here or wherever I am."

She walked slowly toward the doors, finding her way into the foyer, and I followed her, watching her climb the stairs up to the bathroom.

Nothing sounded better than nestling in the warmth of her and her bed tonight.

But instead, I walked past the staircase, through the kitchen, and out the backdoor, locking it behind me as I left the house.

She could be anyone, I told myself. *Anyone*.

And I'd prove it.

• • •

Hours later, I drove Michael's Mercedes G-Class, his brother next to me, and Will and Rika in the back.

Michael had left a while ago, pissed off at Rika for whatever reason and soothing himself with Kai and some booze and leaving her in our care.

It was perfect. I needed this.

I needed someone else. Someone who was nothing.

"Why are you wearing your mask?" Rika asked Trevor who sat quietly in the passenger's seat.

I smiled to myself. She thought he was Kai, because he wore Kai's mask. We weren't going to tell her any differently, because Michael's brother had a bone to pick with her, and so did I.

Nothing personal, kid. You're just a distraction.

"The night's not over yet," I teased.

We raced down the dark, empty highway, heading in the direction of her house—where she thought we were taking her—but that wasn't where we were going.

"You want him, don't you?" I asked, playing with her. "Michael, I mean."

She just looked out the window, ignoring me.

She was sixteen. Did she really think she'd keep him entertained? Satisfied?

Girls that young haven't even grown into their bodies yet. Kind of pathetic really, the hopes they dreamed up. Like we'd fall in love just as we were starting to have fun?

"Shit," Will groaned, his drunk-ass like a limp dick sitting in his seat next to her. "She's ready to ride a fence post with how horny she is for him."

Both of us laughed. "Don't be an asshole, man," I told him. "Maybe she's just horny, period. Bitches have needs, too, after all."

I winced inwardly, knowing how fucking nasty I just sounded.

I shook it off and watched Rika in the rearview mirror, her body going rigid and barely breathing. Her helpless eyes drifted to Kai, probably wondering why he wasn't stepping in and shutting us up, but that wasn't Kai and she had no heroes in here.

"We're just messing with you," Will drawled. "We do it to each other, too."

He smiled at her, his eyes closing as he drifted off.

"You know, the thing about Michael..." I continued, resting my head back against the seat as I drove, "he wants you, too. He watches you. Did you know that?" I shot her a look in the rearview mirror. "Man, the look on his face when he saw you dancing tonight."

She'd looked pretty good, actually, but it was nothing compared to the places Winter took me when I watched her.

I laid on the gas, speeding past Rika's house and racing toward my oblivion where Winter didn't exist.

Forget her. Just forget her.

I saw her shoot up in her seat, watching her house pass and me not stop.

"Yeah," I went on. "He never gets that look over a girl. I'd say he was damn close to taking you home and popping that little cherry of yours."

"Kai?" Rika protested, not wanting to deal with me. "We passed my house. What's going on?"

"You want to know why he didn't take you home?" I asked her, hitting the locks so she couldn't jump out. "He doesn't like virgins. He never wants to be that important to someone, and it's a lot less complicated to fuck people who know there's a difference between sex and love."

She turned her gaze from Will to Kai to me, fear in her eyes.

Sex and love.

Boys will be boys, and she teased you, didn't she? She wouldn't let you have it, I heard my mother's voice in my head.

Sex was power. Degrading, filthy, mean, unclean power.

Love always hurt. Sooner or later.

"Where are we going?" Rika demanded.

But I ignored her. "You saw the girl at the old church today," I mused, remembering her in the catacombs watching the guy and girl on our first Devil's Night stop. "You liked it, didn't you?"

I turned left, down a dark gravel road, and I saw her try to peer out the front windshield to see where we were going.

"You wanted to be her," I said. "Pushed down on that floor and fucked..."

Because even as unclean and degrading as sex was, the feelings were strong, and they were real. Sex and fear were the only things that made you real.

Little girls just don't understand what boys need, my mother would say.

It was the one thing she was right about. We didn't need anything we didn't take ourselves. No questions, no tears, no touching or soft words... Just fucking sit there and don't try to be special.

"You know why?" I asked Rika. How I knew she wanted to be that girl, pushed down and fucked? "Because it feels good. And we'll make you feel so good if you let us."

Her eyes raced from Kai to me to the locked doors as worry set in.

"You know," I told her. "When guys let a girl into their gang, there are two ways for her to be initiated." I pulled the car to a stop in the middle of the woods on the isolated road. "She either gets beat-in." I shut off the car, killed the lights, and locked eyes with her in the rearview mirror. "Or fucked-in."

She shook her head. "I want to go home."

Her voice sounded so fucking pitiful, and she looked like a kid, sinking to the bottom of a river, not wanting death but knowing it was coming.

No, don't. I don't want to, I remember myself saying when I was a kid, and I had no power.

But like me, there was nothing Rika could do.

"That's not one of the choices, Little Monster," I taunted.

Both Trevor and I turned our heads, staring straight at her.

She lost it, realization dawning. She grabbed the door handle and yanked on it over and over again, frantic to get out.

"We can take what we want from you," I warned, opening my door. "One after the other, and no one would believe you, Rika."

I climbed out, moved to her door behind me, and opened it, yanking her out as Will still slept it off in the other back seat.

Slamming the door shut, I pushed her up against it, pressing my body into hers and holding her wrists down at her side.

Was I doing this? For real?

"We're untouchable," I told her, looking down at her. "We can do whatever we want."

She breathed fast, in shallow breaths, squirming against me.

Trevor had gotten out of the car and come around behind me.

"Kai, please?" she begged for his help, still not knowing it was Michael's brother behind the mask. He'd had the hots for her forever, but she couldn't stand him. She wanted his older brother, and he was pissed.

"He won't help you," I muttered.

And then I pinned her hands over her head, against the car as she cried out.

"I'm going to feel so good," I whispered against her forehead and closed my eyes, envisioning Winter in my hands.

If I get it through my head and treat her like trash, then I can do the same things to Winter. I can throw her away.

Like nothing.

Reaching behind her, I grabbed her ass. "You know you want to ride this."

"Damon," she gasped, turning her head away, "take me home. I know you're not going to hurt me."

"Oh, yeah?" I threatened. "Then why have you always been afraid of me?"

Did she really believe I wouldn't do this? Or did she think she could talk me down?

I had no respect for her. She had no value. She was a warm body.

Yeah, she saved my ass earlier when we torched the gazebo in town. But if I couldn't have Winter, then Michael wasn't having Rika. If anyone deserved to come tonight, it was Winter. Who did Rika think she was?

I held her wrists above her head with one hand, pawed her ass with the other, and kissed a trail across her cheek.

I want this.

"Damon, no!" she shouted. "Let me go!"

But then I slammed my mouth down on hers, my teeth cutting into my mouth, and I just tried to see Winter in my head. It was her.

Hurt her. It would be over if I could just hurt her and break her goddamn heart.

"Help!" Rika cried.

"He doesn't want you," I whispered, running my hand up her body and cupping her breast, my stomach rolling with nausea as I felt her struggle.

Please, I don't want to.

Shhh, baby, I heard my mother again.

Oh, God.

423

"But we do, Rika," I choked out, clearing my throat and forcing myself on. "We want you so bad. Being with us will be like having a blank check, baby. You can have anything you want." I bit her bottom lip. "Come on."

She jerked away, growling, "I'll never want you!"

Fine. I grabbed her by the collar, hauled her away from the car, and flung her over to Trevor in his waiting arms.

"Kai," she gasped, a shred of hope left in her voice.

"Maybe you'll want him, then," I said.

Trevor wrapped his arms around her, crushing the little monster.

"Stop!" she yelled.

And then she raised her hand, slapping him across the mask.

A pang of admiration hit me and I faltered, seeing more of Winter in her than I wanted to. She was a fighter.

Hit him again. Like I should've done to my mother long before I finally did.

Hit him again.

Hit me.

But he threw her onto the ground, her body landing on the cold, wet leaves, and she flipped over, scurrying backward, trying to get away.

Trevor lunged for her, coming down on top of her, and I cocked my head, watching carefully.

He looked like he was whispering something in her ear, but I couldn't hear.

Then she belted, "Get off me!"

He grabbed her hair, shouting back to me, "Hold her arms!"

"No!" Rika cried, thrashing and kicking. "Get off!"

I didn't budge.

Trevor held her hands above her head with one hand and her neck with the other, and she tried to get free of his hold but couldn't.

She couldn't.

She couldn't stop what was happening.

I blinked. *No.* I didn't want this. I wanted to scare her. Threaten her, frighten her, run to the edge and nearly lose my balance, but...

She fought. Like many of us should have learned how to do so much sooner.

"Enough," I said.

But he didn't hear me. He kept struggling with her.

I said it louder, "Enough!"

Trevor froze for a moment, turning his head.

I charged over, grabbed him, and threw him off, reaching down and dragging Rika back up to her feet by her sweatshirt.

"Stop crying," I gritted out, holding her by collar. "We weren't going to hurt you, but now you know that we can."

I grabbed her by the back of her hair, her face flushed, upset, and still scared out of her mind, just like Winter that first night I broke in. "Michael doesn't want you, and neither do we," I breathed out. "You get that? I want you to stop watching us and stop following us like a pathetic dog begging for someone to notice her." And then I shoved her away, seeing Winter stumbling back from me. "Get a fucking life of your own, Rika, and stay the hell away from us. No one wants you."

Tears welled in her eyes, and she spun around and ran into the forest, toward her home, as fast as she could.

"What the hell was that?" Trevor spat out, whipping off his mask.

His blondish hair was sweaty, and he scowled at me as he shot Kai's mask to me like a basketball. I caught it and turned away, yanking the car door open and climbing in.

I wanted to fuck with her. Maybe fuck her, too, or anyone just to get my head clear—but goddammit—that wasn't...

He wasn't stopping.

She wasn't having fun.

She believed she was in actual danger, and all I could feel was my mother on top of me like Trevor was on top of her.

It gets hard when I do that. That means you like it.

No, it didn't.

I dropped the mask in the passenger's seat and started the car, seeing Trevor shoot off, racing toward his side of the car.

"What the hell are you doing?"

But I didn't wait. With Will still passed out in the back, I hit the gas and sped off in reverse, ignoring Trevor's curses and shouts as he chased my headlights.

You can fucking walk home.

I drove to the end of the gravel road, not stopping as I launched back onto the highway without a single pause for any oncoming traffic, and shifted into gear, speeding back down the dark, quiet road.

I gripped the steering wheel, gripping the hair on my head as I rested my elbow on the window.

"What the fuck?" I muttered.

What did I just do?

Was I actually going to hurt her?

But I did hurt her.

She came out tonight, saved my fucking ass in town earlier, and I... I fucking attacked her. She stood up for me, and all I saw was trash and a threat.

All that spirit, and I beat it down. I treated her like garbage, and instead of feeling powerful, I only saw a little boy on the ground, crying and heartsick, because he couldn't stop what was happening to him.

Rika would hate me. She'd never look at me again.

I pulled into Will's house and parked right in front, unloading him from the car, and heaving him over my shoulder. Climbing the steps up to his house, I dug his keys out of his back pocket, unlocked his huge iron door, and stepped inside, quickly punching in the security code we all had memorized years ago.

The house was quiet and dark, but I could always smell the hydrangeas his mother kept on the foyer table in various colors. Sometimes they were blue, sometimes white. Today, they were purple and always made the house look happy as soon as you entered.

Out of everyone's houses, I liked Will's the most. It was newer, more spacious with room to walk and breathe, and it was bright with high ceilings. He had two older brothers who left home a few years ago, off making the world a better place. Will was the youngest. And the most trouble for his parents.

I took him up to his room, plopped him down on the bed, and saw him yawn and pull his comforter over his body. He looked like a burrito, and it was the first time all night I actually felt a smile I wore.

Will and I were cut from the same cloth, both always diving too deep for our own good, he with alcohol and drugs and me with the pain I needed to inflict.

Rain started to patter his window, and I looked up at it, the drops streaming down the glass like being in a fountain and watching the falls spill from the bowl above.

Winter.

That was the only place I wanted to be right now. She was alone in that house, the fountain spilled outside, and she wanted me there.

Grabbing a pair of clean jeans and a T-shirt from Will's closet, I strolled into his bathroom and showered, washing my hair and body to get Rika off. To get the cigarettes off.

To just get every shitty thing I did tonight off.

After I was clean, I dressed and left, taking Winter's key, my wallet, and my phone, and quickly jumped back into Michael's car and headed for her house. It was almost two. I would have a few hours with her, at least, until I ran the risk of her father coming home.

But when I arrived, I saw the gates were open. Did he come home early?

I killed the lights and slowed the engine, noticing no cars parked in front of or on the side of the house, and no lights on in the home. Maybe she left the gates open for me. I almost smiled. I liked that idea.

I pulled the G-Class off the side of the driveway, out of sight in the trees on the lawn, just in case, and got out of the car, taking her key with me.

I darted inside and locked the door again, looking around and alert as I climbed the stairs.

When I cracked her bedroom door open, I immediately spotted her body under a sheet on the bed. The shadows of the rain on the window danced across her form as she lay on her side, and I closed the door quietly, stepping up to the foot of her bed and watching her sleep.

Heat coursed through every inch of my body, seeing her there, looking so warm and peaceful.

She was so small and gentle and delicate.

But there was fire in there.

She never lied or pretended she was someone she wasn't. She couldn't see what I was, but she felt it and recognized it in herself, and we were able to find each other and feel that it was right. I didn't know how it happened, but it was why I was always drawn to her. Since we were kids. She saw everything.

I picked up the bottom of the sheet and pulled it softly from her body, seeing she was in a white, silk night shirt, loose and flowing down her arms but bunched up around her waist. I stared at her. My territory.

If my friends touched her like I touched Rika tonight, I'd kill them. Without pause.

She let out a little whimper, taking in a deep breath. "Is that you?"

She pulled her shirt down and propped herself up on an elbow, her head moving around the room.

"Yeah," I replied quietly.

She followed my voice and smiled.

I set my knee down on the bed, coming down on her as she settled onto her back, and I rested my body on top of hers as I planted my elbows under me and held both sides of her head. I slid my fingers into her hair and touched my forehead to hers, breathing her in and feeling her body underneath mine.

She scaled her fingers up my back, whispering, "What's wrong?"

I closed my eyes, having no idea where to start. "I fucked up," I whispered back.

She rubbed me, and I soaked in her heat, the rain hiding us from the world, and still wondering how she got inside me—inside my head and my...

"Need to hide for a while?" she asked, a lilt of comfort in her voice.

And I nodded. "Yeah."

For as long as I could.

We kissed, softly at first, but my body became aware of hers, and she wanted to feel everything, her hands going under and inside my clothes.

And as we stripped, and I thrust inside of her, I knew without a doubt that this is who I would've been if I hadn't become me. If I hadn't learned to cope with pain in all the worst ways growing up in that house and denied taking any responsibility for the man I became.

I would've gone to school, played basketball, laughed with my friends, and snuck into my pretty little girlfriend's house at night to make love to her, delirious in no other need than to be good, because I wasn't so twisted that I needed anything else to be happy.

This is what I might've had forever if I hadn't lied.

A few hours later, we laid together, the rain lighter now as she rested her head on my chest and ran her hands over my body, memorizing every line and chord.

"The scars on your body..." she said quietly. "Your scalp, under your arm, your groin. Places people don't see."

I stroked her arm with my thumb as I held her, already knowing where she was going with it. I stopped cutting when I was fifteen. The night my mother left.

But some of the marks never truly healed. It was a good thing I was smart about where I did it, so my clothes always covered it.

"I had a classmate in Montreal who had scars like that," she went on, "but she didn't bother to hide it. It was everywhere. She had to leave and go to a hospital."

I stroked her arm still, my breathing even and calm.

"Where were you for two years?" she asked.

"Not in a hospital."

I knew what she suspected, but this was all so much more complicated than she knew. Not everyone needed help to stop hurting themselves. Some of us just traded in one coping mechanism for another.

She didn't see me for two years, because Damon was trying to stay away. And then he was at college.

"Someone taught me a long time ago that pain releases pain," I explained. "So when I was younger, I cut, poked, scratched, and burned myself, so I wouldn't feel everything that hurt. And then I realized, it felt even better to hurt everyone else."

"But not me?"

She had a teasing tone, but if she only knew. None of this was a joke.

I smirked anyway. "I did some damage."

She just didn't know how much yet.

"Don't make me answer questions," I told her. "You won't like the answers."

"But I need them." She turned her face up to me.

"I know."

I knew it was coming. Once the sex happened, she didn't want to be away from me.

And in all honesty, I didn't want to be away from her.

I just needed to make sure she listened to me. That she heard me out and couldn't run away. That there was no one around to interfere before she was able to process it.

If I wanted to keep this, it was my only chance.

I tipped her chin up, looking down at her. "My family has a cabin in Maine," I told her. "There's already snow. It's gorgeous up there. One phone call and it's stocked for us. Get dressed and come with me now."

"What?"

"Once we're there," I explained, "I'll tell you everything. Just for a few days, and then I'll bring you home."

She pulled her head up, a puzzled look on her face. "Taking me to a remote location where I can't run away?"

"I'll make sure you won't want to leave," I teased, pulling her back on top of me and holding her face. "I promise."

She'd be unbelievable angry, but it was the only thing I could do to make sure she absorbed it and got a chance to see past it. To make sure she knew the man I was with her was what was real.

"A cabin?" she pondered. "Like for skiing? I don't have to ski, right?"

"We're not going to fucking ski." I kissed her, nibbling and teasing. "We're going to eat and drink and screw and probably fight a little, but we're not leaving the cabin."

A ping sounded from my phone, but I ignored it.

She sat there, straddling me as I kissed and bit, teasing her and luring her, but she stopped moving or responding.

I pulled back, seeing the worried look on her face.

"You don't want to go," I guessed.

But she sighed, looking ready to cry. "I do," she said. "God, I do. I want to be alone with you for days and days. It would make me so happy, but..."

But what?

She paused, more notifications dinged from my phone, but I just held her face, waiting for her answer.

"I am a minor," she pointed out. "Technically, anyway. If my father overreacts, it could be considered kidnapping, taking me over state lines without my parents' permission."

I almost laughed, intrigued by the adventure, but then again, she was right. Even if she got over learning who I was and walked back to this town, her hand in mine, not only would I have to face the reality that I'd just run away for the weekend with the mayor's underage daughter, but that he would undoubtedly know I'd gotten into her pants.

He might forbid us from seeing each other.

But he wouldn't press charges. That was drama and gossip and embarrassing for all parties involved. He'd want to keep it as quiet as possible.

I was who I was, and so was my father. Griffin Ashby wouldn't take it that far.

And nothing would keep me from her. I'd love to see him try. I almost looked forward to it.

Fuck it. We were going.

I snatched up her bottom lip between my teeth, a smile in my voice. "My kind of fun has a price."

She laughed, looking excited, and nothing mattered more than where we'd be in a few hours. Alone, quiet, just us.

I didn't even want to stop at my house for clothes.

My phone started ringing, hers beeped, as well, and she reached for it, but I pulled her hand back, starting to get hard again.

Shit. We didn't have time for this. We had to leave.

My phone dinged again.

And again and again, one right after the other.

What the fuck? If Michael needed his car back that badly, track it and come get it, for Christ's sake. It was fucking early.

I pulled away from her mouth and growled as I reached over the side of the bed and felt for my phone. Finding it, I picked it up and turned it on, looking at the screen as she kissed my neck.

Instagram notifications, tags, tweets, PMs with article links...

What the fuck was this?

It all hit me at once, my nerves firing as I tried to make sense of what I was seeing. And then I clicked on a tag, a dark video popping up with the sound off, but it didn't matter. My heart stopped, instantly recognizing what I was seeing.

Winter and me in the bathroom night before last night.

The video on the group phone. It did take.

After it fell to the bathroom floor, it only recorded the ceiling, but it was still going. All the sounds we made would be on there and...

My eyes raced, scanning for who posted it, the comments, and then seeing my other notification and that it had been posted on multiple social media sites by several people, shared and retweeted like crazy.

Dread rolled through my stomach, and I caught another video I recorded of Kai and Will beating the shit out of a man who had been beating the crap out of his little sister.

Unfortunately, the man was also a cop, and Kai and Will's faces are also visible.

And mine, along with Winter's on our video, wasn't hidden at all.

The comments raged, throwing shit at all of us, and I couldn't look anymore. I closed my eyes. "Oh, my God," I muttered.

"What's the matter?" she asked, still kissing me.

Notifications were piling up, my phone still beeping, and I silenced it.

How did this happen? Where was the phone?

Jesus, my hands were shaking.

Will always handled the phone on Devil's Night. If we were all in on a prank, he filmed it. I gave it back to him after we got into the village last night to go to Sticks.

But it wasn't in his pockets last night when I searched for the keys. Where was his sweatshirt?

And then everything fucking hit me like a truck.

Rika.

The tear in the sleeve I saw when I held her wrists last night. That wasn't her shirt. She'd grabbed the wrong one when she left the warehouse. She'd been wearing Will's hoodie.

I shot up, forcing Winter off me as I sat up.

"Fucking Rika." I rubbed my eyes, wrapping my head around the shitstorm about to ensue. "Motherfucker."

"Rika Fane?" Winter questioned. "What's wrong?"

I didn't know what to say. I couldn't think.

Looks like she'd responded to what happened last night. To what she thought Will and I were in on and Kai was a part of, not knowing it was Trevor Crist instead.

God, I was so stupid. I was afraid she'd hate me and never forgive me, but she found the fucking phone in the pocket and dealt with us for good by uploading those goddamn videos. I'd underestimated her.

It was one thing to get caught with Winter by her father. But no one survived the jury of public opinion. Our mistakes—reprehensible to those on the outside who didn't understand—were laid bare to everyone who had an opinion, and there would be no choice. We'd have to be held accountable.

I quickly texted the guys.

We're so fucked!

And then I added, letting them know:

Rika has the phone! She had Will's sweatshirt last night!

As far as I saw, Michael wasn't in any of the videos. Of course. She wouldn't do anything to hurt her little crush.

I stood up, pulling on my jeans.

"Get dressed," I told Winter. "We gotta get out of here."

But she just knelt on the bed, facing me. "What's wrong?"

"Now," I ordered, sticking my phone in my back pocket and looking for my shirt.

But she didn't move. "You're scaring me," she said.

"So what else is new?"

I gathered up my shit, making sure I had Michael's keys, but when I looked at her again, she still wasn't budging.

"I said get dressed. Let's go."

Her head turned toward her phone, hearing notifications go off for her, as well. One after the other.

She dropped her voice, demanding, "What's happening?"

I stood there, not knowing what the hell I could do to salvage this. How did I get her out of here and gone and make this all go away so she never found out the nightmare that was happening out there right now?

But behind me, I heard an engine racing at full speed down the driveway.

She knew something was wrong. She wouldn't run with me like this.

And they were already here.

Dropping my shit, I dug out a cigarette and lit it, staring at her with the sheet wrapped around her body and just wanting to dive into her hair and lips and the warmth of her bed just minutes ago.

How did so much change in such a short time?

She heard the lighter, smelled the smoke, a troubled look crossing her beautiful face. "You smoke?" she asked so quietly.

I could hear the tires screech to a halt outside and the doors slam.

I darted my eyes to hers. "Don't let me go," I told her, breathing hard. "No matter what you hear or what they say, don't let me go."

She shook her head. "What do you mean?" And then she turned to where her phone sat again, flustered. "My phone's going berserk. What's happening? Please?"

"Winter!" her father shouted from downstairs, suddenly in the house.

And I dove in, brushing her lips with mine as he charged up the stairs.

"Don't let me go," I whispered.

But then her door was thrown open, her father entered with another man in tow, and he charged me.

"Oh, you son of a bitch! Get away from her!"

He threw a punch, and it was the first time in years I hadn't been ready to fight back. I didn't even want to. If I lost her, I didn't even care.

His fist landed across my jaw, and I fell into her nightstand, the lamp on it crashing to the floor with me.

Winter started gasping. "What's going on?"

A kick shot into my stomach, and I grunted, wincing as he did it again.

"Dad, stop!" she cried, climbing off the bed. "Leave him alone!"

The other guy pulled her back, and I recognized him as Mr. Kincaid, my old dean. He gripped Winter by the arms as she struggled to free herself.

"You sick little shit!" Ashby growled at me. "I threatened a restraining order and you do this? You're going to fucking jail for this. How dare you!"

He came down, landing another punch, and I clenched my teeth, holding my stomach.

Winter.

"Restraining order?" she repeated. "What?"

Please no. Please don't find out like this. Fuck.

"How could you have sex with him, Winter?" her father shouted. "What were you thinking?"

She held the sheet around her body, shaking her head. "How do you know that? What's happening?"

She doesn't know anything. She doesn't know about the video being leaked, me...

"Call Doug Coulson," Ashby told Mr. Kincaid. "Tell him we have Torrance here and to get his ass over here on his rounds picking up all the rest of the little shits."

I squeezed my eyes shut, barely feeling him grip my hair as I waited for Winter to understand.

It was over. She'd hate me.

"Torrance," she breathed out, hearing what her father had said. "Damon Torrance?"

I looked at her as he pulled my hair, making my scalp burn. "Winter," I begged.

"What?" she said to herself, still processing.

I tried to move toward her. "Winter." But I didn't know what to say. Instead, I shouted at Kincaid who just stood there with his hands all over a nearly naked girl. "Get her some fucking clothes!" I told him.

Oh, Jesus. He was having me arrested.

But I didn't care about that as much as I worried that she wasn't responding to me. *Please don't leave me.*

"Winter, listen to me," I said. "It's not what you think."

"It's Damon Torrance?" she asked the other men.

"You didn't know?" her father asked. "You didn't know who this was?" And then he glared at me, baring his teeth as the full measure of what had happened between us sunk in. "What did you do?"

"Winter, listen to me," I pleaded.

But she started sobbing and covering her mouth with a hand. "Get out!" she screamed, backing up into Kincaid and as far away from me as she could. "Get him out! Get him out!"

Ashby hauled me up, blood dripping from my lip.

"Winter, please." I begged.

"No more!" she put her hands over her ears, backing up into the wall. "Just die and leave me alone!"

She raged, and the backs of my eyes burned, but I watched as she buried herself in Kincaid's chest, shielding herself from me like I was going to hurt her.

Like I was a monster.

Just die and leave me alone.

"I hate you!" she growled. "You're a horror, and you had to lie, because you knew I'd never want you! No one would ever love you! Get out!"

Kincaid pulled her in, putting a blanket around her shaking body as she cried.

"Don't let him near me again," she pleaded. "Please, don't let him touch me."

I looked down at my hands as Ashby pushed me out of the room, away from her, and all the pain and loss spun like a cyclone in my brain.

I would never want you. No one would ever love you.

I'd defiled her, like I knew I would.

She would never dance like an innocent again.

She'd never have the wonder in her eyes she had when she was on that motorcycle.

I'd changed her forever. I'd bent and twisted and broken everything that made her the most beautiful thing that ever happened to me.

CHAPTER 21

Winter

FIVE YEARS AGO

My hands shook as I navigated the VoiceOver Accessibility option on my phone, listening to us out there for everyone to see online.

My kissing and our breathing. The moans and panting.

I love... I hate you.
Yeah, I hate you, too. I just want a hot piece of ass.
Yeah?

It was like I wasn't even there, experiencing it like this now. Like I was on the outside, hearing a disgusting display of something meaningless and shallow when it hadn't felt like that at all. My face cracked, splintering in pain as I sobbed, hearing his phone fall in the video, but not cut off, and the sounds, whimpers, and everything we did in the shower coming through, so there was no mistake what was happening.

My mother called this morning, before jumping on a plane with my sister to come home, and assured me I was never naked in the video, both of us having moved out of sight when it fell to the floor, but it had clearly kept recording.

My DMs were piling up, and I knew I shouldn't open them, but I hadn't been allowed out all day. The phone downstairs and my parents' cells had been going crazy, and I knew it was bad, but I didn't know how bad for me.

I clicked, VoiceOver reading the first one:

You look like a good time, and I could use one right now.

I clenched my teeth, clicking another and holding it to my ear.

So, Damon gives good D, huh? He has a thing for the blind, deaf, and dumb chicks. Close your eyes, plug your ears, and spread your legs, baby.

God, why were they doing this? My head was splitting, and I cried harder. I didn't know I was being recorded. It was private. It wasn't like that.

Nasty, skanky slut. How much dick do you have to blow to get anyone to love you? You should kill yourself.

Most of it seemed to come from accounts I didn't recognize, and the tears came so hard that no sound came out. I wanted to die. He used me. He did this all for a kick. He did this to me, because he got off on it?

The whole time. The past two years. The dancing, the car, the motorcycle, the janitor's closet, the theater, the fountain in the village square... All of it was Damon Fucking Torrance. I pictured those same black eyes from when we were kids, watching me in the ballroom.

I let out a growl, throwing my phone down on the bed and putting my head in my hands. "I could kill you!"

But then I heard someone barge into my room. "I told you to stay off the phone!" my father bellowed.

I pulled my hands down, still sobbing but feeling him take something off my bed.

I reached for where I threw my phone, but it was gone. "I need my phone," I argued.

"Griffin—" my mother interrupted.

But my father wasn't listening to anyone today. "Enough!" he barked.

"You knew I liked him," I heard my sister say, somewhere around the doorway. "He was arrested, Winter!"

"Good!" I yelled.

"Everyone hates us now."

"Get out!" I shouted at her.

How could she not be on my side? On this one thing?

"You're going back to Montreal day after tomorrow," my father bit out, seething so hard I thought he might hit something. "We'll bring you back if the police need you."

"You can't press charges!" Ari told him.

"Go!" he ordered. "Go to bed, and stay out of this."

I hung my head, and I couldn't stop crying even if I tried. "I didn't know it was him."

"Who did you think it was?" Ari charged. "You were warned they liked to play pranks! They get off on it! Like a regular guy would actually date you? That's what you thought?" And then she mumbled, "Fucking stupid."

Stop. Please stop.

I thought...

I thought it was real. I thought he...

The feel of him on top of me in the shower crawled over my skin, and I covered my face with my hands.

I loved him.

This morning I loved him, and tonight I hoped he suffered unimaginably.

"That is enough, Ari," my mother gritted out. "Go to your room now!"

After a moment, I heard her footsteps head down the hall, and I wondered what Damon was doing right now. Was he sitting in a cell? Or in a room being questioned with the rest of his buddies who also got nicked for other uploads.

But then it occurred to me. None of them would've purposely done this to themselves. This was bad for Damon, too.

He didn't upload the video himself. Why did he take it at all? I told him to take a picture.

But no, he wanted to brag to his buddies.

I tried to find comfort in knowing he might not have intended for the whole world to see it, but it was short-lived. He stole from me.

"You're not to leave this house," my father instructed. "You don't use the phone. You don't answer the door."

"Yes, she knows," my mother told him. "Leave us alone."

I heard my father sigh, and then he said, "I need to go talk to Doug Coulson. I'll be back late."

He left and slammed my bedroom door, making me jump. He hadn't asked if I was okay. Not once today. He hadn't hugged me or...or acted, at all, like none of this was my fault. He was treating me like I was partially responsible.

Ari was having sex. They knew it. And long before she was sixteen, too.

But I'd been willing with someone in that video, and it didn't matter with who. My father thought anyone who wanted me was obviously victimizing me.

And look at that. He was right.

I was the idiot for not knowing better. For thinking a "regular" guy wanted me.

I felt the bed sink as my mother sat down. "Did he hurt you?"

Every muscle on my face trembled. *How do you mean? Bruises? Is that what counts?*

"Yes, I know he lied." She touched my face, trying to comfort me. "But did he force himself on you? We need to know every detail, Winter. The court will need to know."

I sucked in a breath. Court. God, this town would massacre me.

"He lied," I said. "He made me think I was with someone else."

"Who?" Mom asked. "Who did you think he was?"

I opened my mouth to try to explain, but it wouldn't make sense. I'm not even sure it did to me anymore.

He never said he wasn't Damon Torrance. I had sex with him, knowing I didn't know who he was. Not his name, his family, his school...

No one was going to believe me.

There were probably other girls he'd hurt, and they may want to back me up, but his family was too wealthy and he was popular. They might hate him, but they were also afraid not to love him in public.

And the guys. They idolized him. He'd scored with a sixteen-year-old girl, and hey, it was just a technicality. I was legal in thirty-three states. Just not ours, right?

Oh, Christ. How was I so stupid?

"Did he make you do anything you didn't want to do?" my mother asked, clarifying her question.

But I just dropped my head, shaking it, because I didn't know how to answer. No, he didn't make me do something I didn't want to do, but he made me do something I would never have done with Damon Torrance.

She wrapped her arms around my neck, bringing my head into her chest. "It's okay. Shhh. I'm going to fix it," she told me. "We're going to fix it."

She rubbed my back and held me for a long time, calming me down and letting me hide a little. I was kind of glad my dad took my phone, though. Listening to that shit was screwing its way into my head, and I wanted everyone to understand, but I knew it would be pointless. The world loved to hate, and for now, my bubble was the safest place.

She laid me down and pulled my blanket over me, my clothes still on, but I was too drained to change.

"I left a glass of water on the bed stand," she said, "and there's a Xanax next to it if you feel like you need it."

I nodded, knowing I wouldn't. My eyes were heavy, and I'd be asleep soon enough, waking up tomorrow to face the nightmare all over again.

• • •

"Mom?" I called, hearing the music drift up from downstairs as I sat up in bed.

It was so clear.

My door was open. I thought she closed it.

Reaching over, I hit the button on the clock, hearing it read, "Twelve-fourteen a.m."

I patted around for my phone, remembering my father took it, but felt the water my mom left and gulped down a hefty drink.

The night was still so clear, like I hadn't been asleep at all, but I was still too tired to muster more tears just yet.

"Mom, are you there?" I shouted.

Nausea rolled through my stomach, and I needed something. I didn't know what. I hadn't eaten all day. That was probably it.

Yawning, I swung my legs over the side of the bed and rubbed my eyes, just wanting some soup and crackers or something and then maybe I'd take that Xanax and sleep forever.

Patting my way out of my room, I trailed down the bannister, hearing the faint, haunting tune of "Sleep Walk" by Santo and Johnny playing from somewhere downstairs. Any other time, I might smile at the gesture. My mom knew I liked oldies when I wanted to feel better.

But it was no use playing it while I was asleep.

I made my way into the foyer, still wearing a pair of jeans and a tank top from earlier, but before I swung around to head for the kitchen, I heard the beep of the answering machine near the door. Yawning again, I walked toward it.

It could've been a prank call. I was sure lots of those came in today.

But I didn't have my cell, so just in case Dad called...

Finding the button, I pressed it, my head spinning and my heart hammering as soon as I heard my mom's voice.

"Hey, sweetie," she chirped. "Didn't want to wake you. Your sister snuck out, so I left to go find her. Doors are locked. Don't leave. I'll be back as soon as I can."

The music drifted from the ballroom, and I breathed so hard, I was gasping.

Who was in the ballroom?

"Mom?" I screamed.

It was her. The message was from earlier tonight. She came back.

"Mom!" I cried out again.

And a creak split the floor to my left, and I stopped, my face scrunching up and my eyes squeezing shut as the nightmare loomed even though I was no longer asleep.

But I refused to cry. I locked my jaw, fisted my hands, and turned toward him.

"Damon," I said to my ghost who now had a name. "Perks of being rich, huh? You can make bail in record time."

I shook my head.

He was going to get off. Nothing was going to happen to him. Guys like him never paid.

"Your friends were arrested, too, I hear," I said. "The town is in chaos tonight."

I didn't hear him move, but that didn't mean he wasn't. Reaching behind me, I grabbed a gold figurine on the table, with a nice, pointy part on it.

"And you're here." I listened carefully for footsteps. "Why are you here?"

He didn't say a word, and for a moment it felt like the very first time he broke in and terrified me. This time, though, I wouldn't be waking up safe. He'd had his fun, and now he was here to have more.

"You want to shut me up?" I pressed. "Hurt me? Or do you want to see how much you already hurt me?"

Was he here to keep me quiet, or because he just couldn't resist his sick, perverted kink? To survey the damage he'd done on the girl who had been ready to run away with him this morning. Dreaming of waking up in his arms, in a warm bed with a fire roaring in the cold mountains.

It meant nothing to him.

"The best I've ever felt in seven years were the nights with you," I told him, tears springing up. "So just soak it up, because you win. I fucking fell for it. I want to eat my goddamn heart, because it wouldn't hurt as much as what you did to it this morning. I hate you."

My legs started to buckle underneath me as I cried, and my head started to swim.

"I hate you," I said, a sob thick in my throat, "and I'll hate you forever, so do what you're going to do, because I'm dead. I'm dead already."

I would never trust another man again. I'd have to leave my school and my home to escape the gossip.

I was the one paying for his lie, not him, but so help me God, I would drag him down with me. I would make sure he remembered me and know how enormously he failed at being the worst thing to ever happen to me, because he wasn't that important. He was nothing.

I didn't love him. I didn't even understand him.

"My father hates me. My sister hates me," I said. "My mom can't stand on her own. You made me think I wasn't alone. Why would you do that?"

The floor creaked again, closer this time, and I shot out my hand to get ready, but I stumbled, my head spinning, and I fell to the floor.

What was going on?

I swayed my hand on the floor, unable to steady myself.

"What's... what's wrong with me?"

"You drank the water," he finally spoke.

The water. The water? And then I remembered the glass my mother left me in my bedroom.

And my door was opened when she had closed it. He'd come in when I was asleep. He'd put something in the water?

Oh, Jesus. No, no, no…

I started gasping, trying to stand up, but I couldn't get my legs under me. Where was the figurine I had? I just had it in my hand.

"Wh—what did you give me?" I growled.

He grabbed hold of me, hauling me off the floor and holding me upright with his arms wrapped around me.

"Shhh," he said.

But I shook my head again and again. No.

Please, no.

"What are you going to do?" I choked out. "What do you want?"

I tried to pull away—tried to stand up—but my brain was slipping sideways, and I couldn't get control of my limbs.

"I just wanted to hold you," he said. "One last time."

Hold? What? His voice was fading, like it was in stereo down a long tunnel.

"Just wanted to hold you." His voice loomed somewhere over my head as my eyes started to close. "And say I'm really fucking sor—"

"What?" I asked, giving out and falling into him. "I can't understand you."

"Don't let me go," he whispered in my ear. "Don't let go."

"I'm gonna…" My mouth was so dry. "I'm gonna send you to jail."

His lips rested against my cheek, and I thought I felt his body shake with a silent sob.

But as I fell into sleep and oblivion, his words were sharp and clear in my ear. "Then you better hope I never get out."

CHAPTER 22

Winter

PRESENT

I sat in the theater, listening to the latest rehearsals for the annual *Nutcracker* performance and remembering when I was up there with all the little kids, too. The stage was larger than life, and I still remember leaping around as the snow fell, barely registering the audience, because the world up there was far too beautiful to look anywhere else.

Someone squeezed past me in my aisle seat, sitting next to me.

"How are you?" Rika asked.

I just gave her a small smile.

There were no answers to that question. Saying "fine" would seem comical.

I clasped my hands in my lap, chilled from the air, and I dipped my mouth under my thin scarf, breathing out to heat myself up.

"Come stay with us," she said.

She'd made the offer ever since the haunted house the night before last, but I felt numb now, and I didn't want to run. I wanted to win.

"You're helping me," I pointed out. "I appreciate it."

We met yesterday about her and Michael sponsoring a performance, and it wasn't much, but it was a path to get out on my own. They'd get their money back with ticket sales—if I were fortunate enough to have any—and whatever was left we'd split as profit. But she'd called earlier today with more ideas, including a tour. Maybe scouting other performers who weren't getting seen. She was really into it, and it was nice to have another person excited for my dancing. Other than Damon...

"You look a little dangerous," she mused. "Like you've got ideas."

"For the tour or for my sister's husband?"

She snorted. "Whichever one you have that look to kill for."

"I hate him," I said, pulling down the sleeves of my little jacket. "I hate what he did to me. He deserved his punishment."

He deserved to go to jail.

"But?" she pressed.

But my weak heart kept thinking about what he said in bed two nights ago when I'd held the blades to his rib and neck. About lying to me being the only way he felt he could get close to me in high school. Maybe it was just a lie he fed my mother to get rid of her.

Or maybe it wasn't. It didn't make it right, though.

"There were so many moments back then—" I told her, "—they felt real, like he could've been different and I could've been different."

He seduced me with a lie. Why was I having any doubts about the man he was?

"I do hate him," I told her. "I just wish I hated him every second."

"Alex told me after the haunted house the other night about everything that happened to you," I explained to her. "How they mistakenly thought you were the one to upload the videos and they went after you because they thought you sent them to prison." I paused as she remained silent. "She told me what Damon did. But you don't seem to hate him. Why?"

She invited him and our family to her engagement party. She was fine being around him at the haunted house. I heard a rumor they were having business meetings.

But she just sighed. "Why don't I hate any of them?" she asked. "I guess when you hate someone you don't have to hate them forever."

But it wasn't okay. How could she trust him? How could she forgive him?

"I don't excuse what he did," she said, hesitating for a moment, "but...I don't know. I see a chance in there. I can't explain it." And then she continued, "Michael, Kai, Will... They have never disappointed me since."

I didn't know what they'd done to her compared to Damon, but I knew what he did to me compared to her. I would never forgive him.

"He hasn't hurt you, has he?" she asked, like she expected he wouldn't really.

Another hard question to answer. Was he forcing me? No.

Was he threatening me? Playing with my head?

"The mindfucks are a little rough," I told her.

She scoffed, sounding like she understood. "Yeah, they are good at that."

The director was shouting on stage, giving direction, and then the piano started up again as I heard a dozen pairs of ballet slippers hit the stage, the musical number beginning again.

"The only good memory I have of Damon when we were younger was when we were kids," Rika told me. "I was like three or four—the memory is faint but I remember the gist— and we were at the library. Another kid pushed me down and stole my pop-up book." She laughed a little at the memory. "Damon stole it right back and gave it to me. He never talked to me, and my mom invited him to come sit with us and read, but he had to leave with his nanny, I think."

I pictured it in my head, Damon doing what he did and taking control of the situation. I wasn't sure why she told me that, as if an endearing little story would make up for who he was now.

"I didn't start to fear him until high school." Her voice sounded thoughtful as if she were figuring something out herself for the first time, too. "After everything that was happening in that house happened to him."

"It's no excuse," I pointed out.

And she agreed. "No, it's not." she said. "It's a reason. Plain and simple. There's always a reason why things are as they are."

• • •

I returned to the house late, sliding out of my shoes and unwrapping my scarf as I entered my bedroom. I hadn't seen Damon for almost two days, and I wasn't sure where he was or what he was doing, but I was tired.

So tired.

I undressed and slipped into one of my sleep sets, the cool silk of the shorts and shirt refreshing on my exhausted body, and I plugged my phone into the charger, ignoring the notifications from my mother.

I reached my mom yesterday morning, confirmed she and Ari were safe again, and when I asked how she could leave me and when she'd be back, she paused just a little too long, and I hung up. Let her get her excuses straight and leave me a message.

Had she honestly believed that shit he told her? About us being in love and needing time to reconnect?

Or was it what she wanted to believe, because it was easier than fighting back?

I locked my door and lodged my chair under it before sliding into bed and setting my alarm.

But as tired as I was, sleep wouldn't come.

Doors opened and closed quietly downstairs as Damon's security moved about, circulating around the property and keeping an eye on the house while he was away.

At first, I thought it was guards for me. To hinder my coming and going and report back to him on what I was up to. And those were undoubtedly some of their orders, but no one gave me any hassle when I wanted to go somewhere, and I never got any instruction to stop doing that or stop going there.

A driver chauffeured me, doors were opened for me, and if it wasn't them or Damon creeping me out the other morning or in the theater, I actually felt a little safer with them here.

When he was gone.

I clutched the sheet, resenting the thought that wormed its way in. That a part of me wished he wasn't gone.

Where was he? It had been days. Did he still have Mikhail?

Or did Damon go to the Maldives after all? A pang of jealousy hit me, and I drew in a deep breath, pulling my shirt away from my neck, because I felt stifled.

Fuck you.

What the hell was I doing? The sex was good, so I forgot that he was a lowlife? What a cliché.

I didn't care that he defended Rika when she was four or that he was abused as a child. Plenty of people grew up shitty.

I'd fucking loved who he pretended to be, but his lie negated everything that happened between us. He humiliated me.

Why was it so hard to remember that whatever he made me feel had been a lie, too?

The haunted house. The fantastical fear. The pulse in my veins.

But then I remembered his strong arms around me.

I loved the danger. The way he brought me to life.

My fingers rested on my stomach, against the sliver of skin where my shirt rode up, and I glided my hand along it, throbbing between my thighs as my nipples poked through my shirt.

Tears burned my eyes. I hated myself.

Because I wanted him.

He lied so well, didn't he? That I wanted to feel everything he convinced me of when he was in my bed when I was sixteen.

A tear fell, but I tried not to cry. I wanted to feel him again.

But I couldn't. I couldn't let him win.

I heard a car pull up outside, the door open and slam shut, and then the door downstairs slam.

I froze, the pulse pumping in my neck as I listened.

Footfalls on the stairs.

A creak in the floors.

The slow whine in the floorboards getting closer, and I heard Mikhail whine.

I closed my eyes. *No.*

He jiggled my door handle. When it didn't give, because it was locked, he did it harder.

The door still didn't open.

Everything was quiet for a moment, and I clutched the sheet at my sides, waiting, and then...

The door was kicked in.

I sucked in a breath as it flung open, the wood splintering, the handle crashing to the floor, and I heard my chair tip over and hit the wood.

I shot up in bed, shaking my head against the heat rushing my belly and the warmth between my legs. "Don't," I begged.

But I wasn't sure if I was telling myself or him.

I didn't hear him move, but I knew it was Damon. The cloves drifted off his clothes, and the security would've stopped him if it wasn't.

A light sweat made the silk pajamas stick to my skin, and I pulled off the sheet, swinging my legs over the side of the bed.

"Please, don't," I whispered. "I can't think straight."

His footsteps approached, he stopped in front of me, and I heard ice clink in a glass as he took a drink and cupped my chin.

He ran his fingers over my jaw, possessive.

"You don't want to want it," he said in a low, deep voice, "but you do."

"Please." *Just leave.* "Please."

Don't touch me. Don't hold me. Don't take me in your arms.

He set the glass down on my nightstand, and I heard him remove clothes, his jacket maybe, and throw it off somewhere.

"Lie down," he told me.

"No," I mumbled.

I heard buttons go flying as he tore off his shirt and then the jingle of a buckle as he unfastened his belt.

"Lie down, Winter," he said sternly.

He's not him. He's not who I fell in love with.

He was my sister's husband, and he wanted to make sure I was never happy again.

I put my hands on his stomach, holding in my sobs as he threaded his fingers through my hair, bringing my head in close. Bending down, his breath falling across my lips, he said, "On your back, Winter. Do it."

And then his lips caught mine, biting, and I kissed him back, letting his tongue sink into my mouth and feeling the need for him course through my body.

But instead of lying down, I pulled back, touched his face, and pleaded with him as he caressed my cheek with his thumb.

"Just let me go," I told him.

And he growled, throwing me off.

I cried, scooting away from him on the bed as he stalked around my room.

"Let me go," he mocked me, repeating my words. "Why can't you shut up? Why can't you all just shut the fuck up?"

"I will hate you if you do this to me," I fought. "I'll despise you and never stop trying to escape you, because I could never love you. Because you're sick, and I hate the way you make me feel! I could never love you."

A clutter went crashing to the floor, and I knew he'd shoved everything off my dresser.

But I didn't stop. "And I hate myself around you," I told him, saying anything to hurt him. "I hate what I let myself do with you, because the only way I can get you away from me is to get it over with!"

"That's not true," he bit out.

I climbed off the bed, facing where his voice was coming from. "You're such a little boy. A child who can't control himself. A disease!"

More went crashing to the floor, and I heard my mirror shatter in his little tantrum, but I only grew stronger.

"So come on," I dared him. "Fuck me. Do the only thing you know how to do, because it's all you can take from me anyway, and I don't give a shit about any of it! Take the house. Take the family who left me here with you. Take the fucking clothes off my back and make me walk out of here naked!" Sobs filled my throat, but I refused to let them loose. "I would gladly do it if it meant getting away from you!"

He rushed up to me, grabbing the back of my neck. "You were in love with me."

"It wasn't the real you. It was nothing but an act!"

I slapped his hand away and shoved him in the chest.

"You shouldn't have killed her," I said, digging deep for the worst fucking things that would ever come out of my mouth. "She was the only one who was ever going to love you. She was the only one who wanted to touch you and take care of you and be around you!"

He breathed hard, labored, like he was struggling for air.

"Everyone else you have to hold prisoner!" I snarled. "You have nothing and no one! No one can stand you!"

"S...s...stop," he gasped, sucking in air. "Just please stop."

"I hate you!"

"Winter, please don't," he begged, and then I felt him move away, his body hitting the wall and sliding to the floor. "Please stop. Just stop."

He grunted, like he was in pain, and I stood there, still hot from my fury and tears welled in my eyes, threatening to fall.

He said again, barely a whisper, "Please stop. Please."

I stood there, my fingers curled into fists. What was wrong with him?

Why wasn't he storming out or charging for me and throwing me on the bed like he threw me on the floor in the haunted house?

He just sat there, the air pouring in and out of his lungs, turning calm after a few minutes, but I fisted my hands, staying charged.

Who was he? Who the hell was he?

He was a machine. A monster. A liar.

What the fuck was I supposed to do? What did he want from me?

But he didn't say anything. He just sat there. Quiet.

Until finally I heard his voice again, solemn and calm. "My father had this rottweiler," he said, "who was pregnant with mutts when I was about seven. He let me have one of them. Not sure what happened to the rest, though."

I swallowed the tears in my throat, still standing rigid and ready.

"I'd never loved anything so much," he told me. "That little thing wanted to be wherever I was. He followed me everywhere." He paused and then continued, "He had this thing, though, about barking. At the drop of a pin. He barked so much, and I couldn't shut him up, and every time the doorbell rang or a car pulled up to the house or someone knocked on my door, I...I couldn't get to him in time to settle him down before my father heard him and got angry."

Dread knotted my stomach, and I pictured seven-year-old Damon and his puppy with their sliver of happiness in that shitty house.

"Even at seven years old, though," he continued, "I knew the horror of finding my dog hanging from a tree in the woods wasn't as awful as the realization that my father made no attempt to hide what he'd done."

My face cracked, but I stayed silent.

"He wanted me to find him." His voice grew thick with tears. "Even then I understood that the dog wasn't the one being punished, and that next time he'd make me do the deed. I never asked for another dog after that."

I squeezed my eyes shut, tears spilling over. *Jesus Christ.*

"And I learned, really quick, that life wasn't going to be pretty. Not until..."

Until...me?

I put the pieces together. His dog at seven, the party at eleven and how his father yelled at him and how his demeanor had already started to go downhill. I had nothing to do with any of that.

"I was so alone," he explained from somewhere on the other side of my room. "I couldn't talk to people. I didn't have any friends. I was scared all the time." His voice was thick with memory, as if it all happened just yesterday. "I just wanted to be invisible, and if I couldn't be invisible, then I just wanted it to end. I was going to run away, because..." His sad voice trailed off. "Because the only other way to escape was to end it all."

I couldn't wrap my head around it. That's what was going through his mind when I met him that first time? What eleven year old wants to die?

"You were so little," he mused. "When you came into the maze and noticed me hiding and crawled inside and sat down at my side, it was like..."

Like you had a pet again.

"Like I wasn't alone anymore," he finished. "So little. So quiet. But it was everything. Feeling you next to me."

God, what was he doing to me?

"You taught me how to survive that day," he said. "You taught me how to be strong and how to get to the next minute. And the next and the next. I could never forget, and when you came back in high school, and I had changed into this, because I'd seen so much shit," he went on, "and my desires had morphed into something ugly and twisted, but I'd fucking survived, nonetheless, and didn't swallow the bad for anyone anymore, because you had taught me how to get rid of the shit. I finally craved one more thing I realized had been missing when I laid eyes on you again."

I didn't understand. I was eight. What could I possibly have taught him to keep him surviving? To keep him fighting? And what was missing from his existence after he'd gotten through all that?

"I wanted something good," he admitted. "Beauty, maybe? The night of the pool party, the house was quiet. It was just us, but you didn't know I was in the house, too. I watched you dance."

I remembered that night so vividly. For the two years after that, I'd looked back on it, excited and terrified, but also with this weird sense of being safe in that closet with him.

"You made the world look different," he told me. "You always had, and it struck me as odd, because I had hated to watch my mother dance growing up. It was just some elaborate lie that I couldn't stomach, but you..." He trailed off, searching for words. "It was pure, and it was a dream. I didn't want to change you. I just wanted to be a part of it all. Of everything beautiful you were going to do."

He sat there for a moment, and everything in my body hurt. I didn't realize every muscle had been tightened this whole time. This was the first time he'd ever said things like this. The first time he'd ever really talked to me.

"But I was still me, and I scared you that night, because that's what I do," he admitted, sounding like he hated himself. "Something amazing happened, though. You followed. You wanted to feel that edge, too, as long as you were at my side, and for a few incredible days, I felt..."

He didn't finish the thought, but I knew what he wanted to say. It had felt the same with me.

"When it was time to come clean, I couldn't," he said, his voice growing thick. "I just wanted to stay there with you. Behind the waterfall, in the shower, in the ballroom... Just stay with you."

He rose to his feet, and the walls felt too close, and my clothes too tight, and I couldn't get my lungs to open, because there was too much to take in and not enough said so many years ago. *Why didn't you say all of this years ago?*

"Nothing was a lie," he whispered.

And then he walked out, and my chest ached so badly, for air or for him, I didn't know, but I ran to the window, yanked it up, and drew in a lungful of air, feeling everything give way. Slip away, fade, and ease.

My fear. My worry. My hatred.

My anger.

Why didn't he say all that years ago?

Why?

CHAPTER 23

Damon

PRESENT

The elevator doors opened, and I charged into Michael's penthouse in the city, turning the corner and strolling into the apartment.

Walking into the great room, I saw Michael, Kai, and Will sitting on chairs and couches, while Rika stood near the wall of open balcony doors, a rare, balmy evening breeze drifting through.

Michael allowed the doorman to let me come up, so he must be intrigued enough to indulge me, and I was glad most of them were here.

I threw the piece of newspaper that I'd folded into an airplane on the table in front of Michael, watching him take it with very little enthusiasm.

He thought he'd have the first word. Nope. I was controlling this conversation.

I looked at Will. "Do you hate me?"

He fixed me with a guarded stare but didn't say anything.

Then I looked at Rika. "You?" I asked.

She locked her jaw, averting her eyes.

But not answering the question, either.

I'd hurt them the most, and if they could get past this, then I had a chance.

"You're not my enemies," I told everyone. "I don't want that."

"Then what do you want?" Kai retorted.

I saw Michael open up the airplane to see the article that was in the Post yesterday about the Throwback Night being organized at The Cove this weekend, the old abandoned theme park in Thunder Bay.

I knew they were interested in buying it. It was time.

"I want for us to get back to the plan," I answered. "To run things."

We wanted Thunder Bay, and not just a resort. We wanted everything. A whole seaside village as our little clubhouse.

But Kai just scoffed. "We were eighteen. With no clue of the money or connections it was going to take."

"We have money."

"No, Rika has money," Kai shot back. "We have our parents."

I inched forward. "I'll control thirty-eight percent of the hotels on the eastern seaboard, twelve television stations, and enough land to start my own state if I want to."

"When your father is dead," Will pointed out.

Yeah. Which would happen sooner or later.

"You, Michael, and Kai can have the premier resort destination in three years right here in Thunder Bay," I explained, "making it the new Hamptons and drawing the elite of America's major cities."

"We wouldn't even be able to get permits," Michael told me. "Your father and my father have had no trouble convincing the mayor that any jobs a resort will create isn't worth the business it would take away from their real estate and hotels in the city."

I cocked my head. "What mayor?"

The four of them stared at me, looking befuddled as they wrapped their heads around exactly what the hell I'd been doing all this time as Crane helped me gather information the past couple of months. Taking down Winter's father wasn't just to get Winter.

Kai shook his head. "Jesus."

"They'll elect someone new, Damon," Will argued. "They're holding a special election in three months to replace Winter's father."

"Yeah." I smiled. "I know."

And I stood there, waiting for their pea-sized brains to catch up again. Thunder Bay needed a new mayor. One who would give us all the permits we needed to start building over at The Cove.

We had some likely candidates right in this room.

Will dropped his wide eyes, absorbing the idea, while Michael sat back, staring at me.

"You can't be serious," Kai laughed out.

But I just cast my eyes to Rika, holding her gaze.

"What?" she asked, seeing me stare at her.

"You're a good chess player," I teased. "Politics. It's the greatest chess game."

She started laughing. "I'm not running for mayor, so I can protect your business interests, Damon. I don't want to run that town."

"Why wouldn't you?"

She opened her mouth to retort, but got lost for words for a moment. Finally, she blurted out, "Why me?"

"Because Michael couldn't care less, and the rest of us are felons."

"Hey, it's America." Will leaned back, slumping in his chair with a lazy smile. "Anything is possible."

"You want the press digging up your past?" I challenged him and then looked to Kai. "You?"

The Internet was forever. We'd never get an ounce of peace as things got dug up and blasted online. And Kai and Will especially had no interest in bringing that stress onto their families.

"The girls are clean," I said. "Rika needs to do it."

She let out a pathetic little laugh, still searching for an argument, and finally looked at Michael who still hadn't said anything.

"Michael?" she prodded for his help. To offer some excuse why she shouldn't do this.

But he hesitated, looking apologetic when he finally met her gaze. "It's not a *horrible* idea, actually," he said. "It would give us leverage, and you'd do well by the town. It's worth thinking about."

Her eyes flared, looking pissed. "What about Banks?"

"I have bigger plans for her," I told them.

"Oh, you do?" Kai replied. "I'd like to hear the plans you have for my wife."

"In good time."

He shook his head at me, everyone falling silent as they processed what I was suggesting. I already gathered Michael had investors lined up and a bank in his corner for the land and the resort, but he wasn't moving forward, because he anticipated problems with hiring workers and getting permits. That problem was now solved. I'd worked my ass off for a seat at this table.

If the past could be the past and fucking stay there, that was.

They all remained silent, sharing looks with each other and pondering how this would all play out with me involved.

But maybe I couldn't win them, after all. Maybe the past was too much to swallow.

But then Will spoke up, not looking at me. "Say you're sorry," he said.

Sorry?

It only took a moment for me to realize what he was talking about.

He wanted an apology. For everything.

I dropped my eyes, frowning.

He wanted me to cower down? Like we all haven't made fucking mistakes, and I hadn't already proved that I wanted this and I was ready? That I wouldn't go there again?

Words were shit. They didn't mean anything.

I gave Winter a whole fucking monologue last night, and not one word from her since. What we did mattered, not what we said.

But they just stared at me, all waiting for me to say it, like if I said it everything would be fine. Would it be fine?

I wanted them back, though, and while my father taught me powerful men didn't apologize, maybe—just this once—I could choke out the words. I had fucked up, after all, and I was actually pretty lucky they hadn't taken my head over everything.

I swallowed the bitter taste in my mouth. "I'm sorry."

They all just looked at me, frozen, for forever, and my stomach was knotted so tightly, I was about to hit someone if the words hung in the air any longer.

And then Michael rose from his seat and slipped into his suit jacket. "Contact Mike Bower and tell him we want to talk," he told me and then walked over to kiss Rika goodbye.

I almost smiled. Bower ran the city council. We'd need to talk to him to get Rika on the ballot.

Will and Kai stood up after him, gathering their stuff and starting to leave with him.

"And we'll meet at The Cove tomorrow with the architectural firm," Michael informed me as he walked past. "Ten o'clock."

I nodded, accepting his invitation to be there, relief immediately washing over me.

They left—I wasn't sure where—but Rika and I stood there for a moment, silent. I knew there were things she wanted to say—maybe get mad about what just happened and being pushed into a new role with a hell of a lot of responsibility she hadn't asked for—but she picked up her leather school bag and hooked it over her head, walking past me.

I let her go, standing there, but then I heard her footsteps stop and her voice behind me.

"Michael and Kai are smarter than you, you know?" she said.

I listened.

"Because if there's one thing they know about revenge, Damon, it's that it won't feel nearly as good as her love will."

I clenched my teeth together against the ache in my gut, but I felt it anyway.

Fuck you, Rika.

"But I think you already know that, don't you?" she continued.

Fuck you so much.

"She'll make you stronger," she said. "And we need you strong."

I closed my eyes, not wanting to feel the shit I felt when I was nineteen when I let myself...want her.

When I let myself fucking love her.

When I let my guard down and believed what was happening between us was stronger than anything and guys like me could have a completely different life.

But God, Rika was right. I knew she was right.

Nothing in my life had ever felt as good as Winter happy because of me.

I'd told her everything last night. I wanted her to understand.

"You should leave her alone," Rika told me, and her voice was closer now like she'd turned around toward me. "Let her be calm and safe, and give her some room to breathe."

I wasn't asking for your opinion.

I heard her step closer behind me. "And in the meantime, be an adult. Get to work on something and show her you can survive without her. Without her respect, you have no chance."

"No chance at what?"

"No chance at not becoming your fucking parents," she replied.

A baseball lodged in my throat.

Was she right? Was that where I was heading? Was I ever going to be done with Winter? Did I want any other woman?

No.

And what if I got her pregnant? Would my kids hate me for hurting her? Was it just some endless fucking cycle, because I wouldn't face that Rika was right, and Michael and Kai knew what I refused to see?

I wanted her.

I broke last night, because I didn't want this. I just wanted that kid back who sat in my lap and drove my car.

I made her happy. Me.

And instead of sticking to the plan and making her hate that she wanted me, I hated that I still wanted her.

None of it was a lie, except my name.

It was real, and I wanted it again.

I fucking loved her.

Goddammit.

I spun around and walked past Rika, toward the elevator, but I heard her voice behind me again.

"And Damon?" she called.

I stopped.

"When and if she comes around, take her somewhere, just the two of you."

What?

"It's called a date," she explained, "and it's where you do something she likes that makes her happy. You and she will keep your clothes on for this."

Oh, you're funny. I shook my head, leaving her apartment and stepping into the elevator.

I pushed the button for the lobby. "A fucking date," I mumbled.

CHAPTER 24

Winter

PRESENT

I came out of the shower, dressed and drying my hair with a towel as I heard the motors of heavy trucks and a jackhammer outside again.

What were they doing? It had been going on since yesterday morning, but I tried not to care at first, and then I just thought it was more installations from the new security. They'd been installing an alarm system and changing locks, but this sounded like serious construction.

I walked to the end of the hall, past my bedroom, and stood at the window, the warning beeps of a truck moving in reverse sounding off outside and workers calling out to one another. I couldn't hear what they were saying, though.

Damon had disappeared again after the fight in my bedroom, and I hadn't talked to him or heard him in the house for almost two days.

Two days of freedom, rehearsing at the studio, practicing more at home, planning with Rika and Alex and brainstorming ideas for how to get me on some show bills or into outdoor festivals.

Someone climbed the stairs behind me, and I recognized the footfalls. Crane had this way of falling into his steps, almost like skidding, on the hardwood.

"What's the noise outside?" I asked over my shoulder.

I felt him approach and waited.

"Mr. Torrance is having the 'stupid, gaudy, fucking fountain' removed, he said."

I almost wanted to laugh at the way he repeated Damon's words, throwing shade.

But then they sank in.

"Removed," I mumbled.

He was taking out the fountain in front of my house. Throwing it away. Getting rid of it.

Like he didn't want any reminder of the past or what he fell in love with about us as a boy.

He wanted to kill it.

I stopped drying my hair, holding the towel in my hands. "Is he here?" I asked.

"He's close."

Close. What does that mean? Was he always close? Even when he left?

"Do you need something?" Crane inquired. "I don't expect him back to the house today, but I can get a message to him."

I didn't even know where to start. I wanted to say things to him, but everything in my head was still a hodgepodge of feelings contradicting facts.

I didn't want to talk, but I wanted to feel him in the house.

Turning around, I followed the wall past Crane, without answering him, and slipped into my bedroom, closing the door.

I'd tried hard not to think about everything he said night before last—keeping busy with choreography and planning—but if I slowed for a second, he was there again, sitting against the wall in my room, and whispering nightmares I'd never seen and confessing secrets he'd tried hard to keep hidden for so long.

Should I forget everything he did? Was it all suddenly okay just because his feelings had been real?

I moved around my room, putting away clothes and cleaning up. Yesterday morning, after Damon's tantrum, Crane came in and picked up everything his boss shoved onto the floor the night before and replaced my mirror. When I came home later, he'd brought in a contractor who replaced my door. The room was almost back in order. I wished he cleaned up all his messes as quickly.

There is a reason why all things are as they are.

I laid on my bed, hearing the trucks and workers still moving about outside, and closed my eyes, feeling my body relax but not my mind.

The pull of him was everywhere. I remembered so well the feel of teasing each other, laughing through a kiss, the heat of his arms around me, and the way his body craved mine. The way he wanted and the way I've always ached for his roughness and danger, his whispers and him.

The way I always saw Damon Torrance's raven eyes in my head, even before I knew my ghost was Damon Torrance.

"Come on," he says, pulling me through the maze. "You'll like it."

"What is it?"

I breathed hard, stumbling to keep up as he races through the other side of the maze and beyond the hedges.

He wants to show me something, but I really just want to stay in the fountain. It's fun in there—so secret.

But he's so happy now, and I'm kind of curious.

I can't stop smiling. My belly has flutters in it.

We run deep into the backyard, our clothes wet and cold as we near the forest line, and I see it right away. I shoot my eyes up, taking in the long trail of wooden boards nailed to the tree trunk, and at the top sits a treehouse disguised above a line of branches and leaves.

Sort of.

It doesn't look completed, but there's a really big floor and a railing around the outside. It sits between a split in the tree, two trunks locking it in and surrounded by green. You aren't just in a treehouse. You're in the tree.

I let go of his hand. "Wow. You're so lucky."

He stands next to me, looking up at it. "You like it?"

I nod, not taking my eyes off it.

I wonder if he did it himself or if someone helped. It didn't look all fancy like some others I've seen, and his dad doesn't seem like the type to build treehouses, either.

"You go up first," he tells me. "In case you slip, I'll be behind you."

I dart my eyes over to him, his dark ones looking at me under black eyelashes. A somersault hits my stomach, and I turn away.

Why am I nervous all of a sudden? Am I scared? It's a tall tree, isn't it?

"I think my parents might get mad," I tell him. I've never been that high before.

His face falls a little, and after a moment, he just nods, looking disappointed. "Okay."

I feel bad. I want to go up. I want to do things with him. He's so fun. He's not calling me 'chicken' or getting mad at me or anything.

I like him.

"You won't let me fall?" I ask, making sure.

He looks down at me, smiling and excited again. He takes my hand and we run for the ladder, him letting me step up first, the boards still looking new and nailed in tight. My heart starts to pound, because if I slip or lose my grip, I'll fall.

But I feel him right behind me, and I swallow the lump in my throat and start to climb.

One step after the other, one at a time, I scale the tree, refusing to look down and keeping my eyes above me on the door in the floor of the treehouse that I can spot through the leaves.

My tutu brushes against the trunk, the netting getting stuck on the bark, and I tighten my hands on each board as I pull it off and keep going.

A breeze blows across my legs, chilling my wet clothes even more, and before I can stop myself, I glance down, seeing how high we are. I gasp and wrap my arms around the board in front of me.

"I'm scared," I tell him. "It's high."

He climbs up behind me, setting his feet outside of mine and his hands on the boards around me.

"It's okay. I have you," he says. "I promise."

I squeeze my fists one time and then start to pull away from the tree a little. I look over my shoulder, meeting his eyes, and he's right there, staring at me, almost nose to nose.

Something fills my chest, and he's so close, it makes me feel so weird. Like something is pulling me.

I can't look away, and he holds my eyes, too, and it's like I can't stop it. The pull.

His lips touch mine, and I feel like I'm on a roller coaster.

It makes me stop breathing as tickles hit me everywhere, and then I pull away.

I clutch the board tighter, heat rising to my face. "Why did you do that?"

"I didn't do it. You did it," he charges.

"I did not."

God, I'm so embarrassed.

I glance back at him, trying to see if he's mad, but he looks just as embarrassed as me.

I didn't kiss him, did I? It was him.

Or both of us. Ughhhh...

He nudges me. "Hurry. Come on."

And although I'm still mortified, I breathe easier knowing he still wants to go up in the tree.

Cool. Let's just forget about it then.

I climb to the top and stop, waiting for him to catch up behind me and push open the door. He does, and it flies up and tips over, hitting the floor.

I smile, relieved. I scurry the rest of the way and crawl up onto the floor of the treehouse, pulling myself to a standing position.

I rise, the wind blowing against me and the leaves of the tree rustling all around.

"Whoa," I breathe out.

It's like another world.

I turn in a circle, the space kind of an odd-shaped circle but so big, and I can see out over some of the trees, finding the clock tower in town and the roofs of some of the estates in the area.

I point, smiling. "I see the ocean!"

Through the branches, out beyond the forest, lays the silver water spanning all the way to the horizon, and I tip my head back, looking up into the clutter of leaves over our heads and the branches within reach in case we want to climb farther.

He's so lucky. This is the best. I wish I had this at my house. I'd never leave.

He lets me take it all in as he puts his hands in his pockets and walks around me. I scan the treehouse floor, seeing a lantern, a sleeping bag, some drawings, and empty chip bags, and soda cans.

I look at him. "Why do you hide in the fountain when you have this place?"

"Because they know about this place."

He's quick to answer, so he must know from experience. How often does he hide? Is he always alone when he does? He shouldn't always be alone.

I walk to the railing facing Damon's house and see some of the party going on, but I'm too far away to recognize anyone or hear any of the music.

He comes up to my side. "Why are you named Winter?"

"It's a poem by Walter de la Mare," I tell him, still taking in the vast scenery as I recite part of it. "'Thick draws the dark, And spark by spark, The frost-fires kindle, and soon, Over that sea of frozen foam, Floats the white moon.'"

I have the whole thing memorized, but he's probably not interested in hearing it. Any of my classmates who ask aren't interested, either.

"It describes winter," I explain. "My mom said the poem made a cold and bitter season seem pretty. She said the beauty in life is what we live for, and it's everywhere. You just have to look closer."

He just stares out beyond the railing, looking thoughtful.

"I'm not sure why she named me that, but I like it," I add.

He sits down, dangling his legs over the sides, and props his arms up over the wooden board nailed across to keep people from falling, and I hesitate for about three seconds before I join. I plant myself down next to him, hang my legs over the side and laugh at the butterflies taking off in my stomach.

I peer over the side, my head feeling a little dizzy, so I draw back.

We sit there, quiet, and observing the view, but I notice my head ache and start to rub at my hair.

"It hurts," I say out loud, shifting my bun. "My scalp…"

It always happens when my hair is in a tight style all day. It feels so good to let it out.

I pull out a barrette—the only other one in my hair that I didn't leave in the fountain—and start pulling out the pins in my bun.

"Can you help me?" I ask. "Make sure they're all out?"

He reaches behind and feels my hair, pulling out a few more pins, and then he helps me unwrap the twist, my hair coming down. I slide my hands underneath it, rubbing my scalp and sighing, because it feels so good.

I look over at him, and he's just looking at me, his eyes moving over my face.

My skin under my costume starts to get too warm.

He turns away and lets out a breath as he stares ahead. "I might kiss you again when we're older," he says. "Just so you know."

My mouth falls open a little, and I want to make some sound in disgust, just in case he's kidding or teasing me, but...

Is he telling the truth?

I fold my lips between my teeth to keep from smiling. I don't know why I want to smile, but I can't help it.

He puts his hand down next to mine on the floor of the treehouse, and my heart beats so loud.

Is he gonna hold it?

"Winter!"

A shout pierces the air, and I jump.

Searching the ground, I see my father and mother storm up toward the treehouse, their gazes fixed on us.

"Why would you run off without telling your mom where you were going?" he barks.

"Dad," I breathe out, suddenly scared I did something wrong.

Why is he here? He wasn't here earlier. He looks upset.

"Come down, honey," my mom calls, smoothing her clothes. "It's time to leave."

"You shut up," Dad says. "She and Arion are not to come here again. You'll be lucky if I don't sue you for custody."

Custody? Why is he mad at her?

"What's going on?" I look up at Damon.

Did we do something wrong?

He shakes his head, scooting back and pulling me with him. "I don't know."

We move out of sight and stand up, feeling the floor vibrate under us like someone is coming up the ladder.

He's rigid next to me, but he looks just as confused. I should've told my mom where I was going, but she was with Mr. Torrance, and it just happened.

Is that why he's mad?

My father comes up through the door in the floor, his lips tight, and his suit wrinkled.

He stands up, scowling at us both.

"Get away from her," he orders Damon.

Damon and I exchange looks, both of us scared.

My father charges over, and Damon steps in front of me.

"Did he hurt you?" my dad asks.

But Damon just shakes his head. "I didn't."

It sounds like a plea. Why is my father so worried?

"Move." He pushes Damon out of the way.

My dad grabs my hand and pulls me. I stumble, letting out a cry.

"You don't speak to him, and you are never allowed back at this house," he growls. "If Mom brings you, you tell me. Do you understand?"

"But I want her to come back," Damon says. "Please."

"What did we do?" I ask my dad.

He just ignores me, flexing his jaw and squeezing my hand as he yanks me toward the door.

I look back at Damon but stumble when Dad nudges me toward the hole in the floor. I spin back around, looking down to the ground far below and shake my head. My knees shake, and I feel like I'm going to pee my pants.

"I'm scared," I start to cry.

I can't see the steps going down like I could coming up.

"Now!" he snaps.

I jump.

Shaking and tears streaming, I crouch down by the hole, knowing I'm going to slip. My foot will slip. I know it. I won't be able to see the steps underneath me.

But Damon rushes over and takes my hand, pulling me away from the hole and putting himself in front of me again.

"Leave her alone!" he fights. "I'll help her! I'll do it!"

My father charges for him, Damon steps back, digging into my foot, and I cry out.

"Just get out of here!" Damon yells. "I'll bring her down!"

He backs up more, scared, and I'm stumbling, step after step, and we're falling back, and I can't catch myself.

"You little shit…" my dad growls.

"Just leave her alone!" Damon cries out.

I look back, see us heading straight for the railing, and he's not paying attention.

"Damon!" I beg.

He falls into me, our weight snapping the small wooden beam, and I fall backward, crying out and grappling for anything.

"Ah, oh, my God!" I hear my mother scream from below.

I catch the edge of the floor, losing my grip and spilling over, but a hand catches me, and I suck in air, bile rising up my throat as my legs dangle.

I look up, tears filling my eyes as Damon lies on his stomach, struggling to keep hold of me, but I feel so heavy, like I'm being pulled down. My father comes down and grabs for me, but Damon and I can't hold, and I flail, slipping out of his fingers. His eyes meet mine, time freezes for a split second as we stare at each other, knowing I'm gone.

I slip, scream, and fall, his face the last thing I see before I see nothing at all.

I blinked my eyes awake, sweat coating my brow as warmth spilled through my bedroom window. The memory— the panic—still raced through my body as if I went over that treehouse edge yesterday.

That was the first time I recalled so many details my eight-year-old mind had buried away. He was so different. Rika was right.

I sat up in bed, wiping my eyes but still tired.

Tired of worry and hate and anger.

But also tired of feeling like I always lost.

That was my dilemma with Damon. That accident wasn't his fault. I knew now that my father wasn't upset with me or Damon that day. He'd discovered my mother and Mr. Torrance together and lost his temper.

Everything got out of hand, and Damon got scared. We were just kids. He didn't mean to push me over. I knew that now.

But still...

I just never seemed to come out of anything with him unscathed, did I? In body or in mind.

Rising from the bed, I left my room, the house still silent as I walked down the stairs and into the ballroom. I fell asleep so early I missed dinner last night, and I needed some coffee, but I needed to stretch. I started my playlist and walked over to the wall, moving the curtain aside and lifting the first window to breathe in some fresh air.

But as I did, I stopped, hearing the rush of water outside.

A lot of water, and not like rain.

I thought he got rid of the fountain.

I couldn't hear the workers anymore—no trucks or machinery. Did they bust a pipe or something? What was that sound?

Leaving the ballroom, I walked toward the front door, punching in the code Crane had given me and disarming the house.

I opened the door, the sound of water filling the air as I stepped outside.

Inching across the driveway in my bare feet, I held out my hands and went slow, careful for any equipment or cars.

But as I walked, I felt the draft and spray of what felt like waterfalls, and then suddenly, the pavement changed to something else under my toes, and I stopped. Dipping my foot out a little more, I felt water spill onto my feet and a granite floor underneath—no bowl or pool where the fountain was collecting. Simply a massive slab of ground. Maybe with drains?

I stepped in, my heart pounding as I held out my fingers, grazing the towers of water around me.

My mouth went dry, trying to puzzle this together. What was this?

I stepped on a spout, the water spraying everywhere and splashing me, and I sucked in a breath, getting a little wet.

But I kept going, tracing the spouts with my toes as I walked and finding a path. I kept my arms out at my sides, my fingers tracing the water and where it created walls and turns, coming to dead ends and veering around corners. The water shot up well above my head, and as I rounded the paths, finding little alcoves and hiding places, my sleep shorts and top stuck to my body and my hair grew cold and wet down my back.

I closed my eyes, my throat swelling as I mapped the water, gauging the huge circle and all the spouts inside creating this intricate wonderland of nooks and avenues, and I...

Oh, my God.

Tears pooled, realizing. He hadn't taken away the fountain. He'd replaced it.

My eyes stung.

It was a fountain maze.

I stood there in the center, towers of water shooting up and spilling around me as the tears started to fall. Hiding me in a world within a world.

Just like his fountain growing up.

Just like the treehouse.

Damon, what did you do?

My head fell back, and everything crumbled. My heart, my head, my hate, and my grudge, and I just wanted to see him. To feel him and put his forehead to mine and feel him breathe. To have him pick me up and hold me in here, where the water and the walls were high enough to hide us.

I loved him. I still loved him.

Goddamn him.

I cried, the music inside the ballroom drifting out through the window, and I ran my hand through my hair, everything inside just wanting out. I was tired of stopping myself. Of spending more time resenting than getting on with it.

I wanted to fight and scream and laugh and smile and kiss and taste and wrap my arms around him more than I could stomach never feeling him again.

I closed my eyes, starting to spin as Lana Del Rey's "Dark Paradise" drifted out of the ballroom through the open window, and I swept my leg, arched my back, and shot up on the ball of my foot, dancing and twirling as the music filled me up and took me over. My arms sliced through the water, splashing and whipping the spray, and I danced and danced and danced, running my hand over my stomach, my drenched hair flying around me and sticking to my face and body.

To dive and fall.

To have a lifetime of searching for something.

Or to have five minutes of everything.

I slowed as the music ended and stopped, the chill of the water seeping into my bones, but I felt awake for the first time in years. I was alive.

I wanted it. I wanted it all.

I pushed my hair out of my face and over the top of my head, breathing in so deep, because my lungs felt so much bigger all of a sudden.

"Winter?" someone called.

Crane.

I walked across the fountain maze, smiling through the towers of water and smoothing back my hair as I made my way to the edge, following his voice.

"Where is he?" I asked.

Crane was silent a moment, and then said, "Occupied at the moment. Would you like me to give him a message?"

Occupied.

Okay. If he wanted to play, let him come find me then.

I was ready.

"Let him know that I'll be going to the *Throwback* at The Cove tonight with some friends," I told Crane. "So he doesn't send out the hounds."

"And you'll be home by eleven?" he demanded more than asked.

But I just cocked my head, unable to hide the small smile he had to know was pure mischief. "Of course."

• • •

Throwback Night was organized by some of Thunder Prep's alumni as one last hoorah at The Cove before it was sold off, rumors flying for a while now that several investors were interested in redeveloping the property. Back in the day, this was a theme park—rides, roller coasters, fun houses, and games—and mostly everything still stood here, abandoned for years, having been dark since we were kids. I remember coming here once when it was still active.

The sea air breezed through the park as the music blasted and partygoers laughed and shouted, their excitement to go back to when we were high schoolers palpable. Most of them were in college or beyond now, although there were some current students of Thunder Bay about tonight, and I kind of dug feeling the old uniform on me again, not having worn it since I was sixteen. Before I fled town to go back to Montreal.

As part of the party theme, we were requested to don our uniforms in keeping with the school spirit. Unfortunately, my body has grown and developed a bit more since then, so I'd asked Rika if she had an extra skirt and shirt from her senior year, still able to use my old necktie with no problem.

"Come on, dance!" Alex pulled my arm.

I laughed, taking hers instead and letting her lead me out to the dance area where the DJ spun music up off to my right. Michael and Erika were here somewhere, Kai and Banks were on their way, Will had said, and I hadn't heard from Damon, although I left my phone in Will's car, so I wouldn't know if he'd tried to call anyway.

People bumped into me, and I couldn't see the space around me, so I kind of just stood there, unsure about this kind of dancing in front of others. I'd slow danced at school events before, but this was different.

"I can't dance with a crowd," I shouted over the music. "I'll smack someone in the face."

"I gotcha," Will came in behind me, wrapping his arms around me waist and swaying both of us back and forth. "You can dance with me."

Which I'm sure was just an excuse to put his hands on something.

I reached behind me, patting him on the cheek. "A true knight."

"See, she gets it," he joked, probably to Alex.

I heard her laugh.

I felt a little more confident with him holding onto me, and we moved, our bodies in sync to the beat of the music.

"Misha!" I heard him call to someone. "Hell yeah. Didn't think you'd be here."

"Hey, man," another guy said, approaching.

Will stopped dancing but still held onto me, reaching over my shoulder for one of those handshake-hug things men did.

"Wow, you look like shit," Will told him.

"They said to wear school clothes," the guy retorted. "I was always out of uniform back then, so this is it."

Will's chest shook at my back.

"Winter, this is my cousin Misha Lare," he said. "A couple years behind you in school, I think."

I held out both my hands, taking his and shaking it. I knew the name. He was younger, though, so we didn't cross paths.

"And his girlfriend, Ryen," Will introduced her like she was an annoying little sister.

"Hi, Winter," she said.

I smiled, following her voice. "Hi."

"Come on, Ryen," Will prodded. "Wouldn't you have loved to see Misha in his uniform tonight?"

"You look like all the frat boys I'll warn my daughters about when they go to college," she griped.

Misha snorted, and Will laughed.

"You guys dating?" Misha asked, and I guessed he was talking to Will and me.

"No, man. She's Damon's."

"Damon Torrance's?" Misha said it like he was spitting out food.

Will tightened his hold. "I know, right?"

"I'm not Damon's." I shook my head.

"Yeah, she is," Will shot back.

I didn't want to be talked about like I was property. That kind of conversation was fine in private, but Misha's tone definitely relayed that he had an opinion about Damon. And not a positive one. He didn't know me. I didn't want him drawing conclusions.

"Who's Damon?" Ryen asked. "Have I met him?"

"God, no," Misha blurted out. "Let's get some beers before he shows up. Later, man."

"Bye," Will called out as they left.

I let out a sigh, reminded that a lot more people than just me had a past or perception of Damon. He had his work cut out for him if he wanted a future in this town. That was, if he cared about what anyone thought, anyway.

"To be fair," Will said, setting his chin on my shoulder. "Misha hates everyone."

"You don't have to sugarcoat it," I said. "If anyone knows what I'm getting myself into, it's me."

He breathed out a laugh.

And then he stood up straight, still holding me tight. "Having Damon around was the only time I ever felt solid in my life," he told me. "He's powerful. But painful."

The corner of my mouth turned up in a small smile, knowing exactly what he was talking about. The highs with Damon reached the sun.

But our kind of fun had a price.

He pulled away from me, leaving my back, and I stood there as everyone danced around me, wondering where he just went. I moved my hands around my sides to feel for him. Did he leave?

"Alex," I called.

Where did they go?

And then someone was at my back, the height and broad shoulders covering every inch of me, the cloves drifted on the air, and I knew it was him.

His hand reached around my neck, cupping my face and turning my head, as I closed my eyes and felt him come down, pressing his forehead to mine.

Damon.

His other hand came around my stomach, touching me and pressing me into his body, his chest rising and falling behind me. He felt like five years ago. Like seven years ago.

And I wanted it.

"You're supposed to be wearing your uniform," I whispered, feeling the jeans and brushing the hoodie with my hand as I reached up to touch his face.

"This is how you knew me then."

I appreciated he wanted to be who I fell for in high school.

But they were always the same person.

"As long as you're Damon Torrance, I don't care what you wear," I told him.

He kissed me, melting his mouth into mine and tipping my head back, cradling it in his arm so he could deepen the kiss and sink his tongue into my mouth.

A swirl of excitement spun all the way down to between my thighs, and I was already panting as his heat just made me want so much more right now.

A bed. A whole night. Just him.

"Did you like it?" he asked against my mouth.

"Huh?"

Did I like the kiss? Wasn't it obvious? My body was a puddle in his hands.

"The fountain?" he clarified when I didn't respond.

He turned me around and lifted me up, and I could feel the draft under my skirt, so I knew it was riding up, but I didn't care.

Just take me home.

"It was incredible," I told him, wrapping my arms around his neck. "Perfect for sitting."

Just like we liked to do.

We kissed again, harder and deeper, and I gripped the hair at the back of his head, forcing us to go slow every time he wanted to speed up. I hovered, teasing him, and dipped in for a kiss only to pull away again.

"Winter," he growled low.

We stayed there, nose to nose and breathing each other in, not wanting to pull away for a moment, even to get out of here and find a bed.

But he put me down and took my hand, leading me off. "Follow me."

We walked through the crowds of people dancing and hanging out, the music pounding and the smell of grilled food hanging in the air, and I trailed close, holding his hand and his arm, too.

I still wasn't sure how to feel about a lot of what had happened and what was happening now. What was prison like for him? Did I feel badly about any of it?

What about Arion? What were his intentions with both of us, and what about my father? Did I resent that Damon was the one who exposed him?

I gripped his arm, overwhelmed with just the need for him, and I couldn't care about the rest right now. *Just hide with me. Just hide us away.*

We wound deeper into the park, passing some voices here and there, but the music and hustle and bustle of the party were far behind, leaving us on our own the farther we went.

He stopped and rose up. "Steps," he told me.

I followed him, still holding his hand and arm as I followed him up a small flight of five metal stairs.

We took a few steps, and he paused again, telling me, "The Midnight Maze."

I smiled curiously, cocking my head. I didn't remember this, but my pulse quickened at the thought of another maze.

He let me go first, the mobile structure sounding quiet and feeling still. We must be the only ones out here.

Putting my hands out like I did with the fountain this morning, I touched the plastic panels on both sides, hearing them shake as we both walked inside and began down a path. The walls ended here and there, showing me how the maze diverted into different trails, and I stepped quietly in my Chucks, smiling about how silent I could be and getting an idea.

"Marco," I called.

After a moment, he answered behind me. "Polo."

I spun around, and he grabbed for me, slipping his hands up my short skirt, but I pushed them back down again, touching his face.

"Close your eyes," I told him, making sure his lids were closed. "Keep them closed and find me."

"And if I find you?"

I grinned at his loaded tone and backed away, getting a head start.

"You won't," I teased, immediately finding a diversion in the path and slipping off to the left.

I moved slowly, careful of my steps and knocking into the plastic panels, which I assumed were clear, since it felt exactly like the funhouses I'd been in at carnivals when I was younger. He'd better not cheat. He could see me through the panels. I couldn't see him.

Traipsing down a path, heel to toe in soft steps, I felt the wall end, and I turned right this time, slipping through the narrow opening.

I didn't know if Damon was moving, but I heard his voice after a few moments. "Marco?" he called, and I heard his voice echo from off to the right.

"Polo," I replied, trying not to laugh.

I crept along the path, darting into another lane and accidently hitting the toe of my shoe on a panel.

It made a noise, rocking between its screws, and I froze, putting my hand over my mouth.

Shit.

His heavy footsteps made the floors creak, but since this thing was on a trailer, the whole damn floor whined, so I couldn't gauge where the hell he was coming from.

Until he said, "Marco?" And I gasped, hearing him right on the other side of the panel in front of me.

I winced, squeaking, "Polo."

A slam hit the panels, and I jumped, knowing he knew exactly where I was and dashing away as fast as I could, not caring that I was loud and clumsy.

"Marcooooo?" he sing-songed, hitting the panels and taunting me as he got caught up in the hunt.

Jesus. Even blind, he was a lion.

"Polo," I said quickly, slipping into another avenue, unable to control my giggling.

"Marcooooo," he threatened from somewhere behind me.

Oh, my God. I stepped quickly, banging my hands all over the panels and searching for my way out, but I couldn't find it.

Where is it?

"Marco!" he called again.

Where is it? Where is it? I searched, flailing my hands and patting the walls.

Finding an opening, I slid through, relief washing over me and finally answering, "Polo."

But then he was there, snatching me up and wrapping his arms around me. I screamed.

"What's my prize?" he teased in my ear.

I shook, caught between laughing and fighting to breathe.

"What do you want?" I shot back.

"A piece of clothing."

I shook my head, but he pushed me back against one of the plastic walls and knelt down, reaching under my skirt and peeling my panties off. He pulled them down my legs, the rough fabric of the plaid skirt now rubbing against my sensitive skin, and lifted up my feet, sliding the underwear off.

The cool air caressed me, and being bare and exposed made me extra aware and crave him even more. I started to run, but he caught me and pushed me back again, lifting my knee and pressing it back against the wall at my side, opening me up for his mouth as he came down on me, sucking on my clit.

Fireworks went off in my thighs and belly, spreading down my legs as I gasped and whimpered.

"Damon..." I half-moaned and half-protested. He couldn't do this to me here.

But God, it felt so good. He kissed and massaged it with his tongue, and I tipped my head back, unable to not groan, and I didn't care who heard me.

I finally pulled away, stumbling off to the side, and I heard him breathing hard.

"Marco," I panted, digging my nails into the walls.

"Polo," he growled back.

I stepped backward more. "Marco."

"Polo."

"Marc—"

But he grabbed me by my necktie and yanked me into his body.

I sucked in a breath, slamming into him.

He got in my face, still holding me by my tie and asking, "What do I get now?"

"You cheated," I argued. "You opened your eyes."

There was no way he would've found me that fast.

But he ignored my protest. "I want your bra."

Cute. I'd have to take off my shirt, then, too. Clever.

But I was way ahead of him. "I'm not wearing one."

He exhaled hard, wrapping an arm around me and walking us backward, deeper into the maze.

Setting me down, he forced me back up to a wall and ripped open my white uniform blouse, the night air hitting my bare skin as the buttons flew, hitting the walls and floor.

He pressed his body into mine, reaching under and lifting my leg to nudge himself between my thighs. "Winter," he murmured.

I kissed him, caressing his tongue with mine, and letting him know, with every breath, moan, and rub of my hips that I wanted him right now.

He slid his hand farther under my skirt, and I held his bottom lip between my teeth, as I reached down and slid my hand inside his jeans.

I took his cock in my hand, hard and hot muscle filling my fist, and I started stroking him, making it harder and harder.

"Now," I breathed out. "I want you now, Damon."

He sucked in air between his teeth. "Say that again. With my name."

"I want you now, Damon."

He lost it. He gripped my jaw, sinking his mouth into mine for a hard, rough kiss, and then he pulled away to unfasten his belt and jeans while still holding me against the wall.

I leaned back, my shirt ripped open but my tie still hanging from my neck down the center of my chest. I felt him pull his cock out, fit himself at my entrance as I held onto his shoulders, and thrust his hips, pushing himself deep inside me.

Yes.

He hauled me up into his arms, my legs circling his waist as he propped me up against the wall, and I tipped my head back, moaning as he pumped his hips into me again and again. His cock slid out and back in, deep and fast, his hips pounding between my legs and making the whole funhouse shake. I brought my head back down, forehead to forehead as he fucked me, starting to roll my hips in little movements, meeting his thrusts.

"Yeah," I whimpered. "You feel so good."

"Winter," he said like a prayer, and I could hear the pleasure-pain in his voice.

I kissed him again, dying to feel his skin and have all these clothes off, but there was no way I could stop.

We heard a throat clear off somewhere near, and I hid my face on the other side of Damon's, mortified even as need built deep inside me.

Please, no.

But Damon wouldn't stop. He just kept riding me, rolling his hips into my body, the rhythm and pace staying steady.

"Sir, your father is calling, demanding to speak to you," Mr. Crane said.

I squeezed my eyes shut, wanting to tell Damon to stop, but my orgasm was coming, and all I could do was hold on.

"Watch the door," he bit out to Crane. "No one comes in."

"Yes, sir."

His father must be pissed if Crane came in here to bear witness to this. Shit.

Damon held my face with one hand, my body with the other, and my eyes started to tear up, feeling him drive deep and fill me up. And then it was coming.

"Damon," I whimpered, my chest caving again and again.

"Say it again," he growled.

I gasped. "Damon."

"Who's fucking you?"

Oh, God, I was coming. "Damon Torrance," I breathed out.

And then my body convulsed, I held my breath, and I froze, letting Damon finish me as my orgasm exploded all over my body.

My head floated off, heat raced under my skin, and I cried out, feeling my body get wetter as he kept going.

Every limb weakened, and I felt like I was going to fall as exhaustion took over.

He put me down, spun me around, and shoved me into the partition, my breasts crushed against the clear plastic as he reached around and spread my thighs wide, thrusting back inside of me from behind.

He dug his fingers in the inside of my leg, holding me open, with his other hand wrapped around the front of my neck and bending it back to meet his mouth.

He fucked me, pressing me into the wall. "Mine," he said against my lips. "Don't ever leave my body."

His hand on my neck scaled down, squeezing my breast and running over my stomach, and came back up to my neck, holding me tight.

"Don't ever leave my body," he chanted again.

"I won't," I whispered.

"Say you love me."

I swallowed, my throat so dry.

"Say you love me," he demanded.

"I love you," I told him, surprised by how easily it came. "I love you, Damon."

And he wrapped his arms around me, holding me tight, and this was it. Right here. Everything I wanted to feel that brought me even more happiness than dancing did.

He was still the boy, promising to kiss me again someday, and I was still her, never wanting to leave whatever little private world we created when we were together.

Later, after he held me and touched me and kissed me some more, we made our way out of the park, toward the lot where Mr. Crane was parked. Damon had given me his hoodie to cover up my ripped shirt—or Rika's ripped shirt, actually—and he held my hand, leading me past the crowds, the music, and his friends who were smart enough to know to leave us alone when he ignored their calls for him.

We approached the car, and I felt sprinkles of rain hit my hand as he held the door open, and I climbed in.

"Just drive," I heard him tell Crane.

Thunder cracked overhead and rolled over the sky, and I heard shouts of excitement coming from the park as heavier drops hit the roof of the car.

He climbed into the backseat next to me, and I laid my head down on his lap, my eyes heavy and my body already feeling the residual ache of what we did against that wall.

I slid one of my hands in the center pocket of his sweatshirt, feeling my panties and smiled lazily.

I was glad he didn't leave them on the floor in there.

Mr. Crane drove, and I reached up with my other hand, running the back of it over Damon's cheek and neck, caressing his ear, too.

The gravel under the tires crackled, we jostled as he pulled onto the road, and then the pavement turned smooth as he coasted down the late-night highway.

I told him I loved him. But he hadn't said it back.

It was okay. I didn't need to hear it yet. He seemed to need to hear it himself, though. Like in the treehouse when we were kids. Desperate to keep me safe and by his side.

I got the impression from his friends that he was possessive with more than just me. If he found something good, he fought to keep it.

It could be a scary thing.

But it also meant he knew what was important. He worked to keep what he valued. Would he be so devoted to a wife?

His children?

I continued touching him, just savoring the feel of his skin and the feeling of peace at just lying here with him.

"What's your tattoo?" I asked quietly, remembering how my friend noticed he had one.

He didn't say anything for a moment, or ask how I knew, but then he answered, "A decaying snowflake."

I raised my eyebrows. *A decaying…*

"Why?" I asked.

"Because of *Winter* by Walter de la Mare," he replied softly. "Something still beautiful, even after what I did to her."

Her. Me. The snowflake represented winter.

My throat tightened, and I kind of smiled and teared up at the same time. How did he do it? How did he always break my heart, especially in ways I loved?

"I wish you could see the sea," he suddenly said, changing the subject. "The choppy waves and moonlight on the whitewash. The rain spilling from the dark clouds under a sliver of moonlight."

I pictured it, what he was seeing, and I wondered if he felt guilty about what happened to me and all the things I could no longer see.

"I hear it," I told him in a quiet voice as I listened to everything around me. "The drops on the roof, heavier or lighter in certain areas, because the trees are catching some of it not hitting us." I caressed his neck, finding his ear lobe with my fingers as I listened for more. "The storm drains we pass every minute or so, because the tires are hitting where the water pools as it flows into the underground." And then I smiled, telling him, "And the rhythm of the wipers and how they sound like *We Will Rock You* when the two in front go and then the one in the back does, and it's like "swipe, swipe, SWIPE"." I imitated the beat of the song and how the wipers mimicked it.

I heard him laugh under his breath.

I continued. "The way I know he's driving over the speed limit, because it wasn't windy tonight, but the rain sounds torrential as it hits the windows." I wetted my lips, feeling his hand move to my hair and smooth it over and over again. "There's more thunder over the sea than there is over the forest," I said, analyzing more sounds in my head, "and it's getting closer to us."

I brought my hand down, tucking both in the pocket again to keep warm.

"How, with everything going on out there," I went on, "I feel like I'm wrapped in a blanket in here—warm, dry, and safe. And all the world living and breathing and raging outside makes where I am seem like a world within a world. Like a fountain in a maze." I paused, musing, "Like a home."

Everything with him was like home.

"I hear so much more than when I could see," I said, my voice turning to a whisper. "I don't think I'd ever want to not hear all that now."

I missed not seeing things and enjoying the world the way so many others did, but...I also saw the world so much more differently now. One kind of beauty was replaced with another.

I rested my head to the side and closed my eyes, lulled by all the little sounds and hoping that tomorrow would be more of this with no doubt between us.

"I do love you," I told him again before I drifted off.

Just so he knew.

I woke the next morning in Damon's bed, naked under the sheets, everything from last night slowly coming back to me. The party. The maze. The drive in the car.

The whole lot of extra energy he had in bed throughout the night when we got home.

I broke out in a smile, blissfully exhausted but more awake than I'd felt in a long time.

Reaching over, I didn't feel him in bed, though. Patting his sheets and pillow, I landed on a piece of paper, it crinkling under my hand.

He wasn't dumb enough to leave me a note, was he?

I picked it up, noticing the little pokes in the paper, and I laid it in my palm, running my fingers over the raised dots and instantly recognizing the Braille.

Moving left to right, over the cells, I deciphered the message.

> *Stay in bed. I'll be back for breakfast.*
> *Then after breakfast, we'll eat.*

I snorted, realizing the breakfast he'd be back for was me.

> *P.S. Your phone is on the nightstand.*

I crashed back on the bed, feeling my body tingle all over. He wrote me a note. I'd never gotten a love letter before, and that was totally one.

I couldn't believe he had a Braille printer? Nice. With audiobooks and VoiceOver, I rarely read anything in Braille anymore, but if only to get little notes from him, I loved it.

What time was it? We were up so late, and if he wasn't back yet, it must still be early. Didn't he ever sleep?

My phone rang, and I reached over and grabbed it, hoping it was him.

"Hello?" I answered, sitting up and keeping the sheet wrapped around me.

"Winter?" Ethan blurted out. "What's going on?"

I stilled, my smile falling. Why was he calling me?

I kind of wanted to have it out with him about those pictures, but I wasn't in the mood yet.

"I can't talk right now," I told him. "I'll call you later, though."

"Why are there pictures of you online?" he barked, cutting me off. "Pictures of you with him?"

"What are you talking about?"

"At the Throwback last night!" he yelled. "There's footage of you two kissing! People were taking pictures! Did he make you do it?"

What? Pictures... I don't...

And then I remembered Will and I were dancing, Damon came up behind me, we started...

People were everywhere. All around us.

And my shoulders fell.

Winter Ashby sent Damon Torrance to jail for statutory rape, and now she's crawling in bed with him, of age, and here was proof she was totally willing this time.

"How could I be so stupid?" I murmured.

In front of everyone.

But it was going to happen anyway, right? It was a small town. Eventually people would know we were together, and we'd have to deal with reactions, given our past.

"What is the matter with you?" he snapped like I was a child. "You had to know people were watching! You sent him to jail for rape. People were going to remember that. And now you're making out with him? It makes you look..."

Like a liar. Yeah, I knew exactly how it made me look.

Sometimes I longed for the time where everything wasn't recorded and broadcast for the world to see. Of course it looked bad.

And now the people who always maintained his innocence were emboldened more.

"He knew what he was doing," Ethan continued. "How could you fall for it? Why would you let him touch you? Did you not know it was him again?"

I could hear the disbelief in his voice now.

Again.

"Some people were willing to believe you the first time, but now..." he said. "They'll never believe he fooled you twice. I knew he was smart. I just didn't think you were so dumb."

I hung up on him, refusing to listen to it anymore. I didn't do anything wrong. We didn't do anything wrong.

We had a fucked-up start years ago, and we both spent years paying for it, but we were doing this. We wanted this.

I loved him.

And Damon didn't plan that last night. He didn't know they would take pictures. He wouldn't have done that.

But part of me wondered.

Part of me doubted. *He wouldn't have done that, right?*

He hadn't said he loved me? He got me to say it. Twice.

Why hadn't he said it back?

CHAPTER 25

Damon

PRESENT

Walking through the backdoor and Mikhail following, I downed the rest of the bottle of water and tossed it into the trash before dumping some food into his dish and letting him chow down before I headed down the hallway and through the foyer.

I brought my T-shirt to my nose as I climbed the stairs and sniffed. Cigarettes and sawdust. It was probably on my skin, too.

Eh, she'd deal with it.

I pulled the shirt off over my head and walked into the bedroom, tossing it on the floor. "I'm dirty and sweaty," I said, kicking off my shoes, "but you're just gonna have to roll with it."

Leaving the light off, I put a knee down on the end of the bed and crawled up, dying to pin her hands above her head and kiss her until she was begging to get fucked.

But as I reached her side of the bed, it was empty.

"Winter?" I called.

I felt the bed, not finding her, so I reached over and turned on the lamp.

She wasn't here. The sheets were rumpled and still warm, though.

"Winter?" I barked louder.

Dammit, girl...

I climbed off the bed and went into the bathroom and dressing room, finding them both empty. Leaving the room, I headed down to her bedroom and swung the door open, but she wasn't there, either. My heart pumped harder, and I bit the corner of my mouth to keep my nerves in fucking check.

Maybe she was in the ballroom.

I walked to the railing, about to head down the stairs but saw Crane move across the foyer.

"Where is she?" I demanded.

He stopped and looked up, meeting my eyes.

But then dropped them again.

"Fuck you, where is she?" I snapped.

"A car picked her up," he told me, looking like he really didn't want to. "She said she'll be at St. Killian's and back in a couple days."

"And you let her leave?"

He closed his mouth, averting my eyes. Why the fuck did I hire extra security if he was just going to let her come and go like that?

"It wasn't my impression she was a prisoner, sir," he said.

"Was it your impression that I might eat ice cream out of your skull for not telling me she was going?"

He tightened his lips.

"Was she upset?" I asked. *Do you know that at least?*

"She seemed troubled, yes," he answered. "Said she just wanted to have some space to think."

Think.

I pinched the bridge of my nose. When women think, shit didn't go the way I wanted it to.

What the hell was she doing? I did what Rika told me to do. Almost. I got to work on something. I brought in a crew, we tore down that fugly fountain and built the one I had designed and planned, working day and night for two days, so she'd find it and explore it and hopefully love it.

Getting the message that she'd be at The Cove last night gave me hope, but nothing prepared me for how she just let it happen. How she was already ready when I showed up and for the first time, she let me touch her, without a guise or a fight.

It was fucking incredible, and for a little while, it was like the years in between when we were kids and now had never happened. Nothing existed except us, especially all the bullshit in between.

It was kind of a date. I kept her clothes on. Most of them.

But every time the spell started to fade, she let all that other shit back into her head, and I was getting kind of fucking sick of losing her.

She may or may not love me.

But it was becoming clear. She didn't want me.

"Sir?" Crane called out, sounding on alert.

I looked up, the door opened, and men, some I had and hadn't seen before walked in, all in suits and some with gloves.

I closed my eyes, sighing. "Fuck," I mouthed.

My father stepped over the threshold, dressed in a black suit with a gray shirt, his dark eyes looking up and finding me instantly.

He was trying to get a hold of me last night, and I blew it off. He always gave me a long leash, but if he had to snap it, it fucking hurt.

"What do you want?" I asked, descending the stairs.

"Do you care?" he replied. And then he looked around. "Where's your wife?"

I held his eyes. My father's strength hadn't dissipated with age. Although graying, his skin growing more wrinkled, and his voice getting raspy from all the years of cigars, he still had a very healthy appetite.

For everything.

Especially for making sure he had control over all in his domain.

Unfortunately, I never went according to plan and never would. I might not be any better than him, but we weren't the same, either.

He waited another moment, but when I didn't answer, because I already knew that he knew Ari wasn't here and his grandchildren weren't getting made, he flexed his jaw and jerked his chin, gesturing to me.

"Take him," he told his men.

What?

They rushed me, taking my arms, digging their fingers into my shoulders, and I thrashed, throwing them off and growling. "Get the fuck off me!"

I tore away, shoving one of them in the chest. "Son of a bitch!" I yelled.

One grabbed my wrist again. I whipped it away and threw a punch, but more came from behind, and I looked to Mr. Crane who was already being held back, looking angry and helpless.

Gabriel paid for the security. He paid for everything. As much as my own team wanted to do something, they wouldn't.

The backs of my legs were kicked in, my knees buckled, and I fell, coming down to the floor. Three men held me down, keeping me on my knees, one with his grip on the back of my neck.

In front of me, my father crouched down.

"And where's the sweet, little bitch who's twisting your head?" he asked. "Where is she?"

Winter.

I was suddenly glad she wasn't here. Michael and Rika were no match for Gabriel, but she was safer with them than anyone if I wasn't there.

"Your life was going to be blessed," Gabriel told me. "All the money and pussy you could ever want, and all you had to do was follow a simple instruction." His voice was eerily calm. "It wasn't even that hard."

He stood up, and the muscles in my shoulders stretched with someone holding my wrists behind me.

"I should've shipped your ass to Blackchurch ages ago," he said. "We can lock you up still, though, can't we? Give you some time to think."

And then his hand smacked across my face, the sting something I was very used to. I gritted my teeth together.

"And I have all the time in the world," he threatened.

No.

What the fuck did he mean?

"Maybe in a few weeks you'll come around," he mused. And then to his men, "Bring him."

A few weeks. What the fuck?

They stood me up, barefoot and shirtless, and tightened a zip tie behind my back.

Everyone started to walk out, and I looked over at Crane, jerking my chin, knowing he knew I was referring to Winter and the dog and that he needed to take care of things.

But as everyone left, and the man behind me held on to me, an arm suddenly coming around my neck as the guy in back of me whispered in my ear.

"An eye for an eye, motherfucker," he said.

And then a pain hit my side under my ribs, digging into my flesh as some kind of small blade pierced my skin.

I grunted, immediately feeling the blood drip out as I shot my gaze over my shoulder, seeing the asshole who did it.

Miles Anderson.

The guy who had Winter in his car when she was sixteen. The guy who also attacked Rika the same Devil's Night I did.

Fuck. He worked for my father now?

"A few weeks," he lamented, "more than enough time for us to find her and have some fun."

I thrashed, growling as the pain seared my skin.

"She's been fun to mess with these past couple of weeks," he said. "As we waited for Gabriel to give us the go-ahead anyway."

"Motherfucker," I muttered, seething.

It was him, fondling her in the theater bathroom. Him and his buddies who snuck into the house that morning.

We should've taken so much more than a tooth from his skull all those years ago, son of a bitch.

But before I had a chance to fight, he came around and shot his knee into my stomach, sending me doubling over and coughing to catch my breath. He stuffed something into my mouth, forced me out the door, and into the back of one of the SUVs as I tried to whip out of his hold, but pain shot through me every fucking time I moved.

Ironically, that wasn't the first time I'd been stabbed on that same side. This felt deeper, though.

I hit the floor, coughing, and I looked around for my father, but he must've been in another car.

As the SUV took off, I just prayed Michael and Rika would come through.

Keep her safe. Don't leave her alone.

• • •

I stumbled around my old bedroom, throwing open curtains and peering outside. I tried to open the windows, but they were bolted shut.

Fucking asshole. What was I? Ten?

The driveway in front of my father's house glowed with electric lanterns and headlights of sporadic cars coming and going, while men paced in black suits, some with flashlights behind the tree line but every one of them with a walkie-talkie, I was sure.

Even if I broke the window, I wouldn't get far. I was sure Anderson would love another chance at a cheap shot, though.

I pulled the hand towel away from the scratch that asshole gave me, seeing the cloth soaked again. This was the third towel. It was still bleeding.

I blew out a breath, the hair on the back of my neck rising as heat spread over my skin. I charged away from the window, kicking a trunk sitting on my floor.

"Fuck," I growled, tossing the towel off somewhere and grabbing a T-shirt from my dresser and pulling it on.

I had to get out of here. Soon, before I didn't have any energy left. They hadn't fed me all day, and no one had come to check on me. I knew there were guards outside my door, though. I was stopped as soon as I tried to leave earlier.

I should tell them I was bleeding. My father would get me a doctor.

As long as I got back in line, brought Arion back home, played the husband, and went to work for him.

I shook my head. *Fuck him.*

I was going to burn this place to the ground with him in it. If he was lucky.

I had to get out of here before anyone got to Winter. I was the only one who'd be able to keep her safe.

I blinked away the spots in my vision and headed into the bathroom, throwing my fist into the silver-framed mirror above the sink. Shards of glass spilled into the sink, and I grabbed a washcloth, wrapping it around a piece of glass and heading for my door.

I stumbled, though, the room spinning in front of me.

"What the fuck?" I gritted out, impatient.

The wound was bearable, but sweat covered my brow, and nausea rolled through my stomach. I blinked long and hard, but every time I opened my eyes, the room was getting blacker, like I was sinking deeper into a tunnel, the light at the end getting smaller and smaller. Blood slowly seeped through my black T-shirt and down my pants.

Fuck, this wasn't good. I needed food. Or water. And the pain was fucking irritating.

I rubbed my eyes, but instead of moving for the door, I fell down on my bed, letting my head fall back.

The cool comforter felt like heaven, and I swung a leg up, trying to calm my breathing.

Just a minute. Just need to rest for one fucking minute.

I wasn't sure if I fell asleep or how long I was asleep, but I opened my eyes with a start, the room pitch black and a body on top of me.

"Shhh," the shadow said, her hand over my mouth.

What? Who was this?

I reached up, grabbing her and recognizing the feel of her hair and her head in my hands.

Oh, my God. You've got to be kidding me.

"Winter?" I blurted out. "What the fuck?"

"Shhh," she hissed, pressing her hand down on me harder. "Be very quiet. They're right outside the door."

She was saving *me*?

"How did you get in here?" I asked.

She straddled me, her knee rubbing my wound, but I didn't care. I took her in my arms and kissed her lips, her forehead, her cheek...

But then I shook her a little. "Hey, you left me," I bit out.

"I came right back," she said, her hands over mine. "I'm sorry. Michael was bringing me back, and that's when we saw you being taken."

She climbed off me and put her hands on me, helping me up.

"Are you..." She stopped, feeling my clothes. "This is wet. Are you bleeding?"

"How did you get in?" I demanded, ignoring her question and gritting my teeth against the pain as I stood up from the bed.

"When we saw what happened, we got everyone together. Banks told us there was crawl space in the wall, from the cellar to the attic." She took my arm. "She's downstairs with Michael and Kai, distracting your father."

"The attic's across the roof." I took us toward the bathroom, knowing now how she got in. "You climbed across the roof?"

Jesus, fuck. And I was worried about getting to her before my father did.

She could've died. How could they be so stupid to bring her?

"Rika's outside your bathroom window," she said in a hushed voice. "Would you shut up now?"

Fine. She was already here. Damage was done. I'd deal with them later.

Walking into the bathroom, I shot a glance to my bedroom door behind me, making sure it was still closed and no one was onto us.

I stepped on top of the toilet, seeing the small window already propped up and Rika crouched down on the roof, waiting.

Where was Will? Why were the girls the ones doing this?

I could understand Kai not wanting to leave Banks alone with my father, but where the hell were Michael and Will?

I stepped back down and lifted Winter up, the slice in my side burning, but I maneuvered her through the window, Rika taking her arms and pulling her up.

I took short, shallow breaths, trying to tap down the nausea creeping up again. I was going to need some fucking stitches. Goddammit. I didn't have time for this.

Hopping up on the toilet again, I planted my foot on the wall for leverage and shot up, digging my elbows into the windowsill and pulling myself forward on my arms while I slipped up and out.

"You okay?" Rika asked.

"Just go."

I breathed hard, hearing her whisper instructions to Winter before they both found the ridge and began crawling it over to the attic window.

My leg was wet from the blood, but the night air chilled my skin, cooling me off and waking me up.

They would have to have a car nearby. Just five more minutes. I'd get to rest.

Following them over the roof and keeping low, I climbed through the circular attic window, falling in and crashing onto the floor.

Winter rushed over to me, touching my face.

The room was dark, but moonlight shone through, and I looked up, seeing not only Rika, but Alex standing there, too, all three women staring down at me.

"Are you fucking kidding me?" I whined, holding my side and trying to get my feet under me.

"That's how you thank three females who just saved your ass?" Rika remarked, sounding all too amused.

And then Alex tipped her chin at me, taunting, "Who's your daddy?"

Winter snorted, and I just fixed a snarl on my face as I stood up. "Just get me out of here," I told them. "And don't tell anybody about this, for Christ's sake."

The girls laughed and led the way through the panel in the wall where Banks and I grew up shimmying down beams of wood to get around the house in secret, either for fun or for pranks.

Rika and Alex went first, then Winter and then me. We made our way down between the walls, vaguely hearing voices on the other side as we descended floors, and now I kind of understood why the girls were sent. This was a lot tighter space now that I was grown. We went slowly and quietly, since everyone whom we didn't want to find us was only a piece of wood and a layer of wallpaper away.

Landing at the bottom, I stepped through the hole in the rocks which made up the walls of the cellar and summoned every muscle and ounce of determination I had to get Winter out of here, so I could push forward and make it to the car.

I heard a phone vibrate, and Rika's face lit up as she looked at a text.

"Okay, now," she said, glancing at us.

What?

I didn't have time to ask, though, because she ran up the steps and pushed through the cellar doors, Alex, Winter, and I quickly following.

She jumped into the passenger seat of a black SUV parked right there for us, while Alex opened the rear door and dove in, Winter and I doing the same.

Alex sat in a seat, while Winter and I fell into the rear bench seat way in the back.

I didn't have time to see who was driving, but I crashed down, falling back into Winter as she slumped back, too, wrapping her arms around me.

"Go, go, go," I heard Rika tell whoever. "I'll text Banks and tell them to get out of there."

Whoever was driving shot backward instead of forward toward the gate, and I held on as the car bounced over the ground and veered left to right, probably to avoid trees. We must be going out the back way.

Winter's chest rose and fell behind me, but she held me tightly, like she wouldn't let anything hurt me.

I closed my eyes, listening to the terrain under us, hearing what she was hearing to know when it was finally safe.

The car rocked over the bumpy land, leaves kicked up under the tires, but I didn't hear any other engines following, shouts, or alarms. So far, we'd gotten out undetected.

I didn't know what Banks was doing or agreeing to in order to distract my father, but I wanted her out of there now.

And Winter should never have come, either. It was insane to think we were going to get out of this alive.

Why did she even come?

She was pissing me off. Screaming at me one minute, all over me the next, running away this morning, and now she was here. Was she going to decide she needed more space tomorrow?

We pulled onto a paved road, swinging around, and driving forward, and I started to breathe a little easier as the car grew quiet and the engine hummed.

"You left me," I said, her chin tucked on my shoulder as she held me from behind. "Everyone is always doing that."

"I needed to think."

"Think," I repeated, shaking my head. "Fuck you, baby. It was perfect last night. There were no problems."

I reached behind, ruffling her hair.

"You're going to do it again," I said, dropping my hand. "You should've just left me there. Why didn't you?"

She was quiet, nudging her cheek into mine as she found her words. "Because I was afraid of life without the hope of you to look forward to."

I fell silent, understanding instantly what she meant. Looking back, I'd always felt the same way. Whether or not we were together, I wanted her, and I'd always want her.

"We can't hide forever, though, Damon," she said. "Not in our mazes, our fountains, our treehouses... We live in the world with other people, and I want to respect myself. I just...I needed to think."

"You want *them* to respect you," I retorted.

This was about what people were going to say about us. She thought they weren't going to trust her now that she was in love with the same guy she sent to jail.

"People think because I'm blind that I'm dumb," she told me. "They treat me like a child. I want to prove I'm capable. That I'm someone."

"You should've been strong," I replied, my fingers freezing now all of a sudden. "If anyone knew what a vile cunt this world could be, it was us. But all I needed was you, and all you should've needed was me, and fuck all the rest. We would've done it. We would've won."

"I came back," she said again. "I was barely gone fifteen minutes. I came right back." She kissed my temple. "And we will win. We will."

Sure. Maybe.

"Okay, there's Banks and the guys," I heard Rika say and noticed the headlights coming through the rear window. "We have about three more seconds before Gabriel figures it out."

My eyes grew heavy again, and my heart was pounding in my ears. I didn't feel so good.

I swallowed. "I sometimes wonder what I'd be like if I grew up in Michael's house. Or Kai's."

She laughed a little. "You wouldn't be like them."

"Probably not," I agreed. "People are a blend of external and internal influences, not all controlled variables. Sometimes, just sometimes, we are who we are. Even in the sea, a snake is a snake."

"A lion, a lion," she added with a smile in her voice.

Blood from the wound dripped from my skin under the shirt.

"I should've taken you to St. Killian's," I told her. "There's a room down in the catacombs."

I paused to make sure she was listening.

"You turn left at the bottom of the stairs and keep going," I instructed, knowing she was mapping it out in her head. "When you feel a draft from your left, you've hit a hallway, and you turn right. Drag your hand along the right wall until you feel the fourth doorway, and then enter it. Water from the snowmelt on the hills above the church seeps through the ground and spills down the walls like a tiny waterfall." My arms started to fall, unable to hold her anymore. "You can smell the wet rock, and there's a little pool where the water sits before it drains into a well. In the pool, there's something you can have. Something of yours I saved. Something you forgot about."

She waited a moment, probably thinking.

"I'm not missing anything," she informed me. "There's nothing I'm forgetting, Damon."

I closed my eyes. "There is so much you're forgetting, baby."

She moved her hand and then sucked in a short breath. "What is this?" She panted, fear filling her throat. "Damon, what happened? Are you injured?"

She lifted my shirt, touching my wound. I grunted. Jesus, it felt on fucking fire now.

She started gasping. "Will, go to the hospital! He's been hurt!"

"What?" Will shouted.

He must be who was driving.

"Get the flashlight on your phone," Rika told someone. "Look at it."

I kept my eyes closed but winced when a bright light shined on me.

"Oh, my God," Alex cursed. "He's soaked. Damon, how long have you been bleeding?"

I just grunted, their voices fading.

"Will, just go," I heard Rika bark. "Speed. Hurry up."

"Fucking Miles Anderson," I growled under my breath. "We gotta kill that motherfucker."

This was really going to ruin my day.

"Why didn't you tell me?" Winter cried in my ear.

"It's fine." I relaxed into her, her arms still around me. "I could die happily right here."

"You're not dying," Winter argued. "You haven't even told me you love me yet."

Oh, that.

"Someday," I teased.

"Damon, wake up." She jostled me. "Come on, we're doing this, right? We're in love. We're doing this."

Their voices trailed off as if I were listening and not really here, and for the first time in my life, my entire body was relaxed. So completely relaxed.

"Is he gonna be okay?" I heard Winter cry. "Please, Will, hurry! Please, just get there."

"I'm calling the ER to let them know we're almost there," Rika said.

Winter's body shook under me, but fuck if I didn't ever want to move from this spot. I let my body give in—falling, falling, falling—and soaking it up as long as I could, because who knew how long it would last. If I didn't die from Anderson's embarrassing little finger knife wound, she was gonna run off on me again to get more space, no doubt.

I needed to think, she'd said.

My dick was inside you four times last night. Now you needed to think? Really?

CHAPTER 26

Winter

PRESENT

I stood there, the speakers at the nurses' station going off with calls, shoes squeaking against the linoleum floors, and the T.V. broadcasting a news channel as I leaned into the wall, rubbing my hands together and feeling his dried blood now grainy on my skin.

There's so much you're forgetting.

What was I forgetting?

What did he want me to have?

He'd said it as if he were leaving me something. Like he wouldn't be back for it.

Needles pricked my throat, but I swallowed them down.

He was just going to bleed out? Because he couldn't choke down his pride and ask for help?

I couldn't believe him. He was insane.

And—in the back of my mind where I would admit it to myself—he was going to leave me. He was just going to let go.

I steeled my jaw, refusing to cry another damn tear for him.

Banks and Rika wandered about, offering me coffee or to find some scrubs, so I could get out of my bloody clothes, but I was rooted to this spot, waiting for the doctor or a nurse to come and let us know what was going on with him.

Kai and Will had also shown up, and it occurred to me to call my sister to let her know he was in the ER, but that fleeting thought left as quickly as it came. He wouldn't want her here, and all she'd be worried about was if she still got her settlement if he died.

I heard doors swing open and closed and felt people surround me suddenly.

"Well, he lost a lot of blood," a woman told us. "Right now, the doctor is working to close the wound, but Mr. Torrance does need blood. We've gone through our supply of B-negative, but it's one of the rarer blood types, and he can only have a transfusion from other B or O-negatives."

I was O-positive, so I was out.

"We've had to request more from a hospital in Meridian City," she told us. "It'll hopefully be here soon."

"Banks?" Will spoke up. "You're O-negative, right? We all did that blood drive last summer. He can get blood from you."

Oh, good. I started to breathe a little easier, but she didn't say anything for a moment, and I starting worrying again.

"Um...yeah," she finally stuttered, "but I, uh...I can't donate blood, I don't think."

"Why?" Will prodded.

She laughed nervously under her breath. "I'm, um... I'm pregnant."

Everyone fell silent, but I couldn't help but smile a little at the irony.

Uncle Damon. That would be fun.

"I was trying to find a way to tell you," she said to her husband, I assumed. "Something special. Sorry it happened like this."

"Yeah, sorry," Will added, clearing his throat and realizing the sudden announcement was sort of his fault.

There was movement, some kissing, and a few whispered words I couldn't make out.

"Okay, well..." the nurse chimed in again. "We'll get the blood we need. Don't worry."

"I'm B-negative," someone spoke up, and I realized it was Rika.

Her tone sounded like mine did when I had to agree to something I wasn't entirely sure I wanted to do.

"Oh, wonderful," the nurse chirped. "Come with me, then."

"Thanks, Rika," Banks called out as they left.

I drew in a deep breath, relaxing a little, but still not moving from my spot.

"I'm sorry," I heard Banks say.

"Why are you apologizing?" Kai asked, a smile in his voice. "This is the best surprise. My parents will be ecstatic."

"I didn't want you to find out like this," she explained.

"Well, are you okay with it? Are you ready?"

"I didn't think I would be," she replied. "I wasn't sure I wanted kids, but since I found out on Monday, I'm just..."

She giggled, and then I heard jumping and a barely audible little squeal.

"No wonder you've been smiling so much," Kai commented. "And I thought it was because of me."

"Well, technically it is."

He snorted. "We've got a lot to look forward to."

"Let's go sit," she whispered.

I rubbed my eyes, forgetting my hands were covered in blood. Shit. I needed to go wash up.

I started to move, but then I heard Kai's voice.

"What are you doing?" he asked, and I stopped, thinking he was talking to me.

But it was Will who answered, "She said B-negative was a rare blood type. It's actually the second rarest in the country, according to this website. Only 2% of the population has it."

He must be looking at the stats on his phone.

"So?" Kai said.

"So isn't it a little convenient that Damon and Rika both share the same, exact, rare blood type?"

My eyes rounded.

Oh, geez.

But I just made my way down the wall, reading the braille signs to find the restroom Banks told me was a couple doors down from here.

It was one thing after another with this group, and for now, I was just fine without any more drama than I had on my own plate to deal with.

They could have that one.

CHAPTER 27

Damon

PRESENT

"Winter?" I mumbled, feeling her and smelling her everywhere as I searched in the black.

I couldn't see anything, and I couldn't open my eyes as I shifted on the bed under me.

Jesus. Everything was so fucking heavy.

"Shhh..." a voice said. "You're going to be okay. Just close your eyes and rest. You're safe."

Hands touched my face and forehead, like checking my temperature, and the warmth of her skin was like a dream. It felt like being in the shower with Winter the first time. Peaceful.

"Your hands are warm," I said, so weak I couldn't even swallow as I put my hand over hers, keeping it on my face. "I'm really fucking lightheaded. Don't move, okay? Just stay." I breathed shallow. "Just stay."

A kiss touched my forehead. "I've always been here," she whispered.

When I woke up again, it took several minutes, but I got my eyes open, the drowsiness taking forever to wear off.

Was that a dream? Where was Winter?

I put hands under me and scooted up in bed, using every ounce of strength I had and feeling a sharp pain in my side.

Ah, fuck. I coughed, touching the bandages on the side of my torso, noticing my hospital gown was down around my waist. An IV stuck in my hand, and two heart monitors were attached to my chest.

My neck ached, my head hurt, and I was groggy as fuck. What the hell did they give me?

I saw someone shift out of the corner of my eye and looked up, noticing everyone was in the room, either passed out on chairs or waking up.

Will rose from his seat, heading over to me, while Kai was passed out on a recliner with Banks curled up on top of him, and Michael and Rika were asleep on the couch.

"How long have I been out?" I asked him, looking for a clock.

He poured me a cup of water, and I downed the whole thing, handing it back for more.

"A few hours," he said. "You never sleep long."

"I want to leave."

The others started to stir, Banks rubbing her eyes and sitting up, while Rika stretched on the couch.

"Yeah, it's not happening." Will handed me another water. "You need to stay put."

"Fuck that." I ignored the cup he held out and tried to remove the sheet on top of me.

But then Michael was on the other side of me; he and Will both pushing me back down.

"Lie down or we'll lie you down," Michael threatened.

"Aw, you care?"

"With you bed-ridden, you can't cause trouble," he pointed out. "It's nice."

Whatever. I wasn't fucking staying. I'd rather pierce my eyeballs than lie here, *resting*.

I'd rather chug a gallon of piss warm milk than stay in bed, doing nothing.

I'd rather get a third degree burn on my dick.

Or develop a peanut allergy.

"Where's Winter?" I demanded, taking the water and downing it.

Both of them remained silent but exchanged looks.

What? My heart began to hammer.

Will cleared his throat. "Okay, I don't want you to freak out," he started. "We will all handle this. But you need to stay calm, okay?"

Stay calm? She was in the fucking car on the way to the hospital. What happened?

"What?" I barked, noticing Kai jump awake to my left.

Rika and Banks approached the bed, too.

"She's, um…" Will paused, struggling for words.

What the fuck?

And then he broke out in a smile, pulling back the curtain that hid the other bed in the room.

"Right here," he teased.

I looked over, seeing Winter curled up on top of the made bed, still wearing jeans and sneakers, but with Will's sweatshirt on now, it looked like.

"Want me to wake her up?" he asked.

I shook my head, seeing her mouth twitch a little. "No, leave her."

I sighed as everyone surrounded my bed, and I wished they'd all go away. This felt so pathetic, and I wanted to leave now. Why were they even still here? Banks, I could understand, but the rest of them?

Reaching down, I peeled away the surgical tape and gauze on the right side of my abdomen, trying to gauge how bad the injury was.

Peering under the bandage, I spotted a small incision, examining it.

"Three stitches?" I said out loud.

Three?

"Don't worry, there's more on the inside," Banks informed me. "Ten whole stitches. Super manly."

I let my head fall back on the pillows, tightening my abs a few times to gauge the pain.

"The injury wasn't that serious," Will said, folding his arms over his chest. "But ignoring it was. You lost a lot of blood."

"Luckily Rika had the same blood type," Michael stated.

"Yeah, luckily," Kai mumbled.

I almost laughed. Rika gave me blood? Like really?

I shot my eyes over to her, dropping my gaze to the Band-Aid on her arm where they'd drawn the blood.

Interesting.

"You going to say 'thank you'?" Michael prodded.

"Someday."

Rika let out a snort. "Well, now that he's fine, I need to go lock up the dojo."

"I'll go, too," Kai moved around Banks. "Some inventory came in that needs to be sorted."

"See you at home," Rika told Michael, leaning up to kiss him.

"I'm heading out, too," he said.

Kai kissed his wife as he, Michael, and Rika started to leave the room, but then Rika stopped and looked over at me.

"I would say 'I'm glad you're okay'," she told me, "but I'm still deciding."

I quirked a smile, and she shook her head, probably more at herself than me.

They left, but Will and Banks stayed, Banks handing me a bottle of water.

"I'm going to get you some real food and pick up some clothes," she said, smirking. "I gather you won't be here for long."

Damn straight.

"Thanks," I told her.

She leaned down and did something she never does... she kissed me on the cheek. But before she could rise again, I grabbed her arm, keeping her eyes level with mine.

"I, um..."

I trailed off, wanting to say something, but I didn't know what.

Before my friends and before Winter, Banks was my safe place. She could read me, take care of me, and just be there with no talking or expectations. She was the best thing in my life for a lot of years. I was tired of disrupting hers with all my bullshit.

I wanted to tell her that I...

I didn't know.

The words tasted like sand on my tongue, and I knew they'd come off disingenuous and unnatural sounding, because I never said shit like that, but...

I finally just met her eyes and shrugged. "Ya know."

A soft smile crossed her beautiful face and her eyes started to glisten. "Yeah, I love you, too," she told me.

Will sniffled at my side, feigning heartbreak, and I jerked my chin at him.

"Go. Both of you," I told them. "Get out of here."

He laughed as Banks walked around my bed toward the door.

"We'll be back with food," Will called out, leaving the room with her.

• • •

I hadn't meant to fall asleep again, but one minute I was looking over at Winter, knowing why she'd chosen to distance herself all the way over on the other bed instead of curl up on mine, but I was still relieved she decided to stay at all.

What a fucking mess. Every time something good happened...

I needed to take her to Maine. Out in the woods, away from everyone else, no WiFi. Maybe then we'd get some time.

The curtain was drawn again between us, the nurse probably pulling it closed for privacy or to not wake Winter, and I sat up in bed, noticing a brown bag on the tray and some clothes on the chair.

Had Banks and Will already come and gone?

I grabbed the bag, opening it. Looking inside, I inhaled the scent of Marina's piroshki and groaned as my stomach rumbled. Grabbing one of the buns, I popped it in my mouth and ate it before tearing off the sheet and swinging my legs over the side.

"Winter," I said, not bothering to whisper.

She didn't respond and I didn't see her move behind the curtain.

My body ached like hell, but I forced myself to stand anyway, stretching and rotating limbs to wake them up.

Reaching over, I whipped the curtain aside, the rings sliding across the track, but when I looked at the bed, it was empty.

Where was she?

"Winter?" I called.

Was she in the bathroom?

I tried to walk, but the cords attached to me stretched taut. Reaching down, I pulled all the plugs out of the wall, yanked off my monitors, and slid out my IV, a stream of blood following and spilling onto the floor.

"Fuck," I mouthed.

Walking over to the chair, I stripped off the gown and pulled on some jeans Banks brought, a T-shirt, and shoes and socks.

"Winter?" I called again.

I looked around, not seeing a clock or my cell phone. I couldn't remember where I'd left it, but it was dark outside, so I knew it was late. Or really early.

Stepping across the room to the bathroom, I knocked on the door, straightening my back and not feeling as sore as I thought I would be. Will was right, I guessed. It wasn't that serious.

When there was no answer, I opened the door, not finding her in the bathroom, either.

I opened the door to the room and entered the hallway, looking both ways for Winter or a nurse.

"Hello?" I called.

Where was everyone?

All the doors were closed, the corridor was dark, and the only light I could see was from a desk up on the right.

I headed up to it, finding the chairs behind the nurses' station empty.

"Hello!" I shouted, getting pissed off.

What the hell? It was the evening, but there had to be someone here.

Blood trailed down the back of my hand from the IV injection, dripping off my fingers, and I spotted some gauze on a cart, grabbing it and wrapping some around my hand before tearing it off and tucking the end inside the rest.

"Hey!" I barked into the dark.

Something was wrong.

Heading back toward my room, I passed it and rounded the corner for the elevators.

But as soon as I did, someone caught me and shoved me against the wall, putting their hand over my mouth.

I grabbed their collar, ready to shove them off, but Rika pressed her finger to her lips, telling me to be quiet.

Will stood behind her, both of them peering around the corner from where I just came.

Finally, she took her hand off my mouth and backed away.

"What the fuck?" I whisper-yelled.

"Someone tried to take Alex from the dojo tonight," Will told me. "She was able to fight them off and run, but..."

He looked down at Rika.

"What?" I hissed, losing patience.

"One of them was Miles Anderson," Rika said.

Miles Anderson. *One of them.* Which meant there were several, including him.

It wasn't hard to figure out motive. And then suddenly everything dawned.

"My father," I said what I was thinking out loud.

She looked up at me, fear in her eyes. "Yeah, I can't find Michael, and..."

"And Winter's gone," I added. "Shit." I ran my hand through my hair and then met her stare. "He knows."

She nodded, agreeing with me.

"We hired security to guard your hospital door," Will told me. "We'll deal with this—"

"Fuck you," I cut him off. "We're leaving now."

"You're not well enough."

"Who the fuck do you think you're talking to?" I glared at him. "Go get some fresh air!"

Clear your damn head, because you're confused.

He cocked an eyebrow, looking displeased, but then shared a look with Rika, and let out a laugh. "Yeah, we thought so."

And he tossed me a black backpack.

I opened it up, finding some clothes, a pullover, and a cell phone.

I grabbed the hoodie, dropped the bag, and pulled it on.

"Where's Banks?" I asked.

"She and Kai are with Alex, talking to the cops," Rika said. "She's safe. They're waiting for us."

"Do you have a plan?" I snatched up the bag, digging out the cell phone, already finding Rika, Will, and everyone else already programmed in.

"No, that's your domain," she answered.

My domain. So since we played our little mind games, she thought I was that good?

Not when I was aching, hungry, and distracted, though. Jesus. *Winter.* If he hurt her...

I scrolled through, trying to call her just in case.

"Damon," Rika spoke up as I let the line ring. "Gabriel will give me Michael, because of his respect for Evans Crist and a sign of good faith, but Alex is disposable to him. She saw the information we were looking for. He'll find her and kill her."

I knew that. I knew what our problems were, Rika.

But she kept talking. "And he knows that even if we give him the evidence we have about my father's accident, we were smart enough to make copies. He'll want assurance we won't use it. He's going to keep Winter."

"The hell he is."

No one answered, so I hung up and led the way to the elevators. Adrenaline was taking over, and I barely felt my stitches at all right now.

"He's going to ship her off somewhere you can't find her and do who-knows-what with her."

"Fucking hell, Rika!" I growled over my shoulder.

What the hell? Was she trying to give me a heart attack? Winter was with my father right now. Every second was a risk.

We rushed into the elevator and Will pressed the floor for the parking garage.

Rika stayed silent for a moment. When she spoke again, her voice was calm and soft. "Absorb it," she said. "Process it. And then get your head straight again. When you do, tell us what the hell we're doing."

She was right. I needed to calm down. I couldn't fucking think with my mind racing and spinning like a tornado.

My father would have Michael and Winter at his house. He wasn't trying to hide them from us. He wanted to bring us to the table.

But Rika was right. In the digital age, there were no guarantees. He knew we had the evidence backed up.

He couldn't get his hands on Alex tonight, and he couldn't hurt Michael.

Winter was his assurance.

Think.

Negotiation was useless. I would never let him keep Winter.

We needed to get on the property, undetected, and he wasn't going to be dumb enough to fall for Banks as a diversion again.

Fuck, fuck, fuck...

My mind started wandering from one scenario to the next, and finally, I had it.

"David and Lev," I said. "They're still working for Banks, right?"

My father's old employees who left on bad terms, hated my father, but knew the lay of the land and everyone who worked for Gabriel. They worked for my sister now, who also stole my father's cook, Marina.

"Yeah, you want me to call them?" Will asked.

I nodded, all of us charging out of the elevator as soon as the doors opened. "Tell them to meet us at the hilltop gate. Tell them to bring something good from Marina. Something my father's men would miss."

CHAPTER 28

Damon

PRESENT

Since we knew my father's men would be keeping a closer eye on the woods that we escaped through last night, it seemed less of a risk just to get them to open the rear gate for us. With a little finesse and guts, anyway.

"Thanks for coming." I walked up to David and Lev, meeting them as they stepped out of their SUV.

"Banks made us," Lev spat out.

Pissant.

Both of them used to work for my father, but now they worked for Kai and my sister at their home in Meridian City. Doing what, I wasn't sure, but they stayed, so there must be something exciting going on over there.

I jerked my chin at the tin Lev was holding. "What did you bring?"

He popped the lid, but David answered, "She had some vatrushka already made. There's zephyr in there, too."

"Fuck, yeah." I reached in, snatching one of the berry marshmallow things and popping it in my mouth. My taste buds exploded, making my mouth water like crazy, but it was probably more because I hadn't eaten in two days rather than them tasting that good.

Although, they were good.

Marina also worked for my father before Banks stole her away, too. She and my sister were the only things I missed about this house, and now that they were no longer there, I had no reason to visit unless I was forced to.

I grabbed a vatrushka bun, barely chewing it before I swallowed it down, and led them over to a tree. I peered around it, the hilltop gate my father used for deliveries, caterers, and employees sat a hundred yards away, lit up by two lanterns.

Rika stood near, blowing into her hands to warm them up, while Will put on a sweatshirt, pulling the hood over his head.

"We just need you to get the gate open," I told Lev and David.

If we could get them to come out, they'd shut off the cameras, not wanting a secret meetup caught on film.

"And then distract them, so we can get in," Rika added, tucking her hands under her arms.

"And when you need to get out?" David retorted.

I exchanged a look with Rika, neither of us having an answer. "We'll deal with that later," I said.

Grabbing our backpack off the ground, I led Rika and Will to the edge of the tree line, waiting for the tiny lights on the cameras to go dark so we could move.

Behind us, I heard David on the phone.

"Hey," he said.

He was silent a moment and then he laughed. "Aw, you still mad about that?" he joked. "Well, David and I aren't here as friends. We come with a drug deal. We got some of Marina's vatrushka. Bring us a bottle of Mamont, and we'll call it even." And then he added, "We have a little zephyr, too."

He was quiet, and I looked over at him, seeing him hang up the phone and nod once at me.

Good. They were going for it.

I dug out some surgical tape, quickly tearing off three pieces and adding them to my wound to reinforce the stitches and hold the cut together. I'd be lucky if this shit didn't tear open again before the end of the night.

I zipped up the pack, but Rika took it, putting it on her own back instead of letting me carry it. I almost argued, but I didn't need another trip to the hospital, so fuck it.

After another moment, the power lights went off, and we bolted, running across the dirt road, jumping over the low hedges lining the wall, and crouching down, waiting for the gates to open.

Steam from our mouths billowed into the air, and we plastered ourselves against the wall to wait.

Luckily, my side didn't hurt at all, and I didn't know if it was because of the drugs they gave me still lingering or the adrenaline, but I just wanted to get in there. Rika's fucking ideas were thrashing around my head, and every second Winter spent inside that house...

I squeezed my fists, trying to calm down.

A deep creak filled the air, iron bars clanked together, and the gate opened, a black Chevy Tahoe pulling through, its lights flashing on the forest ahead. They pulled to a stop, dust kicking up from the road underneath, and opened the doors, one guy from each side stepping out.

I waited for them to move around the front of their car, out of our line of sight, to talk to our guys, but before I could shoot off, Rika grabbed me.

I jerked my head, glaring at her.

No time to lose. What the fuck?

But she just shook her head, grinning. "I know this trick."

And she rushed forward, crouching down and running for the back of the SUV.

What?

Will and I had no choice. We followed her, racing to the rear of their car as she pulled the back door open and climbed inside.

I shot a glance around us and inside the car to make sure it was empty. The dome lights were already on since the guys left the doors opened, so they didn't notice when she opened the hatch.

Jesus. This was stupid.

"Looks good," I heard one of the guys say in front. "Only she makes it right."

Gingerly, Will and I climbed in after Rika, all of us sitting and slouched, staying down and out of sight.

"This is dumb!" I mouthed to Rika.

She rolled her eyes and pulled the door closed but not all the way.

"Try some," someone said outside.

"Think I poisoned you?"

There was a pause as David or Lev probably taste-tested the food for my father's men, and then I heard David speak up again.

"Where's the vodka?" he asked.

The car rocked under us as someone dug in it for the bottle they were trading.

"Splendid," David finally said.

"New employers too good for the black market?"

"At least I'm getting fed well," David replied. "You?"

There was silence and then my father's guy asked, "This time again next week?"

Come on, come on, come on...

The car jostled under us as the men climbed back in, and I watched Rika as she waited.

As soon as their doors slammed shut, she pulled ours closed, masking the sound, and the interior went dark as the guys shifted into gear and shot off in reverse.

I let out a breath.

If that hadn't worked, I would've killed Rika.

But it did, so... Fine, whatever.

The car turned around, and I heard the gate start to close as we sped down the back road toward the house.

It was only a few hundred yards, but this was faster and we travelled undetected. Good plan.

Once the car slowed, we got ready, and as the guys killed the engine and opened their doors, we slipped out, quietly pushing the back door closed again and diving off to the side of the garage where my father kept his cars and motorcycles.

"Go!" I whisper-yelled to Will, letting him lead us to the next building which would curve us around the side of the house for a better view.

We crept over, hiding in an alcove on the side and taking in the surroundings. I heard the guys in the shop, doing whatever they did in their downtime, but I knew there was another shift on the property, making the rounds.

"Now what?" Rika asked.

"The armory is in the clubhouse," I told them.

"Guns?" she blurted out. "That was your plan?"

"You got a better one?"

"We take him," she said.

"Huh?"

She sighed, looking impatient. "We have no idea where they are or if they're even here?" she explained. "After we got you out, he might not think right under your nose is a great spot to hide them. We take him, and we have leverage."

So take my father, if we can, and hide him somewhere, threatening and/or torturing him until he gives up her fiancé and my...Winter.

That sounded like a lot of waiting.

"I don't have all night," I told her. "We're getting some guns."

"Yeah," Will laughed.

She growled under her breath, exasperated.

We started to move around the side of the next building, but she pulled us both back.

"Look," she said under her breath.

We shot our eyes up, seeing men leave the house, Winter and Michael in tow and leading them to a car. Miles Fucking

Anderson gripped her by the back of her hair, force-walking her into an SUV with her hands tied behind her back.

She squirmed and fought, and I inched forward, ready to kill.

Will jerked me back, though.

"They *are* here," he said. "Where are they going?"

"He's moving them," Rika guessed and looked at me. "I told you."

Michael stumbled after, breaking free and charging one of the guys, but a baton smashed over the back of his head, and he fell to his knees.

Rika sucked in a breath, stifling a sob.

I was more worried, though. Winter was more expendable than Michael to my father. He wouldn't want to kill Evans Crist's son or a star player for a national basketball team.

"We need to run," I said. "Now. Back to the cars."

We didn't hesitate. Whipping back around, we bolted through the trees, past the garden maze, my old treehouse, and down the small incline back the way we came. The wound in my side started to ache, so I put more weight on my right side as we ran, digging my heels in.

How were we going to get out? Fuck.

There were no trees around that wall, and we couldn't climb the goddamn gate. We needed to get around to the main road before they left and disappeared.

But as we approached, the cold night air stinging my lungs, I slowed for a second, noticing that the gate wasn't closed. Not entirely.

It wasn't fucking closed.

Relief washed over me, but we didn't stop to question. We slipped through the opening and raced for our cars buried beyond the trees.

Glancing back, I noticed the cameras hung by their wires, dangling like a dead animal, and something was lodged in the hinges of the gate. I laughed under my breath.

Thanks, guys. David and Lev might hate me, but they knew my sister didn't.

My father's people were going to notice the cameras were offline any second, though, if they hadn't already.

We dashed to the cars, Rika jumping in Michael's old G-Class, and Will and I taking his SUV.

Barreling onto the dirt road, I stepped on the gas, kicking up the gears and storming down the empty path. I kept the lights low, counting the seconds in my head as Rika followed close behind.

They got them in the car. They have to get all the way down the driveway and through the gate. Then pull onto the road, and hopefully they weren't in a rush, so they wouldn't be far ahead of us. What if I lost track of her? Where would my father take them?

We charged out onto the highway, bouncing and skidding as I jerked the steering wheel right and laid back on the gas. Rika swerved behind me, getting control of her car again, and I kept my eyes peeled on the road ahead.

But just then, headlights shone from the right, in the distance, and I immediately slowed, knowing it was them. I breathed hard.

We hadn't missed them. They were just leaving the estate now.

Rika skidded behind me, unprepared for my sudden brake, and Will gripped the handle above his door.

"Shit!" he exclaimed.

His phone, propped up in its mount on the dash, rang, and I saw *Rika* on the screen. Will answered it, the speaker coming on.

"Stay back," she ordered. "Just follow."

"I know!" I fired back.

Did she think I was fucking stupid? Whatever we did would put Michael and Winter in more danger. We had to think.

I hung back, hoping they just assumed we were other drivers on the road, and followed them at a distance, unsure of how many people were in the car.

Other than Winter and Michael, probably two? My father's men always worked in a minimum of pairs.

We kept Rika on the line, while Will dug out his pocket knife. We'd need that for their zip ties.

I followed the car down past the neighboring estates, past the security booth for our community, and onto the highway, but instead of heading toward Meridian City like I thought they would, whoever was driving took the right exit, heading for the village.

Gabriel was keeping them close, after all.

I swallowed a few times, trying to get my dry mouth wet.

They were going to come to a stoplight in another mile at the village center.

"You still handy with that crowbar?" I called out, remembering Rika back when she was sixteen and the antics she pulled that night.

"You want to box them in?" she suggested.

I nodded, even though she couldn't see me. "You take the rear. Let's do it."

Will jumped out of his seat, crawling into the back and digging something out. When he came back, he threw me a baseball bat and my mask, and he held his own crowbar, his white skull with the red stripe already on his head.

I pulled the mask on, completely forgetting about not showing ourselves. There were people on the streets, and while I didn't care if my father's men saw us, I wasn't winding up on more motherfucking videos, since we had to do this in the busiest part of town.

We passed houses, businesses, and streets lined with cars, most of the town closed down for the night, but there were still people about.

Perfect.

Gabriel's guys might be less inclined to use weapons if it was populated. My father kept his shit under wraps, even though most of the town knew how his house operated.

The stoplight appeared up ahead, they started to slow, and I punched on the gas, speeding up.

"Go," I shouted to Rika.

I swerved to the left, she swerved to the right, they stopped, and we swung around, skidding to a halt, Will and I in front and Rika in the back, so they couldn't drive off or back up.

Not waiting a single second, we jumped from the cars, masks and hoods drawn, throwing our weapons into their windows and smashing the glass.

Bystanders gasped or yelped in shock, but I didn't waste time worrying about them.

Breaking the rear glass, we reached in, unlocking the doors, and I came down on the two guys in front as Rika and Will grabbed Winter and Michael.

Anderson and the other guy shouted and laid on the gas, trying to move, but they were locked in, just bumping into our cars in the front and behind. We had everyone out of the car before they even had a chance to reach for their weapons.

Will sliced off Michael's restraints, and Michael didn't wait a moment more. He whipped open the front passenger side door and hauled himself up, shooting his legs into the car and kicking the other guy in the face.

Will took Winter, climbed back in our SUV, and Michael grabbed Rika, running for their car.

"Back at the house," I told them. "I'll send Crane."

Rika nodded, Michael climbed into the driver's seat, blood seeping from his head, and they took off, swerving in a U-turn and jetting past us.

I jumped in our car, pulling around in a circle and seeing Anderson trying to start the car as we blew past.

I didn't care if there were cops or if someone on the street was calling them in right now. I wasn't stopping until we were safe.

I looked over at Winter, sitting in Will's lap as he cut off her zip ties, and I quickly scanned her face and clothes. She still wore the same bloody jeans from yesterday when I'd been bleeding all over her and Will's hoodie. She didn't look hurt, except for some blood trickling from her lip, and nothing appeared ripped like there had been a struggle. Her angelic face and white-blonde hair looked like they'd been through the ringer tonight, though. Eyes red while worry and upset creased her face. I could tell she'd been terrified.

How the fuck did this happen? I wasn't asleep long at the hospital. They didn't have her long, right? God, if they touched her...

I quickly called Crane on Will's cell.

"Hello?" he answered.

"Take any guys left and go set up shop at St. Killian's," I ordered him. "We'll be there soon."

"Yes, sir."

I wasn't sure if my father was paying him anymore, but if he wasn't going to go, I knew he wouldn't tell him where *we* were going.

"You think Gabriel will go there?" Will asked me after I hung up. He still held Winter in his lap.

I shook my head. "No. He'll take time to regroup. He'll come eventually, though. We need to be ready."

"Is there someone behind us?" Winter asked, breathing hard again.

I checked the rearview mirror, while Will glanced over his shoulder.

Bright headlights pierced the darkness as we left the village, climbing our tail.

"And coming up fast," Will said.

How did she know that?

I punched the gas, charging up into the hills, the dark trees looming on both sides.

"Did they hurt you?" I asked, looking at Winter.

She shook her head. "Just scared me."

Will took her chin, inspecting the cut on her lip. "Anderson do that?"

"I think so."

I raced past security, not even bothering to stop as the guard popped his head up, startled. He worked for the families in this community, not the police. He'd call the association to report trouble before he'd call the cops.

I turned the wheel, taking us around the curve, but as I straightened out, the car behind us shot up right on our ass, ramming into our car.

Winter gasped, and we lurched forward, Will holding her tight as he planted his hand on the dash. I sped around another curve, but then Will shouted at me.

"No, take the shortcut!" he yelled.

I jerked the steering wheel right, remembering St. Killian's sat across from a small river buried in the forest. There was a bridge that cut through the space between here and Michael and Rika's, avoiding all the winding roads.

We could go faster without all the turns.

Anderson shot past, but I heard his tires screech to a halt on the other road above as we hurried toward the bridge as fast as we could.

I pressed my back into the seat, my arm locked straight on the steering wheel, and my eyes zoned in on the road and checking my mirror.

My blood raced, and if I weren't so worried about her, I might've been having a little fun. Of course, I wouldn't have run. I would've killed that motherfucker right there in the town square. I'd just been caught up in getting her out.

Headlights flashed through my rearview mirror and the car caught up to us again, charging behind.

It rushed up, and I tightened every muscle.

"Hold on," I shouted.

It slammed into our ass, and liquid heat coursed down every one of my limbs as I tried to outrun them.

I looked to Winter. "We're almost there."

She opened her mouth to speak, but the car rammed us again, and we all lurched in our seats.

"Motherfucker!" I growled.

They slammed into us again. I took the wheel with both hands trying to keep it steady.

And again.

Winter started panting in short, shallow breaths, scared with an arm around Will's neck and one on the dash.

They hit us again.

"Hold on," I told them.

The bridge appeared ahead, and I charged dead ahead, racing onto it and seeing Anderson's headlights chase us again.

The dark river loomed still and black underneath us, spreading far to the left and right as my tires bumped over the slabs of concrete underneath.

Anderson sped up, hit us again, but before I had a chance to recover, he shot around and slammed into my side.

"Goddammit!" I bellowed.

I lost the wheel, the car went spinning, and I slammed on the brakes, and then... He was there—his headlights charging right for us.

Will yelled, wrapping his arms around Winter's head, and we crashed through the railing, the back tires falling over the side of the bridge as Anderson's SUV tipped both right tires over the side, as well. Winter screamed as the car wobbled.

There was only a moment, my eyes locked on Winter's face, and then both cars started to slide. I reached for her, took her hand, and pulled her into my arms, locking her in as we both went over the side, free falling into the river.

Holy fuck!

The car crashed down, my neck snapped back, and the whole world tilted on its side as my head swam.

What the hell?

I heard Winter calling me.

"Damon?" she cried, touching my face. "D...Damon, wake up. Wake up!"

I squeezed my eyes shut, lifting up my head and rotating the ache out of my neck before opening them again.

Did I get knocked out? *Shit.*

Winter sat on my lap, nearly nose to nose, crying but kissing me as soon as she felt me move.

I grunted, rubbing my neck as I looked over to see Will yanking on his handle and throwing his body into the door.

It took a moment to register what had just happened, but then I looked up, out the front windshield and saw what was all around us.

The fucking river. Jesus.

"You okay?" I asked Winter.

"Yeah."

I looked around, seeing the car flooding as water poured in from the vents and under the dash, the car already half deep.

Fuck.

The river rushed over the hood as the car sank nose first, and I looked out the window, seeing no signs of life from Anderson's car. It floated upside down, slowly sinking, as well.

Winter jumped off me, and I pulled my handle, following Will and slamming all my weight into the door. The cloudy water rushed, starting to cover the windows and pour in, and I yanked again and again and again, but the fucking door wouldn't open.

I climbed out of my seat, trying the back doors and kicking the windows. Winter moved from door to door, feeling her way and trying the windows, pushing the buttons, while Will took the baseball bat and threw it into the glass.

"Just calm down a sec!" I yelled at him.

We were under water now. If he broke the glass, water would rush in fast, and we needed a minute.

I pushed against the back door so hard my muscles burned.

Fuck, fuck, fuck, fuck... Think.

Goddammit.

My knees shook as I made my way back up front, sloshing through the icy water and picking up Winter who was chest deep and shivering.

I breathed over her lips, trying to warm her any way I could. "There's like six hundred pounds of pressure on the windows and doors, right now," I told her. "Once the pressure equalizes, we'll open the doors."

"When...when..." she stammered, shaking. "When does it equalize?"

The water chilled my bones. "When the car...fills up... with water."

"If it fills up with water, we can't breathe!" Will yelled, climbing out of his seat, his clothes and hair drenched. "We don't want it to fill up!"

He stumbled, catching himself as his head turned right and left, manically searching for a way out.

"Damon, man..." He stood, almost hyperventilating as the water rose to our chests, slowly consuming the car. "We gotta...we gotta get out of here. I can't... I can't..."

He started feeling the roof and searching, looking everywhere for anything he could find, gasping in short breaths.

I turned from Winter, gripping his face in my hands. "Just breathe," I told him. "Trust me. We're getting out of here."

He met my eyes, starting to break down as his chin trembled. "Please, don't..." he begged. "Please don't leave me."

I clenched my jaw, shame washing me all over again at what I let Trevor do to him. How I left him.

How I would never have lived with it if anything had happened to him that night.

I held the back of his neck and planted my forehead to his. "I never did," I promised.

I turned to Winter, took her hand and wrapped it around my belt.

"You don't let go," I ordered.

She shook, so scared, and her eyes watering. The car whined with the weight of the water filling it as we sank into the depths of the river, and I held her up, so she could breathe as long as possible.

"Tell me you love me," she whispered. "Say it."

I looked down at her, fucking done with this rotten luck. We weren't dying. I wasn't telling her that shit like I wouldn't have a chance to tell her later. She could fucking wait.

I held her close, nose to nose. "Someday," I taunted, forcing a smile into my voice.

She let out a little laugh through her sob, and I wanted so badly to have her back on that motorcycle like the night I promised to show her red someday. Even when I was lying to her like I was that night, it was better than this.

She gripped my belt, my heart pounded in my chest, and Will and Winter gasped around me as we sucked up the last of the air in the car. I pushed us up, farther and farther, getting the last breaths we could as Will caught a mouthful of water, coughed and sputtered, and then we were under, and he was thrashing.

Shit.

I didn't waste time. With Winter holding my belt, I moved to one of the rear doors and pushed, but it still wasn't budging. I fondled the lock, making sure it wasn't secured, and threw my weight into the door as best I could.

Winter held on, calm, but I could hear Will fighting in the water, because he didn't get a lungful before we went under, and I didn't know why the fucking door wasn't opening. It was supposed to open.

Come on.

My hands shook so badly, and I was losing it. They were going to fucking die, because of me. Again.

Please.

I pushed at the door.

Please. Please, Please.

And then I pushed...

And it floated open like magic.

I went dizzy for a moment, wondering if it really just did that.

Oh, fucking yes. Thank God.

I dove out into the river, pulling Winter and reaching inside and grabbing Will.

He kicked his legs, swimming out and fighting for the surface, and I followed, taking Winter's hand off my belt but not letting go as we swam.

We all popped up to the surface, hitting the air and coughing, sputtering, and gasping for breath. The cold water stabbed like needles in my skin, but I couldn't feel my wound at least. One pain at a time.

We needed to get out of this water. I looked around for Anderson and his partner, but there was no one. Nothing else on the surface of the river. He was under.

He was gone.

Good fucking riddance.

"Can you swim?" I asked Winter. She'd been in the pool with Will, but it wasn't deep.

"Yeah," she choked out. "I'll follow you."

I turned on my non-injured side and did the side-stroke toward the river bank, watching her behind me to make sure she could follow my sound and movement in the water.

Will swam next to me, the current pulling us, but we made good strides, and I started to feel the ground under me. My fucking body was done.

We reached the river floor, crawling out of the water and onto the bank, breathing hard and relief washing over me as I collapsed.

"Fuck, we did it," I breathed out.

Winter grabbed my leg, pulling herself up.

"We can't stay here," she said, her voice shaking. "We need to... get somewhere warm."

I rolled over, groaning at all the aches and pains, and I needed ten-thousand things right now, but I was so fucking happy they were here and we made it. Raising my head and looking up, I saw a single light through the trees and knew...

Just fucking knew.

St. Killian's.

CHAPTER 29

Damon

PRESENT

We stumbled toward the church, freezing and covered in dirt as Will crawled up a ravine, and I followed with Winter in tow.

Jesus, it was fucking freezing.

There was no telling if my father knew we had Michael and Winter back or if anyone was on our tail, but we had to get inside and get warm.

Our breath clouded in the air as the wet clothes molded to our skin, but I stayed charged.

We were almost there.

Will hung his head, looking ready to collapse, but it was like he was possessed, almost as if he was trying to get away from something as he crawled and scurried.

But instead of running for St. Killian's, Will veered down what looked almost like a cave.

I peered closely through the dark, seeing an alcove in the earth under a tree. Like a tunnel.

What was that?

Following him, I stopped behind him and held Winter close as she shivered uncontrollably and watched him punch in a code.

The door opened, and we slipped inside.

Will kept going, ripping off his sweatshirt and T-shirt and dropping them along the hallway, and I pulled the door closed again, taking Winter's hand.

I looked around, taking about two seconds to figure out these were the catacombs underneath the church. I knew there was another entrance, but it looked like Michael and Rika had installed a proper door with security.

Last time I was here, it was all rock and dirt, but I quickly noticed the polished hardwood floors, the rock walls that had been repaired and spruced up, and the sconces lining the hallway on both sides, their lanterns creating a subterranean glow.

I followed Will, all of us rushing into the massive stone shower, Will going for one showerhead and me for the other.

We turned on the rainfall spouts, getting them warm and steam billowing immediately, and then I darted over to Winter, peeling off her sweatshirt as she kicked off her shoes and socks.

I fisted my hands against the cold, ripping off my hoodie and shirt, as well.

"Fuck," I growled low, putting her under the warm water.

Will hunched over, still shivering but even worse now as the water cascaded over him.

What was wrong with him?

I shot over to him, grabbing him under the arms. "Come on, sit down."

He tried to rise, but his legs gave out, and he fell into me, both of us crashing down. And I just couldn't. I gave up, my strength gone.

We sat here against the wall, Will's back against my chest and his head lying on my collarbone as the water drenched us. My jeans stuck to my skin, but the heat seeped into my bones, and I started to feel better minute by minute.

Will shook, though, his knee bobbing up and down in short spurts.

I wrapped my arms around him, trying to help. "We're okay," I told him. "Just breathe."

But he groaned like he was in pain, and I squeezed his arms, trying get the blood pumping or something. Anything. But he was ice cold and not calming down.

What the hell?

"Will, are you okay?" Winter asked.

"He's shaking," I told her. "Come here."

She came down on the floor, following my voice and crawling, and I took her arm, pulling her on top of him, both of us sandwiching him.

"Get him fucking warmed up," I told both of us.

"You're okay," she said, straddling him and hugging his chest.

"I almost drowned," he choked out, his breath ragged. "Again."

"Shhh," I soothed him, holding him, because that was all I could do.

There was nothing that would erase what I did, only to hate myself more, because I'd done it at all.

I wasn't sure if Winter knew what he was talking about, but she just held him, not saying anything.

"I feel like something is chasing me, man." He wouldn't stop shivering. "Like it's only a matter of time."

I cupped Winter's face with one hand and him with the other, just holding them both.

"I can't stop shaking," he said. "Fuck, I'm cold."

"It's okay." I held him tighter, not knowing what to do to bring him down.

He wasn't okay. He was anything but okay. Rika was right.

He was fucking spiraling.

And I doubted anyone knew the full measure of the mess in his head.

Winter brought her head up. "Close your eyes," she said, putting her hands on his chest. "Close them for a minute. We've got you."

I peered down at him, seeing his eyes closed.

"We've got you," she whispered again. "We're yours. We're all yours. We're not leaving."

She put her head back down on him, holding him with one of her hands resting on my thigh.

She inhaled long, deep breaths, soothing him with her soft voice. "Damon at your back," she said, "and me at your front. Feel us breathing. Feel it."

I did the same, tipping my head back and closing my eyes, just concentrating on our bodies.

"In." She drew in a breath. "And out."

Will's body shuttered, but he was trying.

In.

And out.

"Slow, Will," she breathed out. "Go slow."

Her fingers squeezed my thigh, letting me know she was here, and I rubbed her arm as we all kept our eyes closed, trying to calm the fuck down.

"Do you feel him?" she asked Will. "Feel his body behind you. And feel me."

The shaking in Will's body started to subside as his chest rose slower and slower, all of us concentrating on every breath and falling into sync.

"In," she told us. "And out."

We all blew out, our bodies melted together and moving like one unit.

In...

And out....

"Slow," she whispered. "Slow with me."

His arms came around her, and all of us just sat there intertwined and warm, Rika and Michael probably pacing upstairs and wondering what happened to us.

Will's and my phones were at the bottom of the river now.

I couldn't go upstairs, though. I didn't want to move.

"In and out," she chanted again.

I ran my hand around her back, finding her T-shirt already pulled up a little and Will's hand tucked up inside it, not rubbing but clutching at her warmth.

"Whatever is after you is failing," I told him. "You're not fucked. You're the strongest of us all, because you've survived the most."

I failed to destroy him. Miles Anderson failed. Two-and-a-half years in prison failed.

And that bitch who treated him like garbage in high school and still rented space in his head would fail, too.

I rubbed Winter's back, and he began caressing her with his thumb.

Her voice and the water lulled us into relaxation, everything quiet and warm and feeling so good, I just wanted more of it. We kneaded her skin slowly, but my hand started rubbing her back harder and more demanding as I chased the hunger for contact.

I drifted down to her ass. I needed to feel what was mine. Feel everything that was mine right here.

"We've all been through some shit," Will said.

"Too much shit," I added.

And nothing felt so good as to hold nearly everything I cared most about in the world right here.

Will and I stroked her skin, more demanding as our breathing grew more labored again, and she pulled her head up—or tried to—but it just hung, dipping into Will's chest as she arched into our touch.

"You guys," she begged.

But she didn't get any more words out.

Will peeled her shirt off over her head, leaving her in her bra, and I cupped her face, caressing it. She laid her head back down, us touching her—her arms, her neck, her back.

She trailed her fingers up Will's arms, and I felt him let out a sigh and relax into me more as her hand left him and found my arm, her touch drifting down the length.

We became a web of arms and hands, our hands on her and hers on us, returning the affection as Will traded one frenzy for another, and the spray of the water drowned out the world outside.

She arched up, holding Will's face, but kissing me, long and slow, teasing me with that tongue, and no sound filled the shower except for the breath between us.

Holding her face with one hand, I gripped her ass with the other and nudged her up into me, forgetting Will was there. Instead, she rubbed up on him, and he let out a breathy growl as their groins met and the friction got him turned on.

Winter froze, her lips layered with mine as she seemed shocked at first, but then a whimper escaped.

I watched her, feeling her body in my hands, and then I kissed her, going at each other as my heart pounded and my groin charged, hot and ready.

I had everything right here. Everything. I hadn't let them go. They were here. I fisted her hair. *Mine.*

I moved her on him again, sucking and biting her lips as his mouth came down on her neck, and he wrapped his arms around her like she was all he had to hold onto, and all three of us were a mess of lips and hands, biting and grabbing.

Will took her bra-covered breast and sucked it into his mouth through the fabric, while she rolled her hips on him, deep and urgent, fucking him through his jeans.

He gripped her hips, sucking in air through his teeth as he helped her move.

"Don't make her stop," he gritted out. "Don't stop."

She planted a hand on the wall behind me, held my face with the other as we kissed, and dry-fucked him.

But then she whimpered and pulled away, climbing off him and rising to her feet all of a sudden.

What...

My blood chilled, and Will couldn't catch his breath, both of us painfully hard and wanting her so badly.

Shit, what did I do? Was she scared?

I closed my eyes, dropping my head back.

"It's okay," I told her, looking back up. "I know I'm fucked up. Just go. You can go."

Jesus Christ. What was I doing?

It just felt so good to have them both here, in my fucking arms, and I knew Will felt it, too. After so long and so much anger...

But she just shook her head. "I don't want to go."

Then why did you leave?

God, she was beautiful. With a wet body that could kill.

I wanted her so goddamn bad.

Why wasn't she here?

But then we watched as she unbuttoned and unzipped her jeans, sliding them down her legs and stepping out of them.

She reached behind her back and unclasped her bra, moving her wet hair over the front of one shoulder as her tits, full and tight, stared at me. Will and I were so fucking frozen, just looking at her.

Smooth and glowing. Wet and rippling with steam.

My cock swelled, and I stared at her red silk panties with lace trim, knowing how good what was underneath them felt.

I could feel the small smile on my face as I leaned into Will's ear. "You see that shit?" I growled, both of us zoned in on the triangle of Winter's panties.

He breathed hard.

"You stay on the outside of it," I ordered.

He chuckled, his playful tone like his old self again. "And if I don't?"

"Then you just might die tonight, after all."

He laughed, and I pushed him off, shooting to my feet.

Stalking over to her, I scooped her up and threw her over my shoulder, smacking her on the ass.

She gasped.

"Turn off the water," I told Will. "Let's go to bed."

CHAPTER 30

Winter

PRESENT

We almost died. A half an hour ago we were sinking to the bottom of a river, and I just wanted to hold them and touch them and never let go all night, so all we would feel was good right now.

That was everything I wanted in this moment. Them safe, Damon to know I was rooted at his side, and Will to know he was ours. We claimed him, and we wouldn't let him fall.

Damon threw me down on the bed, my body wracking with something I couldn't explain, and he came down on me, his wet jeans rubbing against my panties and driving me wild.

I heard someone else close the bedroom door, and Damon was just as charged as I was, not waiting a moment. He unfastened his jeans, yanked my underwear to the side, and I spread my legs as he thrust inside me, sheathing his dick to the hilt.

I cried out, his length touching me deep inside and filling me up so good I clawed his shoulders.

He growled, holding himself up with one hand and sliding his hand under my ass with the other as he fucked me, pumping his hips between my legs hard and fast like he was possessed.

"Damon," I breathed out, rolling my hips to meet him.

I tipped my head back, his mouth devouring my neck, and I heard clothes drop on the floor as Will must've taken off his jeans.

"Fuck, that's hot," he said from somewhere next to the bed.

I whimpered, my breasts bouncing back and forth with his quick, hard thrusts, and the tender flesh of my nipples craved his mouth so bad.

Damon grunted with his attack, pumping so hard, and I loved every second of it. I wanted everything rough right now.

Wild.

And then I heard Will's voice next to my ear as he came down on the bed.

"What does it feel like?" he whispered.

I turned my head, feeling the breath from his lips. "Thick," I moaned. "It hurts so good."

I held Damon's hips as Will's mouth hovered close. "You wet for him?" he asked.

"Mmm-hmm."

"You have an amazing body, girl." He sucked in air through his teeth.

And then his hot tongue, flicked my lip, and heat swirled in my belly, making my clit throb even more.

"I want to play with you," he whispered. "Let me touch your pussy."

I started to pant, almost wanting to cry, because everything felt so good, and I wanted to feel everything, but I was getting dizzy as Damon went deeper, pushing my body back and forth as he fucked me.

Will layered his lips with mine. "Let me fucking touch you."

I nodded.

"I'm gonna touch her, man," he told Damon.

Damon remained silent, and I ran my hands up his chest, feeling his body move as it went on instinct and took what it needed. I wanted this forever.

Him forever.

I wanted to hold this place where we could hide in our dark places and feel everything we didn't always understand. Fantastical fear and falling. Danger, fury, heat, and need.

So strong you're a fucking animal.

Black and red.

And underneath the earth, behind a closed door, in this room, we let it happen. We just gave in.

"Oh, fuck," Will groaned as he reached down and fingered my clit.

His soft lips played over mine, just caressing and teasing, while his fingers taunted me, starting to rub me out as his best friend fucked me.

I panted and whimpered, Will's hot breath mixing with mine, as I closed my eyes and reached for Damon, holding him to me as I waved my hips, meeting Will and Damon's touches at the same time.

The need built inside, and my breath turned raspy as I got more excited and desperate. It was there. I was almost there. Will sank his tongue into my mouth, claiming my lips in a deep kiss, and I wondered if Damon was watching us. What was he seeing? Did he like it?

I could feel his eyes on us.

But then I heard his voice, deep and gruff. "You two..." he said, sounding like a threat. "Are making me so hard."

And then he slowed, both of us enjoying every inch he sank inside me, and came down covering my breast with his mouth.

I gasped, but then Will's mouth tore away from mine as he found my other breast, both of them sucking on a nipple. I threaded my fingers through their hair—Damon's longer and smoother, Will's shorter and thicker—as they kissed, nibbled, and bit me. I tipped my head back, arching my back to meet their mouths with my breasts.

God, to have them both kissed at the same time...

Damon then came up and kissed me on the mouth, deep and hard, and then dipped to my neck, trailing kisses over my skin just as Will came back to claim my lips again. I dove into Will's mouth and taste, holding Damon to me, only to have Damon pull my chin over to him, so he could kiss me again. One after the other, sucking on my body until they wanted their turn with my mouth.

Damon devoured my breasts again while I ate up Will's lips, just for Damon to thrust hard again and come back up again, gripping the top of my hair, and demanding my mouth once more.

I was breathless and dizzy, losing track of who was who.

"So hot," Will said. "Watching him fuck you bare."

I spread my thighs wider, wanting Damon to have it all.

"He says I can't fuck you," he whispered in my ear. "But you're going to feel my dick tonight, Winter."

I whimpered, my breath shaking, because I wanted this with them. Both of them in my arms and the overwhelming feel of them in every one of my senses, because we needed this.

But it was so much. Too much.

Damon pulled out of me, and I only had a moment to wonder what he was doing, before he covered my pussy with his mouth. Will pulled his hand away and moved up and down my body, sucking and kissing.

My stomach rose and fell in heavy breaths as Damon nibbled and teased me with his tongue, and I sucked air between my teeth, the need building again.

"Don't stop," I begged. "I love what you're doing to me."

He ate me up, sucking so hard, I could only hold on.

The orgasm crested, and I sucked in short, desperate breaths, ready to explode, and then he stuck his tongue inside me, and I shuddered, crying out.

My orgasm burst, spreading all over my body, and I shook, holding his head to me as he sucked my clit through it.

"Oh, God," I moaned.

But when he stood up and his jeans fell to the floor, I just wanted more from him before he came down on me again.

Pulling away from Will, I climbed up on my knees, coming to the end to the bed where he stood, and wrapped my arms around his neck, kissing him with everything I had.

"I love you," I whispered.

He was hot and hard, his cock like a steel rod poking into my belly, and I inched back on the bed again, falling on all fours and taking him into my mouth.

God, I wanted this. I wanted him on my tongue. I wanted to feel him everywhere.

I sucked him as far as I could, wrapping my hand around the rest of him, and moving up and down slow and tight, I felt his groan and his breathing grow ragged.

He gripped my hair as I licked and sucked, and I left no part of his smooth skin untouched. He started to pump his hips as he held my head, and I could feel myself getting wetter.

I moved to the side. "Will, come here," I said quietly. "Lie down."

He moved down to us, and when he was in position, I held Damon in my hand and threw my leg over Will's body, straddling him in reverse.

"Oh, fuck yeah," he growled, realizing what I was doing and scooted down more to get himself under me.

Back on all fours, I took Damon in my mouth again and got into a rhythm, weaving my hips on top of Will and rubbing our groins together.

I moaned in the back of my throat as Damon filled my mouth and rode Will, pressing down harder and harder on the long ridge of his cock through my panties.

"Winter," Damon breathed out.

I ran my tongue on the underside of his cock, tasting him drip a little and so ready. Will grabbed my hips, working me harder, so stiff and needy, too.

Damon pulled my head up and came down kissing me as I continued to rub on Will.

"Turn around," Damon whispered.

I climbed off Will and started to turn, but then Damon shot Will an order. "Sheet," he said.

Will threw the silk sheet over his groin, and I climbed back on, feeling his thick ridge through the smooth, silky fabric. The bed dipped behind me, and I felt Damon come up on my ass.

Then he grabbed the back of my panties and yanked, the shrill tear of fabric filling the room as he ripped them clean off my body.

He grabbed my jaw, turning my face to speak over my lips. "Head down, ass up."

A shudder rocked through me, and I leaned over Will, arching my back and waiting to feel what I wanted.

Will held my head to his body, his body shuddering underneath me.

Damon spread my legs wider and pressed down on my back to get my ass up higher, and then he crowned me.

Just like in the haunted house.

The head of his cock pushed inside me nice and slow and then slid the rest of the way in, filling me up and touching me deep. Will's cock rubbed against my clit through the sheet underneath me, and I started moving, knowing it was me who knew how to move to give them both what they needed at the same time. I rolled my hips in a figure eight motion, up and over Will's cock and back and up again on Damon. Up and over, back and up. Up and over, back and up.

And when they started moving to meet me in our rhythm and grunting and panting, I knew I was doing it good.

I held myself up on my hands, riding them both, dry humping Will underneath me and backing up on Damon behind me as he fisted my hair. Will leaned up, sucking on my nipples, one after the other, and the room filled with the sounds of us fucking and needing this. Needing the connection.

Damon pushed hard and faster, and so did I, humping Will as I leaned down and kissed his chest. He held me to him as I sucked and nibbled, and in moments, we were nothing but bodies and mouths and hands and aching deep inside.

I came first, crying out and shuddering, the sensations inside me coursing through my clit and making me throw my head back and lose all control of my body. I just knelt there, the orgasm rippling through me as Will came, his body tightening and spilling in the sheet and his hands gripping my hip and breast.

Damon pushed me down, holding my shoulder at my neck, and thrust inside of me, taking me harder and harder as Will held my head to him again to keep me secure.

Damon growled under his breath, his movements fast and wild, and then he came, driving inside of me once real slow and then again, letting it go.

He jerked a few more times and collapsed on my back, damp with sweat and all three of us trying to catch our breath. My eyelids felt heavy, and I swear I could feel their heartbeats against me.

I relaxed into Will's body, feeling Damon behind me, and even though the fear and worry over what happened earlier tonight would return tomorrow, I couldn't think about it if I tried right now.

Right now, I never wanted to leave this room.

It wasn't until the air grew cold and our breathing turned silent, that I peeled myself up off Will, Damon rising, too.

Will tore the spoiled sheet off the bed, and an hour later I could hear his steady breathing as he fell fast asleep on my left side.

Damon spooned me from behind, both of us still awake, but I knew he'd turned off the lights.

I hugged my arms to my chest as Damon held one of his over me, and now that we were all calm, I waited for the guilt to come.

The shame. The worry. The doubt.

But it didn't. At least not yet.

We'd touched and kissed and fell into each other, and I was grateful they were here. Alive and safe.

I didn't want to think.

"I've never let women do that to me," Damon said quietly, breaking the silence.

"Do what?"

"Put their mouths on me," he replied. "Down there."

He didn't let other women use their mouths on him?

"I just never..." he trailed off. "It's not something I..."

He struggled to find the words, but I realized what he was talking about, and I tried to keep the sadness from my voice.

"I know," I told him, saving him from having to say it.

His mother and what she did to him.

He didn't like that, and the reason had to do with her.

"Why did you let me?" I asked, keeping my tone soft.

"I didn't even think about it until it was over," he whispered. "It was like she wasn't here. It was just you."

He sucked in a breath and tightened his arms around me. "I love you," he said.

I immediately broke down, tears springing to my eyes. Happy tears.

He turned me over, slid on top of me, and kissed me as he nestled himself between my legs again.

"I love you," he whispered over my lips again.

I held his face in my hands. *God, I love you.*

And as I sucked in a breath, feeling him push inside of me again, I knew what he was talking about all those days ago. The anger and fury and heat and need—years of it leading to this moment when we finally knew what we were and who we lived for.

Red.

Out of all the colors, I liked red the best.

CHAPTER 31

Winter

PRESENT

Devil's Night.

I woke up, unsure how long I'd been asleep, but I knew it was late when we came to bed. It had to be morning, which meant tonight was the night. Devil's Night.

I felt bodies on my left and right, and a tiny cyclone swirled through my stomach as my hands rested on my belly, and I clutched the T-shirt I wore that Damon had found in one of the drawers in the room last night.

Everything from the night before came flooding back, and even though my cheeks warmed with embarrassment, I couldn't negate how good I felt right here, right now. Every muscle still slumbered, and my mind was at peace, if even just for a few more moments.

Raising my right hand, I reached up and cupped a face, feeling Damon's jaw and straight eyebrows, his nose and warm neck. Raising my other hand, I found Will asleep on his stomach, his soft hair falling over his forehead.

All three of us.

So much pain and disappointment. I was a little bit scared, but I knew they were, too.

I laid there, listening to the silence, knowing we were underground but surprised I couldn't hear much. No footfalls above. No plumbing. It was a pretty solid little fortress down here. I'd never been before they renovated it, but that shower was impressive.

The catacombs.

Damon had said something about hiding something down here, didn't he? In a shallow pool? Or a well?

I wondered if the room he described was still here.

Leaving them asleep, I quietly climbed out of the bed and found my way to the bedroom door.

Where did he say to go?

Something about the bottom of the stairs.

I walked out of the room, knowing the shower was across the hall, and we had come from my right. I didn't think we'd passed any stairs, so I veered left and walked, hearing music playing, so I followed the sound as I trailed down the wall.

You turn left at the bottom of the stairs, he'd said, *and keep going*.

After what seemed like minutes and minutes, my heart racing a little more every step I took away from Damon, the music was loud now, and I held out my hand, feeling an entrance to a stone staircase. I put my foot on the first step, making sure. This must've been the stairwell leading up into the cathedral part of the house.

With my back to the stairs, I turned left, trailing down the hallway, the floor turning from marble to stone and dirt, and the walls less polished and grainier under my fingers. When I felt the draft, I turned right and held out my right hand, brushing the wall and counting the doorways.

Damn, this underground level was big. I wondered what I missed down here in high school, but then again, I was probably happier not knowing.

Reaching the fourth doorway, I stopped and immediately heard the trickle of water he'd told me about. Fear crept in, because I was far away from anyone else in the catacombs, but my heart leaped, too, because I'd found the place he described.

Stepping inside, I swallowed down my nerves, and followed the wall around to where I felt water spilling down the rocks and dribbling into a small pool. Kneeling down, I patted the rocks and stuck my fingers in the water, feeling its icy coolness.

Dipping my hand in, I felt around, touching rocks, until I came to a straight edge with a corner. I grabbed hold of it, recognizing that it was a box of some sort.

I shimmied it out from where it was lodged and set it down on the ground, finding the clasp, and opening it. Carefully, I grazed my hand over whatever was inside to make sure it was nothing sharp.

Finding a plastic bag, I pulled it out and unraveled it, feeling something hard inside. Opening it up, I felt around, fingering what seemed like beads and another small metal object.

Pulling both out, I held them in my hand, examining them.

Right away, I recognized the cross on the rosary.

It was Damon's. The one he wore in high school, and the one he had in the fountain when we were kids.

The other object was metal, with a sharp clasp, and a design on it. A hair barrette.

And then a memory flashed—me taking this out of my hair. Why did I give this to him?

The rosary, the barrette, the fountain...

I bit him.

What?

The memory was so fleeting, but it was vivid and strong. "I'd bitten him that day," I said out loud, realization flooding back. "Before we went to the treehouse. He let me bite him in the fountain. He was glad I did it. Why?"

What were we doing in that fountain? And why was it more important to Damon than what happened afterward in the treehouse?

Leaving the box and bag, I carried the items with me back out in the corridor, retracing my steps.

"Winter?" I heard Rika's voice.

"Hey," I replied, holding out my hand for her.

"Did you get lost?" she asked, coming over for me to take her arm.

But I just shook my head. "Just exploring," I told her. "Would you take me to the bathroom, please?"

"Are you okay?"

"I hope so," I joked.

I had no idea how to answer that, and the way my life had been going, the answer could be different in five minutes. Ask me later.

Right now, though, I just needed another shower. The floors in that part of the catacombs were non-renovated and filthy.

And then there was last night, so...

She walked us both to the spacious bathroom, and I found the vanity chair and lowered myself into the seat.

"Are they still in bed?" she asked, messing with some items in the cabinet.

I opened my mouth to tell her 'yes', but then the nature of her question hit me, and I froze.

Are *they* still in bed? There was more than one bedroom down here, I was sure. Why would I know if Will was still in bed?

Unless...

"You heard," I said, my shoulders slumping a little.

I couldn't catch a break. I'd never had much of a sex life, but when I did, everyone knew everything.

"I heard a little," she said, and I could hear the amusement in her tone.

"Michael, too?"

When she didn't answer, I knew.

Dammit.

"It's okay," she soothed, coming over and dabbing something on my forehead. I hissed at the sting of a cut I didn't realize I had. Must've gotten it in the accident last night.

I frowned. "What you must think."

Every moan and cry that left my mouth last night raced through my head, and I was a little mortified. Private things needed to stay private, because not everyone would understand. I could just see her and Michael coming down to make sure we were okay last night and hearing what they heard. It must've seemed so shallow.

"I'm thinking... I understand," she told me. "And you don't need to explain yourself to me."

I appreciated her manners, but still...

She cleaned my cut, remaining quiet for a moment, and then affixed a Band-Aid to my hairline.

"Our life is a series of plans," she finally said. "Days, weeks, months, years... And then, there are moments. Moments you don't see coming and you don't plan, but everything you need, all the things you want to feel, are in that moment."

I listened to her, letting it sink in.

"People come together, and for a tiny space of time," she went on, "it's beautiful and raw, because you can't think and you don't want to. You just feel." She paused and then continued. "The moments are what we remember."

People come together. So...

"You and Michael and...?"

"Kai," she answered quietly. "Before he was married, of course."

She put the first aid stuff away, refastening a cap and closing the box.

"So believe me when I say I understand," she explained. "Men don't feel ashamed for enjoying sex on their terms. You shouldn't either."

I gave her a little smile, thankful we all had our secrets.

"You have some marks on your neck," she told me. "Just an FYI."

Marks? Like hickeys?

Splendid.

"So have you forgiven him?" she asked.

"Who?"

"Damon."

I thought for a moment and let out a long sigh. Now that was a question.

"Yes," I replied. "No...I don't know. I've been angry for so long. But I love him."

"You just don't know if you can trust him."

"I don't know if I should," I clarified.

Should I entirely?

I wanted to trust him, and there were things I would never doubt.

I knew he'd always come for me. I knew he loved me. I knew that however long this lasted, it would probably be the happiest and most miserable I'd ever been. He made me so angry, I wanted to punch him.

But then there was nothing like kissing him.

I shouldn't forgive him. That was the textbook answer.

But I didn't want to ever be without him, so in reality... There was never a question of forgiving him.

"Will you forgive me?" she suddenly asked.

I pinched my brows together, confused. "For what?"

She fell silent, and I didn't realize I'd been holding my breath until my lungs started to ache.

"I gave Damon the information on your father," she finally said.

My face fell, and I didn't know how to respond. I'd thought Damon was entirely responsible for that, and it was something I'd already gone through the anger for. With Damon and my father.

But knowing she was working with him. That she knew his plans all along and helped him?

"Rika." A stern voice pierced the silence, and I jumped.

Damon. He was across the room, probably in the doorway, and after a moment, I felt Rika leave my side, walking away.

"Call Banks and Kai," he told her in a softer voice. "Get them over here. And can you get her something to eat?" And then he added, "Please?"

"We have breakfast laid out upstairs. I'll bring a plate," she said. "And some clothes."

I kind of wished I didn't have to borrow her clothes now, but I didn't have a choice. Was I angry with her? She gave Damon information that changed my life forever and sent my father on the run.

But then again, the money we lived off of wasn't ours, and my father wasn't a good man.

One way or another Damon would've gotten what he wanted. I just didn't like that more people than just him were in on it. It made me feel like a pawn in a scheme much grander than I knew. Powerless.

And their families weren't exactly saintly, either, so what right did they have to take mine down?

Damon came over and cupped my face with one hand. I didn't pull away, but I shifted in my seat, not really in the mood.

He knelt down, coming down to my level. "If you don't hate me, don't hate her," he said. "I had info she needed, and she had what I needed. She regretted giving it to me almost immediately."

I knew he was right. I shouldn't hold her to a different standard than I held him.

I'd just already processed my anger with him, and this brought that up again.

He picked up the objects in my hand, and I blinked, remembering I was holding them.

"Why were they here?" I asked.

He didn't answer immediately, but then told me, "They were safe here, I guess. I didn't want to leave them at my house when I knew I was going to jail."

Jail.

For three years.

And I'd been sent back to Montreal to escape the storm and chaos that raged over the town when he, Will, and Kai were sentenced, and to run away from the taunts and whispers of everyone who thought I was a slut.

He lied to me. He shouldn't have done it, and he paid the price.

But there was so much more than that between us. Buried in the cracks of all the broken things, where the words were always true and days were too long without him.

When no one else could make the world look like he could, and even after years, in the quiet parts of my mind, I missed the feel of his eyes on me.

Maybe on those nights, sneaking into my house and taking me on adventures, was the real Damon Torrance.

I dipped my forehead to his and took my barrette back, clasping it in my hair.

"I need a shower." I grinned. "Step into my fountain?"

I heard him exhale a laugh, and then he stood up, pulling me into his arms.

CHAPTER 32

Damon

PRESENT

"Ugh, what the fuck?" I said, wincing as I sucked a drag off my cigarette and watched Banks clean my wound.

It felt like I'd been stuck with a red-hot poker.

She sat in a chair in front of me, eye level with the stitches and shaking her head. "What the hell did you do to this?"

"Lots," Will chuckled, coming into Michael and Rika's luxury kitchen and rounding the massive marble island.

Just as I thought, they completely douched up the place. I couldn't bring myself to look at the rest of the house after I'd come upstairs.

Banks dabbed at the blood from the torn stitch, and I just hoped nothing inside was torn as a tiny wave of nausea rolled through my stomach.

But thankfully, it quickly left.

Will came around to Winter's side, who sat at the island facing me, and lowered his head next to hers, whispering in her ear.

"Get the fuck off," I told him.

He could talk to her. Just not like that.

He looked up at me and laughed, but threw his hands up and backed off.

Nothing had changed. He'd remember that.

"You're going to need to go to the hospital again, Damon," Banks spoke up.

"Fuck that." I blew out smoke. "Just butterfly bandage it."

"Are you kidding?" she blurted out.

Rika blew through, carrying a small duffel bag and wearing a black suit with her hair teased and wild. She plucked the cigarette out of my mouth, quickly looking around for Michael before she took a drag.

But pain suddenly sliced through me, and I hissed, "Shit, Banks."

She just shook her head, and I barely noticed as Rika stuck the cigarette back between my lips.

I blew a few breaths, using what nails I had to dig into my skin around the wound and detract at least a little of the pain.

I swallowed, looking at Rika who unzipped her bag and started adding shit to it.

"We need guns," I told her.

She didn't look at me, only grabbed something out of her bag and slammed it down on the counter next to me.

I looked down at it, arching a brow. "That's not a gun."

It was the dagger we gave her two years ago as a threat. Coincidentally, the same one she stabbed me with then, too, not very far from the wound I had now. Her cut wasn't as deep, though.

"It's our way," she answered, still focused on her task.

"Our way?"

What the hell did that mean?

She zipped up her bag and fixed me with a hard stare. "If you want this town, we are not leading by creating a massacre in the streets," she bit out. "They won't fear us because we're armed. They'll fear us because we never fail."

And she grabbed the bag and stalked off, head held high and shit.

I snorted. "Madame Mayor..."

"Shut up," she fired back.

But Michael caught her, wrapped her in his arms, and led her off himself, smiling back at me. "I knew she'd warm to the idea."

Yeah. We had her. Definitely.

Banks cut two-inch pieces of first aid tape, slicing off triangles to make the butterflies and started fixing them to the incision, keeping the skin together until I could get back to the hospital.

"What are you guys going to do?" Winter asked.

"You mean, what are *we* going to do?" I teased back.

She was coming tonight. We were ending this once and for all.

She shrugged. "I can stay here with Mr. Crane," she said. "I'll just slow you down."

I narrowed my eyes, looking at her. She was beautiful in a tight black turtleneck and black pants, her hair loose and shining down her back, and Rika had even helped with her makeup. She was ready. Why did she think she wasn't coming all of a sudden?

I'll just slow you down.

I pulled away from Banks and headed around the island to where Winter sat. Leaning over the corner, I took her under her arms and lifted her off the seat slowly, bringing us nose to nose.

She tried to face away, but I followed her.

"I'm not in a rush," I whispered.

Her mouth twisted to the side, like she was trying not to get upset.

"I don't want you to worry about me," she admitted. "You need to focus tonight."

I stared at her, thinking about all the times that would come up over the years ahead where she would think we'd move faster without her. Have more fun without her. Get to enjoy the full extent of an adventure without her.

Have more freedom without her hanging on.

I wasn't living like that. I wouldn't let her live like that.

"That's not how we're doing things," I said. "That's not your life anymore."

The corner of her lip twitched, like she might tear up, but she didn't.

If I ever thought I couldn't do something with her, then I wasn't doing it at all.

"Your place is at my side," I told her. "Say it."

She whispered, "My place is at your side."

"Louder." I shook her gently, but my tone was firm. "My woman doesn't ask permission. She's a force. Say it louder."

Her chin started to tremble, but her voice burst out strong. "My place is at your side."

And I kissed her, making sure she fucking believed it. She was always wanted.

I set her back down, a little smile peeking out of her now, and Alex strolled in, carrying something and plopping it down on the island in front of me.

It was a black suit with a white shirt and black necktie. Kind of like Rika's.

There were gloves and shoes, too.

I looked to Alex.

"It's a party, after all," she said.

And then she put my mask on top.

I laughed a little. The irony wasn't lost on me.

We weren't boys in hoodies anymore, I guess. It was time to reintroduce ourselves to Thunder Bay.

A half hour later, I tightened my tie and pulled on my black, leather gloves, heading out the front door to one of the motorbikes Michael had waiting. I had no idea if he owned all of them or what, but the village wouldn't accommodate our cars tonight, so bikes, it was.

I checked the dagger in my breast pocket, making sure it was tucked tight, and mounted the motorcycle next to Michael's. I wasn't sure why I brought the knife, but we had a history. Why not?

"Get on, girl," I heard Will say. "Come on."

I looked over my shoulder, spotting Alex grinning and shaking her head as she swung over the bike, sitting behind him.

Kai and Banks took the fourth motorcycle, while Lev and David backed us up in Michael's G-Class.

Rika and Winter came out, Winter holding Rika's arm as she led her over to me. I took Winter's hand as she felt for the seat with the other one.

I smiled. She wore a blindfold of sheer red fabric. I could still see her eyes, but it was the perfect mask, because it didn't hinder her other senses that she used to see the world.

"You know what you gotta do?" I asked.

She climbed on, wearing a small backpack. "Just tell me when."

She wrapped her arms around my waist, and I unhooked my mask from my wrist, pulling it over the top of my head.

I looked over at Michael, Rika already situated behind him and pulling on her mask. "Your father will be there, too," I warned him.

He laughed to himself, turning on the bike and revving the engine.

"First thing's first," he called out.

We all pulled down our masks, gripped the handles, and took off.

Damn straight.

• • •

It was the perfect setting.

Public space. No kids. Chaos and activity.

It seemed, in the past few years, that absence had made the heart grow fonder, and the town of Thunder Bay decided to institute some Mischief Night activities of their own, apparently lamenting the loss of the horsemen.

Earlier in the evening there was a Halloween parade with a carnival for the kids, but after ten, the curfew went into effect, and anyone under sixteen had to be indoors.

To let the adults play.

Bands set up in a couple pubs, drinks were served on the street, and the entire village square was like one dark, gothic circus with vendors, games, artists, and performers. Decorations hung from everything nailed down, people wore costumes, and masks were heavily encouraged, rumors even of naughtier get-togethers happening privately or by invitation only. The event had even started to attract some people from neighboring towns, too.

It was all very...cute.

Not bad if you wanted to hang out with some friends for a beer, but this wasn't the real Devil's Night. These people wore their black as a costume.

For us, the costume was coming off.

We stopped at the light, the village center ahead, and cast each other a look for any last-minute questions.

Arrive. Distract. Invade.

That was the plan.

I tipped my mask up, looking over my shoulder at Winter.

"You ready?"

"Like a bowling ball," she repeated Rika's instructions for her part tonight.

I felt her move the backpack between us, so she could reach inside easier.

I pulled the mask back down, reached behind and squeezed her thigh, and then revved my engine, joining the others.

The crowd sat ahead, cluttering the tables of cafés and bars on the sidewalks, or loitering in groups around the vendors at the edges of the street, but the road wasn't too packed anymore, the parade having ended hours ago.

"Me Against the Devil" blasted from the sound system in the square as high school and college kids danced and jumped up and down, and we waited only another moment before we shot off, Winter holding me with one arm and getting ready with her other.

We raced into the noise, the high-pitched whir of our engines overtaking every other sound in the square, and people popped their heads up and turned their eyes on what was coming as we raced around the square. Michael and I, carrying Winter and Rika, zoomed around the bend, doing one entire turn around the perimeter of the square, hearing shouts and cheers as we sped and screeched our tires. Kai and Will followed a little slower, checking out The White Crow Tavern as they passed.

The wind rushed us, I clocked the cop cars parked around the square, and Rika pulled out her paint gun, holding it pointed to the sky as Michael took us around the square for another run. The music charged me up, and I gripped the handle bars, speeding ahead.

Ready and... I tapped Winter's right leg twice.

She pulled the ring from a smoke grenade and rolled it out of her right hand just like a bowling ball. It tumbled across the street, green smoke pouring out of it as it hit the curb.

People shouted excitedly as towers of smoke billowed into the air, creating a fog. If there were any kids around, at least, it was non-toxic.

"I did it?" she asked in my ear.

"Perfect."

I wished she could see it. I raced over to the left and screeched to a stop, tapping her left leg as I felt her dig another out already.

She pulled the ring, and rolled one out of her left hand, it falling under a car, purple smoke drifting up out from underneath.

We took off again, and I could hear her laughing as I swerved side to side, firing up the crowd. I noticed the cops watching patiently, wondering how far they were going to let us take this.

I heard a guy from the sidewalk yell. "Paintballs?!"

I looked over to see him with a big red splotch on the chest of his gray sweater.

He pointed, laughing. "I'm gonna get you, Rika! I know that was you!"

I laughed.

We raced, setting off more grenades as Lev and David worked the drones flying overhead, which they'd disguised as reapers with skulls and black robes attached to them as they flew around the square, buzzing people.

We had everyone's attention, the clouds of smoke dusting the air and blurring views.

I tapped her left thigh.

She threw another grenade, pink smoke pouring out of the can.

I sped on, tapping her right leg, and another can rolled, billowing red smoke.

All four corners of the square were covered in clouds of color, Rika punching a couple of paintballs on the brick over her family's store windows.

Banks and Alex, both in their own masks, held their grenades in the air, steaming the smoke behind them.

"All right, just start throwing a few," I called back to Winter. "Make a mess!"

I drove, she threw can after can, draining her supply, and I watched as smoke filled the area, creating a heavy cover to where I had to slow down to see.

She finally took her arm off me, loading one can in each hand and pulling the rings, holding them up in the air.

"Whew!" she screamed, laughing.

We all did a final turn and then raced up to The White Crow Tavern, ending our escapade.

People filtered into the streets, screaming when the drones flew across, and disappeared into the smoke.

I climbed off the bike, lifting my mask.

"Having fun?" I asked her, helping her off.

She tossed the can and moved the pack to her back again. "I don't know." She laughed. "How much does this fun cost?"

"Sticking with me for the rest of your life," I replied, putting my arm around her waist. "That'll suck."

I walked her into the tavern, everyone else following. Once inside, I looked over my shoulder at Kai.

"There were no guards at the door when we drove past," he told me. "He might not be here yet."

He was here. This was an annual get-together and the only time he invited his reputable business associates from out of town to his home. Or as close to his home as he wanted them. My father was methodical about his routine, and his pride wouldn't have allowed him to miss this or cancel it.

"Let's go," I said.

We filtered into the tavern, which wasn't really a tavern anymore. It was a revolutionary-era meeting house with fireplaces, original wood floors in some rooms, and three levels of dining, drinking, and private poker rooms.

The clientele was fancier than outside, which still sat in a mountain of smoke.

Men wore suits and tuxes, while the women wore cocktail dresses and eye masks.

"Spread out," I told them, every single one of us keeping our masks on, as well, blending into the crowd.

We veered, some to the left and some to the right, drifting around the outside of the party. The space was so small, people were packed in here, but we slid in between tables, trying to make out all the guests in the dim candlelight.

I knew he was here. He had to be in the back or on another floor.

But then I spotted him. Dead center of the floor, a spiral staircase winding behind him as he stood with another man and sipped his drink.

He wore his usual black suit but with a white shirt this time and no tie.

Will came over, and I clutched Winter's hand.

"There's too many fucking people," he said.

I nodded. "I thought he'd be in a private dining room." We couldn't do this in public.

"How do we get him alone?" he asked.

I didn't know. I needed to think. I scanned the room, spotting his guards—three standing around the perimeter, and there were probably a couple more outside somewhere.

I knew we'd have to take down the guards, but I assumed it would be on the second or third floor. Less people. Less witnesses. If we started shit here, the cops would be inside in seconds.

"You get everyone else to leave," Winter finally answered for me.

I looked down at her.

"How do we do that?" Will asked.

She pulled off her backpack and dug out a couple remaining smoke grenades.

"For once, everyone will be on an even keel with me," she joked.

Meaning they'd be stumbling around blind in here. I smiled, taking them and giving them to Will.

"Man-to-man," I told him.

He walked off, passing on the basketball defense strategy to the others to cover a guard when the shit hit.

I took off my mask, smoothing my hair and straightening my suit.

"Cover the door," I mouthed to Lev who'd just walked in.

I briefly considered leaving Winter there for the moment, not wanting my father to see her, but that left her vulnerable to any of his men if they got to her.

I took her with me and walked over to my father, keeping her behind me.

Taking a drink off a tray, I approached, the man he was talking to seeing Gabriel's eyes lock on me and taking the hint.

He excused himself, and I walked slowly over.

Gabriel regarded me and then the people around us, probably wondering where I thought I could take this. "What do you want?" he asked.

I stepped forward, stopping at his side and taking a sip of my drink.

"Thunder Bay," I replied in a low voice.

"You can have so much more."

"Leave," I ordered, ignoring him. "Or I will make you leave."

He just laughed and sipped his drink. "It would take a lot more than that to bring me down." And then he looked at me, his long face adorned with a smirk. "You're still a shit kid. Always tough with everyone but me."

Winter gripped my jacket behind me, and I felt her forehead touch my back, reminding me that she was here.

But I stared at him, knowing he was right. Even when I finally started opening my mouth and talking to people as a kid, beating down whatever tried to beat me down, hurting others so I wouldn't hurt, he was the one I feared, because I needed him. How much worse would it have been for me without his money and influence to protect me?

At a certain point, I started wondering—did I behave the way I did because I could? Or did I behave the way I did because it was the only thing keeping me alive in that house? Because eleven-year-olds shouldn't be thinking about how to end their lives.

Commotion started filling the room as I held his eyes, and I knew without a doubt—with my friends back and Winter with me—that nothing he could threaten me with would change my course of action. I didn't need him, his money, or his protection. I just wanted him gone.

Away from this town and away from us.

And if he didn't leave willingly, I would not hesitate to use that little flash drive to send him away. It might not take him down, but I wouldn't feel badly about trying.

Blue smoke drifted up around us, and I heard people start to exclaim as the room filled, the two cans Will covertly dumped pouring thick clouds into the small, tight space.

Our gazes stayed locked, guests shuffling and moving about, trying to get away from the mountains of smoke as they coughed and worried about staining their dresses.

A small smile curled his lips because he knew what was happening and I followed suit, smirking back.

The smoke consumed the entire room, like a cigarette in a jar, breezing between us, and suddenly, everyone moved, heading for the doors and running to get away from the polluted, closed space.

But just then, I lurched forward, someone crashing into Winter who fell into me, and I whipped around, seeing her fall to the ground, lost in the smoke.

Shooting down, I reached for her and pulled her back up as someone ran past, their knee knocking her in the head.

"You okay?" I put her on her feet and held her face.

She nodded, a little shaken. "Yeah."

I looked around the room, trying to see if Will and everyone got to the guards and if Lev was still covering the door, but I couldn't see shit.

I turned back to my father, but it was suddenly empty air. He was gone.

Taking Winter's hand, I moved us through the crowd, finding Lev still positioned at the door as everyone poured out.

He lifted his mask up halfway. "He didn't come through," he told me.

I spun around, heading for the rear exit, but I heard a clank above me, and I peered up the narrow, spiral staircase and saw two men dressed in black climbing the stairs.

"He's going up the stairs," I shouted back to Lev. "Stay there!"

Heading toward the staircase, I put Winter's hand on the rail. "Lots of steep steps."

She gripped the rail and found the first step. "I got it."

"You sure?"

"Go!" she barked.

And I didn't need to be told twice. Running up the stairs, I glanced at Winter behind me, seeing her hold the railing tightly and jog up the steps as I held her other hand.

I tried to see up the staircase, but the smoke had filtered up there, clouding everything, and I had no idea where he went. He couldn't leave. We needed to keep this in a public place, and I didn't want him to have any time to regroup or dig in.

We reached the top of the stairs, Winter vaulting into my back, and I reached around, grabbing her thigh.

"Shhh..." I said.

I looked down the long hallway, seeing multiple rooms. He didn't own this building. Only hosted here. He wouldn't have back-up or anything tucked here, would he?

Will raced up behind us, coming to my side, and Michael, Alex, Rika, Banks, and Kai quickly followed.

"He's in one of them," I told them.

We started down the hallway, but Winter pulled me back.

"Wait," she blurted out. "He wouldn't box himself in. Is there a fire escape?"

Will and I exchanged a look.

"The roof," he said.

I gritted my teeth and leaned over the railing, calling down to Lev.

"Go outside," I yelled. "Guard the fire escape!"

"Okay!" His voice carried up.

I put Winter's hand on my arm and ordered her, "Stay behind me."

She nodded, and I bolted, everyone following as I took the small, dark staircase to the left.

"Steps," I warned her.

She reached out for the railing, breathing hard, trying to keep up, but as soon as she found the first one, she made like a demon and climbed like her legs were on fire.

We darted up the staircase, pushed through the doors, all of us spilling onto the roof, and I looked up, immediately spotting my father with one of his men heading for the edge and the fire escape.

They whipped around, the guard reaching for his weapon, but all of a sudden, something flew past us through the air and slammed right into his forehead, making his neck snap back, his knees give out, and his body crumple to the floor of the roof.

What the hell?

A dagger clanked to the ground next to him, the butt of it must've knocked him out.

I looked over at Rika. She stood in a lunging position with her arm outstretched.

Then she stood up, straightening and breathing hard.

Yeah, okay.

My father looked at his man on the ground, inhaling long and deep as he assessed his current situation.

Then he turned his eyes on me.

"You won't do what it takes," he said, the glow of the town's lanterns and the trees from the park behind him.

Smoke still painted the air.

I took Winter's hand off my jacket, touched her face, and pulled away, approaching him as everyone else stayed back.

"I did once," I said, thinking of my mother. "Did you really think she's just been lying on a beach this entire time?"

He thinned his eyes on me and cocked his head, almost looking impressed. He must've suspected my mother was dead. She hadn't surfaced in years.

And he knew that if she didn't stay away and leave me alone that I'd make her leave me alone.

"You let it happen," I bit out, stepping forward again and then stopping. "You let her do those things to me."

"Spare me your whines," he retorted. "A little pussy is what every growing boy needs."

I glared at him.

"So what did you do with her?" he asked. "Where is she?"

You mean, where's the body?

I held his gaze and reached into my breast pocket, pulling out the dagger tucked there.

His eyes darted to it and then up to me as I fisted the handle.

"Close," I taunted.

I tightened my grip, the leather of my gloves gritting together.

"You won't," he told me. "You can't."

You know I can. And I would.

"Leave," I muttered.

But his eyes glanced behind me. "Is she pregnant with my grandchild yet?" he asked, looking Winter up and down. "As long as that blindness isn't genetic, breed with her as much as you want. I expected bastards from you at some point."

I shot forward.

"I wouldn't lose control if I were you," he said quickly. "You have to keep me alive. How else will I change my will to include you again?"

And I stopped.

Amusement crinkled his eyes as he waited for me to process.

I didn't care about the fucking money.

But if not me, then who?

"Banks is more of a son than you ever were," he went on. "I really should've known better. That kid was born in the gutter. Strength comes from trial. You only ever indulged. You get that weakness from your mother."

I looked behind me at my sister who had removed her mask. She looked at me, concerned.

"Banks…" I said under my breath.

"Is my sole heir," he finished. "I changed my will last year. She's responsible, hard-working, and intelligent. She won't drive my life's work into the ground. If you're good and get back in line, I'll change it back."

Something about what he said made anger knot in my stomach again. Like I still hated that he didn't think I was good enough.

"It's kind of ironic, actually," he went on. "That I put all of my faith and energy into you for so long, believing a daughter could never be what a son could be, and as of right now, it looks like your sisters will be the ones with the real power in Thunder Bay. Not you."

Sisters?

I looked at him, confused, as a slow, vile grin spread across his fucking face.

What the hell was he talking about?

I only had one sister.

CHAPTER 33

Damon

PRESENT

"They are exquisite, aren't they?" my father asked, peering around me at whoever was standing there. "I'm not even unhappy about it. I can't wait to see what they do."

Slowly, I turned, looking over my shoulder, but something told me I already knew who he was referring to. I always knew.

I spotted Rika and Banks standing there, watching us and looking at me questioningly.

I closed my eyes, my heart thumping so hard. *Motherfucker*.

"Sisters..." I repeated, turning back around.

"It was also ironic that I could get any woman so easily pregnant, except my own wife." Gabriel pulled out a cigar from his breast pocket. "Christiane was beautiful, though. I didn't mean to knock her up, but I knew the kid would be good-looking with genes like that."

I couldn't believe it.

But then again, it made so much sense. The stars finally aligned.

He lit his cigar, the puffs of smoke clouding into the air.

"Rika..." I said in a low voice. "She's yours."

"Oh, I wish," he shot out, smiling to himself. "But no, Erika is a Fane."

What?

Then I don't...

"A few years before her, though," he told me, "Christiane had a son."

And then he looked at me, taking a drag of his cigar and thinning his eyes against the smoke.

A son.

I stopped breathing.

They were my sisters, but Erika wasn't my father's. So that meant...

I bared my teeth. "You're lying."

He broke out into a smile, enjoying every second of this.

It wasn't true.

"Natalya Delova was my mother," I maintained. "I look just like her."

"Be that as it may, you didn't come from her cunt," he said.

I stood there, unable to speak. He had to be lying. There was no way that was happening right under my nose, and I didn't know it.

She wouldn't have... How would I never have known that? She would've spoken to me or done something.

My father's laugh filled the air more than the smoke or the noise below.

I raised my eyes back up to him.

"Schraeder Fane was out of the country for a few months," he explained, "leaving his pretty new wife at home alone." He tipped his chin down at me. "I just couldn't resist having my way with his pretty little bride."

Having his way.

Like I knew he did in rooms of our house, late at night, their cries carrying through the walls.

I stilled as realization hit of how I was conceived. "You raped her."

He laughed and then shrugged. "Whatever."

I did the math in my head. She was young. Still. She was Winter's age when Rika was born. She would've been a teenager when I was born. Eighteen? Nineteen?

My father continued, "When Schraeder came home to a pregnant wife, there was no hiding what I'd done. He was prepared to raise you as his own and leave town with his little family, but I couldn't have that. Real men don't let other men raise their sons."

I glared at him. Like he raised me at all? Intimidating me, smacking me around, and treating me like property?

"So the night you were born, I came and claimed what was mine," he stated. "She screamed and cried. And then spent the next several years depressed and drunk. I really didn't think she'd take it so badly, but...things got a little better for her when Rika came along."

Rika's mother was a mess for a lot of years. I grew up, seeing a barely functioning, pill-popping, alcoholic on the rare occasions she was in public.

It was all his fault. Not her losing her husband or anything else. She'd been barely alive, and Rika barely had a mother.

But she was always nice, wasn't she? Now that I thought about it. Always docile and sweet.

"They ended up staying in Thunder Bay," my father went on. "Probably to be close to you."

No wonder he didn't bat an eyelash when he knew Natalya was coming into my room and what she was doing to me. She wasn't my mother in his eyes.

In his eyes, she was making me a man.

"When you were a teenager," he told me, "I found out she and her husband were planning on telling you the truth as soon as you turned eighteen. So I took care of Schraeder. With a little help, of course."

With Evans Crists' help. Michael's father.

Since he had Power of Attorney over the estate and Christiane was all too happy and drugged-out to care, Evans saw his opportunity to control another fortune. The largest fortune in town.

I glanced back at Rika, seeing her brow furrowed as she probably wondered what we were talking about. None of my friends could hear us.

I dropped my eyes to the scar on her neck.

"Didn't expect Rika to be in the car that day, but..." my father trailed off. "And then the town doctor provided Christiane with a nice little cocktail to keep her docile for the rest of her miserable little life."

He stepped up to me, but I wanted to back away. The walls were closing in even though we were outside, and I gripped the blade in my hand as full knowledge of what was happening fell like a ton of bricks on my shoulders.

"You never really took notice of Christiane, did you?" he taunted.

But I barely heard him as I got lost in my head.

I could've had a different life. Christiane would've been different. I would've had good parents.

"The way she'd look at you at parties or on the street in town," he went on.

She was looking at me? No, I don't remember that. What was she seeing when she watched me? What was I doing?

My throat closed up, and my hand with the blade shook.

"Her heart was broken long before Rika was born or her husband died," my father droned on.

She wanted me even with what my father did to her? Her husband wanted me anyway?

"She would look at you for so long, completely obvious," Gabriel continued, inching up to me farther and torturing me with what was happening right under my nose, and I never even knew it. "I actually thought she'd be a liability, and I might have to kill her, too."

What if she didn't like what she was seeing? What if that's why she never approached me? What if she saw me growing up and thought I was turning out exactly like him?

What if she was scared of me?

"You honestly never noticed?" he asked, looking at me like I was the dumbest shit on the planet.

Rage filled my chest, my stomach twisted into knots, and every image of him flashed in my head.

Raping her. Destroying her life. Stealing me away as she screamed.

Forcing her to watch another woman raise me a few miles down the road.

Giving me to that house and the horror I had to swallow.

And I looked up at him, clenching my jaw and channeling it all, knowing I would never give him any grandchildren to get his hands on.

"I thought you were so much more perceptive than that," he told me. "But I guess she wasn't very smart, either, so—"

I growled, grabbing him by the shoulder and shoving the goddamn dagger right into his fucking stomach.

My friends gasped behind me, and I heard Banks cry my name, but it was barely a whisper.

He jerked, his mouth falling open as he stood there wide-eyed for the first time in his miserable fucking life, and looking like he couldn't breathe all of a sudden.

I pulled it out and stuck it in again, feeling it dig into his flesh and feeling a chill spread up my angry arm and filter through my blood, the rage cooling just a little.

I pulled it out once again, stared into his eyes, and rammed it into his fucking body, burying it in his stomach one... final...time.

"Just...die," I bit out right in his face. "Die."

He sputtered and rasped, his knees giving out and his body crumbling to the ground as he slid off my knife and collapsed.

Someone sobbed quietly behind me, but everyone else was silent as we watched him spill all over the roof, his white shirt turning crimson as it soaked.

I stared down at him, holding his eyes. Someone approached from behind, but I waved my hand from where it hung at my side, gesturing for them to back the hell off.

The weight in my gut started to dissipate, and I wasn't running.

I wanted to see this.

I wanted to make sure he died.

• • •

"Are you okay?" Winter asked, wrapping her arms around me as I sat with my hands cuffed. "What's going to happen?"

I nuzzled her, burying my face in her neck.

I had no idea. But I wasn't scared anymore. She was safe. My friends were safe. No matter what happened, I had that, at least.

"It'll be okay," I whispered.

Strangely, I felt only tired, not even worried or upset or guilty, like maybe I should be. I was just happy he was gone and happy she was free. It was worth it.

The coroner was putting my father on the gurney, already zipped into a body bag, while the police talked with each other and waited for forensics to arrive.

Kai made sure none of us said anything until we talked to lawyers.

But I was the one found with the knife and the blood on my hand.

I'd be going in.

"Go with Banks and Kai," I told her.

I wanted her out of Thunder Bay tonight. In the city with new air and space.

Away from this shit.

She held in her tears as she kissed me and whispered, "That's not your life anymore. I don't leave."

I couldn't help the smile that broke out as she kissed me again. I wouldn't admit it to her, but that fucking made my night.

Banks pulled her back as the cop yanked me up and started to take me away.

I watched her over my shoulder, praying like hell that wasn't the last time I touched her.

As I passed Rika, our gazes met, and she knew there were things happening she didn't understand. I wasn't supposed to kill him. That wasn't part of the plan.

But she hadn't heard any of the conversation between me and my father.

That shit was for another day.

For now...

"One down," I told her. "The rest is on you."

• • •

Hours later, I'd received medical attention for my wound and a pre-packaged cinnamon roll which still sat unopened on the interrogation room table in front of me.

My eyes burned from exhaustion, and my stomach growled, but I couldn't get the damn roll, because I was handcuffed, and I couldn't reach it. They knew that.

They hadn't tried questioning me yet, though, probably knowing I was smart enough to know my rights.

But they hadn't taken samples of the blood on my hand or had me remove my clothes, either. I was getting curious about what the hell was happening out there, because no one was coming in, and I hadn't gotten my phone call. What if I had to piss?

I rubbed my face on my shoulder and yawned as the fluorescent lighting beat down on me.

Where was Winter? I pictured her in my head, in our bed and sleeping peacefully like I wanted her to be.

But I knew she wasn't. She was awake and frantic, just as tired and worried as I was. It dawned on me after I arrived that, while I was happy she was out of harm's way with my father gone, I still didn't want her walking through this world without me. I didn't want to miss anything.

For that reason, maybe I regretted doing what I did.

The door suddenly opened, and I turned my head, seeing a short, pepper-haired man in a gray suit but still pretty young and fit.

"Hi," he said, stepping aside and allowing the officer in behind him. "I'm Monroe Cason."

The cop came over, and I watched as he uncuffed me and turned away to leave, only to turn back with tight lips and pick up the cinnamon roll, setting it down in front of me.

Huh?

I leaned my forearms on the table, picking up the roll and turning it over in my hands a moment before I flung it at the door just as he was closing it.

Jerk.

I looked up at the dude, cocking an eyebrow. "I didn't call a lawyer," I told him.

He smiled small and shot his eyes up. I followed his gaze, seeing the video camera, and after another moment, the power light went off.

What the hell was going on?

I glanced at him again.

He dug in his briefcase, pulling out something wrapped in plastic. He set it on the table in front of me.

"I can have it taken care of, if you like, but I thought you'd want to see it destroyed yourself," he informed me.

I leaned over the package, making out Rika's dagger inside. Clean and shining new. Maybe particles of blood could still be found on it, though, which was why he suggested it be destroyed?

Why would they let me destroy my murder weapon?

I thinned my eyes on him. "What is this?"

"You're free to go," he said.

My heart leaped. "Why?"

He let out a small breath and placed his case on the table, unbuttoning his jacket and having a seat. Pulling out a paper from his briefcase, he placed it in front of me.

"No one will mourn your father," he told me. "In fact, there are many who are quite happy—and grateful—that he's gone. The testimony is that you and your friends showed up at the parade to celebrate. When you arrived, one of your father's disgruntled employees had done him in, and you found him lying in his blood up on the roof."

I scanned the paper, the testimony written there.

"Everyone has signed it," he informed me as I spotted the signatures.

That was why they hadn't taken samples of the blood on me. Or my clothes.

"His guards...?" I argued.

What about his bodyguards? They knew things.

But he was quick to answer. "They are now on your sister's payroll, as she is the sole heir of your father's estate. She assures me that she has her house under control."

Her house. It was strange to hear, but it had a ring to it.

The cops, though. The blood that was on the dagger. My prints. People might've been happy to see my father go, but they weren't shoving this under the rug out of the goodness of their hearts. There were many who still didn't like me, either. They were rid of my father, so why not let me go to prison for it and be rid of me, too?

"Who's your employer?" I asked, suspicious. "Who's paying you? Who'd pay the city off to look the other way about this?"

He just stared at me, unblinking and then answered, sounding almost serene. "Someone who wants you to have a chance, Mr. Torrance."

And I sat back in my chair, my eyes finally open and knowing the answer without him telling me.

Christiane Fane.

I unlocked the front door, Winter and I stepping inside her house an hour later.

I couldn't believe I was out of there.

I knew the talk in town was probably bad, and I had no idea what the repercussions would be from Evans Crist as he undoubtedly knew that we knew how Rika's father died. How *she* almost died.

But right now, I couldn't bring myself to care. My father had been the bigger threat, and although we weren't all safe yet, I had every confidence people would have a nice, long, fucking pause now before coming at us.

And if they did, we'd be ready.

I ran my fingers through my hair, just wanting a shower and a bed right now, but there was one thing more I had on my mind to deal with before that.

I closed the door and locked it.

"I kind of just want to go sit in the fountain," Winter said lazily, resting her head on my arm as I held her hand and we walked.

"Plenty of time for that," I told her. "I have another idea, though."

"Oh?" She sounded amused like she could only imagine what I wanted to do right now.

But instead of heading up the stairs, I continued down the hall and through the kitchen.

She popped her head up. "Where are we going?"

"You'll see."

I led her outside, across the patio, down beyond the pool and pool house, and past the hedge line, into the trees. We went slow as she navigated her way over the land and fallen branches, but when we got to the large, white oak tree, I picked her up, carrying her over the debris of leaves and wood I hadn't cleaned up yet.

Setting her down, I took her hand and put it on the tree.

She ran her hands over the bark, feeling up and down until she landed on a board nailed into the tree trunk.

She pulled away, straightening her back and her face falling as she understood why I'd brought her out here.

Her chest moved with her shallow breaths, and I could see the fear on her face.

Moving around her, I wrapped my arm around her waist and kissed the back of her hair.

"I'm stronger now," I whispered. "I won't let you fall."

I felt her body shake, but she didn't say anything. Just stood there, going through the shit in her head.

After another moment, she reached out, breathing hard but determined, and felt for the first step with her foot while grabbing hold of the board in front of her.

I watched as she started to climb, taking her time, one step after the other, and I followed, not taking my eyes off her for a moment.

She paused about halfway up, feeling the wind whip across her hair, but she kept going.

Just one more step.

And another.

"Stop there, baby," I told her when she reached the top. I didn't want her hitting her head.

She stayed put as I closed the distance between us, and then I reached above her head, throwing open the door in the floor.

Waving her hand to gauge the width, she climbed through, crawling up onto the floor and standing up carefully as I came through after her.

She stood there for a minute, getting her bearings, but then took a few careful steps, finding the railing. I kept my eye on her feet, making sure she didn't step over. I'd put the boards in the fencing close enough together, we wouldn't fall, but she could still slip and hurt herself.

I walked around, making sure everything was holding well and inspecting the pointed roof to see if any water had seeped through in the last rain. I'd thought about making it a full house, completely enclosed, but maybe that was better for kids. For now, I liked it open on the sides for the wind and the sound of the trees.

"So this is where you've been going?" she said, still facing out. "Not a hundred yards away from me."

I came up behind her. "Never."

All the nights I was away, I was still here.

I held her waist with one hand and leaned on the railing with the other, staring out at the house and thinking about where we were five years ago today.

It was Halloween, and I'd just been arrested.

"How are you?" she asked.

I knew she meant my father. If I was upset.

I still wasn't sure. I was glad he was gone, but I was still trying to figure out what this meant and what the next step was.

The important thing was I wasn't alone anymore, and that made a huge difference. We were going to be fine.

Unfortunately, not as fine as I wanted, though.

"I have no money, no home, a wife, and a probably pregnant girlfriend," I said, trying to tease.

But even I knew the amount of shit that needed to be cleaned up when I woke up tomorrow. I had a lot to do.

She was quiet for a moment, but then said, "I wonder if it's easier to get an annulment if the marriage was never consummated." She let the words hang in the air a minute. "*If* it was never consummated."

I looked down at her, knowing what she was worried about. Did I sleep with Ari...

I reached around and turned her chin toward me. "It's called fraud," I explained. "When you enter into a marriage with no intention of consummating it. I'm way ahead of you, Devil."

An embarrassed little smile tugged at her lips, and I could see her shoulders relaxing.

Marrying Ari got me into the house and put them all under my thumb. It was a means to an end. It didn't take long to face the fact, though, that I could barely tolerate eating a meal with that woman, let alone take her to bed. I knew who I wanted.

She lowered herself onto the floor, dangling her legs over the side just like we did when we were kids.

"Banks won't want the inheritance," she pointed out. "You can contest his will if you want."

I let out a breath and sat down next to her, leaning back on my hands and looking out through the leaves in the tree that hid us from the world.

"Fuck it," I said. "He was right. She'll do better with it than I would have. And I don't want anything of his anyway."

She nodded, but no worry creased her brow. She almost looked happy, and with her hair blowing behind her and those same dark pink lips, she was eight again, and I was eleven, unable to stop looking at her.

She faced out toward the house, and I was glad she seemed to like it up here.

"What do you see?" I asked.

She inhaled a deep breath and then fell slowly back, lying down on the floor with her legs still hanging over the side.

A little smile played across her lips. "I see us spending the night up here."

I came down on her, taking her face in my hands and heading for her mouth.

Hell yeah.

Chapter 34

Damon

Present

Slamming the car door, I clicked the lock and walked around, jogging up onto the sidewalk as I shivered.

It was going to snow soon. I could feel it.

I yanked up the zipper of my pullover and stuffed my hands into my jean pockets as I opened the door to the theater and walked inside. Warmth hit me, and a couple of employees made eye contact, but looked away again when they realized it was me.

I'd been coming every day to drop Winter off and pick her up, so they knew why I was here.

Plus, the whole town knew what really happened at the tavern last week, and even though no one was crying about it, they still moved to the other side of the street when they saw me coming. They put their heads down, stayed out of my path, and answered extra polite with one- or two-word sentences when I ordered food or got gas in my car.

In fact, I'd noticed they were doing the same thing when they saw Will or Rika or Kai, too. All of us, in fact.

It was like the town had a changing of the guard or something and people weren't sure if they should be scared.

I headed past the concessions and the stairs leading to the mezzanine and gallery levels, and opened the double doors, heading into the ground floor of the theater.

Music filled the room, while Winter moved about on stage, sliding and turning, her whole body in every move she made like it was all a single unit instead of individual parts.

I descended the small pathway toward the orchestra section, watching her, the long, gauzy gray costume flowing in layers around her legs and her hair flying around her as she spun and bent backward. There were no words to describe how beautiful she was.

But everyone was soon going to find out. Michael and Rika were sponsoring a small tour for her as an opening dance at other theaters and festivals, and if it went well, we'd go from there. Her twenty-minute show would take a couple more months to get ready, but she was already rehearsing and outlining the performance.

And while it was good, she deserved everything coming to her, and I wouldn't stop anything or do anything to discourage her. I wondered what the hell I was going to do now, too. The only thing I was ever good at was basketball, and that ship had sailed. I didn't have the temperament to work well with others, and I wanted absolutely nothing to do with my father's money or his businesses. Banks had it, so it was staying in the family. That was all I cared about.

I wasn't taking his money, and I wasn't fucking asking my friends for anything. Everything Winter and I built would be ours.

"Damon, are you here?" I heard Winter call out.

I looked up at her, not realizing the music had ended.

"Coming," I told her.

I climbed the few steps off to the side of the stage, and walked over to her, picking her up and wrapping her legs around me like I'd done every day the past week when I picked her up from rehearsal at five.

She smiled down at me, threading her fingers through my hair, and kissed me.

"Lookin' good," I said.

"Yeah, you're prejudiced."

"I don't lie."

She snorted, and I carried her backstage, toward the dressing rooms, so she could get her things.

She started kissing my cheek, leaving little butterflies across my face, to my ear, and down my neck. I wanted to get her home and in the shower with me. Right now.

"How was your day?" she asked, nibbling my ear.

"Fine," I mumbled, enjoying her attention too much to think of more to say.

I'd dropped her off at eleven this morning and went to Kai's house to collect my snakes that Banks had been taking care of, and then I went to my apartment at Delcour and my room at my father's to clear out the rest of my things.

I should've been looking for work, but right now, I just wanted her home before the snow started, and then I'd keep her up all night trying to make a kid we definitely couldn't support yet.

We reached her little dressing room, and I let her down, watching her go pack up her bag and pull out her change of clothes and strip right there. I took the bag, half-tempted to plant her ass on the vanity and go right now, but...it was cold. I'd wait for the hot shower.

"Ready?" she asked, dressed in jeans, flats, and a cable-knit sweater.

Giving her my arm, I led her out of the room, through the backstage area, and out the rear exit and into the alleyway.

"Can I drive?" she teased.

I laughed under my breath. "You know the rules."

Late, dark, and no witnesses.

We walked around the corner of the building, coming to the street, and I dropped her bag in my trunk before unlocking the car. As I opened my door, though, she stopped at hers and spoke to me over the hood.

"You know," she said. "There's stuff in the house we can sell. Art, furniture, rugs...I have some jewelry, too."

"No."

"Damon—"

"I'll handle it," I cut her off but kept my voice as gentle as possible. "I'll get a job. I'll deal with it. Don't worry."

It wasn't that I expected her to do nothing, or that she wasn't a partner in this, but I exposed her father. It was my responsibility to fix this and give her back the life she was used to. A life she deserved.

And it was definitely not okay for me not to be doing something.

I'd find an income. A legit one.

She opened her door, and we both climbed in, Mikhail jumping from where he waited in the passenger's seat to the backseat to make room for Winter.

I ruffled the fur on his head, but my phone rang in the console where I'd left it, and I picked it up, seeing a local number.

"Hello?" I answered.

"Damon Torrance?" a man asked.

"Yes."

"This is Grady MacMiller," he introduced himself. "From Hiberian Bank?"

It sounded vaguely familiar.

"Yes?" I stuck my key in the ignition and started the car.

"Listen," he said. "I know this is going to sound extremely odd, but I have to try. I came by to appraise the Ashby house yesterday while you were gone."

That's why his name was familiar. Banks owned the house now as part of my father's assets. She was trying to get the books in order, and she'd warned me someone was coming by.

It was also a reminder that Winter probably couldn't sell anything inside the house. Banks owned every stitch. I rubbed my eyes in frustration.

"Well, I brought my children with me," he continued. "Unfortunately, the nanny was sick, and my wife has been—"

"Yes?" I interrupted.

Jesus.

"I'm sorry," he said quickly. "Excuse me. Anyway, we saw the treehouse, and the fountain maze, and I inquired with the security at the house, and they told me you're the designer. Is that true?"

"The designer?" I repeated, seeing Winter quietly listening beside me. "I—uh, no. I built them, if that's what you mean. What's this about?"

"Well, my children loved both features," he burst out. "Absolutely adored them. It was like it was Christmas morning. I feel so weird asking, given who your father is—or was—I'm sorry for your loss, sir," he added. "But I have to ask. You wouldn't be willing to build another like it, would you? At my home? For my children?"

"Another what?"

"Treehouse and fountain maze."

I scoffed. "Uh, no. Sorry."

"Oh, I uh…"

"I have to go," I told him, shaking my head.

I hung up, laughing under my breath. For Christ's sake. What was I? Neighborhood dad, around to help with science projects, too? Maybe come by to help you move?

"What was that?" Winter asked.

I dumped my phone back in the console and shifted the car into gear. "Someone liked the shit I built at your house," I replied. "Wanted me to make a treehouse and fountain for their property."

"And you said no?"

"I don't have time for that," I shot back. "I need to get a job and figure out what we're doing." And then I paused, my back straightening and understanding dawning on me. "Ohhhhh."

"Yeah, dumbass!" she screeched.

He was trying to hire me.

To design and build.

It had never occurred to me whether the features I built at Winter's house were any good or not, but I'd had fun planning them out. I was completely focused on the job at hand, and I definitely enjoyed doing something where I could be left alone. To dive into all the little nooks and crannies I still kind of wanted to spend my life hiding in. Only with her now.

I wouldn't mind doing that for work if I could. I just hadn't thought of it. I had a dozen more blueprints of other designs when I was brainstorming the builds.

But...

"I can't work for the people in my own town like I'm a servant."

"Ugh." She rolled her eyes. "First stop Thunder Bay, next stop world domination. How about that?"

Meaning it was a starting point. It could grow into a lot more.

A lot more.

But then I remembered.

"I went to jail for a sex crime," I reminded her. "No one will want me working around their families."

"And I don't think your history has escaped Grady MacMiller's notice, either," she pointed out. "He still wanted to hire you, Damon."

Yeah, I guess so. He knew the nature of the trial. Once I married Winter, people would know it was a lot more complicated than what happened in court.

And then maybe, with word of mouth...

"Dial him back and give me the phone," she told me. "I'll pretend to be your assistant who buffers between the client and the temperamental, asshole artist."

I smiled, hooking my finger in her collar and pulling us together, face to face. "First, a shower."

And I drove off, taking us home as quickly as possible.

• • •

Later that night, long after the sun had set, and I'd left Winter to work on some marketing ideas for the tour with

Alex, I walked up to a front door I'd never knocked on and never thought I would.

There was so much I'd missed over the years, that when I pieced them together now, it all fit like a puzzle.

The ice cream she gave me when I was seven one day on the street, saying they gave her and Rika one too many.

The way she looked at me at graduation, and I wondered why she was even there at all, but then I just thought she showed up as a family friend, because Michael was graduating, too.

The way I heard through the grapevine my senior year that she'd told Rika to stay far away from me when she was an incoming freshman, because she knew we'd be at the same school. I'd thought it was because my reputation preceded me, but it was because she was afraid something would happen between us.

She was right to warn her off. To think how many times I taunted that line with Rika...

Jesus, fuck.

Oh, what the hell. In the long scheme of things, it was just another rung on the ladder of fucked-up shit I'd done that just made our little group a little more interesting. We'd get over it.

Ringing the doorbell, I slid a hand in my pants pocket, dressed in a black suit and black shirt, because it wasn't Winter's Damon I needed to be tonight.

The door opened, and I looked into her eyes, her smile fading and her chest caving deeper and deeper as she breathed.

I stared at her face, seeing it with new eyes and studying her features to try to detect any parts of me. Blonde hair, same as Rika's, in a stylish, messy bun with strands of hair around her face. Thin, toned body—much healthier than a couple years ago when she was hopped up on pills and alcohol.

She wore a slender pair of black pants, a black, sleeveless blouse, and her makeup made her look so much younger than her mid-forties.

I didn't see much of me, though. Or maybe my pulse was thundering in my ears so hard, I was just too impatient and distracted to think straight.

"Is it true?" I demanded.

She dropped her hand from the knob and stood there, as if in a trance.

"Is what true?" I heard someone say.

Rika came out from somewhere behind her mother, her fingers threaded through the handle of a coffee cup and looking at me.

They, on the other hand, looked a lot alike.

When no one said anything, her gaze shifted to her mother. "Mom?"

But Christiane's eyes dropped, her lips trembled, and she knew it was over. There was no hiding this anymore.

"My grandfather would tell a story..." she finally said, still carrying a hint of her Afrikaner accent, "about an ancestor from Persia. Centuries ago. A woman named Mahin." Her solemn eyes rose, meeting mine. "He said that's where he got his black hair and raven eyes."

My black hair and raven eyes.

"And he said," she continued, "every few generations she shows herself again."

Liquid heat charged through my blood, and I was so angry, but I wasn't sure I should be, and even if I shouldn't be, I wanted to be, because there had to be someone else I could take this out on.

How could anyone be that weak?

I tried to understand her position. My father was a dangerous man, and I knew he threatened her, killed her husband, and no doubt, threatened to hurt Rika, but...

How do you live like that? In this town, under his fucking nose, knowing your kid is a mile away, living every day without you? How do you not snatch him off the street when he was five or eight or eleven, and just run?

Schraeder Fane was wealthy. They had resources. Did she have any idea what that house was like for me?

But then I realized, too, if I hadn't grown up in Gabriel's house, I would never have been there for Banks.

Still, though...

Rika looked between us, a confused pinch to her brow.

"It was you at the hospital," I said to Christiane, remembering the voice and the comforting touch of her hands on my face.

Tears welled in her eyes, and she sucked in a breath. She took a step toward me, but I backed away, keeping her at a distance.

"I have no use for a mother," I warned. "Not anymore." And then I gestured to Rika. "But I have plenty of use for her. This changes nothing, just don't come between her and me."

"What the hell is he talking about?" she asked her mom, concern hardening her voice. And then she turned to me, "Damon?"

I broke eye contact with Christiane—done with fucking parents—and locked eyes with Rika. "I told you you'd never escape me," I reminded her. "I always felt it."

She glanced at her mother, worry written all over her face. "Mom? Please? What is it? What's going on?"

I started to back away, toward my car, but still looking at Rika. "We're going to rule the world, Rika." I held out my hands, grinning. "You, Banks, and me."

I spun around and headed for my car, hearing Rika beg her mother to snap out of it.

But to no avail.

I drove off, Christiane Fane still standing in the doorway watching me.

That was all she ever did.

And hopefully she knew better than to try for more. She wasn't welcome now that my father was dead and out of her way.

I didn't respond well to bad parents. She'd do well to remember that.

EPILOGUE

Damon

I pulled my phone off the charger and held it up, the light hurting my tired eyes as I looked at all the notifications that had slowly woken me up over the last half hour.

Fuckin' Will.

Missed calls, texts, pictures... He was having the time of his life in Rio.

Or Cartagena. I forgot.

Him on the beach. Him with what's-her-name. Him in the sun and sand, not freezing his ass off back here in Thunder Bay in January. Eating good food and laughing.

In the nearly three months since Devil's Night, we'd gotten him clean but not dry, and as Kai, Michael, and I settled into the holidays, our homes, our women, and our work, he broke away and did some traveling. He said he needed a change of scenery, but he'd been gone a while, and although the pictures looked great, and he looked happy, I knew he was spinning and spinning until he eventually lost his balance and fell.

And, at twenty-four, his family would only tolerate the self-destruction for so much longer before they cut him off and made him come home.

Throwing the sheet off, I grabbed some sleep pants and pulled them on, dialing Will.

No answer, though. I sent a text, letting him know I was awake, and he could call.

Walking over to the floor-to-ceiling window, I peered out at the master bedroom balcony, taking in the blanket of fresh snow falling, making it look like cake frosting on the stone railing as the wind howled outside, making the trees creak.

Picking up the cigarettes on the table, I pulled one out and slid it under my nose, smelling the tobacco and cloves. My lips burned, and I stuck it in my mouth, rolling it and feeling the comfort of its feel already.

Winter was trying to get me to quit. It was a non-option for much of the argument. I wasn't a *non-smoker*.

But then she mentioned kids and it being on my clothes and how secondhand smoke kills, and do I really want the baby to smell like shit?

Ah, fuck it.

I walked over to the French doors, picking up my lighter off the table, and sparking it up as I put on my shoes and opened the door to go out, but then I heard her sleepy voice from across the room.

"Hey," she said from the bed. "Anything wrong?"

I growled silently, tearing the cigarette out of my mouth and crushing it in my fist.

Dammit. She would've smelled it on me when I came in, but at least I would've gotten a smoke in.

I tossed the lighter and broken cigarette on the bureau, kicking off my shoes and heading over to her.

"Everything's fine," I soothed, sitting on the bed and leaning down to kiss her.

"You were trying to smoke, weren't you?" she said, sitting up.

I sighed, setting my phone back on the bedside table. "I'm dying here, babe."

She snorted. "You don't have to quit," she told me. "I'm not going to leave you over it. It's just healthier."

Then she climbed up on me, straddling me as I sat on the side of the bed.

"I know." I ran the backs of my knuckles under her V-neck, over her stomach, touching the soft skin that still wasn't showing signs that there was a kid in there.

She was only about eight weeks along, and with all the dancing, she was working off a lot of what she ate, and I worried the baby wasn't getting enough, so everyone was feeding her all the time now. Thankfully, her tour was short, and she only had a few more performances before a nice, long break.

We'd gone 'round about putting herself in danger and the kid in danger with the shows, but she was determined to assure me she could finish it and be safe.

Things had gone well for her the past couple of months, and she already had more projects lined up for after the baby was born.

I tried to be at every performance—no matter where—but after the work I did for Grady MacMiller, jobs started coming in, and I had to work. A couple of families sent me to their summer houses down south to build things, and I was busy planning out more projects already booked for spring and summer.

I made sure either Rika, Banks, or Alex was with her if she had to go out of town overnight for a performance that I couldn't attend.

And although I was paying the bills and building us a future, I did relent when Banks gave the house back to Winter, including ownership of everything in it. Banks advised Winter to keep it solely in her name, though, so she could kick me out whenever she wanted.

They laughed about that one.

And Banks also honored my father's deal with Margot and Ari for a nice settlement, even though the marriage didn't make it a year and was now annulled. They'd moved into the city, Ari refusing to ever be in the same room with me again.

Somehow I'd find the strength to go on living.

And we still hadn't heard anything about her father. I hoped it stayed that way.

Winter planted her forehead on mine, gliding her fingers down my arms.

"It's snowing," she whispered.

"How'd you know that?"

We weren't outside. She couldn't feel it.

"I can hear it," she said. "Listen."

We sat there, so still and quiet, and I closed my eyes, trying to see the world how she did. I inhaled, smelling the cold air, but the silence rang in my ears, and I couldn't hear it at first.

But then I picked up a hint.

"On the glass," I told her.

She nodded, smiling. "I love that sound. Like the world is asleep."

It looked like it, too, remembering the blanket of white over everything outside. How water kind of had a habit of quieting the world around me my entire life, and in one form or another, I sought it out and reveled in hiding behind it.

Looking over her shoulder, out the window, the snow fell, charging the air with a little more beauty, the animation making the Earth look alive even when everything else was still. A little more pretty. A little more peaceful. A little more cover.

She always got that about me. She felt it, too.

Even when we were kids, she knew.

I sit in the fountain, the water spilling over the sides from the bowl above, down around me, and hiding me from her.

My finger stings, dripping with blood where I'd sliced myself on a thorn as I ran through the maze, but I don't dare make a sound or even breathe.

She's searching for me, and I just want to be left alone. My chin trembles. Just leave me alone.

Please.

"Hello, sweetheart," she says, having bumped into a little girl. "Are you having fun?"

I close my eyes, imagining I'm far away. In a cave. Or out at sea. Anywhere away from here. I rub the little scratches on my wrist that I'd put there yesterday, trying to see if I had the balls to do it. Maybe I won't do it. Maybe I will. If I did, I wouldn't have to stay here with them. I wouldn't have to live here. It would be over.

"Have you seen my son?" *I hear her say, and I open my eyes, my hair and tears blurring my vision.* "He loves parties, and I don't want him to miss this."

I don't like parties. My knee shakes uncontrollably. I don't like anything.

"No," *the little one says.*

But I see her staring at me through the water, and I wait, terrified she'll tell my mother I'm here.

Don't, please.

My mother finally leaves, and the little girl moves toward the fountain, checking behind her to see if anyone is still there.

Approaching, she calls my name. "Damon?"

She can leave, too, for all I care. I want to be alone.

"Are you okay?" *she asks.*

Just fucking go. I don't want to talk. I won't say the right thing, and I don't want to answer questions. Just leave.

"Why are you sitting in there?" *She peers through the spills of water, and I shiver, the cold seeping through my clothes.* "Can I come in, too?"

I notice she wears a tutu—everything white—and her hair is twisted into a tidy little bun. She's younger than me, clearly one of the students from my mother's school. Winter, I think? She's been here before, and I was in the same grade as her sister.

"I see you at Cathedral sometimes," she tells me. "You never take the bread, do you? When the whole row goes to receive communion, you stay sitting there. All by yourself."

The nanny takes me every week—my parents making me attend but never bothering themselves. It's the one thing that bitch lets me fight her on, too. It all felt so fake, like the makeup women put over their bruises to hide what's happening to them. It's an act.

"I have my first communion soon," she says. "I'm supposed to have it, I mean. You have to go to confession first, and I don't like that part."

My lips twitch, my anger fading just a little.

I don't like that part, either. It never stops me from making the same mistakes. It seems weird to receive forgiveness for repeatedly doing things I know are wrong but I'm not sorry for.

"Do you want me to go?" she finally asks when I don't say anything. "I'll go if you want."

I sit there, not as frustrated as I was a moment ago. I've even forgotten about the pain in my hand and my parents for a minute.

"I just don't like it out there very much," she explains. "My stupid sister ruins everything."

I feel like I understand. I don't like it out there very much, either. We can hide.

Together.

If she wants.

"I'll go," she tells me and starts to turn.

But I reach my hand through the water, inviting her in instead.

She stops, seeing me, and turns back around. Her eyes light up, and there's almost no waiting. She takes my hand and steps in.

The water splashes, and she sucks in a breath as the cold water hits her. She giggles as she comes to sit down next to me.

"Wow, this is cool," she says, looking around at the space, the shade of the bowl over us and the water spilling around.

I notice her white ballet slippers in the water as she hugs her knees to her chest, and everything on her is so small.

"What happened to your hand?"

I look at it, turning it over and rinsing off the blood in the water and wiping it on my jacket.

"Does it hurt?" she asks.

I still don't speak. But yeah, it hurts a little.

"My dad taught me something cool. Wanna see?"

Her voice is so...relaxed. Like she doesn't know how awful things can be.

"It'll help get rid of the pain," she informs me. "Let me show you."

She takes my hand, and I try to pull it back for a second, but then I stop and let her have it.

She holds it up in front of her. "Ready?"

Ready for what?

She finds the cut on the inside of my index finger, toward the knuckle, but puts her teeth on the other side of the finger, pressing down enough to stretch the skin but not break it.

Her eyes meet mine, and that's how she stays for several seconds, increasing the pressure just a little.

It doesn't hurt, though. Not at all. It actually feels kind of good, because the annoying sting of the cut is suddenly gone. Just gone. Like a kill switch.

She stops biting, explaining it to me. "He told me if you're hurt in more than one place, your brain only registers one pain at a time. Usually the stronger one. I had a hangnail one day, and it really hurt, so you know what he did? He bit my finger. It was so weird, but it worked. I didn't feel the other pain anymore."

One pain at a time. So if something hurts, you can make it hurt less by adding more pain?

The sting starts to return but not as strong, the feel of her bite still lingering.

She does it again, and again, the sting disappears.

"Is that okay?" she asks. "Better?"

I want to smile, and I think I do a little as I nod.

Amazing. I wonder if the cut were deeper, would I have to bite harder? And does it have to be biting? Can I do something else to make the pain go away?

She releases my hand and smiles up at me. "It doesn't make me happy like Oreos in ice cream, but it's relief."

Oreos in ice cream, huh? Yeah, I like that, too.

We sit there for a while, enjoying the noise of the waterfalls, the maze falling quiet and the lightning bugs starting to spark up around the hedges. The music and party and nothing else exist except our little hideaway.

"I wish we didn't have to leave the fountain," she says.

We don't. Not yet anyway. Let them come find us.

"Why do you wear the rosary?" she asks.

I follow her gaze, looking down and seeing the wooden beads peeking out from under my shirt where they're caught on my collar.

"They get mad when kids wear it like a necklace, you know?" she points out.

A laugh escapes me, and I can't help it. I swallow. "I know."

That's why I do it. They give the girls white ones and the boys wooden ones for first communions. Father Behr was really mad when some of us put them around our necks.

When I found out how wrong it was, I started wearing it like that all the time.

There isn't much I can do to fight back—at home anyway—so I pick dumb things I can get away with.

I pull it off over my head and hold it over hers, slipping it on.

"Now you're bad, too," I tell her.

She looks down at it, rubbing the cross between her fingers, the silver over the wood.

"You can have it," I say.

She can remember me, then.

"Are you mad I'm here?" she asks all of a sudden.

Do I seem mad?

When I don't answer, she looks up at me.

I shake my head.

"Can I come back again, then?" she presses hopefully.

And I nod.

"Let's do this," she says, taking off the rosary and then unclipping the silver jeweled barrette from her hair.

She takes both and sets them up on the little alcove under the upper bowl, hiding them in the niche there.

"Since it's our secret hiding place," she tells me with an excited look in her eyes. "It's like part of us is always here. In our spot."

I tip my head back against the fountain, looking up at the items that claim our nook, and I smile. She's nice. I like how she talks to me.

And she likes it here, too.

Winter's mouth hovered over mine, our lips teasing each other as I pulled the white V-neck over her head and dropped it to the bed.

Her chest rose against mine, and she all but begged my name, "Damon."

I kissed her slow and soft, her hands torturing me with featherlight touches and her body so warm I was drunk on it.

"Damon," she breathed, tipping her head back and letting me taunt and nibble her neck.

"Shhh," I teased in a whisper. "Quiet as a mouse."

The snow outside turned to water, and the sounds of it rushed my ears as the fountain fell around us again, lulling me and my body into the only girl who ever really knew me. The only woman who needed who I was and who was all I needed.

I didn't deserve anything I had, but I was doing everything to make sure I'd deserve whatever came. We'd have the family we would make, our friends, and our home, and every fucking night, I'd have her right here, surrounding me and getting lost with me where the rest of the world didn't exist, and it was just us.

Always just us.

I slid inside of her, and she started rolling her hips, taking me in and out as she tipped her head back, and I squeezed her breast and bit her neck.

The snowy, silent night raged outside, our entire world right here, right now.

I wish we never had to leave the fountain.

We never did.

THE END

Thank you for reading Kill Switch!
Please keep reading for a glimpse of Nightfall,
Devil's Night #4.

*This is a preview of *Nightfall,* the fourth and final installment of the Devil's Night series. Enjoy!

Emory

PRESENT

It was faint, but I heard it.

Water. Like I was behind a waterfall, deep inside a cave.

What the hell was that?

I blinked my eyes, stirring from the heaviest sleep I think I've ever had. Jesus, I was tired.

My head rested on the softest pillow, and I moved my arm, brushing my hand over a cool, splendidly plush white comforter.

I rolled my eyes around me, confusion sinking in as I took in myself burrowed comfortably into the middle of a huge bed, my body taking up about as much room as a single M&M inside its package.

This wasn't my bed.

I looked around the lavish bedroom—white, gold, crystal, and mirrors everywhere, palatial in its opulence like I'd never seen in person—and my breathing turned shallow as instant fear took over.

This wasn't my room.

Was I dreaming?

I pushed myself up, my head aching and every muscle tight like I'd been sleeping for a damn week.

I dropped my eyes, taking inventory of my body first. I laid on top of the bed, still fully clothed in my black, skinny pants and a pullover white blouse that I'd dressed in this morning.

If it was still today, anyway.

My shoes were gone, but on instinct I peered over the side of the bed and saw my sneakers sitting there, perfectly positioned on a fancy white carpet with gold filigree.

My pores cooled with sweat as I looked around the unfamiliar bedroom, and my brain wracked with what the hell was going on. Where was I?

I slid off the bed, my legs shaky as I stood up.

I'd been at the studio. Byron and Elise had ordered take-out for lunch, and—I pinched the bridge of my nose, my head pounding—and then...

Ugh, I don't know. What happened?

Spotting a door ahead of me, I didn't even bother to look around the rest of the room or see where the two other doors led. I grabbed my shoes and stumbled for what I guessed was the way out, and stepped into a hallway, the cool marble floor soothing on my bare feet.

I still went down the list in my head, though.

I didn't drink.

I didn't see anyone unusual.

I didn't get any weird phone calls or packages. I didn't...

I tried to swallow a few times, finally generating enough saliva. God, I was thirsty. And—a pang hit my stomach—hungry, too.

"Hello?" I called quietly but immediately regretted it.

Unless I'd had an aneurysm or developed selective amnesia, then I wasn't here willingly.

But if I'd been taken or imprisoned, wouldn't my door have been locked?

Bile stung my throat, every horror movie I'd ever seen playing various scenarios in my head.

Please no cannibals. Please no cannibals.

"Hi," a small, hesitant voice said.

I followed the sound, peering across the hallway, over the bannister, to the other side of the upstairs where another hall of rooms sat. A figure lurked in a dark corridor, slowly stepping into the landing.

"Who is that?" I inched forward just a hair, blinking against the sleep still weighing on my eyes.

It was a man, I thought. Button-down shirt, short hair.

"Taylor," he finally said. "Taylor Dinescu."

Dinescu? As in Dinescu Petroleum Corporation? It couldn't be the same family.

I licked my lips, swallowing again. I really needed to find some water.

"Why am I not locked in my room?" he asked me, coming out of the darkness and stepping into the faint moonlight streaming through the windows.

He cocked his head, his hair disheveled and the tail of his wrinkled Oxford hanging out. "We're not allowed around the women," he said, sounding just as confused as me. "Are you with the doctor? Is he here?"

What the hell was he talking about? *'We're not allowed around the women.'* Did I hear that right? He sounded out of it, like he was on drugs or had been locked in a cell for the past fifteen years.

"Where am I?" I demanded.

He took a step in my direction, and I took one backward, scrambling to get my shoes on as I hopped on one foot.

He closed his eyes, inhaling as he inched closer. "Jesus," he panted. "It's been a while since I smelled that."

Smelled what?

His eyes opened, and I noticed they were a piercing blue, even more striking under his mahogany hair.

"Who are you? Where am I?" I barked.

I didn't recognize this guy.

He slithered closer, almost animalistic in his movements with a predatory look on his face now that made the hairs on my arms stand up.

He looked suddenly alert. *Fuck.*

I searched for some kind of weapon around me.

"The locations change," he said, and I backed up a step for every step toward me he took. "But the name stays the same. Blackchurch."

"What is that?" I asked. "Where are we? Am I still in San Francisco?"

He shrugged. "I can't answer that. We could be in Siberia or ten miles from Disneyland," he replied. "We're the last ones to know. All we know is that it's remote."

"We?"

Who else was here? And where were they?

And where the hell was I, for that matter? What was Blackchurch? How could he not know where he was? What city or state? Or country even?

My God. *Country.* I was in America, right? I had to be.

I felt sick.

But water. I'd heard water when I woke, and I perked my ears, hearing the dull, steady pounding of it around us. Were we near a waterfall?

"There's no one here with you?" he asked as if he couldn't believe that I was really standing here. "You shouldn't be so close to us. They never let the females close to us."

"What females?"

"The nurses, cleaners, staff..." he said. "They come once a month to resupply, but we're confined to our rooms until they leave. Did you get left behind?"

I bared my teeth, losing my patience. Enough with the questions. I had no idea what the hell he was talking about, and my heart was pounding so hard, it hurt. *They never let the females close to us.* My God, why? I retreated toward the staircase, moving backward, so I didn't take my eyes off him, and started to descend as he advanced on me.

"I want to use the phone," I told him. "Where is it?"

He just shook his head, and my heart sank.

"No computers, either," he told me.

I stumbled on the step and had to grab the wall to steady myself. When I looked up, he was there, gazing down at me and his lips twitching with a grin.

"No, no..." I slid down a few more steps.

"Don't worry," he offered. "I just wanted a little sniff. He'll want the first taste."

He? I looked down the stairs, seeing a cannister of umbrellas. Nice and pointy. That'll do.

"We don't get women here." He got closer and closer. "Ones we can touch anyway."

I backed up farther. If I bolted for a weapon, would he be able to grab me? Would he grab me?

"No women, no communication with the world," he went on. "No drugs, liquor, or smokes, either."

"What is Blackchurch?" I asked.

"A prison."

I looked around, noticing the expensive marble floors, the fixtures and carpets, and the fancy, gold accents and statues.

"Nice prison," I mumbled.

Whatever it was now, it clearly used to be someone's home. A mansion or...a castle or something.

"It's off the grid," he sighed. "Where do you think CEOs and senators send their problem children when they need to get rid of them?"

"Senators..." I trailed off, something sparking in my memory.

"Some important people can't have their sons—their heirs—making news by going to jail or rehab or being caught doing their dirty deeds," he explained. "When we become liabilities, we're sent here to cool off. Sometimes for months." And then he sighed. "And some of us for years."

Sons. Heirs.

And then it hit me.

Blackchurch.

No.

No, he had to be lying. This place was an urban legend wealthy men told their kids to keep them in line. A secluded residence somewhere where sons were sent as punishment but given free rein to be at each other's mercy. It was like *Lord of the Flies* but with dinner jackets.

But it didn't exist. Not really. Did it?

"There are more?" I asked. "More of you here?"

A wicked smile spread across his lips, curdling my stomach.

"Oh, several," he crooned. "Grayson will be back with the hunting party tonight."

I stopped dead in my tracks, lightheaded.

No, no, no...

Senators, he'd said.

Grayson.

Shit.

"Grayson?" I muttered, more to myself. "Will Grayson?" He was here?

But Taylor Dinescu, son of Dinescu Petroleum Corporation I now gathered, ignored my question. "We have everything we need to survive, but if we want meat, we have to hunt for it," he explained.

That's what Will—and the *others*—were out doing. Getting meat.

And I didn't know if it was the look on my face or something else, but Taylor started laughing. A vile cackling that curled my fists tight.

"Why are you laughing?" I growled.

"Because no one knows you're here, do they?" he taunted, sounding delighted. "And whoever does, meant to leave you anyway. It'll be a month before another resupply team shows up."

I closed my eyes for a split-second, his meaning clear.

"A whole month," he mused.

His eyes fell down my body, and I absorbed the full implication of my situation.

I was in the middle of nowhere with who-knew-how-many men who'd been without any source of vice or contact with the outside world for who-knew-how-long, one of them who had a great desire to torture me if he ever got his hands on me again.

And, according to Taylor, I had little hope for any help in the next month.

Someone went to great lengths to bring me here and make sure my arrival went undetected. Was there really no attendant on the property? Security? Surveillance? Anyone with control of the prisoners?

I ground my teeth together, having no fucking idea what the hell I was going to do, but I needed to do it fast.

But then I heard something, and I shot my eyes up to Taylor, barks and howls echoing outside.

"What is that?" I asked.

Wolves? The sounds were getting closer.

He shot his eyes up, looking at the front door behind me and then back down to me. "The hunting party," he replied. "They must be back early."

The hunting party.

Will.

And how many other prisoners that might be just as creepy and threatening as this guy...

The howls were outside the house now, and I looked up at Taylor, unable to calm my breathing. What would happen when they came inside and saw me?

But he just smiled down at me. "Please do run," he said. "We're dying for some fun."

Thank you for reading!
And thank you for your reviews.
Your time and feedback are the
best gifts you can give an author.

The horsemen will return!

Acknowledgements

First and always, to the readers—so many of you have been there, sharing your excitement and showing your support, day in and day out, and I am so grateful for your continued excitement and trust. Thank you.

Nightfall (Devil's Night #4) will be the final installment in the series.

Add *Nightfall* on Goodreads: https://bit.ly/2EC6sJA

Now on to the rest...

To my family—my husband and daughter put up with my crazy schedule, my candy wrappers, and my spacing off every time I think of a conversation, plot twist, or scene that just jumped into my head at the dinner table. You both really do put up with a lot, so thank you for your patience.

To Jane Dystel, my agent at Dystel, Goderich & Bourret LLC—there is absolutely no way I could ever give you up, so you're stuck with me.

To the PenDragons—you're my happy place on Facebook. Thanks for being the support system I need and for always being positive. And thank you for the playlist suggestions! It helps so much! And also to the hardworking admins, Adrienne Ambrose, Tabitha Russell, Kristi Grimes, Lee Tenaglia, Lydia McCall Cothran, and Tiffany Rhyne. I couldn't do it without you.

To Vibeke Courtney—my indie editor who goes over every move I make with a fine-toothed comb. Thank you for teaching me how to write and laying it down straight.

To Kivrin Wilson—long live the quiet girls! We have the loudest minds.

To Milasy Mugnolo—who reads, always giving me that vote of confidence I need, and makes sure I have at least one person to talk to at a signing.

To Lisa Pantano Kane—you challenge me with the hard questions.

To Jodi Bibliophile—no cowboys. Got it. No pubic hair. Never. No condoms. Eh, sometimes. Eye rolling—welllllll, I tried. Thanks for reading and supporting, and thank you for your witty sense of humor and always making me smile.

To Lee Tenaglia—who makes such great art for the books. I'm so glad you love these devils as much as I do!

To all of the bloggers—there are too many to name, but I know who you are. I see the posts and the tags, and all the hard work you do. You spend your free time reading, reviewing, and promoting, and you do it for free. You are the life's blood of the book world, and who knows what we would do without you. Thank you for your tireless efforts. You do it out of passion, which makes it all the more incredible.

To Jay Crownover, who always comes up to me at a signing and makes me talk. Thank you for reading my books and being one of my biggest peer supporters.

To Tabatha Vargo and Komal Petersen, who were the first authors to message me after my first release to tell me how much they loved *Bully*. I'll never forget.

To T. Gephart, who takes the time to check on me and see if I need a shipment of "real" Aussie Tim Tams. (Always!)

And to B.B. Reid for reading, sharing the ladies with me, and being my bouncing board. Can't wait to climb inside your head. Wink-wink.

It's validating to be recognized by your peers. Positivity is contagious, so thank you to my fellow authors for spreading the love.

To every author and aspiring author—thank you for the stories you've shared, many of which have made me a happy reader in search of a wonderful escape and a better writer, trying to live up to your standards. Write and create, and don't ever stop. Your voice is important, and as long as it comes from your heart, it is right and good.

About the Author

Penelope Douglas is a *New York Times, USA Today*, and *Wall Street Journal* bestselling author. Her books have been translated into fifteen languages and include *The Fall Away Series, The Devil's Night Series,* and the standalones, *Misconduct, Punk 57, Birthday Girl, and Credence.* Please look for *The Hellbent Series (Fall Away Spin-Off)* beginning in 2021 and the stand-alones, *Tryst Six Venom and Motel,* coming soon!

Subscribe to her blog
https://pendouglas.com/subscribe/

Follow to be alerted of her next release:
http://amzn.to/1hNTuZV
Or text DOUGLAS to 474747
to be alerted when a new book is live!

Follow on social media!

Spotify: https://open.spotify.com/user/pendouglas
Instagram:https://www.instagram.com/penelope.douglas/
BookBub: https://www.bookbub.com/profile/
penelope-douglas
Facebook: https://www.facebook.com/
PenelopeDouglasAuthor
Twitter: https://www.twitter.com/PenDouglas
Goodreads: http://bit.ly/1xvDwau
Website: https://pendouglas.com/
Email: penelopedouglasauthor@hotmail.com

And all of her stories have Pinterest boards!
https://www.pinterest.com/penelopedouglas/

Printed in Great Britain
by Amazon

29603443R00381